Fran O'Brien is a Company Dire ————————— ...shed Just
Curtains Limited with her sister Ma₁y Lucherini in 1978. This
is her day job and very demanding, but Fran still manages to
run McGuinness Books with her husband Arthur, and on top of
all that, finds time to write, something she loves.

Her first novel – *The Married Woman* – was published
in 2005 and raised over thirty thousand euro in sales
and donations for The LauraLynn Children's Hospice
Foundation. Getting to know Jane and Brendan McKenna,
founders of the LauraLynn, has brought a new dimension
into the lives of Fran and Arthur.

All proceeds from sales of *The Liberated Woman* will
also go to the LauraLynn and, with your help, Fran and
Arthur hope to raise even more money for the charity
on this occasion.

Also by Fran O'Brien

THE MARRIED WOMAN

THE LIBERATED WOMAN

FRAN O'BRIEN

McGUINNESS BOOKS

THE LIBERATED WOMAN

This novel is entirely a work of fiction.
The names, characters and incidents portrayed
in it are the work of the author's imagination.
Any resemblance to actual persons, living, or
dead, events or localities, is entirely coincidental.

Published by
McGuinness Books
19 Terenure Road East
Dublin 6.

A catalogue record for this book is
available from the British Library

ISBN 978 0 9549521 1 2

Typeset in Sabon by Martone Press

Printed and bound in Great Britain by
Cox & Wyman Ltd, Reading, Berkshire.

Cover design based on an original painting by
Trudi Doyle
www.trudidoyle.com

www.franobrien.net

For Jane and Brendan

Acknowledgments

Very special thanks to Jane and Brendan McKenna to whom this book is dedicated, and for their wonderful friendship which has meant so much to me.

Thanks to all my friends in the Wednesday Group, and particularly my editor Muriel Bolger. Also thanks to the artist Trudi Doyle, who painted an original work on which the design of the cover is based, to the writer, Anne Dunphy, for her encouragement, and Vivien Hughes, who did the final proof-reading, thanks so much.

Many many thanks to my family, friends and clients, all of whom help us to raise funds for the charity.

Thanks to Yvonne and Martin Malone of Martone Press for their encouragement and great design ideas. To my printers, Cox & Wyman Ltd, who are so helpful, and efficient beyond belief. And to the booksellers in shops nationwide who promote this book with so much enthusiasm.

Grateful thanks to Coca-Cola Ireland, Craftprint Limited, FindlaterGrants Wine & Spirit Merchants, Mackenway Distrbutors Ltd, Reads Print and Design, Tipperary Natural Mineral Water.

And a huge heartfelt thank you to Cyclone Couriers, who last year distributed free of charge my first book, *The Married Woman,* and for their continuing support for the LauraLynn by distributing *The Liberated Woman* also. I deeply appreciate their amazing generosity.

And to Arthur, who is always there for me. I love you.

Chapter One

There he was, unchanged, her own sweet Jack. Leaping down the steps two at a time, his tall figure moving so fast he almost knocked into her.

'Kate?' he yelled. It was a calling out, a shout demanding an answer of recognition, and they reached out to each other, thrusting close. Her heart thumping as fast as his own, a bloodrushing drumbeat. Tears filled her eyes as she held him tight, so aware of his lean body, warm through the thin cotton of the blue shirt, the fine stubble on his chin hard against her cheek.

'I can't believe you're here.' Breathing fast, he looked down at her. 'Is Dermot with you?' he stared beyond, an anxiety in his dark brown eyes.

'No.' She had a sudden reluctance to tell him that she had separated from her husband almost a year ago, and had come out to Spain on a whim to fulfil some crazy urge to see her love again before he left for Brazil - too far away to catch up with him. Her first couple of days spent in Mojacar, and then dashing to Torrevieja when she heard that he was staying there with his sister, Chris.

'Thank God. I don't know what I'd have done if he suddenly arrived around the corner. It would be pistols at dawn no doubt!'

She managed a tearful smile.

'Where are you staying?'

'I've just arrived.'

'I'm sorry. I'm being too pushy, as usual. You're here - I can see you - touch you - and that's all I've wanted for months now.' He cupped her face in his hands and his lips gently explored, so warm

1

and moist she immediately responded. 'I love you, Kate. You're in my blood, a permanent virus. I thought I could get you out of my system, but no matter how hard I tried, you're still there in the heart of me dominating everything I do.'

'I called to Chris - I was hoping to see you before you left.'

'When was that?' he was puzzled.

'About an hour ago. She wasn't too pleased to see me.'

'What? She never told me you were there.' A shadow crossed his face. 'Only I spotted you on the beach I would never have known.'

'It doesn't matter.'

'No, you're right. Let's go back up, there's a party in progress, and I want to celebrate.' They began to walk slowly up the path, arms around each other, but then he stopped suddenly and looked down. 'You've no shoes on?'

'I forgot to put on my sandals. I was rushing back up to the house to have another word with Chris. I was furious!' Her anger forced its way to the surface again.

'I'm so sorry my love, we'll talk to her together. Look, you've a cut there. It's bleeding.' He bent down and touched her foot.

'I never even noticed it.'

'Let me clean it.' He helped her to sit down on the small stone wall at the side of the path and gently dried the blood with his white handkerchief. 'I'll carry you the rest of the way,' he smiled, 'which shouldn't be difficult, you've lost a lot of weight.' His expression changed to one of concern. 'You're not...ill?'

'Of course not.'

He tore a section off the handkerchief and covered the cut. Then he eased on the sandals. 'Can you manage to walk as far as the house?'

She watched him; surprised to find that he still cared about her, and loving it. Cared about - that description of how one person felt about another which said it all. Her husband, Dermot, always professed that he loved her deeply, but had kept secret the fact that he had an affair with her stepmother, Irene. Typically, she had been the last to find out. God knows what else went on in his life. Bastard. There were a million miles between the two.

'I'm sorry, but I'm not going,' she said.

'Why?'

'I don't want the door banged in my face for a second time.'

'What? She did that?'

'You go. I'll see you later.'

'You're crazy if you think I'm going to leave you for one second.'

'She blames me because you're going away.'

'Don't be ridiculous. She doesn't really give a damn whether I go or stay. I live in Mojacar half the year as it is.'

'I'll wait for you in that bar on the corner.'

'Promise me?'

She nodded.

'I won't be long.' He kissed her.

*

'Well?' Chris glared at him.

'What is your problem? I believe Kate called earlier and you were extremely rude to her. And deliberately told her I wasn't here!'

'You don't need that one in your life. A woman who deceives her husband, plays around with you for months on end and then dumps you when it suits her.' She took a deep pull on a cigarette, a picture of annoyance.

'I'm forty-five, Chris, and it really isn't any of your business what I do! Now I think I'd better go before I say any more.' He turned and walked up the stairs.

'This is your going-away party, what am I going to say to my guests?' She followed.

'You'll think of something, Chris. Anyway, most of them are so intoxicated by now, they won't even remember why they're here, so I wouldn't worry about it.' In the bedroom he pushed the last of his possessions into a backpack.

'But we're taking you to the airport in the morning.' She blocked his way.

'I'll get a taxi.'

Jack and Kate drove back to Mojacar in a relaxed companionable mood, as if they had never been apart. That night they had dinner at a new restaurant - Casa Memorias. In the beautiful central patio of the old Moorish house, tables were arranged between intricate carved wooden screens. A guitarist played Flamenco, accompanied by a young man who sat on a box, beating out the rhythm. Another clapped in time to the music. The resonance of the wonderful melodies rose and fell as the guitarist strummed the strings. His fingers coaxed the tune, the notes soft as the stroke of a feather, or beautifully fierce like the gypsy music of long ago.

'To you, my beautiful Kate.' Jack raised his glass. 'What brought you here now, on this very day?'

'The paintings.' She sipped her wine.

'Which paintings?'

'The ones you did of me. I saw them recently and ... I was surprised you sold them.' She was unable to explain how deeply she had been affected when she saw them hanging in the studio of a well-known celebrity.

'I gave them to the Nestor Gallery just before I left, but never discussed price, or possible buyers with Vincent. I just wanted them out of the house.'

'*Señor?*' The waiter appeared beside them.

Jack murmured something in Spanish and he moved away.

'How could you expect me to wake up every morning, and go to sleep at night with those paintings staring me in the face? Every highlight, shadow and brushstroke held a part of you. All the love I felt was there, all the happiness we had known and lost, I couldn't bear to look at them ever again,' he beseeched, 'you obviously have no idea how I felt at that time; how I still feel.'

'I assumed you would just head off to Spain and work.'

'I once told you that my painting would take second place to you and it has turned out that way. I couldn't go back to Andalucia, the memories were too painful, and so I went north to Santiago de Compostela. But I soon discovered that there was something missing. I had lost the urge to paint. I haven't done anything worthwhile since. That's why I decided to go to Brazil - to find some

4

inspiration,' he smiled wryly.

'I'm sorry.' She reached out her hand to cover his. 'I can't believe you're not painting.'

'Maybe it's gone altogether. I might have to go back to accountancy as a career.'

'Don't say that. I'm sure Brazil will give you a new challenge.' Feeling guilty, she tried to encourage him, aware that Chris had been right and that it was her fault that he had lost his motivation.

He held her hand in both of his now.

'When are you going?' She had been wondering about that all evening, and even though he had loaded his stuff into the jeep, collected her bag at the bar where she had left it, and driven back to Mojacar, she was afraid to assume that this meant anything at all.

'I'm booked on a flight to Madrid early in the morning.'

'So you would have to leave at?' She tried to calculate the time.

'Somewhere between three and four,' he grinned.

'You'll be up all night at that rate.'

'Doesn't matter.'

'I've really upset your plans.' Suddenly, the reality of his departure made itself felt and she had to struggle to hide her disappointment.

'My plans are flexible.'

'What do you mean?'

'I could easily change my mind.'

'But what about new inspiration?'

'I have all the inspiration I need in front of me.' He leaned across the table and kissed her.

Chapter Two

Dermot held the whiskey bottle up to the light but when he saw the dribble which was left, threw it into the fireplace where it shattered into pieces. Frustrated, he went into the kitchen, opened the fridge and stared bleakly at the meagre contents. There was some hard sliced cheese, an orange with a blue fur of mould on its skin, the remains of a Chinese takeaway in a tinfoil container and a charred sausage which looked particularly unappetising. He crashed the door closed, the bang accompanied by a shout of colourful invective. Aimlessly, he wandered around the house, his footsteps echoing hollowly. They had all deserted him - Kate, Conor and Shane.

Later he decided to go over to see Irene and tried to make an effort with his appearance. In the past his shirts were laundered by Kate; the suits always freshly aired and pressed, the sweaters folded in colour coordination, the casual gear in their own particular section. His numerous pairs of shoes were polished to a bright shine, and underwear, socks, ties and handkerchiefs lay in their neat positions in the tallboy drawers. He longed for those days when she satisfied his every whim. Now when he slid open the wardrobe doors an untidy mess greeted him. Shirts were thrown on the shelves, mixed up with a motley collection of other clothing. From the suits which hung crookedly on their hangers, out of shape and crumpled, he finally chose a grey stripe and a blue shirt which wasn't too badly creased. Clothes were a very important part of Irene's life and she would no doubt make some very caustic comment on seeing him.

'Looking like something the cat dragged in, I see.' Her eyes swept over him with contempt.

'I was in a hurry.' He closed the middle button of the jacket and straightened his shoulders, longing to tell her what she could do with herself.

'I suppose you'd better come in,' she sighed and marched ahead of him, beautiful as ever in a cream full-length skirt and embroidered top.

'You're looking well,' he said in his most confident tone, watching her bottom wiggle from side to side. But that sight did nothing for him. Irene was Kate's stepmother. There was a time when he had been fascinated by her, so alluring and looking a good ten years younger than her age – which was supposedly just over forty. And she had been besotted with him. The sexual attraction between them was electric, thrilling and, most of all, forbidden. But now that passion had waned and he hated the control she had over him.

'Thanks.' She nodded in a disinterested way, poured a whiskey and handed it to him.

'Cheers.' He raised his glass and gulped, badly needing a drink. At least he could always depend on Irene for that.

'I don't know if cheers are in order. Any word from that bastard Manuel?' She sat down at the other end of the couch, slid the shining mahogany box of Havanas along the glass-topped table towards him and took a cigarette from a silver case. Rolling the cigar in his fingers he watched her light up. Flick. Flame. Flick. The tip glowed red as she inhaled and blew a haze of blue smoke towards him.

He shook his head and drew deeply. The Spaniard had ruined his life.

'I don't know where your brains were to get involved with him again. You should have known he wasn't trustworthy.'

'He sounded genuinely sorry that the project in Calpe collapsed. A lot of people had their fingers burned,' Dermot muttered, his expression surly. He should never have trusted the man that first time, much less the second. But doing business with the sharp operator had filled his head with ideas of getting back to where he had been a couple of years ago. So he fell for the suave excuses, the halting explanations in broken English, and had decided to take another chance with him.

'A likely story!' she humphed, 'you're a sucker, always were, and he could see you coming a mile away.'

'You thought it was a great idea at first.'

'But I didn't know the full details of the Calpe collapse; you were so full of enthusiasm to get back into business, you'd have climbed into bed with anyone.'

'Not with him, not my scene.' The joke was weak, and she grimaced.

'It wasn't such a big deal, ten apartments, chicken-feed compared to Calpe.' In the new company which Irene fronted and funded, she held two thirds of the shares, split with Dermot by verbal agreement only. Manuel held the third share.

'I think there's much more to him anyway.' She squinted suspiciously.

'What do you mean?'

'Had he got an office in Alicante?'

'A huge place, filled with art. He collected paintings and had a number on the wall by Jack...whatever his name is. You know the guy Kate did business with.'

'I wouldn't mind getting my hands on a few of them to make up for all the money I've lost. To lose the apartments and our deposits because that little tap dancer didn't come up with the money was disastrous.'

'It never happened to me before, I was always on top of things. Nobody could pull the wool over my eyes.' Dermot had been a very successful property developer, both in Ireland and Spain. When the project at Calpe matured he had intended to buy a tropical island in the Caribbean, which he would develop into a haven for the very rich. He had imagined himself a billionaire in a couple of years, until Manuel disappeared with all the profits and his glorious life had collapsed around him.

'What about the address he used in Dublin, have you checked it out?'

'No record of him.'

'Why did he come over here at all?'

'He wanted to invest.'

'But there are plenty of other places he could do that, Hungary, Turkey, Bulgaria, property is dirt cheap out there. Did you know anyone else connected with him, surely there were other investors, friends, even the people who worked in his office?'

'I knew his secretary, Carmen.' He remembered the dark-eyed *señorita* who had followed him back to Dublin when Manuel threw her out because she was playing around with another man. It hadn't been a wise dalliance.

Irene raised her eyebrows. 'You didn't happen to hit on her, by any chance?'

He looked at her, with a deliberately shocked expression on his face. 'What do you think I am? You're the only one for me, Irene.'

'I often wondered what you were up to over in Spain. Those warm velvet nights are very seductive.'

He remembered many a night with Carmen, and all alone now, he was often sorry that he had sent her back to Spain.

'Spaniards are very hot-blooded and possessive about their women. It could easily have been enough to send Manuel on a vendetta.'

'You're crazy, Irene, off the wall.'

'There must have been something going on.'

'I invested five million euro in the company, and lost it, that's all I know.' His face was sullen.

'Probably a con. Most of those property developers are chancers, fooling the innocent eegits who think they're buying a dream home. A high percentage of them only ever see an abandoned building site.'

'There was nothing like that. The development was complete. I was just waiting to get my share of the profits, but it never arrived in my bank account.' Dermot swallowed nervously. The moment she mentioned the word "con", he felt sick.

'Why didn't you go over there to investigate?'

'I did, but when I was met with a policeman toting a gun I wasn't hanging around for a chat.'

'But you were just an investor. What did your solicitor say?'

'Nothing could be done,' he barked, knowing that he had been up to his neck in the fraud which was perpetrated on people who purchased property in Spain through his company.

'It's all very odd.'

'Past tense now.'

'And your life is a shambles.'

'I'll get myself up and running again, all I need is a helping hand. That's why I can't do without you, Irene.' He moved along the couch and put his arm around her, but she stood up.

'How much is it this time?'

'Just enough to keep me going for a week or two.'

She opened her handbag and threw him a couple of hundred. 'Only I know you were stung by Manuel, I wouldn't give you a cent. But this can't continue, and it must be repaid eventually. Remember that.'

'Thanks so much, Rene, you're so good to me.'

As he waited to pick up a taxi, he took the phone from his pocket and punched in a number. 'Dermot Mason here, I want to put two hundred on Dusty Fellow to win in the three o'clock.'

Chapter Three

Later that evening Kate and Jack walked through the dark narrow streets of Mojacar. Turning a corner there was a sharp gust of wind and she shivered, pulling the collar of the red linen jacket closer. He drew her against him into the shadow of an archway.

'Tell me - are you and Dermot still together?' he asked urgently.

'No, we've separated. I'm not Mrs. Mason any longer, it's Ms. Crawford,' she smiled.

His arms tightened, and she could feel him shudder.

'My love.' He bent his head and searched for her lips. She leaned against him, feeling the narrow contours of his body close to hers, and let all the anguish and stress of the last couple of days drift away. She held on to him tightly, her fingers smoothing his short dark hair, breathing in the aroma that was so distinctly Jack. A mixture of the Spanish soap he used, aftershave and moisture from his skin, like no-one else. But there was something missing. That hint of paint and turpentine which she always associated with him had gone.

Without another word, they walked back to the house, moving across the courtyard, the quiet of the night broken by the musical sound of water trickling in the fountain. The shape of the blue dolphin glimmered in the soft light which splayed from the base of the stone basin.

'I've missed him.' She ran her fingers along its curved back.

'I've missed you.' He pulled her close.

It was like that first time they had been together. The bedroom bathed in moonlight, the split shadows on the terracotta tiles when he drew the slatted blinds, the crisp white bed linen. But the room was devoid of personal possessions, which reminded Kate that he was booked on a flight in the morning which would take him on the first part of his journey to Brazil.

He didn't switch on the lights as he undressed her and threw off his own clothes. His fingers delicately followed the shape of her face, neck and shoulders, across her breasts, the round of her stomach, her narrow hips. He was like someone searching for identification. A person without sight who was reading Braille. Then he embraced her and she moved with him on to the bed. With frantic haste they clung to each other. This is you. This is me. Lips pressed deeply, tongues sending messages from the brain through nerve-endings to every part of their bodies, a delicate communication which enflamed and had to be satisfied now.

They slept with their arms around each other, curled like children on the white bed as the moon waned and a gold yellow radiance crept through the slats. Kate awoke, immediately aware of Jack beside her, his head snug in the curve of her neck and shoulder, his arm loosely across her body, heavy in sleep. She lay there, quite still, and revelled in this opportunity to watch him. The flicker of his eyelids as if he was dreaming, that slight tremor through his fingers, the way he hugged close to her even in sleep. When at last his eyes opened, he smiled immediately. 'I love you,' he kissed her. 'I love you, Kate.' His arms tightened around her. 'I didn't mean to sleep.'

'You've missed your flight,' she whispered softly.

'What flight?'

He fussed over her. Rushed out to shop for breakfast, and came back with fresh, still warm, rolls. He scrambled eggs, squeezed oranges, and brewed strong coffee. They sat on the balcony, the morning surprisingly warm for January, and she suddenly discovered she was ravenous.

'I'm glad to see your appetite's improved, you only picked at your meal last night.' He held the basket of bread towards her, and she took another piece.

'I still have to watch what I eat, you know,' she remembered the years of being overweight. Every diet in existence tried, only to end in failure.

'You're so much thinner, I'm afraid to catch hold of you in case I break you,' he laughed, 'but I love the longer hairstyle.' He ran his fingers through her soft shoulder-length blonde hair.

She smiled shyly.

'But don't lose any more weight, you know skinny women don't appeal to me.'

'It fell off really. I suppose it was stress.'

'I hate to think of you under that much pressure.'

'It was a combination of things, but mostly Dermot. When you and I ... after that night ... I tried to fit back into the shoes of Mrs. Mason. But Dermot only wanted me as a housekeeper. He was drinking heavily, and when he sold the beautiful diamond necklet and earrings you gave me, that was it.'

'I'll buy you something even nicer.' He covered her hand with his. 'When was that?'

'Early last year.'

'That long?'

'I needed to be on my own for a while, and anyway, I didn't think you'd want to know me again. You were pretty angry the last time we met.'

'I'm sorry, I shouldn't have been. But when our plans for a new life together suddenly collapsed ...'

'I never regretted anything so much.'

'I don't know why you didn't call.'

'I had to get my life in some sort of order, so I stayed with Carol for a few weeks, and when the tenants vacated Berwick Road I moved in. It's great having my own place. I can come and go as I like. Eat what I like. When I like. No-one looking for football gear to be washed, or sandwiches made for friends, or dinner for ten at the drop of a hat. It's heaven.'

'You've certainly made a lot of changes. No doubt there are hoards of people looking for you to design their homes?'

'I was very busy coming up to Christmas, but it's quiet now.'

'Then you might be able to spend some time out here with me?' he grinned.

'I might,' she smiled, 'have you decided about Brazil?'

'Forget about Brazil.' He kissed her.

Those first days they did nothing much at all except to make love. Long mornings spent in bed, only struggling up to eat brunch at Pedro's across the square somewhere in the mid-afternoon, and then walking along the beach, hand in hand, catching up on what had been happening in their lives.

'You'll have to start painting again,' she encouraged, very concerned at his almost empty studio. 'Come on, sketch me. You can start now. Have you got a pencil?' She ran ahead of him, and turned back in dramatic pose, arms outstretched, hair flying wildly in the stiff breeze. 'You used to enjoy painting me, I seem to remember,' she smiled coyly.

'You know, I might just do that.' He took a small camera from his pocket and snapped.

'You'll soon be arranging another exhibition at the Nestor Gallery.'

'Vincent was on to me recently, but I had to admit that I had done nothing at all, the same with my agent here.'

'What about commissions?'

'There are some in the pipeline, but they'll hold.'

'I'll take the blame.'

'Lack of motivation is probably some fault in my make-up. Painting is such an emotional thing for me.'

She put her arm around him, but said nothing for a while as they followed the curve of the rolling surf, green blue in the sparkle of sunshine, white foam spuming at the tops of crashing waves.

'Kate, I don't want to push you. Sorry, I'm doing exactly that. But I need to know how you feel. I don't want to have a relationship like we had before. I hated the secrecy. I can't do that again.' He looked bleakly at her.

'I haven't really thought about the future, and had no idea how you would react to my turning up unexpectedly. There might even have been another woman in your life by now.'

'You don't know me very well.' He stopped walking and turned to her.

'Maybe I should get to know you all over again,' she smiled.

'Does that mean?'

'Let's see how life pans out. All the secrecy will be a thing of the past, no looking over our shoulders any more.'

A couple of days later, he woke her early for a change. 'We're going on a trip, so pack something warm, it could be chilly there.'

'Where?'

'It's a surprise.' He kissed her.

'I hate to be in the dark.'

'Don't worry, I'll bring along a few candles, I'd never leave you like that.'

'Go on, tell me, where are we going?'

'You're such a curiosity box!'

'Tease!'

The morning was bright, and they listened to the music of Paco Peño as they drove along. Kate's phone rang. She took it out of her bag, looked at Jack and raised her eyebrows.

'It's Paul Kenny here.'

'How are you?' She had done a lot of work with Paul while working in her last job with Mags and Carol. It transpired now that he needed her to design and fit out an apartment block. As he explained, excitement bubbled up and she was immediately challenged. 'Give me the details.' She scribbled. 'What's the timescale? I'll just have to check my diary.'

'As soon as possible. We've only just made the decision to sell them to investors fully-furnished, so speed is vital. Are you very busy at the moment?'

'Busy enough,' she told a little white lie, 'but I should be able to organise it for you.'

'Great, I knew I could depend on you.'

'Thanks for thinking of me.'

'You don't think I'd go to anyone else, do you?' he laughed.

'You'll give me a swelled head. Thanks again. Talk soon.' She put away her phone and whistled. 'Would you believe that?'

'What?' Jack asked.

'It's a fantastic job. A whole apartment block,' she grinned at him in delight, 'it's exactly what I need, a real challenge!'

'Sounds like it could be very demanding. If you're living with me, you don't have to work at all. I hope I can scrape enough for the two of us to live comfortably.' He put his hand across and touched hers.

'Thanks, my love, but I can't depend on you for everything.'

'Why not?'

'I suppose I want to build up the business, become a name in interior design.'

'That means you'll be spending most of your time in Dublin?' His eyes were clouded.

'I'm sure I can come out occasionally, and you'll spend some time at home surely?'

'I was hoping you might stay here with me for a while.'

'I would have, if I hadn't got that call.'

'But we've only just got together again.'

The atmosphere in the car grew tense.

'Jack, I must work.' She was disappointed that he wasn't happy for her.

'I can give you anything you want.'

'I can't lean on you, and … I want to do the job. It's a great chance for me.'

'So when are you planning to go back?'

'I suppose I'll have to try and get a flight as soon as I can.'

'But we're heading for Morocco, what about that?' There was an edge in his voice.

She didn't know what to say for a few seconds. 'I'm sorry, my love, but can't we go another time? Have you booked a hotel?' She was worried then, and felt guilty, hating her intransigence.

'Would it matter?'

Chapter Four

Dermot made an attempt to press a white shirt, but the creases stubbornly remained after five minutes of pushing the iron back and forward on a yellow towel he had folded and placed on the kitchen table. Then he remembered that when Kate used to tackle a pile of ironing there was always that hiss, so he turned on the tap and impatiently watched the water level rise in the little glass window. The steam made a considerable difference and he was pleased with the result as he carefully smoothed the front. But as he worked his way around he left the iron down for a few seconds too long and discovered a nice brown impression on the white cotton. He swore. To hell with it. No-one would see the back.

The busiest pub in the group owned by his sister Mary and her husband Des was situated just off Grafton Street. It currently basked in the popularity of being one of the "in" places for the trendy set. Dermot had resisted looking for any kind of job since the collapse of his business, hating the thought of toeing the line for someone else. But as the money which Irene threw him from time to time usually went to the bookies, he had to have another source. One of these days his horse would romp home and he needed to be out there playing. Recently he had even put two hundred euro on the possibility that it would snow on Christmas day.

Mary was in the office at the back, and Dermot knocked politely. It was very important he made a good impression.

'Come.'

He put his head around the door and she looked up from a pile

17

of papers on the desk. Usually dressed impeccably, today there was a rushed look about her, as if she had overslept and just thrown on the elegant black suit. Her short blonde hair was slightly tangled and she peered at him short-sightedly through gold-rimmed reading-glasses as if she didn't know who he was.

'What are you doing here?'

'I wanted to see you; it's been a while since ... ' He sat down on the chair in front of the desk, and leaned forward towards her in what he hoped was the friendly confident manner of old.

'I didn't think you'd have the neck to show your face around here again for quite some time, you behaved disgracefully that last night you were in.'

'I'm really sorry. My life is in a mess since the bankruptcy and then Kate leaving ... that's had an awful affect on me.'

'You got what was coming to you. The way you treated that girl over the years was terrible. There was many a time I wanted to say something, but of course I couldn't interfere, you'd have probably taken the head off me as well.'

'It was the drink,' he mumbled.

'That's an excuse, and a weak one at that. You took her for granted. And you ridiculed her in public too. I remember the night of the New Year party when you made the most scathing remarks about her weight in front of everyone. The poor thing was devastated. And you always had an eye for other women. You've been seen out and about too, don't think it wasn't noticed! I was delighted when she left, good enough for you,' she glared at him.

Dermot quailed, and shifted uncomfortably. Mary always put him down, in just the same way his mother used to do. Even when they were young, she had been the favourite, and although he was the eldest son, somehow he couldn't manage to reach his Mam's expectations. And when he announced that he was going to marry Kate, who was pregnant with their first son, Conor, she told him to get out of the house and not to come back. They had never spoken again. Over the years he had always thought he didn't care, but that day when the police had taken him down to the station for questioning about the Spanish property deals, something had cut into him, and he had cried in his heart for the only two women he had ever truly loved - Kate and his mother - both gone now. 'I want a job,' he whispered hoarsely, 'please?'

Her blue eyes widened. 'A job?'

'Yes, I need something to do, Mary, I'm going crazy.'

She took off the glasses, a sudden puzzlement in her expression. 'I don't know, Dermot,' she sighed.

That very hesitation fired something, and anger spiralled. The cheek of her wondering whether she might give him a job, he thought, remembering how he helped with money when they bought their first pub, put them in touch with the right publicity people, and was always there if they needed anything. He wanted to march out. Let her see it didn't really matter, and that he wasn't prepared to kowtow. But need was greater than anger. He couldn't afford to alienate her. 'I'll do anything, serve drinks, clear up the place, anything,' he muttered.

'We're not looking for lounge boys,' she smirked.

At that he almost lost it again, but he steeled himself, knowing that she would insist on having her say before agreeing to anything.

'But I suppose I could do with a hand in the office.'

It was good at first. When it was busy he served behind the bar. Otherwise, he did the paperwork, and handled the money. They paid him well, but not quite enough to cover Dermot's lifestyle, and he still resented Mary's attitude on that first day. They had him here just like any employee, and he couldn't even take a drink, scared anyone would smell the alcohol from his breath. And that began to gnaw at him too, with bottles grinning at him from the shelves, pints of creamy-headed Guinness, cool beer, whiskey, vodka and so much more. With dry mouth, and an empty craving inside, he winced as he watched drinkers down that first slug, glug glug, cool, delicious.

But while he had to deal with his addictions, to the outside world he managed to present himself as the Dermot people knew a couple of years ago. And most of all, Mary was happy.

'You've surprised me,' she said, 'I don't know what I expected, but the main thing is you've stayed off the drink when you're working, which is great.'

'I'm trying, Mary.'

'And I admire you for that.'

But he made up for it later in one of the clubs in town. Finally getting home in the small hours, he usually fell into an intoxicated coma, to wake up bleary-eyed in the morning. 'It's been very difficult,' he muttered.

'I can imagine.'

What would you know? he thought, loving your benefactor role, doling out alms to the poor like a blooming nun. You haven't got a clue. Living the high life in your fancy house in Donnybrook, with a string of pubs raking in the money. Jealousy surged.

'We're having a few people around next Saturday night, why don't you come over? Invite Conor and Michelle as well. How is Shane getting on in Berlin?'

'Seems to be doing all right.' Dermot was glad he didn't have to cope with his younger son. But he wouldn't have minded Conor being at home, or even calling occasionally, just for the sake of having another person visit for a short time, instead of listening to his own footsteps echoing in the empty rooms. It was something which always unnerved him. Reminded of childhood days. Opening the front door with the key, walking up that hallway with its brown lino and the brightly-flowered yellow wallpaper. The colours of his nightmares. He always hoped that his mother might have come home early from work, just once, but she was never in the kitchen ahead of them; and the clatter of his shoes on the hard floor haunted him still. In her absence, every day Dermot had looked after his sister and brothers; insisted they do their homework, which was difficult enough to achieve; and peeled potatoes and vegetables for the evening meal.

But his own son, living with his partner, Michelle, had no time for him and declined any invitations to call. He grew to hate the large house in Rathfarnham. Loneliness was something he had never felt before. Cosseted and loved by Kate for all those years, he realised that he hadn't appreciated her. Hadn't told her how much he really loved her, always too involved with his own life outside of their home. His property development company, business associates, and his women, particularly in the latter years of their marriage. Carmen in Spain, Irene here, and other one-night stands along the way.

He never bothered asking Conor and Michelle along to Mary's on Saturday night, but went on his own, only interested in having a few free scoops.

Chapter Five

'Do you mind terribly if we don't go to Morocco?' Kate put her hand on Jack's shoulder.

He sighed, a long despairing sound, and then indicated to exit the Autovia, taking the turn which would bring them to the other side and back to Mojacar. They drove for a couple of miles in silence, but then he pulled off the road into a service station and stopped the jeep. The expression on his face showed how disappointed he was. 'I've only just found you again, and you're leaving me after a few days.' He put his arm around her.

'I don't want to leave you either,' she murmured, very much aware of how much she loved him.

'Stay then.' He kissed her, a long slow persuasion.

'I want to, but ... '

'There's always a "but", isn't there?'

She stared at him, guilt rising inside, and realised that he was referring to her difficulty in dealing with their relationship in the past. Afraid to be seen in public with him. Never taking telephone calls on the mobile. Unable to tell her friends, Mags and Carol, even though she was aware that Mags fancied him too. And worst of all, she had seemed to be incapable of finding the right time to leave Dermot. There was always a "but".

'I thought now that you'd finally parted from Dermot we'd be able to plan for the future.'

'Of course we can.'

'I want to live with you Kate, all the time, every day, every night; not see you occasionally while other things take precedence. I refuse to be in second place,' he said bluntly.

'You're the most important person in my life, but my business is also very important to me. It's who I am. You must understand that, my love.' She kissed him, regretting that she couldn't give him what he wanted, even now. 'What are you going to do? Will you still go to Brazil?' she asked tentatively.

'Of course not, unless you come with me,' he growled, 'but you needn't worry, I'm not going to put pressure on you to go that far. Anyway, the reason I chose Brazil was to try and get away from the memories. So now there's no reason to do that, unless ... ?' His brown eyes stared into hers.

'I love you, Jack. But our lives are very different, and maybe we'll have to compromise a little. I seem to remember that you once said you were willing to do anything for me,' she cajoled.

'And I meant it. But I was hoping to spend a little longer with you before we begin to face up to the realities of life - you, me and no-one else.'

'So did I. But this is a great opportunity and too hard to turn down. It seems crazy to let the business die at this point. You're a painter. I'm an interior designer. I've given up the housewife role, you know!' she smiled to lighten the tone of her words.

'I want to live in a fairytale world of love. Business and money are just materialistic,' he grinned unexpectedly.

'You can't live the life you imagine without money. You've been so successful, you don't have to think about it.'

'You're wrong there. I've done no work in the last year, and my financial situation isn't what it used to be.'

'Then I'll have to pitch in to keep us going,' she laughed, so relieved the anger in his eyes had faded.

'Maybe I should go back with you, and begin work on those commissions?'

They left that day together, travelling overland. Kate had only booked a single ticket on the way out so it seemed the ideal thing to do, and as Jack had been packed and ready to go to Brazil, they were able to head off without much delay.

She enjoyed the sojourn of the few days together on the road, passing through Spain and France, glimpsing places in the distance, the names of which she knew, but had never visited. With overnights in small towns, this was a fast spin along motorways, numbing at times. We are on our way home. That phrase echoed in her head more than once. Together. A couple. Partners. Happiness flared through her.

Not even bothering to grab a few hours sleep, as soon as she arrived back, she went over to the property to survey the job, immediately full of ideas. Spending the day searching through her fabric swatches for appropriate designs, talking to her various suppliers, and working on a presentation, only remembering after six o'clock that she had promised to call Jack.

'When am I going to see you?' he asked.

'By the time I finish this, I'll be completely shattered, so I'm hoping to get a decent night's sleep. I need to have a clear head when I meet Paul tomorrow.'

There was a silence at the other end of the phone line.

'And you should do the same, you must be exhausted.'

'I was hoping you would come over here tonight. I don't fancy sleeping in a bed on my own any longer. All that space, cold and lonely.'

'I'm no company, let's wait until tomorrow evening.'

'I don't want to talk, I just want to hold you close to me for the night and wake up refreshed in the morning.'

'I'm sorry Jack, but I don't know what time I'll finish. It could be all hours.'

'OK, we'll leave it.'

'Don't be annoyed, please?'

'I'm not,' he protested.

'No? Could have fooled me!' she laughed, 'right, kiddo, I've to get on with my work, I'm not a person of leisure like you. In the meantime you can unpack and sort yourself out.'

'I've done all of that.'

'Well, make a start on one of those commissions.'

'You're right; that's exactly what I should do. I love you.'

'Love you.'

Kate put down the phone and continued working, but at the back of her mind, uncomfortable niggly thoughts persisted, and it was only when she had finally completed the presentation that she was able to sit back and let them in. She made herself a cup of tea and went to bed. Lying back on the pillows she was aware that suddenly her life was changing and, without any conscious decision, she was being swept up into this new situation with Jack. That's what you want, isn't it? she asked herself, isn't it? You love him. You want to spend the rest of your life with him, don't you? It was yes, yes, yes, to all of the questions, but there was another side of her which wanted in then. That independent streak which had been born when she left Dermot, determined to stand alone for the first time in her life.

Earlier, she had phoned her sons, Conor and Shane, to see how they were. Both seemed in good form, particularly Shane, the rock band having a lot of success in Germany. He was full of excitement as he told her they had been taken on by one of those big recording companies and were working on a CD which would be released under the well-known label. She was so glad her boys were both following their own chosen paths now, and that they had come to terms with the fact of their parents' separation. It wasn't so unusual these days, they had assured her, many of their friends were in the same position. And it seemed there was no need for the guilt which had consumed her when she had left home. Finally, before her eyes began to close, she called Jack again.

'You've been working until now?'

'Just a short time ago.'

'Have you had something to eat?'

'Stop fussing over me, Jack,' she giggled.

'Can't help myself. I worry about you.'

'For God's sake, Jack, I'm all grown up now.'

'I'm very much aware of that.'

'Let's do something tomorrow evening,' she suggested.

Exactly on the dot of seven, the bell pealed. Upstairs she pulled on the black halter-neck chiffon dress and slipped her feet into strappy high-heels. She had taken ages to choose the right outfit, so anxious to look as good as she possibly could, the first night that Jack had picked her up at home.

'Sorry, I'm not quite ready.' She let him in.

'You're looking wonderful.' He stepped inside and hugged her. 'I don't know how I managed to put in the hours today.'

'It was work work work here,' she laughed.

'And now it's time to celebrate. I've a taxi waiting.'

'I'm not even sure if I'm properly dressed.'

'Which particular part of your wardrobe is missing?' he grinned.

'I know I've got them on so don't get carried away! Give me two minutes.' Upstairs, after applying lipstick, and spraying perfume, she stared at herself in the mirror for a few seconds. Not bad at all, she decided.

'Where are we going?' she asked as they drove towards town.

'First, we're going to take a walk.'

'But I'm in these really high stilettos!'

'It's not such a long walk. You'll be able to manage it. If not, I'll carry you!'

They were dropped off on St. Stephen's Green. Jack paid the man and took Kate's hand. 'I've dreamed of this, you know, but I didn't think I'd ever live to see it.'

'What?' she smiled at him, puzzled.

'Just to walk down Grafton Street with you, hand in hand, and not care who sees us.'

They strolled, arms around each other, stopping to stare into shop windows. Laura Ashley. Richard Alan. Dunnes Stores. Pamela Scott.

'That's nice.' She pointed to a cherry-coloured top.

'I'll buy it for you tomorrow.'

'No you will not, I'll get it myself. Anyway this is only window shopping, probably if I take a closer look I'd hate it.'

'Let me.'

'Could prove very expensive if every time I admire something you buy it.'

'I just want to make you happy.'

'What about your bank balance, I thought you said it wasn't great at the moment?'

'It's not that bad, I exaggerated. What about those shoes, they'd look good on you.' They stopped in front of Fitzpatricks.

'No, not my taste.'

They reached Brown Thomas and he admired a casual black jacket.

'What size are you?'

'You mean you don't know that?'

'I'm teasing you,' she laughed.

'I hope so. I think I know everything about you. Size 40 - which I still think is just a bit too thin. Thirty-eight in shoes. Hat size six. Glove size seven. Other sizes I could guess but I think I'd better not. How am I doing?'

'Go on with you, hats and gloves!'

They moved on to a window display of lingerie.

'Now there's something I'd like to see you wear.' He indicated a white chiffon creation.

'Looks like a wedding dress, not something for bed.'

'Isn't that very appropriate, I wish you were choosing something for our wedding.' He turned to her. 'I don't think I've ever formally proposed so here goes - Kate Crawford, will you marry me as soon as you're free?'

She had an immediate impulse to laugh, conscious of a couple who were standing nearby, but stopped herself as she realised that to Jack this wasn't play-acting. There was no amusement in his eyes, just deadly serious intent. 'Yes, yes I will,' she whispered.

'I hope that wasn't a quick yes because there are a few people around?'

'No, of course not, come on,' she laughed.

'Hey, you're supposed to kiss the guy you know, that's the usual response.' He put his arms around her, and stopped her rush. Then he gave her a long slow kiss. 'You've no idea how happy you've made me.'

27

'Sorry, I was embarrassed.' She pushed her arm through his, hugging close, and they wandered on until they reached the end of the street.

'I'm only sorry we met no-one. I really wanted to introduce you as my other half to as many people as possible.'

'There will be plenty of chances to do that.'

'Tonight was special somehow.'

At the Trocadero, the Maître d', Robert, promised a table in a few minutes. They sat at the bar and had a drink, enjoying the busy atmosphere of the restaurant. Many of the diners were people from the world of theatre and the literary scene, a few of whom Jack knew. He had his opportunity then. For Kate, it was a nice feeling, all the guilt and angst a thing of the past.

He raised his glass of G & T and clinked hers. 'To the real beginning of our lives together!' he grinned.

'This is the place I decided that I couldn't survive another day without seeing you again. It was on the opening night of the play you designed, remember that?' She looked around. The décor was warm and atmospheric with colour tones of pinks and reds which glowed in soft lamplight. The walls were hung with photographs of actors and actresses, a record of theatre right up to the present day.

'I thought I'd never get through it; me at one end of the table and you at the other.' He held her hand.

'I was insanely jealous. Mags was sitting beside you, and she took all your attention.'

'I had no choice. It would have been too pointed if I had tried to arrange the seating plan at the table. Anyway, at that time I didn't know how you felt, maybe I was afraid you would reject me.'

'Foolish man.' She leaned towards him. 'I was drawn to you like a magnet; you had put a spell on me. Just over there at that table you looked at me with those eyes and I was lost.'

'I hope that spell still lasts, or do I have to mutter the incantations again?'

'No, it's permanent, lifelong and will never diminish.'

After a few minutes, they were taken to their table. Kate slid along the red velvet-covered bench seat and Jack sat opposite.

'How are you, we haven't seen you in quite a while,' Robert asked.

'Just back from Spain. I'd like you to meet Kate.'

They shook hands. 'Have you another exhibition coming up, I missed your usual one before Christmas at the Nestor.'

'It didn't happen; I've been doing other things.' Jack looked a little uncomfortable.

'More theatre?'

'Not at the moment.'

'You should do another play, that last design was stunning, I've heard more than one director mention it.'

'Maybe I will.'

'Look forward to it,' Robert excused himself, busy this evening with such a crowd in the place.

Their waiter was Martin, a Syrian, and they had a pleasant chat with him before they perused the menus. To start, Kate decided on Thai prawns in a sweet and sour sauce, and Jack had pate. For mains, she chose duck, and he had succulent fillet steak. The wine was Chilean and they enjoyed its smooth full-bodied flavour, slowly sipping, taking their time, in no hurry anywhere this evening. They had coffee to finish, accompanied by a delicious creamy liquor.

'To us!' Jack raised the little glass.

'To us!'

That night for the first time he came back to Berwick Road with her. They lit the fire in the sitting-room and pulled the big comfy couch closer to it. Candles flickered in the shadows and gave a mysterious magical quality to the room. Jack opened a bottle of wine, but they drank little. Both glasses put down and forgotten as he kissed her, slowly undoing the halter strap of the dress and unzipping.

'Do you know what's really wonderful?' His fingers outlined her face, and trailed across her body. 'To come in here and spend as long as I want with you, and not care who notices.'

'You can come here as often as you want,' she murmured.

'I'll hold you to that,' he smiled and kissed her again, his body taut, and they moved against each other until their passion demanded fulfilment, and they lost all sense of time and place. Now the flames blazed, candle-light danced, and their orgasms were wonderfully satisfying as they climaxed at exactly the same time, held in that position of exquisite pleasure for an unending moment, and then sinking back on to the soft cushions, so happy together.

It was an affirmation of how they felt. After everything that had happened, it seemed now that the way lay clear and uncluttered ahead.

Chapter Six

'It's great to see you.' Carol hugged Kate.

Mags waved her glass from where she lounged on the couch. 'You're looking radiant! Must have had a very good time?' she grinned mischievously.

'Yes!' Kate smiled and sat down, noting that Mags looked stunning as usual. Her red hair spiked, with the longer section at the back in various colours. The strip of a mini was brown leather and even though it was winter, the clinging gold top revealed a considerable portion of taut brown stomach. By contrast, both dark-haired Carol and Kate herself were dressed casually in jeans.

'G & T for you, K? Top up Mags?' Carol handed Kate a glass and put the bottle on the coffee table. 'Help yourself.'

'Right, tell us all. How did it go?'

'Pretty well.' Kate sipped her drink.

'Coy! Come on, give us the raunchy bits. Did you click?'

'Yes, I suppose you could say that.'

'None of us ever guessed what was going on. You put up such a good front over the years. To tell you the truth, the first night I saw you two together I was gobsmacked!' Mags poured more gin into her glass.

'That's mild. You were like an alley cat, all spit and hiss. You could have torn Kate to pieces with your claws, green-eyed monster,' Carol reminded.

'I was in love with him then,' Mags sighed.

'Jack's not your style, it would have fizzled in a week; can you imagine trying to persuade him into town every night, drinking and dancing until the small hours in some dark noisy club. He'd have you in bed by twelve. Isn't that right, Kate?' Carol grinned.

'That's what I wanted - to get him into bed! But I couldn't seem to persuade him,' she sulked, 'no matter how much bare skin was visible.'

'Yea, he's really boring, not your type at all,' Kate smiled, although she still felt a little uncomfortable in Mags' company.

'I was so certain he was mine when he agreed to paint my portrait.'

'You're so blooming sure of yourself. Spoiled rotten by all those other bods over the years; click your fingers and they fall at your feet. Good enough for you to find your charms don't work on every man,' Carol reached to top up all of their glasses again.

Kate put her hand over hers. 'I have to drive.'

'You can stay here for the night,' Carol offered.

'I'll be staying anyway, wherever you put me,' Mags said.

'Is Keith still around?' Kate asked.

'Yea, but I'm trying to get up the courage to tell him it's over.'

'Poor guy.'

'I can't fake it any longer.'

'Now, change of subject. It's great about that job you've landed, Kate. The first big step to success, we're delighted for you. But we have our own little bit of news as well. You could describe it as a very interesting development.'

Kate waited.

'You know Brent Sherwood in the States?'

She nodded.

'They're moving over here, and they want to buy the company!'

'What?'

'They've offered us a fair whack too,' said Mags, a wide grin on her face.

'How much?'

'Guess.'

'I haven't a clue, tell me.'

'Think of a figure.'

'Half a million?'

'Double it!' shrieked Mags.

Kate was astonished.

'And double that,' Carol added excitedly.

'Am I hearing you right, girls?'

They nodded, and grinned like children on Christmas morning.

'Wow!' Kate leapt up and threw her arms around them both. Then all three danced around the room in a wild explosion of mirth, laughing, screaming and shouting.

'Champagne!' Carol disappeared into the kitchen and returned with glasses, and a bottle of Bollinger. The cork popped out loudly, the fizzy drink overflowing as it was poured. 'To a great new future!' Carol shrieked.

'Are you resigning or staying on?'

'I'm going to take the money and enjoy life.' Mags sat back, the tiny skirt riding up as she crossed one slim leg over the other.

'I'm lodging it in the bank and staying put,' Carol smiled.

'I'll call you from somewhere exotic, and you'll both be green with envy.' Mags pointed a long white-tipped finger.

'You haven't got a nineteen-year old daughter.'

'No, thanks be to God, I'm fancy free.'

'That's what marriage does to you.'

'Whatever about getting hitched, kids certainly won't be on the agenda.'

'Is Amanda enjoying London?' Kate asked Carol.

'Loves it apparently. Still I wouldn't want to be on the other side of the world if there's a problem. Now, tell us, Kate, how is the love of your life?' Carol asked.

'He's fine; busy working on some commissions.'

'I wish I had a man who would change all his plans for me.'

'He took me completely by surprise, I don't know where I am,' Kate grinned.

'It's nice, you have to admit that?'

'Yes, but scary.'

'Scary?' They both rocked with laughter.

'Seriously, girls, while I do love him to bits, he wants to make decisions about the future, and I'm ...' she hesitated.

'What?' The two stared at her.

'Not ready.'

'For God's sake, weren't you going to move in together at one point?'

'That was a spur of the moment decision. I probably just needed to get away from Dermot. Now I've more time to think about it, I'm not so sure.'

'You mean there's still a chance for me?' Mags asked excitedly.

'Shut-up you!' Carol admonished, 'this isn't a joke, it's serious stuff.'

'OK, OK!' Mags put up her hands in mock surrender.

'I like my freedom, but I want him too,' Kate admitted.

'Could be tricky.'

'Anyway, I've decided that whatever I do, it has to be on my terms.'

'Didn't he say at one time that you'd be first and his work second?'

'Yes,' Kate laughed, 'but that's all very well until it's put into practice, I wouldn't want to cramp his style.'

'Sounds like you don't want to cramp your own,' Carol smiled.

'Seeing each other at weekends, and a couple of nights during the week is perfect for me. Then we can both do our own thing the rest of the time. If I move into Harrington Place, then I'll have to rent Berwick Road, and as I'm working there during the day, that would be impossible, so I'm stymied.'

'I think we're seeing another side to our Kate, what do you think, Mags?'

'A new surprisingly aggressive side.'

'I'm not aggressive! I've enjoyed living on my own during the past year and I have to admit I love the freedom. I get up and go to bed when I like, leave the dishes in the sink, cook or order in, whatever suits, I'm just being me.'

'Selfish biddy.'

'And that poor man is pining for you.'

'Don't be ridiculous,' Kate laughed.

'You should live life to the full before you get too old.' Carol opened a box of hand-made chocolates and handed them around.

'No thanks.' Kate managed to resist, immediately reminded that it could be her downfall if she wasn't careful. 'What's going to happen to May and the girls in the workroom?' she asked, suddenly anxious to change the subject.

'There's a redundancy package on offer. Brent Sherwood are slimming down the operation.'

'That's awful.'

'They'll be well compensated.'

'When is all this happening?'

'As quickly as possible. We've already signed the deal.'

'You were lucky that you resigned to set up your own company, otherwise you would have been out of a job.'

'Should have hung on until I got the package as well, would have made a big difference,' Kate said, but really didn't mean it. She felt sure that she had chosen the right time to leave and was glad her business was already established. It had made such a difference to have a challenge during those first months living alone, a rather daunting one considering that her financial situation had been so precarious.

'You won't need to work now that you've got Jack to look after you,' Mags giggled.

'You're pissed,' Carol accused.

There was a beep from someone's mobile.

'A text.'

'It's mine.' Kate fished in her handbag, took it out and read the message. 'I can't believe it,' she smiled, 'my brother Pat is coming home from Boston next week for a few days, and then the whole family will arrive. He's got a transfer here!'

Chapter Seven

Jack worked furiously, trying to finish the painting before the light faded. It had been a dull cloudy day and there were times he really missed the wonderful translucent light of the Sierra Nevada as he completed the last of the commissions. He had used some of the many photographs and video footage he had built up over the years but the joy of painting in the open air, seeing the landscape right there in front of him, and being able to touch it, made him feel he wanted to go back to Mojacar for a few weeks. But he needed Kate with him. He couldn't bear to be without her for that length, although she was so busy these days, their time together was limited to say the least.

He had announced her existence to the family when he had arrived unexpectedly for lunch last Sunday. He had quietly opened the front door and just walked in as they all sat around the table. Mam and Dad, his sisters Rose, and Kathleen, with husbands and offspring, his brother Ken with his twin daughters. He had stood there at the door and grinned when he saw the astonishment on their faces, and heard the chorus of shouts and screams.

'Jack! What are you doing back so soon?' His mother pushed through the throng and threw her arms around him.

'I never went.'

'I was waiting for you to help me with the garden this morning, you're late,' his father seemed cranky.

'This morning?' Jack was puzzled. He hadn't seen his Dad since Christmas.

'You told me yesterday you'd be over at eleven.'

'I'm delighted to see you.' His mother dabbed her eyes with the corner of a pink flowered apron. 'Kathleen, will you lay a place for Jack, there's plenty of lamb and vegetables.' She hurried into the kitchen.

'Mam, I'll get it myself.'

'Leave this to me.'

'Why didn't you go to Brazil?' Rose asked when they had sat down again.

'There's a woman in my life now,' he smiled, 'and she is more important than Brazil.'

They looked at one another with eyebrows raised in surprise.

'It's the first time you've ever mentioned that you were even interested in the female sex. We all thought you were gay, didn't we?' There was a burst of loud laughter in response to Kathleen's remark.

'I was married at one time, don't forget.'

'We thought that was the reason why it failed.'

'Stop that talk!' Mam interjected.

'No son of mine is – gay - whatever that means these days,' Dad growled, and his blue eyes flashed under craggy brows.

'Girls, I'm not gay, I can assure you, and Kate isn't the first woman I've known over the years.'

'Kate? What's she like?'

'Beautiful.'

'No doubt! But is she a young slip of a thing? You men are so lucky, age means nothing. You can have your choice of women.'

'For your information, we're both middle-aged. She's just a couple of years younger than myself, so we suit each other.'

'Was that the lady we met over at your house?' Mam asked.

'Yes.'

'She was nice.' There was a little smile on her face as she cut apple-pie portions. 'Bring her over next Sunday, we'd all like to meet her.'

His father cleared his throat. 'I don't know what things are coming to these days. You're a married man, Jack.'

'Divorced, Dad,' Jack tried to keep his tone light. His father could get him going so quickly with his old-fashioned attitude. He still treated his adult children as kids, and Jack was often on the point of telling him to mind his own business. But he knew there was no sense in having a row, his father's generation just didn't understand modern living.

'That means nothing in God's eyes. You've made your bed and you have to lie on it.'

'It's a bit late for that,' he said, trying not to laugh as he noticed the stifled grins of the others.

There was an uncomfortable silence for a moment, no-one in the family keen to argue with Dad. Whatever his views, he was still the head of the house and respected for that.

'Who's for tea?' Kathleen asked, 'or coffee?' She counted the hands.

'This pie is really tasty, Mam,' Jack smiled at her as the tension eased.

'No-one can cook like Mrs. Linley of Tyrconnell Park,' Rose quipped.

The awkward moment passed, and the subject of Jack's lifestyle wasn't mentioned again. Even when he went outside with his father to look at some paving he had laid, there was no further comment. Dad would come out with some sort of tactless remark when they were all gathered together, but he wasn't good one to one. Mam was the person with the communication skills. She always came straight out with whatever was on her mind. Never off the cuff; it was considered, weighed up and mentioned when she decided the time was right. The irritation with his father soon disappeared. He was seventy-nine years old, and extremely fit, but Jack was very much aware that he might be taken from them in a second. He couldn't bear to lose him in the middle of a row, he loved him too much.

'Sorry, I'm not quite ready. Pat's arrived and we've been catching up,' Kate kissed him.

'Will I cancel the restaurant?'

'No, I won't be long, come in and meet him.'

The tall well-built man was about his own age, a little on the

38

heavy side, with a ruddy outdoor look on his full face. 'Jack?' He gripped his hand. 'Good to meet you.'

'How are you, Pat?'

'Just give me a minute.' Kate hurried upstairs.

'Can I get you a drink? I have some good whiskey.'

'No, thanks, I'm driving.'

'Well!' He stood looking at him, hands on hips. 'So you're the latest in my sister's life?'

Jack nodded, bristling a little at the inference that there had been a succession of other men before him.

'It's great to be home. I haven't been over as often as I should, so when I was offered the position here I just jumped at the chance.'

'You're in software?'

'Yea, the company's doing well in Ireland.'

'The economy is vibrant. Where are you based?'

'Blanchardstown; Susie and the lads will join me in a couple of weeks. We'll be staying here until we get our own place.'

Kate appeared, pulling on her navy wool coat. 'Sorry about the delay, love.'

'We've been getting acquainted. We're old friends already,' Pat chortled.

'Would you like to join us for dinner?' Jack felt he had to ask, although the rather brash loud-speaking man didn't particularly appeal to him.

'No thanks, tonight I need a few decent hours of shut-eye. You go on ahead and enjoy yourselves.' He put his arms around Kate and kissed her soundly. 'It's so good to see my sister again, how long has it been since I've been home?'

'It was Dad's funeral, about seven years ago.'

'That long?'

Kate nodded.

'Well, I'm going to have to catch up with a few people. Dermot, Conor, Shane - and I suppose Irene is still making trouble?'

'I don't see much of her nowadays.'

'Just as well, never liked the woman. She could see Daddy coming a mile away, a victim.'

'We'd better head, Kate.' Jack moved down the hall.

'I'll see you in the morning, Pat, sleep well.'

'No worries.' He opened the door.

'Help yourself to anything you want.'

Jack kissed Kate slowly before starting up the car. 'How was your day, my love?'

'Very little done. And there are two apartments needed for next week so I'm going to have to get down to it.'

'I hope you didn't take on too much,' Jack murmured. When he had suggested that Kate didn't need to work at all, he had received such a strong vibe that this definitely wasn't what she wanted, he had refrained from mentioning the fact again. And now with the arrival of Pat's wife and family in another few weeks, he was worried that Kate would slip away from him altogether and become embroiled in her family, to the extent that he would become unimportant in the scheme of things.

After dinner, they sipped coffee, the conversation of the other diners buzzing around them. Kate was quiet, and seemed preoccupied.

'What are you thinking?' he smiled.

'About Pat and Susie.'

'It must be great to see him again.'

'It is.'

'He's a nice person,' he paused, 'how old are the children?'

'Rob is sixteen, and Donal fourteen.'

'How do you think they'll fit into the Dublin scene?'

'Kids fit in no matter where.' Kate stifled a yawn.

'You're tired, let's go.' He stood up, and took her hand. 'Come back with me, we haven't been together since last weekend.'

'Sorry, I couldn't, not with Pat there,' Kate said hesitantly.

'I'll stay with you.' He put his arm around her as they walked back to the car.

'I'd feel a bit strange, do you mind?'

'Of course I mind.' They stood close together in a doorway, his lips sliding warmly on hers. 'I need you so much.' Sudden passion whipped through him. He wanted her now. 'I love you.' His kisses become more demanding. 'Please come back with me for a little while?'

'Sorry, my love, it's a bit awkward.'

He said nothing else for a while, just held her tight, his heart thumping with disappointment. 'OK, suppose we'd better go. The police could pick us up for loitering, or worse.' He made an attempt at a joke.

'Two middle-aged people having a snog. They'd have a right laugh at that,' she giggled.

*

Although she was tired, Kate couldn't sleep that night. Worried about Jack and the fact that she had so little time for him these days. What if he got bored, she wondered. What if he decided the type of relationship which she wanted didn't suit him, she argued the toss with herself. She loved him. But why was it necessary to be with each other every minute of the day and night? They could be together most weekends, and she wouldn't be as busy as this for ever, in another month or two there might be nothing to do. But the expression in his eyes as he left her to the door didn't encourage confidence that he was happy. Then an idea occurred to her.

'It's great to see you,' Kate welcomed May.

'I never thought I'd meet you again.' There was a glimmer of tears in her eyes.

'How do you feel about the redundancy, it must have been a bit of a shock?'

'I was glad. The place just wasn't the same without you. Both Carol and Mags tried to organise the department but it was chaos most of the time. We've all received a nice bit of money, so there's no need to work for a while.' May's thin features were lit up, but her angular body still had an air of tension about it.

'Sit down.' Kate indicated an armchair. 'I'll make a cup of tea, or would you prefer a drink?'

41

'Tea would be nice, thanks.'

They sat and chatted for a while and then Kate suggested she might like to look at the workroom.

'Well?' She opened the door.

'It's a good size.' May moved inside.

'I chose this room because of the French windows which lead into the garden. It's lovely and bright even in winter if the sun decides to shine. I've only one large table, but the smaller one is useful too, and the sewing-machines are in here.' She showed May the set-up in the adjoining room. 'This was the original breakfast-room and a sitting-room, so it was perfect for what I wanted. I've a tiny office here too. Have you ever thought of setting up on your own?'

May smiled, an expectant look on her pleasant features. She was about Kate's own age. Single. Living alone. A quiet woman, whose main interest was playing bridge. 'I've thought about it.'

'So you're not going to retire just yet?'

'No, I'll have to get a job of some sort. What would I do all day?'

'I'm very busy at the moment, but that mightn't continue, so I'm reluctant to employ staff at this juncture. But how about this? Why don't I rent the workroom to you?'

'That sounds interesting.' A wide smile softened her features.

'We can agree a price for the rent, and I'll pay you so much a curtain width. But you can also take in work yourself because I mightn't have enough to keep you going all the time. Maybe Sinead or Phil might be interested in getting involved?'

'It's exactly what I wanted to do, but without the uncertainty.'

'Why don't you have a think about it and come back to me?'

'Can I book you for the weekend after next?' Jack asked.

'Certainly,' Kate agreed. She didn't have the courage to mention that she might be busy.

'And can I book you next Sunday as well.' There was a twinkle in his eyes.

'Sure, although you don't have to do that, you know, I'm here for you whenever you want.'

'We're going away for the weekend and that is a surprise, but I want you to come and have lunch with the family.'

'To meet them all?' Kate gasped.

'I know you've met Mam and Dad once, but I've told them that you're the woman in my life now and they want to be introduced formally. It's just the usual Sunday lunch, nothing special.'

'I hate the thought of your large family giving me the once-over. And I won't be what they expect, you can be sure of that. No doubt Chris has described me in great detail already.'

'She won't open her mouth, believe me.' He seemed unconcerned.

'How do you know?' she remembered the attitude of his sister.

'She's in Spain at the moment, so you needn't worry. Fancy any more pasta?' He took the top off the dish to serve second helpings of lasagne.

'No thanks, at this rate you're going to have me as heavy as I ever was. You're so lucky, the thoroughbred racehorse type who never puts on an ounce no matter how much he eats,' she forced a laugh, and tried to put the thought of being scrutinized by Jack's family out of her head. But that proved difficult and an unexpected resentment built up. She wasn't going to put herself out there for criticism by a bunch of strangers, even if they were Jack's relations. An excuse would have to be found.

Chapter Eight

It was almost closing time and Dermot served pints and shorts expertly. He had become quite accustomed to this side of the bar and felt he could run the whole place without any difficulty. Opening the cash register he noted that the takings had built up over the last short while and that it was time to clear the till again. He pressed a button and heard the click that told him the notes section had slipped into the compartment below. He bent to pick up the container, tucking it under his jacket. This was a simple security system which meant that money could be removed easily and quickly, undetected.

He went into the office and locked the door. His hands had begun to sweat profusely and his heart thumped erratically. It always hit him at this point. Wiping his forehead with a rather grimy handkerchief, he counted the money quickly. All the time looking over his shoulder at the door, then glancing up at the barred windows and back to the door again, afraid Des or Mary, or one of the staff, would knock. He took a mix of twenties and fifties and quickly stuffed them down his sock. After that the speed of his racing heart began to slow and, more calmly, he continued to count. Then he opened the safe door with the combination and placed the rest of the money carefully into the allotted sections. For a few seconds he stared into it, his mind doing a quick count of how much it contained, and then reluctantly he closed the door again, only sorry that he hadn't the courage to take more. He wiped the sweat from his forehead, straightened his shoulders and returned to the bar again, the most trusted employee in the place.

He was off on the following day and decided to go to a race meeting at Leopardstown. To his delight a surprise twenty-to-one win in the first race meant that his financial situation improved considerably, and he had the confidence now to wander into the bar. In the past he had networked religiously at as many events as he could attend, and although he had been out of this particular circle of acquaintances for some time, he still felt he could pull a stroke or two, anxious to prove that he hadn't lost his touch.

'Dermot?' A burly man grabbed his arm as he pushed through the crowd.

He turned to greet the man, recognised him, but couldn't recollect his name.

'I heard you were in a spot of trouble,' the man said, taking a gulp of a pint of Guinness.

'Got stung by a chancer in Spain. I had a large investment in property over there.'

'Caused you to go belly-up, I believe?'

'That's all sub judice at the moment; can't discuss the details,' Dermot said in a jocular manner. He wouldn't have admitted for the world how bad his situation was.

'Best of luck. See you.' He turned away.

'Dermot, how are you?' Another person stopped him and they talked for a moment or two.

'I'm involved in some new developments, lucrative stuff,' Dermot said.

'I heard things weren't too good?'

'Actually, this new investment could be your type of thing, although it's only in the early stages. How about taking an in-depth look at it? You might be interested in coming on board?'

The man took a swig of his whiskey. 'All tied up at the moment, no spare cash. Sorry about that but thanks for the offer. Must see someone, catch you later.'

Dermot felt excluded. Bastards. With their shifty eyes always looking somewhere beyond.

'I've been talking with the accountants, the company has got to be wound up. I'm not prepared to lose any more money,' Irene announced, doing her business executive thing, dressed in a stark black suit, and crisp white shirt.

'Irene, losses are part of any new business, particularly in the first year. You can't expect to make money in that short space of time,' Dermot protested.

'I was willing to invest some money in the venture, but enough has gone into it. I'd be better off buying and selling just one house for myself and making a few bob, than going for the big bipps and getting stung.' She sat up straight, crossed one leg over the other, her patent leather shoe pointing sharply. All the time she puffed rapidly on a cigarette. Deep drags and blows like a steam train, he thought, and wanted to laugh. But there was nothing funny about this situation at all.

'Please Irene, let's give it another go,' he begged.

'No, forget it,' she looked at him coldly, her blue eyes unsympathetic. 'I've no admiration for a man who has let himself sink so low. You used to be so different, Dermot. So vibrant and alive. I couldn't keep up with you. I was fascinated, excited by your success. I wanted to share in it too; don't you remember how we used to talk of going to live in some exotic place? You were going to buy your own island in the Caribbean with white beaches, blue seas, and palm trees, a magic romantic place. And you promised to leave your dull life with sensible Kate behind, and come with me. What happened to all of that?'

'We could still do it. Let's go away, rekindle what we once had. We loved each other then, you've just described how it was,' he whispered softly.

'You've changed out of all recognition, Dermot. I think a week away would be almost too much to bear. You need to jizz yourself up. Get going again under your own steam and stop begging money from me. Be a man, not a wimp.'

'I'm not a wimp. Never was,' he growled, and knocked back the rest of the whiskey in the glass.

There was a ring on the doorbell.

'That must be Ted.' She stood up and hurried out of the room. Hands fluttering, patting a blonde hair into place and repositioning the fall of her jacket.

Dermot's eyes followed her and he wondered who this Ted guy was. He listened carefully, trying to discern the nature of their relationship by the murmurings in the hall. When they walked in, hand in hand, smiling at each other, his stomach sank.

Irene introduced the stocky man. 'This is Dermot, my step-daughter's ex-husband,' her laugh was high-pitched, 'complicated, isn't it?'

They shook hands and Dermot was astonished to note that he was even younger than himself, mid-thirties at most.

'Ted's an investment broker.' Irene led him over to the black leather couch. Then she poured him a drink and, almost as an afterthought, offered Dermot another. Suddenly he was savagely jealous.

'Well, Dermot, what business are you in?' Ted asked with an affable smile.

Dermot hesitated for a few seconds. 'I'm in property,' he said then, hating the other man with his suntanned skin and large white glimmering teeth. The jacket he wore was exquisitely cut, probably Gucci or one of those other designers, judged Dermot. Everything about him screamed wealth.

Irene said nothing.

'I've invested some money myself, but it's only a sideline. No doubt you're in it in a much bigger way.' He covered Irene's hand with his and they smiled intimately.

Dermot was furious as he realised that any chance of getting money from Irene today had disappeared. He sat awkwardly in the armchair, moving slightly forward, the soft leather squeaking under him, until finally he couldn't bear the tension any longer. 'Irene, I'd better go.' He stood up.

'Sure Dermot, I'll see you out.'

She led the way down the cream marble-tiled hallway. Pieces of sculpture positioned in alcoves along its length were lit from behind. Irene was well off, all her money inherited from Kate's father. If she hadn't fluttered her eyelashes at him, that money would have come to Kate and me. Dermot thought as he walked slowly to the lift, his face twisted into a grimace of resentment.

Outside, he wandered on to Merrion Road and decided to walk some of the way into town rather than take a taxi, his preferred mode of transport since he had sold his Mercedes. He hung around a couple of pubs in the hope of seeing someone he knew who would buy him a drink, but there was no-one out tonight. Eventually he took a bus home. Sitting at the back with his head down, his usual explanation at the ready about the car being in the garage and not being able to get a taxi. His phone rang just after he stepped off. It was Kevin, an auctioneer friend of his.

'Sorry I've been so long getting back to you, but it's been madness here.'

'I'm gutting the house, throwing out all the furniture, can you put it into one of your sales?' Dermot asked.

'Yea, sure, I can take it next week.'

'I'll make a list of everything. It's difficult to get rid of stuff these days.'

'What have you?'

'The dining-room suite, Regency, seats twelve, with sideboard. Some good tables. A desk. Cabinets. You know Kate always chose good stuff.'

Everything sold on the day, and he ended up with more than a few thousand. His immediate impulse was to rush down to the bookies to increase its value. But something held him back. For once he didn't do it. He went home. A very lonely place now. The rooms far too big, like school halls in the holidays. He lived in the TV-room and kitchen, denuded of everything other than the table, chairs and the couch. The television provided the only life in the house and he could occasionally persuade himself into thinking for a few seconds that there was someone else there.

Chapter Nine

Kate knew that Jack wasn't fooled when she used the excuse of having to work on the day she was invited to Tyrconnell Park, but if she was to get away for the following weekend it would have to be done. It was very busy, but May and Sinead started on Monday, and made a considerable difference. Even so, she had just rushed back from the hairdressers when he arrived.

'Sorry, I'm not ready yet. I've to check progress with May and Sinead.'

'Can I do anything?' he asked.

'Pack for me please, my clothes are on the bed. I've a couple of calls to make.'

'That reminds me.' He looked at her with a mischievous grin. 'I was about to suggest we turn off our mobiles when we get going.'

'My phone? I don't know if I could.'

'I can see by your shocked expression that you would go into withdrawal if you did that, so just promise me that whoever rings won't drag you away this time.'

'OK, if anything turns up, it can wait until Monday.'

'This place is stunning!' Kate gazed around the elegant foyer of the eighteenth-century house on the outskirts of Kilkenny. The décor was in gold, the rich furniture of the period gleaming, the lighting subdued. 'Come on. Let's walk up this staircase instead of taking the lift. Lady Kate!' Jack took her arm.

In the suite, he tipped the young porter and closed the door.

Kate wandered around the spacious sitting-room and into the

bedroom which was dominated by a huge mahogany four-poster bed, the colour scheme a deep crimson and ivory. 'I feel like I've been transported back in time.' She threw herself into the middle of the soft quilt. 'Thanks so much for arranging it!'

'I love you, never forget that.' He kissed her gently.

'And I love you.' She wound her arms around him.

He quietened her with his lips and moved closer. 'It's so good to have you all to myself,' he murmured.

She curled around him and put everything other than Jack out of her head. Without any haste at all, their clothes were taken off and floated into the space beyond. No thoughts of how creased her good black trousers, pin-striped jacket and silk blouse might become crossed Kate's mind as they languidly came together, making slow sensual love. Jack teased, his hands gently playing, touching all those sensitive places which sent delicious ripples of pleasure through her. She loved the feel of his smooth sallow skin. It had a permanent suntanned hue, with only a light growth of body hair. She enjoyed to look at him. The shape of his shoulders, broad chest, flat stomach and narrow hips, not an extra ounce of fat there.

'You are so beautiful,' he whispered. His lips moved slowly. His breath flowed warm on her skin and left her aching for him so much so she took the dominant role on top. Coaxing him to a climax, their bodies moved in perfect unison, until they were exhausted. Slick with perspiration, they breathed fast, blue eyes devouring brown, and still aroused, drew closer again, reluctant to part.

The next morning, in the warm cosiness they made love before and after breakfast, until eventually, about twelve, Jack murmured something about going out.

'Where?' Kate enquired sleepily, 'let's stay in bed all day.' She reached for him.

'I want to take you out for some fresh air and after that we'll come back if you like.' He kissed her. 'Now, it's time to surface.'

They wandered through the narrow streets of Kilkenny, exploring the ancient heritage of the city. Then they visited Rothe House, and after that, made their way to the castle, where Frank was going to take them on a tour. A friend of Jack's, he was an extremely pleasant man who proved to be a mine of information about the home of the Butler family. They spent a very enjoyable couple of hours in his company and walked through the grounds following the river back into the city. The skies above were overcast and there was a chill wind, but their excited mood dispelled any affect the grey clouds might have imposed. For Kate particularly, it was just wonderful to be away with Jack, the two of them alone, nothing else to interfere. And she had actually turned off her phone! She was enjoying the slow wander through the streets, when Jack steered her towards a small jewellers. 'Rudolf Heltzel!' he announced and pushed open the door.

'He designed the necklet and earrings you gave me?'

The exquisite pieces were displayed in glass cases and Kate was enthralled by the beauty of the unusual designs, deeply regretting that Dermot had sold the jewellery Jack had given her. He introduced her to Rudolf and Maeve, and they chatted for a while. Then he drew her attention to a tray of rings which Rudolf had put on the counter.

'Choose one, my love,' Jack said softly.

'But I ... ' Kate hesitated.

'Look around at the other pieces, maybe you'd prefer one of those.'

'They're all beautiful.'

'Happy Birthday.' Jack kissed her.

Kate's heart missed a beat and she could feel her face grow warm. So busy lately, she had forgotten her birthday was on the following Tuesday.

'That one is very unusual.' Jack pointed. Fine gold rods veered upward from a thick band, a gold daisy on top with a sparkling diamond nestling in its centre.

'It's amazing,' Kate whispered in awe.

'Do you like it?' Jack asked.

'I love it.'

'Let's try it on.' Jack nodded to Rudolf, picked up the ring and turned to Kate. His eyes met hers, questioningly, and she held out her right hand. He smiled and slipped it on to the third finger.

'How's that for size?' he asked.

'It seems fine.' She splayed her fingers, the light catching the large stone. 'It's fabulous!'

'Do you like it?'

'Of course I do!' she smiled, excited.

'We'll take it.'

'I'm over the moon! Thank you so much.' She knew that this ring had significance, regardless of which finger it was on.

'Some day I hope you'll wear another one on your left hand.'

'I will,' she smiled but didn't meet his eyes.

The ring felt strangely out of place, never having worn any other than her engagement and wedding rings which were now in a box in the dressing-table drawer. It was large, but light, and because it fitted so perfectly, it didn't really move very much at all.

'It looks lovely on you.'

'Thanks so much. You're far too generous.' She kissed him.

That evening they ate at the Fleva Restaurant. Jack knew Michael, the owner and chef, and he managed to come out of the kitchen for a couple of minutes to chat and then disappeared again. The restaurant had a number of interconnecting rooms with bright colourful décor. An interesting collection of art hung on the walls. The food was delicious, and in the tranquil ambiance of the place, Kate realised how much she was enjoying this time with Jack.

'Wish we could get away every weekend.' He sipped his wine and smiled at her.

'Neither of us could squeeze work into a five-day week?' she laughed.

'I could.'

'Your clients are not screaming at you to meet targets, you can take your time.'

He put down his glass, and poured more wine for both of them. 'It's nice to be able to drink and not worry about driving. We'll get them to phone a taxi later. There's no hurry.' He leaned forward in his chair and covered her hand with his, smiling. 'When we get back, stay with me, work in Berwick Road, but live at Harrington Place. It's too lonely without you.'

Kate's heart jerked and she took a quick swallow of wine.

'It was a clean break with Dermot, wasn't it?' His voice was uncertain.

'Of course it was. I have no interest in seeing him again, ever.' The last time they met, he had come around to the house with a bottle of wine and a gift. What had started as a pleasant chat had quickly turned into a violent attempted rape which left her shaking, and furious.

'Do you miss Rathfarnham?' Jack asked.

'No.' Kate had a sudden vision of their house, the home she had made. 'That's past tense now. I love you, Jack.' She looked into his eyes. 'I want to share my life with you, but I'm not quite ready yet. I need space, time to breathe. Can you understand?'

'I'm too impatient, I want you now.'

'Don't push me, please.'

'All right, I can see how that would be the worst thing for me to do. Please forgive me?' He pressed her hand gently.

They didn't stay too long on Sunday, the day rather wet and windy and headed back to Jack's house where they intended to loll about in front of the fire and read the papers. As Kate put on the kettle to boil water for tea, Jack listened to the messages on the answering machine, while looking into the fridge.

'What do you fancy to eat?' he asked.

'Couldn't eat a thing after that big breakfast.'

Jack's mother's voice echoed into the room. 'Give me a ring, please?'

'I'll have cheese.' He took some crackers from a tin.

She took out a couple of mugs and poured milk into a small jug.

'Jack, haven't seen you in ages, and I believe you're back from wherever you'd gone.' A man's voice.

'That's Eamon. I must call.'

'Jack. This is Mia. You probably don't remember me but we met about five years ago. Could you phone me?' There was a pause, a number sharply rattled out, with a breathless "please" tagged on.

Chapter Ten

'Your home is wonderful. It's so good of you to have us.' Susie put a small handbag on the hall-table with a tired sigh, although she hadn't carried anything other than that from the taxi.

'Thanks.' Kate let the two heavy suitcases sink to the floor.

'Come on, Susie, let me show you around the house.' Pat took her hand and brought her into the sitting-room. 'Isn't this wonderful? Of course, it needs some work done to it.'

'Just let me get my hands on it, I'll really turn it into something.' She lifted the corner of the cream throw and glanced underneath. 'That can go for starters. Out!' She wandered around the room and stopped at the rosewood desk. 'Not bad.'

Kate stood watching, an uncomfortable feeling in her stomach.

'Susie's making plans for the house already, Kate, you know how good she is at this sort of thing. We've renovated and moved so many times I've lost count. And we made a heck of a lot of money as well.'

'Fourteen times, Pat!' She pointed a finger at him.

'And Dublin is the last, honey.' He put his arm around her.

'This house is just crying out for a make-over. I must do some reading up on Georgian Dublin or is this Victorian? I like everything to be exactly right.' She whirled around and ran her fingers across the fabric of one of the curtains, a disdainful look on her face. She was quite pretty. Kate had to admit. Blonde hair piled on top of her head and held with a grip. A tight-knit sweater and blue jeans hugged a very slim figure, quite tall in teetering high heels. 'I'm really looking forward to this,' she smiled, 'I'll be like a hurricane;

you won't know yourself.'

'I hadn't planned to do any more to the house just yet. It takes a lot of money.'

'But you can't let a house like this fall into disrepair, it will lose its value. You'll have to take out a loan.'

'I'm quite happy with it,' Kate tried to smile, but found it difficult, recalling how much Susie used to irritate her. 'Now what would you like to eat?' She changed the subject, refusing to let herself be intimidated.

They walked downstairs into the kitchen.

'My God, this is like the last century. And I don't mean the twentieth,' she screamed out loud, 'you mean to say you use that antique thing there?'

'It's quite adequate,' Kate said, 'I've cooked Christmas dinner here without any problem.'

'In all my homes, the kitchen was the most important room.'

'Susie is a cordon bleu cook, you know, Kate, certificated. She once managed a top-notch restaurant.'

'You'll give me a big head, darling.' She opened one of the cupboard doors and peered inside. Then, without any comment, examined another, and another, including the cutlery drawer. Kate watched with rising annoyance. Stop looking at my things, you curiosity box!

'Where are the boys?' Susie asked suddenly.

'I think they've gone exploring.'

'Do you want to see your rooms before you eat? I sleep in the large front room. You'll be in the back. And the boys will have the two smaller rooms.'

'Are they en suite?'

'No, sorry, there's only one bathroom in the house.'

'Rob hates to share,' she grimaced.

'Well, he'll have to join the queue here,' Kate dismissed Rob's sixteen-year-old dislikes.

'Donal isn't going to be pleased about it either,' Susie pouted.

'I'm sorry, honey, but this is only temporary, until we get our own place,' Pat tried to placate her.

'I hope it won't be too long.'

I hope it isn't either, thought Kate.

'Hey Mom, there's a neat garden, and an old shed at the back. We could set up a basketball court down there.' Rob and Donal rushed in.

'Yea, sure, no prob. Now come and eat.' The boys crowded in, tall muscular lads who seemed to take up all the space in the kitchen.

'I have a chicken dish ready, and there's dessert as well.' Kate opened the oven door and a delicious aroma wafted out. 'Why don't you sit down in the dining-room?'

'We might try a little of it, but the boys ... ' Susie wrinkled her nose.

'Smells good to me,' Pat sniffed appreciatively.

'We'll get MacDonalds,' Rob said, flopping on Uncle Bill's armchair which Kate still kept by the fireplace.

'You have to go out and get that. Drive. I'm not even sure where there is one,' Kate tried to remember, 'why don't you have something else? I could cook pasta.'

'No way.' Donal, the younger one, made a face.

'We can't let them starve,' Susie said.

'What about fish and chips, or pizza?' At that suggestion Rob's eyes lit up.

'Yea, pizza.'

'You help yourself to some chicken and there are vegetables in the oven as well,' Kate said to Pat and Susie, 'I'll take Rob out.'

'I'll come too.' Donal stood up.

They drove to the nearest take-away and the boys stood looking at the pictures of pizza with puzzled looks on their faces.

'They're different.'

'Well, you're in Ireland now,' Kate laughed. Eventually, they decided on whatever they wanted, with French fries and cans of Coke. As they sat waiting she quizzed them. 'How do you feel about living here?'

'We didn't want to come over, Dad forced us.'

'It will be a new experience.'

'Yea?' His expression didn't auger well.

They returned home, but only picked at the food, really more interested in flicking through the television stations, trying to find something which they liked. But Kate didn't have Sky Sports or any of those satellite channels and, finally bored, they went outside and threw ball at each other in the dimming light of the evening, until Pat hounded them up to bed.

'What's the shopping like in Dublin?' Susie lay back in the chair, sipping a glass of wine. She had mellowed as the first bottle emptied and another was opened, and was a little less brittle in her responses.

'There are some good stores in town and large shopping centres in the suburbs.'

'I love to shop,' she smiled at Pat.

'Does my little girl like to shop!' He reached over and patted her hand.

'Are you getting at me?' She straightened up suddenly, and the softness which had been so attractive in her a moment before disappeared.

'Honey!' he laughed, 'I was just stating a fact, an irrefutable fact. I hate to think of what percentage of my salary you spend on clothes, make-up, cosmetic surgery and whatever else you girls do.'

'Pat!' she glowered at him, 'how dare you give the impression that I shouldn't. It's all for you, to keep myself looking beautiful.'

'But does it have to cost so much?' He swallowed the last of the wine in the glass and topped up again. Both of them well on by now and probably just ripe for a row, Kate thought.

'What does it matter about the cost, once the end result is worth it?' she asked pettishly.

'I'm the one who signs the cheques.'

'I can't believe you're saying this in front of Kate.'

'We have no secrets,' he grinned.

Kate wondered how she was going to stop the pair of them drinking. 'It's getting late, maybe we should call it a day?'

'Call it a night,' Pat's loud lazy laugh boomed around the room.

'It's been one hell of a night,' Susie hissed.

'I've enjoyed myself, good vintage wine, very nice.' He waved his glass in the air.

'That's all you're interested in,' Susie snapped.

'I enjoy a drink. I'm an Irishman. We're famous for it.'

'No wonder you're going to seed.'

'I'm still growing wild.'

She finished her wine, a disgruntled expression on her face. 'Well, I'm not growing wild with you, I'm more particular about myself.'

'At my expense.'

'If you keep on about that I'll ... ' she flashed, turning her head around so sharply long tendrils of blonde hair began to drift downwards.

'You'll what?' He pushed his nose close to hers in a puggish way.

'I'll make you sorry.' She raised her hand and slapped him hard across his cheek.

'Susie, what did you do that for?' He felt his face with a puzzled look.

'And you'll feel my hand again if you don't stop going on about what I spend. I work hard, I deserve every dollar.'

'Awe Susie, don't be so aggressive, it doesn't suit you.'

'Sometimes you have to be assertive, which is a different thing, Pat. A woman can't let her man ride roughshod. I trust you wouldn't let that happen, Kate?'

'Our Kate is a lady,' Pat retorted.

'Are you suggesting that I'm not?' her voice rose into a high-pitched scream.

Kate felt embarrassed.

'You take that any way you like,' he leered at her.

The situation was getting out of hand, so Kate stood up. 'Let's all go to bed, you must be exhausted after the journey.'

'You're a bastard,' she shouted.

'Bitch.'

'Bastard.'

'Pat - Susie - please, the boys,' Kate tried to intervene, but was unsuccessful.

'Bitch,' he roared.

'Bastard.'

Kate was mesmerised by the two of them, snarling at each other like dogs. It was obvious they were not going to take the slightest notice of her, so she slowly walked out of the room and closed the door, leaving them there to taunt each other. She locked up and went to bed, but now had to listen to the continuing argument as it wound its vicious way up the stairs and into the room across the landing. She couldn't believe this.

Chapter Eleven

Jack picked up the phone and dialled the number. Mia answered immediately. Her voice was soft and husky and he could immediately visualise the beautiful Swedish woman, who was almost as tall as himself, and a good ten years younger. They made a little superficial chitchat at first, and then he was stuck for words, unusual for him. There was a pause before he asked, 'are you working these days?'

'No, not at the moment.' The Americanised accent was even more accentuated than he remembered.

'That's a pity, you used to be so prolific.'

'Could I meet you perhaps?'

Taken aback, and somewhat puzzled, he said nothing.

'It won't take long.'

'Yes, of course.'

'I might call.'

'Do that, and you can meet Kate, my partner.' He slipped that in. A slight fear that her reason for making contact might have deeper motivation.

'I would prefer to talk to you alone. Is this possible?'

She came the following afternoon, exactly on the dot of three, as arranged. Dressed in blue jeans, blue shirt and cream jacket, the collar turned up. He was surprised by the change in her appearance. The long fair hair had been cut off and she now wore it very short. The style accentuated the size of the almond-shaped eyes, full lips, high cheek bones, her classic features beautiful. He ushered her into the lounge and she sat down on the chair by the fireplace. Then she smiled. A wide warm smile which transformed her severe expression, and suddenly he remembered. The weeks they spent together were colourful snapshots of heady days and nights in Spain after he had had a particularly successful few months painting in the Sierra Nevada. It had been a crazy in love thing which fizzled as quickly as it had begun.

'Would you like some coffee or tea?'

'Thank you, no.' She shook her head.

'Something stronger then?' he grinned.

'Perhaps some water?'

'Yes, sure, I'll have coffee myself. Just give me a minute.' He went down to the kitchen and quickly poured a glass of Ballygowan, added a slice of lemon and ice. The coffee was already perking and he poured himself a cup, put some chocolate biscuits on a dish and took up the tray. He sat down and sipped his coffee, still wondering why she was here. 'I loved those bronzes you used to do.'

She made a slight inclination of the head. A rather sad gesture.

'You're obviously busy with other things,' he smiled.

She nodded.

'How's life in general?'

'Good.'

'Have you been back to Stockholm or are you spending all your time here?'

'I have no family in Sweden other than distant cousins.'

'Oh yes, I remember.'

There was an awkward silence between them. She drank some water and he sipped his coffee, trying to think of something else to say.

'And you are well, Jack?' For the first time she asked a question of him.

'I'm fine, thanks, I've an exhibition arranged at the Nestor Gallery in December.' The tension eased.

'You mentioned you have a partner now, and ... children?'

'Kate has two grown sons from her previous marriage.'

'I'm glad for you,' she said softly.

'No doubt there's someone in your life as well?'

'Yes.' She lowered her eyes, and put the empty glass on the side table.

'Would you like some more water?'

'No thank you.'

He was going to ask about her partner, but she seemed reticent so he decided against it. None of his business. Another silence yawned, and lengthened, until eventually he spoke again.

'Did you want to talk about something in particular?' he had to ask.

'It's difficult.' Her half-smile was timid, and he was suddenly worried.

'You remember when we parted and I came back to Dublin?'

He nodded.

'Shortly after I arrived, I discovered that I was pregnant.'

Shock waves swept through Jack. His heart thumped. He could feel his chest almost burst open. 'What?'

'I didn't tell you. Our relationship was so short, just a few weeks.' She stopped and then suddenly spoke faster as if she had to get the words out before something happened. 'But I was very happy to have a baby. Maybe I didn't even want you to know, I wanted her all to myself.'

'Her?'

'Yes, my Marie Elaine.'

'Am I hearing you correctly? You had my baby?' He was stunned.

'Yes.'

'I can't believe it.'

'She is beautiful.'

'Why are you telling me out of the blue like this?' he stuttered.

'I felt it was time.'

'How do you know that it's ... she's ... mine?' Anger rushed through him.

Her large eyes met his, wide and shocked. 'There was no-one else, she had to be yours.'

'Are you sure?'

'I am positive.'

'I need a drink!' He stood up. Opened the cabinet. Poured a glass of whiskey and took a quick swallow. His heart did a drum solo inside him, his bewildered mind unable to get around this unexpected situation.

She stared fixedly at him, her eyes luminous, tears about to spill on to her cheeks.

'A child belonging to me has been living in this world for four years and I didn't even know. Why now?' he demanded.

She seemed to shrink in the face of his venom. 'I simply wanted to tell you of her existence,' she whispered.

'There has to be more to it than that. Are you looking for something? Do you need money?'

'No.'

'If you're not looking for anything, then what's the point?' He took another gulp of the whiskey, and tried to be gentler with her, aware that he had handled it very badly so far.

'I thought you ought to know.'

He was silent then.

After a moment, she rose and walked slowly into the hall.

He followed. 'When was she born?' he asked.

'October 6th.' She tucked up the collar of her jacket, opened the front door and stepped across the threshold.

'Do you want me to take her out to the zoo every second weekend? MacDonalds? Have her stay over at Christmas and Easter?' It was sarcastic, and he knew it.

'No, that isn't the reason.'

'Then what the hell?' he burst out, but she had already begun to walk slowly down the drive, head down, hands pushed into her pockets. 'Mia?' he called her back but she ignored him.

He banged the door closed. Then he flung himself into the lounge and grabbed the whiskey bottle, pouring another glass and drinking it quickly. He sat down on the couch, staring into space, but his view of the room was suddenly blurred, as tears filled his eyes and he began to cry. Great surges of emotion burst through him. The death of his first child jumped back into his mind with all its ghastly horror. He remembered the joy when his wife Paula had told him she was pregnant, and then the awful despair which followed when she decided to have an abortion, because she didn't want the inconvenience of a baby to interfere with her career. Now here was a woman with whom he had only a brief relationship, at maximum three or four weeks, telling him that he had fathered another child. He simply couldn't deal with it.

'I thought I'd come around,' Kate said when she phoned later, 'I'll bring a bottle of wine and we can relax.'

'No, I've had enough to drink.'

'You've been drinking already?'

'I'm not good company tonight,' he blurted out, his only thought to try and stop her coming over. He couldn't bear for her to see him in this state.

'What's wrong?'

'I've had a tough day.'

'I'm sorry, love.'

He could sense her growing anxiety. 'My ... eh ... the work didn't go well.'

'I think you need a break, I'll be there in ten.'

'Kate, I'd rather keep at it here, try and make something out of what I've been doing,' he reached out to her, but when he heard nothing else, realised that she had put down the phone.

He picked up the glass of whiskey and finished it, his mood so low he couldn't even imagine how he would string two words of normal conversation together.

Kate floated in, looking particularly gorgeous in a cream poncho over a long lacy skirt and suede boots. She put her arms around him and kissed him. He held her tightly.

'Are you out of sorts? Come on, what's making you feel so bad?' She ran her fingers across his forehead and around his face and then kissed him again slowly. 'Tell me, am I not your closest friend, your lover, your baby?' she smiled teasingly.

'Of course you are,' he said wearily.

'You seem so tired.'

65

'I know.' He sat down on the couch and looked at her. How could he tell this beautiful woman whom he loved so deeply about Mia. Although all that had occurred before he knew Kate, now it seemed that he had committed the worst of sins and was experiencing the guilt that went with it.

She sat close beside him, and put her arm around his shoulders. 'What you need is an early night and a cuddle,' she giggled, but her voiced trailed off suddenly and he became aware that she was staring across the room, her attention on the plate of biscuits which still stood on the table, the mug, and glass beside it.

'You had a visitor?'

'Yes, a friend.'

'Who?'

'One of the lads,' he couldn't look in her eyes.

'I must say you're very reticent,' she grinned, 'aren't you going to divulge his identity?' she paused for a few seconds, 'or is it hers?'

'It was...'

'Forget it, I'm only joking, I really don't want to know.'

'Eamon.'

'He's more a can man, I'd say, hardly tea and bickies.'

'He was driving.'

'Oh.'

'Glass of wine?' She drew the bottle towards her. 'I'll get the opener.'

'Not for me thanks.' He shook his head.

She stared at him for a few seconds. 'Jack, has something happened?' There was real concern in her deep blue eyes.

'I'm sorry.'

'My love, what's wrong?' She cupped his face in her hand.

'Today was ... '

She put her arm around him and drew him close. 'Tell me?'

He shook his head.

'You can't?'

He was very much aware that things were slipping out of his control.

'Jack, I thought we were friends and much more than that. Surely you can tell me, whatever it is? It can't be all that bad. Go on, exaggerate, make it ten times worse than it really is and see whether I'll understand or not.'

He said nothing.

'If you can't share it with me, then obviously I've been mistaken in you.' She tossed her head, stood up abruptly and strode through to the hall.

'I'm sorry.'

'You keep saying that. But it doesn't mean anything obviously.' She opened the front door.

'I don't want you to get the wrong idea, my love.' He reached for her.

'Well, you're not going the right way about that,' she snapped and walked out to the car.

He stood watching with a dreadful sense of loss as she drove away.

Chapter Twelve

Kate didn't know what to think, really puzzled by Jack's mood this evening. She sat into the car and started the engine, pushing her foot down on the pedal with vehemence, causing the car to jerk forward and hurtle into the roadway. What was up with him? She drove along, becoming more and more angry. Why couldn't he have shared whatever it was with her? She stopped at the lights, and moved on when she thought it had turned green, but had to stand on the brake immediately as a car came across. Idiot! She could have been clobbered. The rest of the journey home was taken at a more careful pace, and she arrived in to find Pat walking up the hall carrying a tray of drinks.

'We've some friends in this evening, come and meet them,' he smiled jovially.

She tried to think of an excuse. 'I'm wrecked, I think I'll just go on up to bed.'

He pushed open the door. 'Here she is, my sister Kate,' he announced, and she had no choice but to follow him inside.

There were two couples there chatting with Susie, work colleagues of Pat apparently. Forced to make small talk for a while until finally she excused herself, pleading tiredness. But as she closed the door, a sudden fury burst through her. Why had she let herself be marooned into such a situation by Pat. They had taken over her home. A place which had become a safe haven from the world and all its frustrations. She felt it all the more so tonight, puzzled and upset by Jack's attitude. Although she loved him and wanted to be part of his life, something intransigent inside refused to let her turn her back on all she had achieved. There was more to be done. Much more. And she could feel it at her fingertips, and knew that she wanted to follow the path which seemed to run parallel with what he needed from her. Now perhaps he had decided that he wasn't going to wait any longer. Maybe there was someone else in his life already. And this Mia person, how did she fit into the scheme of things? Jealousy sent a wave of sickening discomfort through her, and she wanted to rush around to him again and demand an explanation. As she lay in bed trying to sleep, her mind painted images of ghastly scenarios of other women, his protestations of love suddenly meaningless.

The following morning she tried to put the events of the night before to one side, and was preparing the orders when the phone rang.

'Kate?'

'Yes.'

'I'm so sorry, my love, for last night, I don't now what got into me.'

She didn't say anything, as a sudden rush of emotion swelled through her and tears moistened her eyes.

'Kate? Are you all right?'

She pulled a tissue from her pocket and dried her eyes. This was an unexpected reaction. She had intended to give him a piece of her mind this morning, but that plan had suddenly disappeared, and left her like a snivelling child.

'I'm ... OK.'

'Can I call over, I must see you.'

'We couldn't talk here.'

'Would you come here, please?'

'I can't just now.' A sense of relief swept through her, and all the fears which had beset her during the night suddenly seemed less threatening.

'What about later, for dinner, or we could go out?'

'I'll be there sometime after six.'

*

69

She was very upset, he could tell that from her reaction and it made him feel even more guilty. But he couldn't tell her the reason for Mia's visit. Not yet anyway. If Kate thought he had deliberately kept the existence of this child a secret from her, it could mean the end of their relationship. She would have limited tolerance for deceit he was positive about that. He had been so anxious to persuade her to make a commitment to him and move into Harrington Place, and was disappointed that she had not yet made that decision. He had put it down to the pressure of business, and the fact that Pat and Susie were staying with her. But now a question pushed its ugly head into his mind. Surely it would have been a perfect solution to come over to live in Harrington Place now. Why had she not thought of that herself?

'What did you do all day?' she asked, but it was an impersonal query, and as Jack embraced her, he could immediately sense the tension within her.

'I have to finish a commission by the weekend, although I'm not happy with it. Perhaps it was the pressure to complete which sent me off the deep end yesterday,' he lied. She shifted in his arms and bent to put her handbag on the hall-table. 'Can you forgive me for being so awful to you?' He pulled her around to him again.

'I'm still annoyed that you couldn't tell me what was up with you,' her expression was cold.

'It was just a low mood; you've never seen me at my worst, the depths of despair are unattractive.'

'That's all?'

'Yes.' He hated himself.

'But maybe I could have helped? I don't like to be shut out.'

'This is something I have to deal with myself. It's happened before and luckily doesn't last very long. Usually I'm feeling my usual optimistic self again by the following day,' he created the myth of the tortured artist, and kissed her. 'My love, I know I've hurt you, and I really regret it. Please tell me that you forgive me?'

'Perhaps I did over-react,' she said slowly, 'but I was jealous, and imagined that you had another woman in your life.' She looked at him.

'You are the only woman in my life, the one I love above anyone else, how could you think that?'

'When someone excludes you, all sorts of things come into your mind.'

'I'll try never to do that again, I promise.' He held her very close to him and they clung to each other then. After a short while, they moved into the lounge and he picked up a bouquet of red roses and handed them to her.

'Thanks,' she smiled and touched the buds, bringing them close to her face, breathing in the delicate scent. 'They're beautiful.'

'And this ... ' He handed her a small box.

'There was no need, Jack, but thanks again.'

She opened the box and took out an exquisite gold chain, its strands entwined together to create a modern celtic design. 'It's fabulous!'

'It's nothing really, you deserve much more.'

'Help me put it on, will you?'

She went into the hall and stood in front of the mirror while he closed the clasp and kissed the back of her neck.

'It's lovely, I don't know what to say. You've made me feel guilty now.'

'It's not you who should feel that way, it's me.'

'This is like my birthday all over again,' she laughed.

'Then let's celebrate, I've got some champagne on ice.'

'You have?'

'I must wipe out last night. I never want you to go home again in that way. In fact, I want you to consider this house as your home, or anywhere else, once it's with me. How about we sell both of our houses, and buy somewhere new?'

'That doesn't make good economic sense.' She followed him into the kitchen.

'Perhaps not, but who cares about economics. I just want to have you with me all the time in a house big enough to accommodate your work and mine. You have to admit, they complement each other?'

'Pat and Susie have taken over. I'm worn out,' Kate sighed when they had settled down after dinner. 'You've no idea what they're like. All arguing the toss. The kids just have them wound around their little fingers. I let them do their own thing as regards food, Susie never cooks, it's all take-away. I'm reminded of my own lads at that age. The younger one wants to use my computer; his own hasn't arrived yet. Apparently, Susie said he could go into withdrawal if he didn't have the net. I refused point blank to let them use my laptop. I even take it with me when I go out in case they start messing. It's in my car now, would you believe that?' She took a sip of coffee. 'You've no idea how good it is to come over here and get away from it all.'

'I hope that's not the only reason,' he said softly, and kissed her, 'stay tonight.'

'I have to be there for the girls in the morning.'

'We can get up early,' he tried his best to persuade.

'I don't want those kids to have free rein in the house, God knows what they'd get up to.'

'Surely Pat or Susie will keep an eye on them?'

'Pat's OK, but he's gone all day. Susie doesn't get up until near lunchtime, and spends her time painting her nails, doing her hair, make-up and shopping.'

'How long do you think they'll stay?'

'Haven't a clue. There's no mention of looking at houses or sites so far. But in one way, I suppose I'm glad to have them home again, they are my family, you know.'

'Let them have the house until they get their own. What I wouldn't give to have you to myself. Going to bed and knowing that when I put out my hand in the middle of the night you'll be there, and first thing in the morning too, please?' he begged.

'They would take over if I left.'

'Kate, you're letting them use you,' he said dispiritedly.

'No way, I'm my own woman now,' she retorted.

He leaned back on the couch, longing to talk to her about Mia, and the child, but afraid. She might walk out on him and never come back.

'When will we be together? Sometimes I think it'll never happen.'

She took his hand, and he looked at her, a sadness in his brown eyes. 'Hey, you're reversing things now. I'm persuading you that I love you above anyone else in the world, and I wanted you to do that for me earlier.' She put her arms around him. 'OK, so we're not together all the time, but we love each other, isn't that what counts?'

He reached for her. 'Prove it!' he laughed, and enfolded her in his arms. 'My beautiful Kate, never leave me, promise?'

'I promise.'

Very gently his hands explored. Pushing up underneath the silk knitted top she wore until she raised her arms, and he took it off. They clung together, soft skin against soft skin, and played with each other leisurely. Tonight was different somehow. A getting to know you again. A finding their way back to where they had been before yesterday. Their lovemaking was languid, almost dreamy, their passion out there on the edge waiting to explode, until they reached such a state of excitement that they couldn't hold back any longer, soaring to a place of the most exquisite delight.

But later, in those dark hours when you are most alone, Jack felt the loss of such love keenly. How could he live without Kate? Could he turn away from the knowledge that this child might be his? Or should he take it further? And if it was proved that she was his daughter, would he want to see her, know her, be a Dad to her?

He wasn't in the mood for sleep and got out of bed again. He was painting a large canvas for the chairman of an international company, and in the studio set out his palette. The mountains of the Sierra Nevada reached up into a blue sky, thick wedges of paint created the light and dark of shadows, the paler edges of cliffs, the deeper tones of blues, rusty reds, gold yellows, and a myriad of other shades which all combined to create a mass of colour which almost jumped out at him in its vibrancy. He worked for an hour or so putting the finishing touches to the painting, and then let his hand fall. It was done. The client would be pleased with it, he had a gut feeling.

He made himself a coffee, and slumped into a kitchen chair as memories of his first child flooded back again. That life which had been abruptly ended by a surgeon in some clinic in London. The pain came in waves, leaving him open and exposed to emotions which had been pushed deep inside since he had split with Paula. Eleven years ago, he had run away from everything he knew. His comfortable life, and successful career in accountancy. Their home had been sold, the mortgage cleared, and the balance divided between them. Jack had invested the money for the future, and headed off to Spain where he lived simply, earning money by working in bars or restaurants, anywhere he could find a job. During the day, he painted. Throwing himself into his art was therapeutic and slowly the pain of loss eased, and drifted into that place where the real soul of Jack, sensitive and vulnerable, was hidden. In a battered truck, he drove into the mountains. Losing himself in the vast stretches of terrain inspired colourful paintings which he hawked around the galleries in Andalucia, until at last they drew attention and began to sell.

He dozed off in the chair. A fitful disturbed sleep, out of which he awoke tired and exhausted the following morning, still undecided as to what he should do, but knowing deep down that this was only the beginning of something which could very well change his life.

It was difficult to begin new work, and in the meantime, he continued working on a painting of Kate from one of those photos he had taken on the beach at Mojacar. He wanted to surprise her with it on some special occasion. Almost complete, he put it away and again was left wondering what to do. He tried out new ideas, none of which seemed quite right, until suddenly one evening his mind took him on to another level, somewhere he had not allowed himself to go before now. This was a place where previously unimaginable possibilities put features on a four-year-old child. Would she look like his first child? A half-brother or sister who had no bright eyes or smile, never laid to rest in a place he might have visited, to say a prayer or put a flower. A wave of regret sent his heart hammering as he accused himself of not trying hard enough to persuade his ex-wife to have their child.

His first stroke was bright yellow sunshiny, deepening darker further down the canvas to a place of death. A forgotten resting place with crooked headstones, the only fertility rampant grasses and weeds licking old markers. Names had faded to nothing, the people who lay here were unidentified. He worked furiously on this first painting for some hours, and then left it; immediately beginning another, an urgency in him as he went backwards in time.

This was the journey of a man never taken before, when he held the hand of his child and walked with it through those first embryonic weeks as the cells formed into a human being. All to waste when somewhere about the seventh, the oxygen was cut off, the heart stopped, and it was lost for ever.

Chapter Thirteen

'Yes Paul, the furniture is in-situ. Steve will be fitting the blinds in numbers five to twelve tomorrow.' Kate flicked through her diary. 'About eight-thirty.' Her mobile rang and Debbie picked it up, nodding and making eye contact. 'I'll be in touch regarding the curtains; should be a little later in the week, certainly by Friday. Sorry, must go, I've another call holding.'

'Kate Crawford?'

'Yes.'

'It's Fiona McStay, I'm with the Gazette. I'm doing a series of articles on entrepreneurs in the property-related areas, and I'd like to feature you.'

'Thank you,' Kate was excited at this unexpected opportunity.

'Could I call to discuss some preliminary ideas?'

'Yes, sure.' Kate checked her diary and they arranged a date later that week. She picked up a call on the other line then and dealt with the enquiry from a client. The morning flew past, the phone constantly ringing, interrupting the flow of work. Just after midday she took a break and went into the kitchen intending to make a sandwich for lunch. But what she found there made her fume. The place was a mess, the boys lay on the couch watching a video, while Susie drank coffee and leafed through a fashion magazine. Although it didn't suit her, Kate began to clear everything away. Noisily she emptied the dregs, scraped the crumbs into the bin and put the dishes in the washer. It was to make a point. An angry frustrated hint that she wanted them to clear up after themselves. 'I don't have much time, so I'll leave you to finish up,' she said, rinsing her hands under the tap and wiping them on a towel.

'We're going to meet Pat for a late lunch, he's got business in the city.' Susie threw down the magazine. 'Then we'll do some shopping. Donal, Rob, let's get going. Do you want anything before we go?'

'I'll have a Coke.' Rob opened the fridge and looked inside.

Kate waited.

'There's none there,' he stared at her accusingly.

'No Coke?' Susie joined him.

'Coopers on the line for you.' Debbie put her head around the door.

Kate went into the office, glad to leave them wondering why one of the staples of their diet was inexplicably missing. She couldn't help grinning and satisfaction bubbled up through her. Good enough for them. What do they think this is? A free hotel?

The day progressed. The girls were going flat out to finish the last of the Roman blinds needed for the apartment block. Kate was pleased with the overall look, a similarity of theme between the different floors. But all the time an underlying worry pushed its way in and out of her consciousness. She knew that it would have to be dealt with sooner or later, and may as well be sooner before she went around the twist.

Pat, Susie and the boys all arrived back about six and ordered in dinner from the take-away menu. They were eating Chinese today, and were almost finished when Kate cooked her own pasta with carbonara sauce, put together a salad, and sat down at a corner of the table.

'Have a glass of wine.' Pat poured. 'We're celebrating. Our stuff is arriving tomorrow,' he grinned, and raised his own in a toast.

'That's good.' Kate sipped a little of the sweet red wine.

'Golf clubs, tennis rackets, computers and the rest of our clothes. We've been lost without them. I've booked the lads into Rathgar Tennis Club. Rob could well go on to play the professional game.'

Kate nodded and smiled enthusiastically, hoping to get an opportunity to have her say, which came later when the boys watched a video and Susie dozed on the couch. She walked with Pat into the garden, the evening quite pleasant still.

'This place is exactly as I remember it. Even the flowers are the same. I've been thinking that you really should renovate the mews, it has great potential. I walked around the back the other day and noticed that most of the others have been converted. They're all upmarket homes now, worth a packet I'd say. The price of property in this area is amazing compared to the States. But I love being home. Susie tells me that I'm losing my American drawl and speaking with an Irish accent now. Did you notice?' he grinned.

'That happens, I suppose.'

'I am Irish after all. My family grew up here, all gone now unfortunately, rest their souls. But what is most important to me is to continue on the line of the Crawfords. There's another generation living here now and when the lads get hitched their children will carry on.'

Kate didn't say anything and they continued on down the long garden.

'Is your relationship with this Jack guy serious?' he asked.

'Yes.' Kate didn't like his tone.

'You'll probably be shacking up together soon?'

Irritation swept through her. It was none of Pat's business.

'Any chance he might want to move in here?' His voice was suddenly sharp.

'Perhaps,' she said, just to give him something to worry about, although truly she didn't see that happening at all.

'Well, there's room for everyone. If the mews was converted, you could live down there and also use it for your work and we'd have the main house,' he said, with an expansive wave of his arm.

'But I thought you were going to buy your own home?' Kate asked, suddenly worried.

'I've been looking at that possibility, but the cost of everything is astronomical over here. I don't think we'll be able to do what we want at all. So that's why I'm thinking of living here.'

'I presume you made some money on the sale of your house in Boston?'

'Oh yes, that sold very quickly. But the longer I stay here, the more I like it, and so do Susie and the boys. It's centrally located and the value is going up all the time. We could get a mortgage together to convert the mews and restore the main house.' He plucked a blade of grass from the border and teased it through his teeth.

Kate stared at him, unable to believe what she was hearing. 'Pat, I don't like saying this, but it's my house and I don't wish to do anything with it at the moment.'

'It's also the family home, Kate, and I'm still a Crawford, the direct male line. If I hadn't been away, Uncle Bill would have left it to me. I don't know why he didn't.' He looked around the garden. 'Instead he leaves it to you, a woman on her own who has no need of a home this size.'

Kate was stunned. But she summoned up her courage and decided that now was as good a time as any to be equally blunt. So she plunged in.

'Pat, as we're talking about the house, and all of us living here together, there are a few aspects which are giving me grief.' She could feel his eyes bore through her, but took no notice. 'I know you get the washing and ironing done outside, but it's the housekeeping, cleaning, tidying up after meals, the boys particularly.'

'I'm surprised you don't have a woman coming in every day to do all of that. In the States we've always had a girl. Susie isn't used to working around the house, never was.'

'It isn't easy to find a trustworthy person.'

'What about one of those Russian or Polish girls? We have quite a few in the factory, and the cleaning staff are all foreign.'

'I don't need someone to come in a couple of times a week and flick a duster.'

'You can't expect Susie to do it,' he barked.

'She could clean up after yourselves at least,' Kate wasn't going to leave it.

'Do you want me to be divorced?' he laughed.

'If we're all living here together, then she has to pull her weight.'

'Then we'll have to get someone, even if I have to pay for it myself,' he grumbled, 'I'll ask at the office, maybe one of the cleaners has a friend.'

'Maybe it would be best,' she gave in.

'And another thing, when are we going to meet Jack formally?' Susie suggested we all go out together some evening. What do you think?'

Kate shrugged.

'I'll make a booking. We found a very nice restaurant the other evening, Italian, you'll like it.'

'I'll have to ask him.'

'And why don't you invite Conor over as well, and his partner, what's her name again?'

'Michelle.'

'Oh, that's right.'

Kate had been thinking of arranging something herself. Conor had met Jack briefly, but she was anxious to introduce the new man in her life to the family circle. Although that reminded of her own reluctance to meet the Linleys, and she realised that it would also have to be faced before long.

Chapter Fourteen

Kate walked slowly along the narrow pathway between the graves, the markers of the last resting place of so many people. She glanced at the words carved on the headstones. In loving memory of my dear husband. Cherished wife. Never forgotten. The best Daddy in the world. Our darling baby. Sister. Brother. A wonderful mother. Gran. Grandad. We love you. She was always sad to see that many of the graves were unkempt, with weeds bursting through concrete, or moss covering gravel. Withered bunches of flowers still wrapped in cellophane were propped in holders, or lay crookedly to one side. Others, particularly those of children, were so full of flowers, it was poignant. Her eyes were drawn to where the Crawford name was carved in gold leaf on the back of the black marble headstone, and she noticed an elderly woman standing at their double plot with bowed head.

At her approach, she looked up, and Kate saw that her eyes were filled with tears. She smiled. There was something about the people you meet in cemeteries. In this quiet place, strangers nodded to each other and even stopped sometimes to have a chat, all of them there for the same reason.

The woman dabbed her eyes with a small lacy handkerchief. 'I sometimes come here to say a prayer,' she said softly.

'I like to keep the flowers fresh.' Kate opened a plastic container and poured water into the planter which held a colourful array of pansies, geraniums and begonias.

'They're beautiful. I remember that Bill was very fond of his garden.'

'You knew him?'

'Yes, a long time ago,' she smiled then.

Kate thought how attractive she was. The pink jacket and navy skirt suited her slim figure. The silvery-grey hair was cut short, and she wore only a little make-up.

'He just slipped away in the end,' Kate said, 'and didn't suffer.'

'I'm glad about that.'

Kate bent to pick the dead heads from the purple pansies which this week seemed to have withered quicker than some of the other flowers. After that she said a short prayer and picked up her empty water container. 'I'm sorry, but I must go.'

'And so should I.' The woman crossed herself and together they walked towards the gates.

'Can I give you a lift?'

'There's no need for you to go out of your way, but thanks for asking.' The woman patted her arm. 'I'll catch a bus.'

'It's not easy from here. Where do you live?'

'Palmerston Park.'

'I'm going to Berwick Road, that's quite close to you.'

'Berwick?'

'That's right.'

'Are you Kate ... by any chance?'

'Yes.'

'Bill talked so much about you.'

'I was always very close to him.'

'I'm Grace.'

Kate stared at her in surprise. 'I can't believe it! I read some of your letters and wondered what happened between you and Bill.'

'It's the old story. My parents didn't approve and I married someone else.'

'I thought it was very sad that you never got together. It was obvious from your letters that you cared very much for him. Sit into the car, we can talk there in more comfort.' Kate opened the door and helped her into the passenger seat. Then she sat in herself.

'Where did you find my letters?'

'I was going through his things and came across them.'

'He had kept them?'

'Yes, in a bundle tied with blue ribbon.'

She seemed very surprised.

'Did you keep in touch?' Kate asked.

'Oh yes.' Her eyes twinkled with humour. 'We always met when he came home from sea on leave, three or four times a year.'

'Secretly?'

'Yes.'

'I'm amazed.'

'When you love someone you don't think about the rights and wrongs of it. I just had to see him. When he arrived the first thing he would do was to leave his bicycle against the railings of the park, and when I passed, which I did every day, I would see it and know. The next step was to go the following afternoon to the Savoy Cinema and sit in the back row. He was always there waiting for me.'

'Why didn't you go away together if you felt so strongly?'

'We should have, but my parents were still alive, and I hadn't the courage to do such a thing. We had planned to move to England when Bill retired, but by that time my husband was seriously ill and I couldn't leave. He never forgave me. Years later I often walked past Berwick Road but I never knocked, I couldn't, somehow.'

'That's so sad. I wish you had made more of an effort, I'm sure he would have come around.'

'Perhaps I should.' She stared out of the window.

'When I read your letters to Bill it made a difference to decisions which I later made. He had a very lonely life. An old man with his garden and a television set.'

'I wasn't much different. A woman living in a house which was far too big for one person, with a dog and a cat for company. I had no brothers or sisters, or children, so there are very few people who call.'

'I'm sorry.'

'That's life,' she smiled, 'sometimes we make a bad decision, but can't gather enough courage to face up to it. Perhaps that's the way I was with Bill.'

There was a brief silence between them.

'I suppose we'd better get back.' Kate started the car engine and drove to Grace's home, one of those very large nineteenth-century houses on a corner overlooking the park.

'Your house is beautiful.' She pulled up outside, and walked around to help Grace out of the car. They walked to the gate. 'And the garden too.'

'I have a man who helps me, but it's becoming harder every year, I'm not getting any younger.'

'It's been wonderful to meet you.'

'And you. Call some day and have tea with me?'

'I'd love that, thank you.'

They exchanged numbers. Kate waited until she stood at the front door and then headed back home, absolutely astounded at the coincidence of meeting Grace. A person who lived so close to Bill all those years since his retirement and who could have been such a wonderful companion to him in the latter decades of his life, and hers too.

As soon as she had an opportunity, Kate went upstairs into the attic where all of Bill's things were stored. Within a few minutes, she found the packet of brown-tinted envelopes, but now she couldn't read them, they belonged to Grace.

Chapter Fifteen

Jack was working on a number of paintings, on a thrust of energy which had taken over these last few weeks. It was like the old days when he would spend months up in the mountains of Andalucia. Then it had been a need to create his own interpretation of the landscape, to capture the light and mutation of colours. But now there was a deeper meaning in the images. The feelings which had been contained over the years were released, and he expressed them the only way he knew how. In contrast to his previous work, these paintings were dark, spare, and with a theme of the family in the figures which peopled the canvas, layering on the paint, delineating the background against which they existed. Always a suggestion of life and death, the delicate line between the two barely discernible. Today, he painted a mother and child. Not in traditional pose, but apart from each other, back to back. A feeling of loneliness there.

In the afternoon, someone pressed the doorbell. He ignored its interference, until it was repeated again and again. Suddenly there was something about the demanding rhythm that reminded, so he put down the brush, wiped his hands, and went to open the door. His sister Chris stood outside, looking chic in black, sporting a healthy golden tan. The last time they had met had been unpleasant. The way she had treated Kate when she had come to her house in Torrevieja to look for him had been so harsh and unfeeling he hadn't spoken to her since. He hated rows of any sort, and regretted it.

But she didn't burst in as usual, waiting until he ushered her inside. He closed the door and they were face to face. For the first few seconds there was an awkward silence between them, until finally Chris spoke. 'I'm sorry, very sorry, that I behaved so badly towards Kate. Can you forgive me?' Her blue eyes misted over with tears.

Jack was very surprised to receive this apology from Chris, who usually ignored any arguments which exploded between them as if they had never happened. But seeing her rather desolate face and brimming eyes, his next impulse was to clasp her in his arms. 'There's no need for that, Chris,' he murmured gruffly.

'Thanks be to God.'

'I've missed you,' he said, smiling.

'And I you.' A tear trickled down her cheek and he pulled out his handkerchief and dried it.

'Enough blubbering, you'll have a drink, I presume? To celebrate?'

'You hardly have to ask,' she grinned.

He poured two glasses of wine and they talked then without rancour.

'I hope my attitude to Kate didn't upset things between you,' she asked worriedly.

'No, it didn't. That day the two of us were so delighted to see each other, everything else was unimportant.'

'Is she living here now?' she asked.

'No.'

'Are you happy?'

'Yea, Chris, happier than I've ever been.'

'What about Dermot?'

'They separated last year.' He sipped his own drink, reluctant to reveal his disappointment that Kate hadn't agreed to come to live with him in Harrington Place as yet.

'In spite of that you still seem a bit, well, not your usual happy self,' Chris observed.

She could always see through him. From the time he was a boy, Chris had been closest to him in the family.

He looked down at the glass of red wine in his hands and swilled the contents.

She pulled a cigarette packet from her bag and waved it towards him, but he took no notice. So she lit up, the cigarette held loosely between her fingers.

'There's something,' he murmured, thinking about Mia and needing to share the burden of this extraordinary situation. He had always opened his heart up to Chris, the only person who knew about the abortion of his first child - and the real reason behind the break-up of his marriage. So he began and as he slowly explained the sequence of events, she sat up straight and let the cigarette burn down into a long narrow taper of ash which finally broke off and fell on to the tiled floor. Neither of them noticed.

'That's some story,' she whispered.

'It took me by surprise, I can tell you.'

'But is the child yours? This Mia could be pulling a fast one.'

'That was my first reaction.'

'What is she looking for?'

'Nothing, apparently.'

'Why did she turn up then?'

'I was puzzled about that too.'

'It's probably not yours anyway.'

'But what if she is?' he asked.

'She?'

'A girl, four years old.'

'I think you should just wait until Mia makes contact again, you'll probably find she's approached all the men she's been with. Forget about it.'

'I wish I could, but I'm finding it difficult. I've been working on a series of paintings which seem to have some relevance. Come upstairs and have a look.'

In the studio he waited while she wandered from canvas to canvas. Chris was always a good judge of his work and he valued her opinion.

'Very stark.'

'I know.'

'They seem to reflect your thinking about this child and maybe also that first time too.'

'I can't get it out of my head.'

87

'Maybe that's a good thing. You've never really expressed it before. No harm at all.'

The doorbell rang. Two short and one long.

'It's Kate.' He moved across the studio.

'Oh my God, what am I going to say?' Her face flamed. 'Can I go out the back way?'

'No, you can't. It's time all this nonsense stopped.'

'Please?'

'Don't be silly.'

'Surprise, surprise!' Kate laughed and they embraced each other.

'I didn't know when to expect you, or whether you'd manage to spare the time at all today.'

'I was at a meeting with Paul about another job which is coming up soon, so I thought I'd come in for a few minutes. I'll be tied up later at a reception for the launch of a new magazine.'

'You're looking great, new outfit?'

'Yea.' She twirled and the silky frilled skirt floated around her.

'That's a wonderful colour, so vibrant.'

'Flame!'

'All on fire then?' he laughed.

'Go on with you!' she smiled, but then suddenly looked upstairs. 'Is there a client in the studio? I noticed a car outside.'

'There is, and she's a bit embarrassed about meeting you,' he spoke in a low voice.

'Who

'Chris.'

'Oh.' Her expressed changed.

'Do you want to come up?'

'Actually no, I don't have anything to say to her, not after that last time,' Kate bridled.

'She has apologised to me, something I never would have expected from Chris.'

'And you've accepted on my behalf?'

'No, it related to our own disagreement.'

'Which was about me?'

'Yes.'

'It's the same thing then.'

'My love, let's not keep it up?' he begged.

'Well,' she hesitated, 'just for you, then.'

'Thanks, I'll go up and get her.' He took the stairs two at a time and returned a moment later with Chris.

'I'm so sorry for my behaviour that day, Kate, I don't know why I reacted like that, perhaps because I knew both you and Dermot for so long, or maybe because I had other hopes for Jack, a family, children ... ' her words echoed in the already tense atmosphere like gunfire.

'I would give anything to be able to have Jack's child, but I've had a hysterectomy so it's not possible,' Kate snapped.

'I was very confused, and I'm sorry.' She moved closer to her. 'I want us to be friends again.'

Kate glared.

'Chris, a family isn't important to us, I'm just happy to be with Kate,' Jack put his arm around her shoulders.

'You're good together, I could always see that, even as far back as the night of Gerry's sixtieth birthday party, although maybe I didn't want to admit it.'

'I loved Kate even earlier than that. We were introduced on the opening night of my first exhibition at the Nestor Gallery. A brief few words among a crowd of people, but when she was leaving she looked back and our eyes met. I was lost from that very moment.'

'I remember the night,' Chris said.

'We were fated to be together no matter what obstacles stood in our way. Isn't that right, my love?' Jack said with a grin, and Kate couldn't help smiling then as her anger faded a little.

'I'm really happy for you, and I hope you can forgive my stupidity?' Chris begged.

There was a few seconds of silence and then Kate nodded. 'Let's not talk about it any more, it's in the past and forgotten about.'

'Thank you, Kate, you've no idea how happy you've made me, both of you.' She put her arms around them and they stood closely together for a moment. When they parted, there were tears in her eyes again. 'All this emotion is too much, I'll need another drink to calm me down,' she laughed.

'At that rate I insist on driving you home, or you can take a taxi. I'm not having any more, Kate, what about you?' Jack asked.

'I'll make tea.' She went into the kitchen and flicked on the kettle.

'Maybe tea would be best for me too,' Chris laughed and sat down at the table.

'How is Gerry?' Kate asked as she filled their mugs a few minutes later.

'He's fine. And will be glad to hear about you two, I know that.'

'You never told him?' Jack was surprised.

'No, I felt so guilty about the whole thing I couldn't tell him. Why don't you come over some night for dinner?'

'When are you heading back to Spain?'

'Three or four weeks.'

'Well, there will be plenty of time for that.'

'We're arranging an evening out next week with my brother and his family, so maybe you'd come along as well, Chris?' Kate asked.

'I'd love to,' she smiled, 'have you met our crowd yet? No-one said a thing at home, so I assumed not.'

'Mam invited us to Sunday lunch, but so far I haven't got a definite yes from Kate, she's too shy, I think,' he smiled at her.

'You didn't tell me your mother asked!' Kate retorted.

'You'll have to come to Dad's eightieth birthday party, all the family will be there so no-one will take any notice of you,' Chris suggested.

'I was waiting for the right moment to mention that.' Jack put his hand over Kate's.

He was delighted. It meant a lot to have his sister and her husband back in their lives. He hardly had any time to talk to Kate as she left later with Chris, and his good mood lasted until he went back to work, when he faced again the questions which dogged him these days. His chat with Chris hadn't helped, and he realised that no-one could do that. It was his own problem and he had to deal with it.

Chapter Sixteen

Dermot slowly ran his finger down the list of names. Anyone he had approached lately had refused his plea for help. Past business colleagues and friends all had excuses. We're doing a major renovation on the house, just bought the wife a new BMW, sons and daughters were heading off to Australia or other far-flung places and had to be financed, or the deposit must be found for their first attempt to get on the property ladder. It was a never-ending litany of excuses. Even Irene had declined, busy with her new boyfriend, the operative word being "boy". Dermot was still angry that he had been replaced.

His phone rang.

'Dad, I'm at the airport, can you pick me up?' Shane's voice was rough and sounded as if he had been drinking all night.

'Dublin Airport?'

'Yea.'

'I thought you were in Berlin with the band?'

'We've split up.'

'But what about the record deals and all that?' Dermot barked.

'I'm going solo.'

'Well, good for you.'

'How soon can you get here?'

'That's a good question. Since I don't possess a car any longer, I'll have to hitch a lift, so I suppose you'll have to do the same.'

'I've no dosh left.'

'I thought you were earning good money?'

'We were, but it's gone now; things are expensive there.'

'I've no money either.'

'Come on Dad. If I get a taxi, can you pick up the tab?'

'I told you I'm broke, I can barely manage on what I earn at the pub.'

'Ok, I'll try Mum,' he muttered.

Dermot thought about the prospect of Shane returning penniless. He can go and live with Kate, I'm not putting up with him here, he grumbled out loud, a habit recently picked up. He had long imaginary conversations with people; persuasive diatribes during which he would trot out various reasons why they should help him. He felt isolated, lonely and resented the whole world.

'Mum coughed up for the taxi.' Shane dumped his bags in the hall.

'She must be flush at the moment.'

'I can always depend on her.' He wandered into the kitchen, looking more like a rock star that he had ever been. He had tattoos on his arms and torso, visible through the tee-shirt which seemed to be the worse for wear, and had added a few more piercings on his lips, nose and ears. 'What's for dinner?'

'Not much, I'm going out,' Dermot said, watching him open the fridge and stare in.

'It's almost empty.'

'I live a simple life now, Shane.'

'Anything in the freezer?'

'No. There was an electricity cut, had to throw the lot out.'

'But I'm hungry,' he groaned.

'That's your problem.'

'Mum only gave me fifty euro,' Shane presented a picture of despair; in sharp contrast to his gothic look.

'You can stay here but it's bed only, no board, so I suggest you get a job,' Dermot snorted, determined not to be pushed into a corner, 'I work. Why don't you try it?'

'Dad, I'm putting together another band, but it's going to take time.'

'That's the deal, Shane, bed only.'

'Dad, I'm really stuck for cash,' Shane poured milk on his cornflakes.

'What about the fifty euro?'

'That's gone.'

'Good enough for you.' Dermot opened the sports page of the newspaper. He checked the list of runners at Aintree and decided that he could place a sizeable bet on one or two good possibilities. 'Hope you enjoy those cornflakes. You didn't book in for that little extra.'

'Thanks a bunch.'

'Listen Shane, I've had enough of you. I'd need to win the Lotto to repay all I owe. Why don't you go and live with your mother?'

'There's no space down there.'

'Well, I can't help that.'

There was a silence between them for a time, broken only by Shane's slurps and the crackle of Dermot's newspaper.

'Maybe Mary might give me a job at the pub too?' Shane said suddenly.

Dermot was astounded, it was the first time Shane had ever shown any interest in getting a regular job. And when Mary agreed to take him on for a few hours, it didn't suit Dermot at all. His slick handling of the money had meant that quite a considerable sum had gone into his pocket and now suddenly, he could see his little empire shake. Damn Shane.

Chapter Seventeen

'You look gorgeous!' Jack kissed her.

Kate wiggled in her turquoise dress as they walked down the driveway to the jeep. 'Thank you, number one fan!'

'The only one I hope.' He opened the door.

'Jealous?'

'Could be, with all those male clients who are flocking around you.'

'It's the price of success, you'll just have to grin and bear it.' Kate sat in and pulled down the mirror. Refreshed her lipstick. Combed her hair. Still not satisfied with how she looked this evening. 'The cleaning lady started today. Her name is Olga, she's Lithuanian, a lovely girl. I have to admit that while I wasn't keen on the idea at first, now I think it's going to be just great. I'll be relieved of all that housework, and guess what, she loves sewing, so May might ask her to do a few hours. And I think I'm going to have to get someone in to help with the admin as well,' Kate chattered away as they drove into town. This was the night of the meet-the-family dinner and she was nervous.

'I can't keep up with you,' Jack grinned, *'entrepreneuse extraordinaire!'*

'I'll just remind you that I have to go with the flow and grab the work while it's there.'

'Why not keep it part-time? Then we'll have more time together.'

'For God's sakes, you'd be sick looking at me.'

'Want to try it?' he laughed.

'You don't seem to understand how much I'm enjoying this; I

love the challenge. It's been an amazing rollercoaster this year.'

'Perhaps if you do get someone, you won't be quite so busy. But can the business sustain another employee?'

'If the company is to expand I need help. And I'm going to get someone to design an interactive website as well.'

Jack parked the jeep outside the restaurant and Kate said a little prayer that her sons wouldn't respond negatively to his presence.

'It sure is great to meet everybody,' Pat beamed, as the waiter handed around the menus and the first few minutes were taken up with orders being placed. Then they sat back and looked at each other.

'How're you settling into the old home place?' Gerry enquired.

'Wonderful!' Pat grinned.

'We're loving it, even the boys,' Susie added.

Rob and Donal grinned sheepishly but said nothing. They could be noisy and boisterous at home, but this evening were quite well-behaved.

'You'll miss the warm weather,' Chris said.

'But imagine digging yourself out of three foot of snow in winter? At least it's a milder climate here,' Pat looked over at Kate.

'You're going to buy a house, is that the plan, or will it be an apartment?' Conor asked.

'Not sure yet. We're enjoying ourselves so much at Berwick Road, we won't want to leave.'

'Although it needs one hell of a make-over,' Susie remarked, looking good tonight in a clinging grey outfit.

'We know someone who will sort you out!' Gerry chortled.

'But she doesn't want to, that's the problem,' she pouted.

'Why not, Kate? Surely that's right up your street?'

'I'm not ready to do it yet.' Kate took a deep breath and concentrated on her starter. She forked smoked salmon, but didn't even taste it. Gerry's bumbling had created a situation; somewhere she didn't want to go. And certainly not in public. She glanced across at Jack, who was in deep conversation with Conor. At least they seemed to be getting on. 'Michelle, I haven't seen you in ages.'

She chatted to Conor's partner, a really pretty dark-haired girl, who sat on her other side.

She smiled shyly.

'More wine?' Pat picked up the bottle.

He topped Kate's glass up, but Michelle refused.

'Come on, have a drink to celebrate,' Pat encouraged, and immediately began to pour red wine into the glass in front of her.

'I'm just having water, thanks.'

'No-one at this table drinks water when I'm the host, except those under eighteen of course. Raise your glasses now.'

Kate glanced at her, concerned to see a flush creeping over her cheeks. The poor thing was embarrassed.

'You drink what you like, Michelle, leave that there if you don't want it,' she murmured.

'Thanks, Mrs. Mason.'

'Kate will do, Michelle. And it's Crawford. I'm not Mrs. Mason any longer.'

The girl smiled.

'Now, to the returned immigrants!' Pat stood up and raised his glass.

'That's us, you shouldn't be doing it,' Susie whispered, her remark quite audible to everyone at the table, who by now had raised theirs as well.

'And good health to all of us.'

There was plenty of chat. Chris, Gerry, Susie and Pat seemed to get on particularly well. Kate spoke mostly with Jack, Michelle and Conor, ignoring the banter which went on at the other end of the table. Shane was late as usual and turned up in the middle of the meal, all apologies. As the evening continued, Kate could see that he was as pleasant to Jack as anyone else there, and began to relax.

It was just after dessert had been served that Conor rapped his glass with his spoon and the loud chink drew everyone's attention. 'We want to make an announcement, Michelle and I.' he hesitated, a wide grin on his good-looking features. He put his arm around her shoulders. 'We're going to have a baby.' He kissed her.

There was an immediate hubbub of congratulations from

everyone. Kate stood up and threw her arms around both of them. 'I am so happy for you.'

Jack kissed Michelle and shook Conor's hand. Then he turned to Kate and kissed her too. 'Congrats, Grandma!'

A grandmother? The very thought of it seemed to age her twenty years and she had an instant vision of grey permed hair, pink cheeks and the merest scrape of lipstick. She could see her mother dressed in neat silky floral dresses, low-heeled shoes and handbag, not necessarily matching, but large, in spite of only containing a handkerchief, perfume, comb and a small amount of money in a purse. She pushed the image out of her mind. That was the way it was forty years ago. Nowadays grandmothers were young, trendy and smart. But deep down the feeling of time catching up with her suddenly assumed unexpected proportions.

'Champagne!' Pat waved to the waiter.

Conor did the honours, twisting the cork to the usual accompanying pop and overflowing bubbles. Then everyone toasted the happy couple. It made the night.

'Come back with me for a while.' Jack leaned over and kissed her as they were stopped at the lights.

'I've an early start,' Kate said hesitantly.

'Come on, it's only eleven,' he persuaded. Running his hand underneath the silky dress.

'Stop!' she grinned and removed his hand. 'I'll try and finish early tomorrow evening.'

'Should I hold my breath?' He had a wry smile on his face.

'Come on, don't be a grumpy old man.'

'What, me? Grumpy? Who are you kidding? I'm the happiest guy on the block. And as for the old, now that's just a bit much!' He drove off when the lights turned green.

'Sorry, you poor thing, are you very upset?' Kate stroked the back of his neck, which was soft, warm and suddenly so inviting.

'Hey, what are trying to do to me?' he laughed.

'I can't resist you, that's the problem.'

He caressed between her knees again.

'Get your hand back on the wheel!' she ordered.

'Let's pull in somewhere, I don't think I can drive for much longer,' he moved further up her thigh.

'Jack!' she giggled.

'Right miss, where to? Any chance of a change of mind?' He removed his hand and stopped at another set of lights.

'Ok you, Harrington Place!'

'I'm really excited about the baby,' Kate confided later, as ever oblivious to time when she was with Jack. They had made love on the couch. It was slow and tender, and she was very conscious of every tiny nuance of this man who meant so much to her.

'There's something about new life ... ' He didn't finish the sentence, and Kate suddenly realised what was probably going through his mind.

'I'm sorry, I've been going on about the baby and I never thought of you.' She put her arms around him and hugged close. But a slight disappointment made itself felt. Would she have to restrict the amount of time she might spend with her grandchild? How would Jack react to him or her?

*

When Jack heard the news that Michelle was pregnant, immediately he was reminded of Mia's little girl and his own long-dead baby, and it was like a professional boxer had given him a lethal left hook and sent him reeling. He regretted that Kate had seen through him. It wasn't fair to spoil her obvious joy. But it was the impetus he needed and the following morning he punched in the digits of the mobile number until it rang once, twice, three times and was picked up.

Chapter Eighteen

Mary and Des took Shane on. He started in the same pub as Dermot and served behind the bar for a week or two. But then they gave him an opportunity to arrange gigs in the various establishments they owned around the country, over a dozen from north to south, and were really pleased to have found someone who could develop this side of the business for them.

But Dermot felt very resentful of the fact that Shane was working it for himself and getting thirty percent of the take on the door. The more he thought about the amount of money going through his son's hands, the more he envied him and wanted a share of it.

'You seem to be doing well, Shane.'

'Yep, Dad, it's cool. I can't believe it. Des and Mary are delighted, and they might arrange for a company van later on if all goes well.'

'What?' Dermot's face froze.

'Yea, I'm on the way up!'

'I wish I could have a share, I'm broke at the moment.'

'Dad, you're always broke,' he grinned.

'Lend me a few euro, please? All the door money is cash and it will never be noticed. Just for a few weeks?'

Shane stared at him with a worried expression on his face.

'If Des and Mary found out there would be hell to pay.'

'I'll have it back to you in no time, it's just a loan,' Dermot begged.

'But I give all the money over to the manager of the pub and get paid by cheque.'

'Take it out of that.'

'No Dad, I couldn't.'

'How could you leave your old Dad down? Remember all the money I gave you over the years, I never asked for that back, did I?'

He shook his head. 'It could wreck everything.'

'Not at all,' Dermot persuaded.

'I'll try and give you something myself.'

'You need all your money, it will be reduced anyway when we take something off the top.'

Shane sat down slowly and Dermot pulled his chair closer.

Chapter Nineteen

Carol sat beside Kate in a corner of the pub. 'It's great to relax!' She sipped her G & T. 'Must say that article in the paper was super, and the photo wasn't bad either. Amazing what a decent bit of lighting can achieve!' she laughed.

'Thanks! It hides all those lines, and shadows no doubt!' Kate grinned.

'I'm joking. You haven't got a wrinkle!'

'You're good for my ego, keep that up.'

'This is only the beginning; your star is in the ascendancy.'

'The article covered everything, and should raise our profile. I've already had a few calls since it appeared.'

'Publicity is everything, it doesn't make any difference whether it's bad or good. Cheers to the future!' Carol raised her glass.

'I hope I can keep up with it.'

'How's the love of your life?' Carol asked, mischievous as ever.

'Busy.'

'Are his paintings similar to the ones we bought? Great big colourful things?'

'No, they're completely different. Very dark.'

'At least he's got his inspiration back again.'

'Thank God. His sister Chris took great delight in telling me that it was all my fault.'

'Another drink?'

'Why not,' Kate laughed, 'although if he walked in here now, he'd have a blue fit.'

Carol waved to the barman. 'Why?'

'Because I don't spend enough time with him.'

'You're lucky he feels so strongly. Although hopefully he doesn't become too possessive.'

'He's not so bad,' Kate laughed, 'but enough about men, let's talk about something else. How are things going at work?'

'I'm afraid the transition from employer to employee hasn't gone very well. The targets are high and the pressure is on if we don't achieve.'

'When you ran the company we all just worked our butts off and hoped for the best.' Kate added tonic to her drink.

'We did very well, thanks to people like you.'

'How's Mags?'

'Enjoying herself in San Francisco at the moment; you know she has friends everywhere.'

'Might as well make the most of life, she's young.'

'Don't remind me!' Carol grimaced, and picked a few peanuts from the dish on the table.

'What are you talking about? You haven't changed since I've known you, in fact you look better if anything,' Kate smilingly reassured.

'Thanks! But having to drag myself daily into the company I once owned is becoming more and more difficult,' she groaned.

'Do you regret it?'

'Big time.'

'But the money you received surely makes up with having to put up with someone else telling you what to do?'

'Makes no difference. I've gone past the stage of bowing and scraping. Can't do it any longer.'

'I'm sorry to hear that, what are you going to do?'

'I don't know. I'm envious of you running your own scene.'

'Why don't you join me?' Kate made the suggestion in an unthinking way, a surprise to herself. While she had clashed with Mags, she had always worked well with Carol.

Her friend stared at her, eyes open wide with surprise. 'Gosh, it's so good of you to ask.'

'Think about it.'

'For God's sake, Kate, this is happening more and more often!' Jack snapped heatedly.

'I'm speaking at a meeting of architects tomorrow afternoon and I have to prepare a paper.'

'Why don't you come over here and do it, then at least I could see you, and I'll make dinner, say yes, please?'

'But all my files are here,' she explained.

'Bring them over.'

'OK, I will,' she agreed after a moment, knowing by the tone of his voice that this could explode into something before she knew it. Lately, his mood had been very unstable. He could fly off the handle in seconds and sometimes she wasn't even sure why.

'Sorry, I was very impatient today, my love!' Jack put his arms around her. She clung to him, and he kissed her. Softly at first and then harder, passionately. 'How long has it been? I've lost track. I just know I'm aching for you.' He covered her lips with his again and the stress of her day faded away as he opened the zip of her jeans and eased his hands around her waist.

'I'll never get my work done,' she whispered.

'Later.' His hands explored slowly, massaging, tickling, until she almost screamed with desire. Then he took her upstairs to his room where the strength of their passion put everything else out of her head including all the work she had to do.

'You're a bad influence on me,' she giggled.

'I'm glad of that, my love.'

They kissed slowly, mouths open, exploring sensually. Lips caressed. And slowly their need for each other built up. Then he moved down her body, to that very intimate part of Kate that only he knew how to excite. His slow delicate arousal sent her clinging closer to him and they came together, these moments of perfect communication the very best of their love, when all irritants vanished and they were at one. They lay silently for a while, eyes closed, until eventually Jack kissed her and made some mundane remark about being hungry.

'Don't care about food,' Kate murmured.

'Making love is hungry work.'

'Is it that much effort?'

'I'm joking, making love with you is the most fantastic exciting delicious experience of my whole life. It is without comparison.' He kissed her again.

'Liar!' she pushed against him, laughing.

'What do you mean?'

'What about all those other women you know? I'll bet there are scores of them. What about that Mia person, remember her?' she giggled, kissing his eyes, nose, forehead, and lips. 'Kiss, kiss, kiss I love you.'

'Come on, let's have a shower.' He pulled her by the hand from the bed and under the warm spray of water they soaped each other leisurely and, wrapped in white bath towels, they went back into the bedroom to dress.

'While I get dinner, why don't you start work?' he asked, going ahead of her downstairs.

'I don't feel like it now.'

'I thought it was vital? If you don't do it then the next time I suggest you work over here, you'll have every excuse to say no.' He steered her into the dining-room. 'Now sit down. Put your lap-top and papers here and I'll give you a shout when dinner's ready.'

'Yes, Daddy,' she grinned and picked up her briefcase. But as she worked on the speech, she couldn't get this woman out of her head. Who was Mia? And why did Jack make no effort to explain his connection with her?

Chapter Twenty

Jack ordered coffee for himself and Mia, and they waited in silence. He stared out across the crowded café which was not quite the same as the old Bewleys but still had many of its features. In particular, the beautiful Harry Clarke stained glass windows which had been threatened with storage in some dark warehouse until the café was taken over by a new owner and the tradition which had been part of Grafton Street since the 1920's was rescued.

He tried to make conversation, but she was very quiet and as on the last occasion they had met he had to drag the responses out of her.

'Who looks after Marie Elaine if you're not at home?'

'A friend.'

'Is she going to school yet?'

'She starts in September,' she murmured, twisting the half-filled cup in her hands and staring down into its dark contents. At that angle her bone structure was sharply defined and he thought again how beautiful she was.

'I'm sorry I have to ask you this, and I don't want to, but ... '

She nodded.

'Were you seeing anyone else at the same time as myself?' he felt embarrassed, asking her such an intrusive question.

She shook her head fiercely. 'I was never promiscuous!' Her voice trembled.

'I wasn't suggesting that.'

'You were!'

He swallowed uncomfortably. 'You could have had someone in

your life before you met me?'

'And so I would pick up the first man I met? You think I am like that?'

'I'm sorry Mia, try and see it from my point of view, I'm in the dark here.'

A tear dribbled down her cheek.

He felt bad and put his hand over hers for a few seconds, noticing that her white fingers were icy-cold. 'I don't want to hurt you and I hope you'll understand that there are things which need to be done to prove ... for me to have a child would be amazing and was something I had simply deleted from my life,' he stopped speaking for a few seconds. Then he took a deep breath. 'So, I'm going to take a DNA test.'

An expression of shock chased across her face.

'And Marie Elaine will also have to be tested.'

She pressed a tissue against the tiny beads of perspiration which had suddenly gathered on her forehead and under her cheekbones.

'Are you all right?' he asked, concerned at the paleness of her face.

She nodded.

'Can I get you some more coffee or anything else?'

'No, thank you.'

'I'm going to have another cup.'

'Perhaps some water?'

'The DNA, how does one go about it?' she asked later.

'It's a simple saliva test.'

'Is it painful?'

'No, they take a swab from inside the mouth.'

She sipped the water, but her face was still drained. 'How long must we wait for the results?'

'I don't know, it could be weeks, or even months.'

'Months?'

'Easily.' He noticed that two bright pink spots suddenly appeared on her cheeks, in strange contrast to her pale marble-like skin. 'I'm sorry this is all so upsetting for you.'

'Perhaps I worry too much?'

'No, it's natural.'

The minutes passed.

'It must have been very difficult for you to phone me in the first place.'

'It was; I had never intended to do it.'

'I'm still puzzled as to why now?'

'Marie Elaine is four years old and, as I told you that last time, I thought perhaps that you should know about her.' The green eyes sparkled suddenly. 'She is beautiful, so lively and independent. I have a photograph; would you like to see it?' She reached for her small leather handbag.

'No, no thanks.' His pulse raced. He couldn't bear to look at a photo of this child who might or might not be his. Questions rushed into his mind. Would she be fair? Or dark? Small? Tall? Thin? Chubby? The images flashed before him and the responsibility was terrifying. He withdrew from the conversation, his mouth dry, unable to think of another word to say. They parted shortly after that with an agreement that he would contact her when he had set up the appointments for the tests.

Chapter Twenty-one

'Is that offer still on?' Carol asked when she called in on her way to work.

'It sure is,' Kate said.

'Right, I'm going to draw up my letter of resignation as soon as I get into the office.'

'I presume you have to give a month's notice?'

'Three months, but I can work part-time for you, evenings, weekends.'

'You said you didn't want to work long hours.'

'It doesn't matter for a short while.'

'Come around at lunch-time, we can go out and have something to eat at that little Italian place. We need to talk, make decisions.'

'See you then!'

But it was one of those days. In the end she had to cancel the lunch appointment with Carol as there were delays with deliveries which would hold up the schedule. Sinead had phoned in sick. A friend of Paul's needed an urgent survey and quotation for a client of his. And as she tried to train Debbie in on her systems, Irene called.

'I haven't seen you in ages, what are you doing these days?' Irene was her usual hyper self.

'I'm very busy.' She took her into the sitting-room, feeling awkward. The suspicion that Dermot had been having an affair with her before Kate left him still rankled.

'So you say every time I ask you to do me a favour; no-one's that busy,' she pouted.

'It's the timing, Irene,' Kate replied with mixed feelings.

'Anyway, I've the most wonderful news!' she smiled broadly and waved her left hand towards Kate. 'I'm engaged! Isn't my ring fabulous?'

Kate stared at the glittering diamond ring, but couldn't say anything for a few seconds.

'Aren't you happy for me?'

'Of course I am.' Kate brushed Irene's cheek with her lips. A light impersonal touch. 'Who is he?' she tried to be enthusiastic.

'His name is Ted, I met him a few months ago in the Virgin Islands.'

'Congratulations.'

She launched into an intimate description of this guy who was good-looking, successful, rich and some years younger than herself. Until finally, Kate had to murmur something about finishing an urgent quote.

'Sorry, I've been rabbiting on, but before I go I want to ask you something very important, and I'm praying you won't say no.'

Kate was aware that Irene was putting on the pressure as usual, so she strengthened her resolve.

'Promise you won't.'

'How can I say yes or no when I don't know what it is?'

'Right, here goes – Kate, I want you to be my matron of honour and Dermot must give me away. You're my closest family, there's no-one left on my side except a few cousins in London I haven't seen in years, so I'm depending on you. I'll need help with everything, the reception, trousseau, the lot. I've never had a big wedding. Your Dad and I only had a simple ceremony on a beach in Barbados, so I'm really looking forward to it. I'm booking a wedding planner who will have all sorts of amazing ideas, but I'll still need your input.' She pulled a diary out of her handbag. 'Now, when can we get together?'

Feeling positively wrung out at the end of the day, Kate stopped at the flower shop and bought a bouquet for Grace. This was the first time she had been able to accept her invitation to visit and she was not feeling a bit in the mood for polite conversation, tea and delicately-cut cucumber sandwiches. But as she pulled up outside the house, her phone rang.

'Fancy having my services a bit sooner than three months?' Carol asked excitedly.

'Yea, sure.'

'How about Monday morning?'

'What?'

'They told me to clear my desk. Don't want me to work my notice.'

'The cheek. Did they think you'd run off with all their secrets?'

'They don't have any secrets.'

'How do you feel about that? Are you upset?'

'No. Couldn't give a damn. Glad to be out of the place.'

'Welcome aboard, I'm delighted.'

Walking up the path to the house, she suddenly felt in much better form, and when Grace met her at the door dressed in a Japanese kimono, that took her breath away altogether. The delicate fabric was scarlet red satin, with a dramatic white and gold embroidered flower design. Her grey hair was caught up with a tortoiseshell comb, and the whole affect was quite beautiful.

'It's wonderful to see you, Kate, come in.'

'You look lovely, that kimono is exquisite.' She handed Grace the flowers.

'Bill brought it back to me from one of his trips to Japan a long time ago.'

'Did he ever see you wear it?'

'No, it wasn't something I could put on going into town, but I wear it now in his memory,' she laughed softly and ushered her into a bright pleasant room at the back of the house. It had that lovely old-fashioned feel of Berwick Road. Pink floral chintz covers on the Chesterfield suite matched the curtains, the furniture was shining mahogany, with lots of delicate ornaments on the mantle, pictures on the walls and flowers everywhere. It was delightful and Kate was immediately at ease. They talked for a while and then Grace served a meal of various Japanese dishes.

'I hope you like oriental food.'

'I've only eaten Japanese once or twice.'

'This is sushi - seafood in dried sheets of seaweed, and tempura.' She pointed to another dish. 'Also seafood with vegetables in batter. And these are yakitori – chicken on skewers.'

'Mmmm, looks delicious. You've gone to a lot of trouble, thank you.'

'My pleasure. Since we first met I've wanted to get to know you better, so I'm glad to have the opportunity.'

'Bill wouldn't have believed it.'

'Probably not.'

'It's such a tragedy that you were apart all those years.'

'The timing was wrong and I suppose it was immoral too.'

'When I first met Jack I was still married to Dermot. It's very difficult if you love someone.'

'Sometimes we have no control over life. We are whirled along like spume on a wave, helpless.'

'My life turned head over heels one day and was never the same again. No matter how hard I tried I couldn't go back.'

'You moved on. Grew beyond your capabilities at that time. Look on it as a broadening of the self. You're happy now?'

'Yes, of course.' Kate looked away, unable to meet Grace's candid gaze.

'Maybe it's not possible to have true happiness. What we want is like a mirage, always shifting ahead of us, and when we catch up, we discover it's not quite as we expected.'

'That's exactly right,' Kate agreed.

'We have to prioritise.'

'There's so much going on in my life, it's hard to do it.'

'You should identify the most important aspect of your life and never lose sight of it. Something I didn't do.' Grace looked sad.

'How long has it been since your husband died?'

'Eighteen years.'

'All that time living here, yet you and Bill were only a few streets apart; it's a wonder you didn't bump into each other by accident, at the shops or the church or somewhere.'

'That was another thing, I'm Church of Ireland. Needless to say, neither family wanted us to get married.'

'It was such a pity.'

'*C'est la vie.*'

'You must be lonely sometimes.'

'No, not now.' She stood up and led the way into the garden through the open French windows.

Kate followed, but stopped suddenly, amazed.

Sheltered from the neighbours by high trees, the very large garden was designed in Japanese style. Soft green lines were created with miniature conifers, which had been trained into various tapered shapes. There were many other lush plants, bamboos, and particularly beautiful weeping willows which hung over the pond spanned by a narrow curved bridge painted a bright red. Beyond, on a raised area, was a small wooden building.

'Harmony is everything and, when it's achieved, the evil spirits leave me alone. I hope you'll find the same thing and put the exigencies of the day behind you.' Grace walked along a series of stepping stones which zigzagged across a gravelled area. Roughly in the centre were placed three large rounded rocks and a fountain from which the water trickled into a stone basin. 'The rocks represent the universe - heaven, earth and men,' she explained.

'I can see your hand in every little leaf and bud, although it must be a lot of hard work to keep it in this condition,' Kate smiled.

'It doesn't require as much attention as the front, and my gardener friend has become as enthusiastic as I am.' They walked across the bridge and at the entrance to the small building, Kate followed Grace's example and washed her hands in a stone bowl filled with clear water before going inside, stooping to enter the low door. It was a plain unadorned windowless room, without any furniture at all, painted white with a pale wooden floor. There was a single Japanese scroll hanging on the wall.

'We will sit on reed mats on the floor and have tea, I hope it won't be too uncomfortable for you?'

'No, I'm reasonably supple, although I can't always achieve the full lotus position,' Kate laughed, 'but you seem to be very fit.'

'I practise yoga every day.'

'I don't get a chance.'

As she spoke, Grace wiped clean various containers which stood on a tray in front of her. With slow careful movements she boiled water over a small charcoal fire which had been lit some time earlier, prepared the tea and poured it into a bowl. Then she bowed and handed it to Kate. The tea had a strange taste, but it wasn't unpleasant and she passed the bowl back to Grace and they continued until it was finished.

Kate listened, fascinated, as she explained how Bill had brought her the utensils for the Tea Ceremony from Japan, and that after her husband's death, she had become interested in the philosophy of Zen Buddhism.

'The Zen monk, Murata Juko, originated the Tea Ceremony about five hundred years ago, and nowadays the serving of tea is studied by many people in Japan. But it's not the final outcome, or how well you perform the ceremony that's important, it's the achievement of presence of mind, to live for the moment, all other extraneous thoughts pushed away.'

It was something about the unhurried pace of Grace's actions that soothed Kate, listening to her gentle voice explain how the various ways to serve tea in front of guests were developed into the spiritually uplifting form practised today. She had no notion of the time spent, and was without inclination to go home until Grace put everything away, and they went back into the house.

'I've really enjoyed myself.' Kate embraced her.

'Me too. There are very few people I'd ask to take tea with me. I am only at the very early stages of study; it's a life-long search for self-realisation.'

'I should probably go on that search myself,' Kate murmured.

Chapter Twenty-two

Jack's father was eighty today and Kate was particularly apprehensive about meeting the family *en masse*. While she had been introduced to his parents on one occasion, and knew his sister Chris, the rest of his family were strangers. She stared frustrated into the wardrobe. Maybe the black suit? Too sombre. What about the red with the silky cardigan? Too bright. She flicked through the hangers, undecided, aware that time was against her. Perhaps the deep purple frilled skirt and matching jacket? Yes. Quickly she dressed, brushed her hair, clipped on her gold earrings, took the ring out of its box and slipped it on. She didn't wear it very often and Jack had commented on the fact more than once.

'This is it, you're about to go into the lion's den. Everyone will be here tonight, the Irish crowd, the contingent from Chicago, London, and South Africa.' Jack pulled up outside the small terraced house.

Kate stared out the window and tried to calm the palpitations which had started just a few minutes before. 'I'm nervous.'

'Don't be, they'll take to you like I did.' He kissed her.

'Spoofer!' she laughed.

'Right, let's go.' He came around to the passenger side of the jeep, helped her down and they walked up the narrow pathway to the house. 'This is where I grew up.'

'I wish my parents were still living in my old home.' There was a sudden nostalgia for her own Mam and Dad, and regret too that they had both died in their early seventies.

'Yea, we're lucky.' Jack put his key into the lock and pushed open the door, to be met almost immediately by Rose.

'You're late, they could be back any minute, it depends on which priest is saying Mass this evening.'

'I forgot the surprise element. I'll just move the jeep.'

'Trust you! Come in Kate, it's lovely to meet you at last.' She kissed her.

'Thanks for inviting me,' Kate smiled.

'Aren't you part of the family now?'

'Not quite.'

'You are as far as Jack is concerned. Once he makes up his mind about something there's no stopping him. Although I'm sure you know that already. Where is he?' She stared down the road until he reappeared a couple of minutes later. 'Go on upstairs, and be ready to come down as soon as they come in the door.'

Jack took Kate's hand. 'Come up to my room and I'll show you my etchings?'

'God help you, Kate, if his etchings are anything like his pictures!' Rose quipped.

They ran up the stairs and into the small front bedroom, but it was already occupied by Chris and Gerry, who were looking out through the net curtains.

'This is a bit of fun isn't it? They'll be bowled over,' Chris said excitedly.

'You're right, seeing some of his sons and daughters after all these years will definitely send him into shock,' Gerry drawled, and put his arm around Kate. 'Would have thought you'd have more sense than to get involved with this family, you may well live to regret it.'

'There they are,' Jack said, 'look, down at the corner talking to Mrs. O'Connor.'

'She'll keep them there for ages,' Chris hooted.

Jack squeezed Kate's hand and smiled into her eyes, 'OK?'

She nodded, feeling her heart begin to dance even faster.

They waited until the front door was opened and rushed down the stairs to join the cheering throng in the sitting-room. Jack's Mam and Dad shed tears of joy when sons and daughters who had come home especially for the occasion appeared in front of them. After a while Jack managed to push through to where they stood and introduced Kate. She wished his father a Happy Birthday, kissed his mother, and handed her a bouquet of flowers. Jack gave his father a card which Kate knew contained an extremely generous cheque.

'Thank you for coming this evening, Kate, it's lovely to see you. I'm looking forward to talking to you later when all this fuss has calmed down.' His mother patted her hand.

'I'd like that.' She moved away, as someone else threw their arms around the old couple.

'I'm sorry,' Jack murmured.

'What about?'

'My father.'

'What do you mean?'

'He didn't say anything to you.' There was disappointment in his eyes.

'He was fine, don't be silly.'

'Now am I going to be introduced to this gorgeous woman, or are you going to keep her to yourself all night?' A good-looking man asked.

'This is Kate,' Jack said with a smile, 'meet my brother Noel, who now hails from South Africa.'

'About time.' He kissed her. 'I believe this is your inauguration into the family circle?'

Kate laughed, very much taken by this pleasant man, 'I suppose it is.'

'God help you. Have you got a glass of champagne?'

'I had one earlier, but I put it down somewhere.' She looked around.

'I'll get another.' Jack disappeared for a moment, then came back and handed her a glass.

'Now, tell me all about yourself Kate?' Noel cornered her then and they talked avidly. She heard all about his home in Johannesburg, the hotel group he owned, the children, their great life.

'You'll have to come out, we'll make sure you have a wonderful time.'

'I'm very busy, I haven't had a decent holiday in ages.'

'All work, no play - you know the old saying.'

'It goes in one ear and out the other.' Jack's eyes met Kate's over the rim of his glass, and she felt suddenly guilty realising how inflexible she must seem to be.

'You mustn't have the right touch, Jack, if it was me! Ah, there's Yvonne, my ball and chain, come and meet.' He propelled her across the room to be introduced to another group of people.

'Kate, when are you and Jack going to shack up together?' Kathleen asked.

'We've no plans just yet,' she replied vaguely, a blush stealing over her cheeks.

'You need to be getting on with it, you'll be hitting the half-century before too long!' Gary grinned, and punched Jack in the arm.

'We'll be waiting for the patter of tiny feet,' someone else said, and they all roared with laughter.

'I don't think we'll be going down that road,' Kate smiled, aware that although Jack was beside her, he had made no response to their jocose comments. 'I've two sons in their twenties.'

'And dead right too, have a decent life yourselves, without the hassle of kids, drive you mad,' Ken remarked.

'Have you formally separated from Dermot yet?' Chris asked.

'No.' Kate replied, a little swirl of annoyance growing inside her.

'Is this a clandestine affair?' Gary asked, sotto voice.

'Hey come on, that's enough,' Jack said.

She could feel his arm tighten around her.

'Sorry, didn't mean to infer. Just a joke.'

'Trust you to put your foot in it, Gary,' they laughed again.

Kate forced a smile on her face. Why couldn't Chris stay out of her life? It was none of her business. She glanced at Jack, aware of a sudden tension in him.

'Come on, Rose, let's organise the food,' Kathleen said.

'Can I help?' Kate asked.

'Sure. Never refuse a pair of hands.'

'Don't let her out of your sight, Jack, she might never come back,'

Tony said.

'You're right, I won't!' he grinned, and together they went into the kitchen where they both helped to serve up the food to the large crowd of people. She was glad to do something, and get away from Chris, feeling so annoyed and embarrassed too as she had asked that question about Dermot, conscious of the cold critical look in her eyes. Had it always been like that? In previous years, herself, Dermot, Gerry and Chris had been quite friendly, but now in hindsight she wondered if their relationship had ever been much more than superficial.

When everyone else had been served, they had something to eat themselves and Jack found a chair for her near his mother, while he stood and talked with his father. But after a couple of mouthfuls of the tasty chicken dish, Kate began to feel claustrophobic. Noise droned above her head. She could hear snippets of conversations. People jabbering. 'A new house - I didn't know – it was a great game – another drink – London - she's a pain - when we scored – help yourself – I – we – you – us – they - me.' On and on and on. A litany of disconnected words which made no sense at all.

Mrs. Linley beckoned and she moved her chair closer to where she sat on the couch.

'Jack is lucky to have found you,' she smiled.

'I don't know about that, I'm not the easiest person in the world.'

'He's very fond of you, I know that. It's a long time since ... and he's been alone too much. All those years he spent in Spain; I never agreed with it, and we couldn't even phone him, you know, months would go by without hearing from him.'

'I'm sure it must have been hard for you,' Kate didn't know what else to say, very relieved to hear a burst of applause as Rose carried in the cake, which was decorated with marzipan flowers, green icing, and a picket fence. Kate stood up and moved closer to Jack, as his father blew out the candles and everyone sang Happy Birthday. She was hoping that this might be the end of the celebrations, her mood had never recovered since Chris had asked that question about Dermot.

'Can I get you some birthday cake?' Jack took her hand. 'Another drink?'

'No thanks, I've had quite enough for one night.'

But it wasn't the end, unfortunately. Later, Jack, Noel and Gary took out their guitars and together provided the musical accompaniment for the session which was traditional on any occasion in the Linley family. Kathleen played the piano and then Rose stood up and gave them a rowdy session of ballads which got everyone going. Sitting uncomfortably on the arm of the couch Kate tried to look as if she was enjoying herself. In spite of her longing to go home, she particularly enjoyed Jack's rendering of some Neil Diamond songs, and later his father and mother sang the old tunes they used to sing together in their youth, still lively and wide-awake at three in the morning, when Jack made an attempt to put away his guitar.

'Come on, give us another tune!' they encouraged.

'It's all hours,' he laughed, glancing at Kate.

'The night is young, although maybe you're not. Showing your age!'

'And he's the baby!'

So they stayed on.

'Hey, I didn't know you could sing so well!' Jack kissed her as they sat into the jeep much later.

'Only in a crowd.'

'We could be good together if we're ever out of work; might do well on the continental busking circuit,' Jack laughed, 'I hope you weren't upset by some of their remarks, but it's all just innocent fun; you'll get used to them.'

Will I? Kate wondered.

*

Jack flicked through the Irish Times. But he only glanced at the headlines briefly, put it back on the table and sat staring at the thick carpeted floor of the consultant's waiting- room. A young couple sat opposite, a man on his own in the corner. All of them silent, staring into space. There was a tense uneasy atmosphere.

He had had the saliva test carried out some time ago, and arranged for Mia to have Marie Elaine tested also. In the interim, he had managed to put it to the back of his mind with some difficulty, but during the last few days had been so irritable that even Kate had noticed and almost lost her cool with him more than once. When the other people had gone in, he was unable to sit still any longer and stood up to look out the back window into a courtyard. The day was dull and the uninteresting view only increased his gloom, so he turned back and began to pace, constantly glancing at his watch to check the time, but it was a good twenty minutes before the secretary called him.

The doctor shook hands. 'Sorry for keeping you. Sit down while I look at your file.' He shuffled the papers on his desk and seemed so disorganised Jack hoped he wouldn't mix his results up with those belonging to anyone else.

'Ah! Here we are. Don't know what I'd do without that girl out there,' he laughed and pulled out a file.

Chapter Twenty-three

'Shane, have you arranged a band for the Waterford gig?' Mary asked at their regular weekly meeting.

'Not yet, but I have a contingency plan. I'll be in Cashel on Thursday, Kilkenny on Friday, and Limerick on Saturday.'

'You're doing really well. The turnover is very good, amazing really.'

Des came into the office, and shook Shane's hand. 'Great job!'

'And here's your cheque for last month.' Mary handed it to him.

'Thanks very much.' He glanced down at the sum written there, and was surprised.

'You treat us well, and we return the compliment.' Des patted him on the shoulder.

'But there is one other thing we'd like you to do,' Mary paused for a few seconds, 'it's because you're family and maybe you might have a fresh eye on things.'

'We're having a bit of a problem with cash,' Des said, 'the levels are not consistent with the computer readouts, so there is a possibility that someone is pilfering. We've caught people before. While the amounts are not huge, it's happening every week.'

Shane's heart thudded uncomfortably. Dermot hadn't begun to repay the money he had given him yet.

'So we want you to work a few hours behind the bar again for us, we'll pay separately. Note anything suspicious at all. It's only the receipts in this particular pub, but we're determined to catch whoever it is.'

'Dad, I can't take any more money from the takings, I'm afraid it will be noticed.' Shane handed Dermot a mug of coffee.

'Sure how would that happen?' Dermot barked. He wasn't feeling well. His stomach was bothering him and the antacid tablets were useless.

'Mary and Des are sharp, and I don't want to take any chances with the job.'

'They're not going to suspect you.'

'Never know.' He kept the other matter to himself as he had promised.

'Rubbish! Anyway I told you I'd pay it back, didn't I?'

'When will you have it?'

'Soon, Shane, soon.'

'I'm worried about it, Dad.'

'Don't be an old woman, Shane, you have to take risks in life.'

Shane couldn't get Dermot to understand how it was for him. He loved what he was doing. This was a real job. And while it wasn't international stardom, it would do fine for now. The promotion business was lucrative and there were contacts to be made which could mean his singer-songwriter capabilities might be recognised. He didn't want to jeopardise this chance.

Back home now and settled, he had caught up with some old friends and he was closer to Conor and Michelle too.

'You've certainly changed,' he told Conor.

'So will you when someone like Michelle comes into your life.'

'How's the job? Have you reached the top of the IT ladder yet?'

'I'm three rungs from the top!' Conor grinned.

'Is it a big or a small ladder?'

'That's classified! But there's a possibility of promotion soon and, if I get it, we'll buy a house. With the baby coming there's just not enough space here.'

Shane grinned, 'that's a long way down the line for me.'

'You might surprise yourself! Beer?' He handed him a can. 'How's Dad?'

'Not in good shape. Drinking too much, and he has a stomach

problem. I told him to go to the doctor but he won't hear of it.'

'Typical, never could tell Dad anything. He knows it all.'

'Would you call around sometime? He might listen to you.'

'Drives me to distraction. Every time I see him he borrows money and I never get it back.'

'I suppose we used to be the same. He's obviously not able to manage to pay everything on what he's earning at the pub, although I'm doing fairly well out of Mary and Des.'

'You have no expenses, why don't you give him a few bob for your keep?'

'I'm constantly giving him money.'

'Hi Shane.' Michelle came in, very obviously pregnant at this stage, wearing a blue T-shirt and white skirt.

'When's the baby due?'

'October.'

'So soon?'

They smiled at each other and she took Conor's hand.

'Hey, I'm going to be an uncle, I hadn't really thought about that. Uncle Shane,' he grinned broadly.

'How would you like to stand for him or her?' Michelle asked softly.

Shane raised his eyebrows. 'Me? You'd risk your child's life in my hands?'

'Why not?' Conor laughed, 'could do worse.'

'You've some confidence in me. Who's the godmother?'

'My sister, Tracy,' Michelle said.

'You're lucky you two, all happy families.'

'We were like that once,' Conor muttered.

'Excuse me, I'll just start the dinner.' Michelle kissed him, and went into the kitchen.

'Have to say I never expected Mum to walk out!' Shane swallowed his beer.

'She's a different person now.'

'Looks younger too.'

'And that guy Jack, what do you think of him?' Conor asked.

'Seems OK, I don't know how serious they are. Has she told you anything?'

'No.'

'I wonder what his intentions are?' Conor guffawed.

'And are they sleeping together?' Shane joined in his laughter.

'I nearly broke up the first time Mum mentioned a condom.'

'And she'd talk about STD's, and drugs, and ask were we straight, things Dad would never mention.'

'She's a great Mum.'

'But I don't think I'd push anything with her these days.'

'When I came back, she gave me fifty euro, and there wasn't another cent offered. Luckily I got the job from Mary and Des; couldn't have survived without that.'

'I hope it works out for her, she deserves another go at life.'

'Do you think Dad and herself might make up?'

'Who knows, I don't think they've gone down the road of a legal separation, and they can't divorce yet. I think there's a four year wait.'

'It would be nice if things could be like they used to be.'

'Too much has changed. The house is like an empty shell. Down to the bare essentials. Regardless of that, it's nothing without Mum.'

Shane's phone rang and he pulled it from his pocket. 'No, I'm over with Conor at the moment. I'll see if I can get hold of him.' He keyed in another number. Listened for a moment and then put it away. 'Dad's not at work. Probably on his way in, late as usual.'

'Very likely sleeping off a bottle of whiskey,' Conor laughed.

Chapter Twenty-four

The doctor stared at the file for a few seconds. Then he lifted his head and smiled. 'The result is positive, you are the father of the child Marie Elaine Ekman.'

The hammering in Jack's chest increased rapidly.

'It's always a bit of a surprise, whatever way you hear about fatherhood,' he said, 'I'll write to your GP to confirm this, but if there's anything you want to discuss now, fire away.'

Jack shook his head. His mind was blown apart by this news. It was as if that first child had suddenly come back to life. Born perfect. Beautiful. His own. He couldn't have formed a question. So he left. Outside he began to walk. A slow meander along the canal bank, passing bridges and locks, thinking about her. Imagining how she might look. Talk. Laugh. He had nieces and nephews but had never taken too much notice of them, and couldn't imagine how he would communicate with a small child.

He phoned Mia. But the voice which replied didn't have her slightly accented English and sounded like a more mature woman, definitely Irish.

'Can I speak with her?' he asked quickly, frustrated at the delay.

'No, I'm sorry, she's away at the moment.'

His heart sank. He hadn't anticipated this.

'How long will she be away?'

'I'm not sure.'

'Will it be days or longer?'

'Hopefully, days.'

Leaving his number, and cursing the inopportune timing, he

continued walking until he reached the stretch near the Naas Road. Having grown up in Tyrconnell Park, this was his playground. He sat down on the grassy verge and stared across the dirty green water of the canal, but couldn't see the beauty of the white swans gliding past, or the ducks swimming among the reeds. His mind took him on a wild hurtle into his own childhood. To those days of ultimate freedom when there were no cares in boys' minds other than how much money they needed to buy sweets or lemonade. How long it would take to help his father in the garden, wash the dishes or polish the floor. In the Linley family, everyone had a job to do, from the eldest to the youngest. There were no favourites.

Suddenly, he noticed a rapid movement in the water, and for the first time his mind concentrated on something other than himself as he saw an animal try to climb on to the bank. He reached and scooped up a small bedraggled puppy into his hand. He looked around for the owner but could see no-one, the only people in the vicinity were occupants of cars driving by. It seemed to be only weeks old, and was a mixture of a Scottie and something else, judging by the little square face. Jack walked down the bank, his eyes intent on the water. Then he saw another, but it was floating in the centre of the canal and he realised that someone had tried to drown the litter and this little lad had managed to escape. But what to do with him? He stood for a moment looking at the shivering bundle of wet fur and then turned for home, the dog cuddled under his jacket.

Kate called around that evening, an unexpected visit. He was so glad she was here and threw his arms around her. 'I love you.'

'And I love you.'

'You're very important to me, Kate.'

'You can't live without me!' she giggled.

'That's so true. I ... there's something ... ' He stuttered, badly needing to tell her about Marie Elaine. A little girl who shared his genes, traits, personality, and was part of him. He tried to express what he felt but his courage failed.

'Something?'

He took her hand. 'Let me love you forever?'

'You'd better!' she smiled.

'All our lives *'til death us do part?*'

'Hey, what's with you tonight?'

'Nothing, I'm just so glad to see you.' They walked down the hall and into the kitchen, but were met with a scene of devastation, a mess of newspaper twisted and torn on the floor. Water spilled. Biscuits scattered.

'What's going on? Have you been painting in here?'

'No, it's the puppy.'

'The what?'

'I found him.'

'Where is he?'

'In the box.'

'He's gorgeous.' Kate tickled the black curly fur. He immediately woke up and climbed out.

'What a mess, I was only up in the studio for half an hour.' Jack cleared the papers.

'Where did he come from?'

Jack vaguely explained the sequence of events.

'This is what happens when you let a baby into your life,' Kate laughed.

'He'll be going to the pound first thing tomorrow morning.' The puppy rushed towards the door, and Jack opened it.

'No, they'll put him down.'

'Someone will want him for a pet.'

'I don't know about that. What's his name?'

'Doesn't have one.' Jack poured disinfectant on the floor.

Kate waited in the doorway until he ran in and immediately began to jump up on her feet.

'He wants you to play with him, little chancer.'

'That's a good name, Chancer, let's call him that,' Kate decided.

'Whatever, I don't care, he's not going to be here for very long.'

Kate sat down, lifted him up on her lap and cuddled him. 'I love him.'

'You can take him home.'

'Sorry, no dogs allowed in our house.'

'Then it's the pound.'

'It's so sad.' She tickled the puppy under his chin.

'You're trying to make me feel guilty.'

'But he chose you to be his daddy, you can't ignore that.'

Chapter Twenty-five

Pat, Susie and the boys were away for the weekend so Kate immediately took her opportunity to invite Grace, Carol and Jack around for a barbecue. She spent the morning preparing the food - a tasty celery and apple salad, fresh young spinach leaves with artichoke, a mixed pepper, with various dressings, and other side dishes. The *pièce de resistance* was a confection of summer berries, meringue and fresh cream. She was enjoying herself, loving the chance to have friends in. It was a pleasant sunny day and the garden looked particularly good with a profusion of colourful flowers. The wooden table and comfy cushioned chairs were shady under the big cream umbrella. Jack was on duty over the hot charcoal, wearing Kate's red and white striped apron, cooking chunky fillet steaks, toasted skewers of marinated pork and chicken. New potatoes and shallots cooked the same way with a garlic and mustard dip. They drank crisp cool Chardonnay from tall John Rocha wine glasses which had been a gift from Jack.

And Chancer was there too. Still with Jack in spite of his threats to take him to the pound.

'I never saw such a variety of gorgeous food,' Grace smiled, looking particularly attractive in a pretty lilac dress.

'Cook of the year is our Jack.' Carol sipped her wine and munched an olive.

'He's not entitled to all the credit, I've done my bit too,' Kate laughed.

'You've got a really nice man there,' Grace murmured.

'I'm lucky,' Kate smiled over at Jack who turned corn on the hot coals.

'I heard that, it's all a front!' he grinned.

'Temperamental, creative, and liable to lose the head at the slightest provocation.' Carol helped herself to avocado.

'I've known men like that,' Grace smiled, 'and they're often the most interesting.'

'There's a certain amount of security in the guy-next-door type, my ex was one of the unpredictable ones, I couldn't live with him in the end. What are these little golden things here?' Carol asked.

'Potato polpettes – with feta cheese, dill and lemon; try one.' Kate handed around the plate.

'Mmmm delicious!'

'You can't choose who you love, it's a lottery,' Kate added.

'And I won first prize,' Jack grinned.

'When you meet your heart's desire, you should give him or her everything, all of you. To hold back only twists you up inside. I've been there,' Grace said slowly.

Suddenly they were quiet.

Kate put a hand on hers.

'I'm sorry, but I think it's because I'm here, in the garden which Bill's dear hands created. He used to bring me flowers from here, roses mostly. It's lovely to see you have kept it much the same.'

'I wanted to do that in his memory. After all, when someone leaves you a gift in his will you have to look after it,' Kate said.

'It's beautiful.'

'Right, everyone ready for steak?' Jack asked.

'Cheers!' They raised their glasses, and were just about to eat when Kate heard her phone ring in the kitchen, and excused herself.

'Hello?'

'Mum, I've just got back from Cork, and Dad's still in bed, but there's something wrong, I can't wake him up,' Shane sounded worried.

She sighed, not very pleased at the interruption. 'He's probably hung over, he'll wake up eventually.'

'But he doesn't look so good; his face is puffy and there's

130

perspiration on his forehead, could you come over?'

'Does he seem to have a temperature?'

'He's burning up.'

'Get a wet cloth and put it on his forehead. See if that helps, and ring me back.' Suddenly, she was concerned about Dermot, but didn't say anything when she rejoined the others. It was particularly awkward with Jack there, and she couldn't tell how he might react. Lately he had seemed rather down and today was the first time that he was in his usual good form.

'I put your steak back on the fire, ready now?' Jack forked it on to her plate.

'This is hot!' Grace gulped her glass of water.

'Spanish chilli potatoes; sorry, I should have warned you,' Jack grinned.

'What are the ingredients?'

'Chillies obviously, garlic, cloves, tomatoes, paprika and a few other things I threw in.'

'I'd forgotten how good Spanish food is.' Carol made short work of her portion.

The phone rang again.

'That didn't work, Mum.'

Kate's stomach dived. 'He's still asleep?'

'Yea, but he's groaning every now and then, and twisting in the bed. I don't know what to do.'

'Call Dr. McKenzie. I'll come over straight away.' While initially she had been annoyed with Dermot, it sounded far more serious than she had imagined, and Shane couldn't be left to deal with it alone. It just wasn't fair.

In the garden the others were laughing at some joke Carol was recounting.

'I'm sorry, but Dermot isn't well, and Shane doesn't know what to do. I told him that I'd go over.' She stared into Jack's eyes, praying he would understand.

'Do you want me to go with you?' he asked.

'No thanks, but would you mind entertaining our guests? My

131

apologies, Grace.' Kate kissed her.

'Don't you worry, I hope Dermot will be all right.'

'Sorry Carol.'

'Go on, will you?'

'Thanks.' She rushed through the house, followed by Jack.

'Let us know how he is, if you want me to do anything just phone.' He kissed her.

She drove to Rathfarnham, really fuming with Dermot. Her one chance to spend some time with friends in Berwick Road and he had to ruin it all.

'Mum, he looks even worse now. And there was only an answering machine at the surgery, and I rang the other number, and they said a doctor would come over.' Shane met her on the landing, his face white.

Kate went into the bedroom and knew instantly that it wasn't a simple matter of a bad hangover. She touched Dermot's forehead which was hot with fever, and that swelling described earlier by Shane was quite obvious.

She called to him, but there was no response. Then she wrung out the facecloth in the bowl of water and placed it on his forehead. He groaned.

'Ring for an ambulance, Shane, he needs to be in hospital.'

'What's wrong?'

'I don't know, but he's got a very high temperature and seems to be in some pain.'

While Kate kept sponging Dermot down, Shane opened the gates, and cancelled the appointment with the other doctor. Within minutes the noise of the siren broke the stillness and the paramedics took charge of the situation. Kate went in the ambulance with Dermot, while Shane followed behind. At the hospital he was rushed into a crowded A & E on a stretcher and transferred to a trolley. To her relief he received attention immediately.

Shane managed to find one chair, and she sat beside the trolley. It was a tense worried place. White-walled. Green-curtained. Staff

132

rushed here and there taking care of people. The elderly all wore oxygen masks; others had more obvious injuries, a woman with a black eye, a man with his skull split open, a broken leg. Wounds, blood, pain, the anxious faces of family members.

'Do you think he'll be all right?' Shane asked.

'I'm sure he will, it may be a virus of some sort. Once they identify it and begin to treat him, he should improve,' Kate tried to give the impression of confidence.

'Hope so.' He stared down at his father. Hands pushed into the pockets of torn blue jeans, shoulders sagged, very dejected.

It was some time before a doctor attended to Dermot, and the delay really worried Kate. But eventually, he was wheeled away and disappeared through a door at the top of the A & E ward. They looked at each other. Kate was about to ask one of the nurses where he had gone but she whirled past and it was impossible to make eye contact.

'Possibly X-ray. Yes. More than likely.'

Kate phoned Jack to say that she wouldn't be home until later, and he assured her that he would look after everything. She sat beside Shane in the packed waiting room, until finally, some time later, they saw a doctor who informed them that Dermot had peritonitis, caused by a burst appendix. They were going to operate immediately. Whatever she wanted for Dermot, and any revenge she might have longed to exact on him, it wasn't this. Somehow things had gone wrong for them, and where the fault lay was probably impossible to say.

Chapter Twenty-six

During the night Jack kept in touch with Kate, and he was glad for her sake that Dermot had come through surgery, but didn't really care about him if he had been truly honest. Somewhere deep down in the recesses of his heart was a thought that if Dermot wasn't around he could have persuaded Kate to marry him, perhaps even that time he had bought her the ring in Kilkenny, and life would be so different now. Frustration boiled up in him. Why couldn't his life be uncomplicated like so many other people he knew?

To escape his morose thoughts he went to work in the early hours. Gripped the knife and applied thick paint on to the canvas which gave a little with the pressure he applied. This was the painting of a man, in sepia-toned colours like an old photograph, and he wondered if it might be a self-portrait. He had never deliberately sat down and completed one, hating the vanity of it. Now as he stared at the figure he recognised something there. Perhaps it was the isolation, the lack of identity. Like himself, a man alone, without anyone to share each moment, to make him feel he was at least human, except for that dog downstairs. Suddenly, he scored across his work. Taking a tube of black he squirted it directly on to the canvas and obliterated the figure. Then he dug the knife into the taut fabric and the threads ripped jaggedly. His final lurch sent the easel toppling backwards until it hit the floor with a crash. He stood staring at what he had done for a moment, his chest heaving with emotion, then turned and left the studio.

He phoned Mia again, but to his disappointment, it was the same woman who answered.

'Is this Jack?'

'Yes.' Hope surged.

'I'm Margaret, a friend of Mia's, I recognised your voice.'

'Have you any idea when she will be back?'

'No, I'm sorry, but I will let her know that you called.'

'Thank you.' A terrible fear crystallised inside him. Had Mia decided to cut him out of her life because of his initial response to Marie Elaine's existence? Would he ever see his daughter?

Later, he decided to go for a run, and took the dog with him. Chancer had had his shots, and it was the first time Jack could have taken him out. He was hard to control, dragging on the lead, sniffing here and there, rushing madly towards any other dog he saw nearby. Usually much larger animals who immediately rounded on the yapping lump of black fur, and snarled, forcing Jack to yank him back and take him up in his arms until they were out of sight. The dog population diminished as he approached Inchicore and, reluctant to return home yet, he decided to call to see his parents.

He was persuaded to have lunch and it proved to be a much longer visit than he had intended. There was a lot of fuss over the puppy and much discussion about how he was found and who might have been the person who tried to drown him. And how many others there were? And who has a dog like that? And what type is he anyway?

'A mixture of something,' Jack said.

'I'd say he's a bit of a Scottie and a poodle.' Mrs. Linley cuddled him on her lap.

'Not at all,' interjected his father puffing on a cigarette, 'he's just a mongrel, no pedigree blood there at all. You don't know what he might grow into. Some big bowser which will drive you mad.'

'He'll be a good guard dog for you,' she said.

'Sure hasn't Jack got all sorts of fancy alarms, what does he need a dog for?'

'He can take it for a walk in the evenings with Kate,' his mother argued, 'like a lot of couples do.'

Jack smiled at the image his mother described.

His father slowly extinguished the butt in the ashtray. An action which heralded a change in the conversation. It was his way. A cigarette enjoyed as he thought about what he was going to say behind the lightweight chat about the dog.

'Who's Kate?'

'She's Jack's girlfriend. You met her at your party, Dad. She's very nice. We like her, don't we?' His mother put the dog down on the floor where he immediately began to chaw at the fringing on the mat by the fireplace.

He humphed and cleared his throat. 'I don't remember her. What does Paula think about it?'

'I don't see Paula any more, Dad, you know I'm divorced now.'

'She was up here for lunch last Sunday.'

'No Dad, it's been a long time since we've seen her,' Mrs. Linley said gently.

'She's Jack's wife, and I talked to her about the garden. She admired my flowers.'

'Dad, we don't live together any more,' Jack explained.

'I don't know what Fr. Byrne will say when he hears that.'

'I won't be discussing it with him.'

'And where is she living then?'

'I don't know.'

'Have you thrown her out?'

'The house was sold.'

'Over her head?'

'No, it was agreed.'

'I can't believe what I'm hearing. Poor Paula. God knows where she is. Have you got her phone number, Mam, we'll have to ring and find out.' He stood up, agitated now.

'Dad, all that happened a long time ago. It's well over ten years.'

'And what about your children? Where are they?'

Jack stared at his father, shocked.

'Dad, Jack doesn't have any children,' Mrs. Linley said.

'Why don't you? Our family has always been very ... ' He stopped for a moment and lit another cigarette. 'All your brothers and sisters have children and the cousins too.' He inhaled deeply. 'I didn't pass on any of those, whatever they're called, it wasn't my fault.' His face grew flushed.

For a moment, Jack was about to retort that he had fathered two children, but he held himself back with difficulty. Now wasn't the time. His father seemed very confused.

'You're getting yourself all worked up, Dad, you'll need one of your pills.' Mrs. Linley crossed the room to the dresser, opened a small container and tipped a tablet out on a plate. 'Now take that with a drop of milk, and no more talk for a while.' She stood over him as he obeyed her instructions with a childish pout.

Concerned, Jack watched, but said nothing until he was alone with his mother in the kitchen.

'Why didn't you tell me that Dad was on medication?'

'He doesn't want anyone to know.'

'How long has this been going on?'

'Only a few weeks. He had a bit of a turn one evening and I made him go to the doctor, which was some achievement I can tell you.'

'What's wrong?'

'Heart trouble. Something about the arteries they said.'

'I wish you'd told me. I wouldn't have let that argument develop,' Jack was worried.

'He never learns.' She shook her head.

'How serious is it?'

'Serious enough. He went to the hospital for tests, but they've decided against an operation, so he just has to watch himself.'

'I'd like to talk to the doctor. What's his name?'

'He's in James's Hospital.'

'You're not telling me,' he said.

'Dad doesn't want anyone to interfere, and we'd best leave it that way.'

'What did the doctor say?'

'I couldn't understand half of it.'

'I'm sure they told him to give up the cigarettes, and ease back on the gardening.'

'They did. But it's like talking to the wall. Anyway he said that the garden would be the best place to die, out there among his flowers and plants.' There were tears in her eyes.

'But I'd prefer it to be later rather than sooner.' Jack looked out the window at the mass of colour. Pinks. Purples. Blues. A rainbow.

'Whenever it comes, it will be God's will, son.' She blessed herself.

He followed his father out on to the patio.

'Who owns that dog. He's digging up my flower bed.' He walked slowly after Chancer. 'Get out of there, out!'

Jack hunted the puppy away.

'Can you mow the grass?' His Dad asked.

'Yea sure.'

'My son usually does it for me, but he's not here now, always away somewhere,' he muttered.

Jack walked up and down the long back garden with the old push machine. But it was easy enough, the grass cut down to a smooth pile, like a length of dress velvet.

'Keep straight there, you're running off line!' his father barked.

Jack never could get it quite right. But eventually his Dad was reasonably satisfied, and he went on to cut the edges, although they were not up to his satisfaction either.

'Do that bit again, it's untidy. And there, look at the corner!'

Finished at last, Jack put away the machines in the shed.

'How much do I owe you?' his father asked.

'Dad?' he laughed.

'Do you think you could come over again?' He stared around the garden.

'Maybe next week.'

'How much?'

'I'm very expensive.'

'You're talking to a pensioner, you know.' He pulled a twenty euro note from his pocket.

'A very young one,' Jack grinned.

'My family wouldn't agree. Particularly Jack. He thinks...God knows what. Hasn't been around in a long time.' He held out the note and when Jack didn't take it, let it drift slowly on to the grass.

'Bring the dog up to us any time you want, he's a pet,' his mother said and hugged Jack.

'But you'll have to keep an eye on him, he's destructive. Where's Bonzo?' his father asked.

'I think we buried him in that corner, under the hydrangea,' Jack said with a smile.

'What?' His father walked over to the spot.

'Bonzo has been dead for years, Dad, don't you remember? The kids were small then.' His mother put her arm around him.

'Nobody told me,' he grumbled.

'Come inside, I think it might rain.' She ushered him back into the kitchen and he went with her, like a docile child.

Jack was worried. As he walked home, other strange incidents over the past few months came into his mind. Things he hadn't noticed at the time, but which now, added to what had happened today, suddenly assumed enormous proportions. How tragic it would be if this was the onset of Alzheimers disease.

Chapter Twenty-seven

Kate watched model after model swan down the catwalk. Blondes. Red-heads. Brunettes. All skinny as rakes. They wore the most exquisite wedding dresses. Traditional dazzling white. The richness of ivory. Even some coloured gowns, all fantastic. But Irene couldn't make up her mind.

'If you could give us something to go on we might be able to make progress. A choice of fabric – colour – style – anything?' The wedding planner, Pru, lay back in her chair with a groan.

'There are too many choices.' Irene waved her arms helplessly.

'Natasha's going to do her nut; timing is everything, any delay at all and she won't be able to make the deadline.'

Useless. Kate thought. Pru was as much help as she would be herself on a space mission. At that thought she intervened. Was it going to be off-the-shoulder. Embroidered. Beaded. One-piece or two-piece. Lace. Silk. Satin. They went through the possibilities until finally, Irene managed to make some decisions.

'Can Natasha create something along those lines?' Kate handed Pru her sketch.

'Of course!' She rushed off in excitement, legs stick-like in pink and green check leggings and short mini-skirt in purple, a garish combination.

'I'll have to go soon, Irene,' Kate said.

'But we have to decide on the design for your outfit,' Irene protested.

'Whatever she produces will be fine by me.'

'But she has to see you.'

'My measurements have already been taken by one of the staff. Email the design and I'll confirm.'

'Please stay, I'm no good without you.' Irene put on her helpless act.

'Sorry Irene, but I have another appointment, best of luck, bye.' She couldn't have given it any more time, it would have driven her crazy.

'Mum, could you call around to see Dad, it might do him some good.' Shane phoned just as she left the salon.

'It's a bit difficult between us, try to understand that.' Dermot had almost fully recovered now but was still staying with Mary in Donnybrook.

'I think he misses you a lot.'

Shane had put her on the spot, and the inference beneath his words was quite clear. 'I'm sure when he's well again … ' It was the first time she felt certain that all her decisions regarding Dermot had been right. Although on that first night in the hospital when her mind and emotions had been solely concentrated on him, she had wondered if through some manipulation she would be drawn back into her old role of Mrs. Dermot Mason. But now she knew that had only been a temporary sentiment born out of loyalty and old love.

'He really needs you.'

'I'm sorry Shane, but our marriage is over; we both have to try and get on with life as best we can,' she experienced a pang of guilt, wondering how much her words might hurt him. 'I know it must be difficult for you.'

'It doesn't bother me, Mum, it's just, if you only saw the way he lives.'

Kate walked quickly along St. Stephen's Green, trying not to let herself become too caught up in Shane's obvious concern for his father. She had arranged to meet Grace in a small café off Grafton Street and, rushing in, found her already sitting at a corner table. 'I'm so sorry for keeping you waiting, but the meeting at Natasha's just went on and on.'

The older woman dismissed her breathless words with a smile and quickly ordered coffee for them both.

Kate was really glad to see Grace. In her late seventies, she always looked absolutely pristine; skin quite unlined, softly pink, grey eyes wide and full of laughter. They had become close these last months. It was a slow getting to know each other, and there were times Kate felt that her mother's spirit possessed Grace, seeing the same gentleness and wisdom in her.

'I'll have to make up for these few hours off later.' Kate sipped a latte. 'But it's lovely to get a break.'

'You do too much. All work and no play?'

'Please don't go there,' she implored.

Grace's eyes twinkled with humour.

'I'm building up the business, so it's par for the course. Although I wouldn't mind having a bit more time to spend with Jack.'

'You should.'

'Lately he seems preoccupied with other things. There are times I don't think I matter so much any more.' Kate cut a square of Danish pastry and munched.

'Perhaps you're going at such a pace you can't see his needs and that's his reaction.' Grace's gentle words drifted like fine sand and nestled in Kate's subconscious.

'He doesn't seem to understand what I want out of life. Sometimes, I feel afraid that he'll turn me into a housewife again.'

'Remember the day of the barbecue at your house? He was quite prepared to do the cooking. I was pleasantly surprised.'

'He wants me to work part-time – I know that's probably the ideal for a relationship - but it's not possible to run the business on a few hours a week.' She folded the napkin in squares. There was a finality about her movements which seemed to set out parameters.

'It's the possession thing; deep down in the psyche,' Grace smiled.

'Nowadays men don't have a choice, most couples both work. And even though I love Jack to bits, I must do my own thing. There's something inside that demands I face up to the challenge.'

'Don't lose sight of the love you have with him. It's a delicate balance and can be destabilized very easily. Remember how I mishandled my own life. Instead of being more open about my feelings, I asked your Uncle Bill to accept a relationship which had nothing in it at the end of the day.'

'I want Jack. But it has to be on my terms,' Kate admitted with a sinking feeling in her stomach. Maybe she was the one who was being selfish? 'I can't go back to the old days, breakfast, lunch, and dinner. Washing, ironing, cleaning. I used to feel like a slave. Do this. Do that. Have you got my whatever? Where did you put the other? It wore me down in the end.'

'But surely he wouldn't expect you to run after him to that extent?'

'No, he wouldn't, I know that. But I felt liberated after leaving Dermot. Free to make my own decisions about every aspect of life. It wasn't easy in the beginning. There was no money. The prospects were bleak. Anyway, I got there and I'm not giving that up,' she said fiercely, 'sorry, I'm losing it, sorry.'

'Talk to him,' Grace advised.

'He won't understand.'

Chapter Twenty-eight

Although Jack couldn't see beyond the next day, he had to follow up on the business side of his work which had been very much neglected lately. There were unanswered letters on his desk and lists of phone-calls to be made. He finally tackled it on a Monday morning. One particularly urgent missive was from Vincent, the flamboyant owner of the Nestor Gallery, who was anxious to come around and view the paintings which would form the basis for his next exhibition in December.

'Is the work in your usual style?' Vincent lit up a cigarillo.

'No, it's quite different.' Jack poured two glasses of wine. 'Darker.'

'Is there a theme?'

'It's personal, probably won't be apparent to anyone else,' Jack muttered. He hated having to discuss his work, but knew that it was necessary.

'Come on, let's have a gander.'

Jack led the way upstairs, followed by the tall man, his long black coat swirling out behind him.

'Quite different is right.' He peered closely at the canvases. 'But interesting. I like them. They should do very well for you, such depth.' He waved his hands. 'What type of frames have you in mind.'

'I haven't decided yet.'

'Something unusual is needed, perhaps none at all.'

'I thought of using a slightly wider canvas behind the main one, but I'll have to play around with the idea.'

'I'm looking forward to seeing the finished product hanging. You're booked in for the fourth, is that still OK?'

'Yes, I have it in my diary.'

'Good, good, now I must be off. Keep in touch.' He hurried down the front steps, climbed into his sleek red sports car and roared off.

Jack was relieved that he liked the work and it gave him new impetus. He decided straight away to finish the commission he was working on and then go back to the collection. If he was to be ready by December, there was a lot of work to be done. Closing the door, he noticed the post on the floor and picked up the envelopes. ESB. Phone. Junk mail. And one other. His name was written by hand. The round curved letters had an almost childish look. He slit the top jaggedly with his thumb and pulled the letter out. His gaze swept immediately to the end of the page, and finding that it was from Mia, his pulse began to race.

"Dear Jack,

When you receive this letter I may not be in a position to talk to you about Marie Elaine. I had no intention of ever telling you about her, being far too selfish and loving my baby so much. But circumstances changed when I was diagnosed with a severe form of breast cancer, the prognosis of which was not good. So far I have had chemotherapy and radiotherapy, but now it has spread and I have very little time left. I know this is an enormous thing to ask of you, but my mother and father are both dead now, and apart from distant cousins in Sweden, you are the only person I can ask to take care of my Marie Elaine. Although she is very close to my friend Margaret, it would be too great a request to make of her as she has her own family.

So it is to you that I entrust my precious baby. She is your daughter, as you now know, and deserves to have at least one natural parent in her life.

Thank you. Mia"

145

He stared stupefied at the letter, unable to believe what he had read. Cancer? Dying? Dead? The words spun through his mind like a ricocheting table-tennis ball. His throat felt constricted as he read it again, hoping to find another meaning there. But as he came to the end, it was clear that his understanding had been correct, and suddenly everything fell into place. Her gaunt appearance. Pale glistening skin. That tight-cut hair.

Margaret was a woman about his own age. Heavy-set with a pleasing attractive face, straight dark hair, and warm hazel eyes. As they shook hands and murmured their first words, he was immediately at ease.

'Sometimes Mia knows us, but then there are other times when she doesn't, so I want you to be prepared,' she said as they walked into the Hospice. 'I don't know how long it's been since you've seen her, but she has lost a lot of weight.' She pushed open the door of the room and he followed her inside, shocked when he saw the slight figure in the bed. Mia was only half the size she had been when they last met, and looked like a child lying there, so pale and still.

They sat down on chairs by the side of the bed. Margaret gently took her emaciated white hand which lay on the quilt. 'Mia, how are you feeling today, love? Jack has come in to see you, and he's brought you a lovely bouquet of flowers. Are you going to wake up for me, you can't be sleeping all the time, particularly when you have guests.'

Her eyes partially opened, but she didn't seem to register their presence.

He covered her other hand with his, almost afraid that the roughness of his touch would cause the delicate skin to crumble. 'Mia?' he murmured softly, 'how are you?' What a stupid question, he thought. But he was rewarded when her eyes moved in his direction, widening large, the pale lips parted in a half-smile.

He moved closer.

'Look after Marie Elaine for me,' the whisper was barely audible, her breathing uneven.

'Of course I will, don't worry, she'll never want for anything.'

146

'And please try to love her.' She leaned forward towards him, but the effort proved too much and she fell back on the pillows and closed her eyes.

'I will, I do ... love her already.' Tears welled up and he bent his head.

Margaret reached to pick up a little silver-framed photograph which stood among some of the other items on the bedside locker and handed it to him.

He stared at the image there of a little girl, with dark curly hair and large brown eyes. She had a heart-shaped face, and the sweetest smile. She was, without any doubt, a Linley.

Chapter Twenty-nine

Back home in Rathfarnham now, very early one morning Dermot's doorbell rang and rang, until finally he pushed himself out of bed and padded downstairs wearing dark blue pyjamas, the top of which gaped open as a couple of the buttons had gone missing. 'Shut-up will you, I'm coming, for God's sake, quit it!' he grumbled. He pressed the gate control, and contrary to his usual habit, only then looked out, shocked to see three cars swing into the driveway, one of them a Garda car. A group of men, some wearing uniforms, others in plain clothes, jumped out and rushed up the steps to the front door.

*

Mary and Des were still at the pub, and had been there since they had closed the night before.

'I don't believe it.' She stared at Des, a shocked expression on her face.

'Neither can I. Dermot must have lost it altogether.' Des clicked the computer keyboard.

'Of course he's been in considerable financial difficulty over the last couple of years.' Mary totted up the list of figures she had scribbled in a notebook.

'But why didn't he come to us for money?'

'I gave him a wad of cash a couple of times, but he hasn't asked lately.'

'He didn't need to ask, he was stealing it. Only for the CCTV we would never have found out.'

'He must have been desperate.' Mary was very upset.

'And his own son suggested we install a camera, what do you think of that? Were the two of them in on it?' Des flashed.

'Shane would hardly have done that if he was involved himself,' Mary argued.

'It stinks. They'll both have to go,' Des glared at her.

'But he's doing so well organising the gigs.'

'We can do that ourselves if we have to.'

'But what if he has the bands under contract and they won't deal with us?'

'He'll release all contracts to us, or I'll beat the shit out of him.' He banged the desk. 'Bloody relations!'

'But we don't know that he's guilty of anything.'

'You're soft.' He left the office.

Perhaps Des was right, Mary thought. But Shane was family, and like one of her own.

*

Shane was still asleep when his phone rang and, only for the fact that it was on the bedside table, he would never have heard the tinny jangle. 'Yea?' he grunted.

'Shane Mason?' an officious very wide-awake voice enquired.

'Yea?' He pushed himself up on one elbow.

'This is the Gardai; we have your father here.'

There was a short delay.

'Shane! I want you to contact Martin Purcell,' Dermot's voice was low and he sounded extremely nervous.

'What's happening?' Shane asked in astonishment.

'I've been arrested - obviously!' he snapped.

'Why?' Shane's stomach did a somersault as he thought about the money which had been stolen from the gigs. As Dermot hadn't repaid anything at all, using his own funds he had gradually begun to replace what had been taken each night, and the total amount was reduced to a few hundred euro at this point.

'This whole thing has been trumped up and I need to get out of here immediately.'

'What whole thing?'

'Phone at nine, Purcell and Somers, Merrion Square.'

Shane could hear a gasp as the line cut off. Confused, he sat on the edge of the bed. If this was about the money stolen from the gigs, then he had an involvement as well. But why was his father arrested? He hadn't actually done anything. Then, suddenly terrified that the Gardai would crash through the door of the hotel room, he got out of there fast.

With growing trepidation, he drove to Dublin and a couple of hours later he arrived at the house in Donnybrook. Mary opened the door and he knew by the expression on her face that she knew about it.

'Would you like a cup of coffee? Something to eat?'

'Thanks,' he said nervously.

'Toasted sandwich, how does that sound?' She put bacon on the grill and flicked on the kettle.

'Great, I haven't eaten.'

He was silent as she prepared the food, unsure of what to say. Then she sat down opposite him and sipped a coffee as he ate.

'We've been up all night doing the figures, Shane.'

His stomach churned.

'The CCTV cameras proved that it was Dermot who was taking the money. When he was ill, the figures tallied, but as soon as he came back they were down again.'

'I know,' Shane muttered.

She seemed puzzled. 'How do you know?'

'Dad rang me from the Garda Station.'

'Has he been involved in an accident or something?' Mary's face paled.

'He wouldn't give me the details, but I ... ' His voice trailed off as he suddenly realised that he could be implicating himself.

'We've only just done the figures to support what we saw on the tapes last night.'

'So you didn't go to the Gardai?'

'No.'

'I'd better find out what's going on.'

At the Garda Station, Mary and Shane were allowed in to see Dermot for a short time, and found him in a very fearful state.

'It's about the Spanish project. They interviewed me a good while back and I thought that was the end of it. But seemingly they've come up with something else. It's probably all to do with Manuel. I knew he'd stitch me up in the end, the bastard!'

'What's happening now, was the solicitor in with you?'

'Yes. I'll be in Court tomorrow. But that means I've to spend the night in this place.' He looked around with a disgusted expression on his face.

'But have you done anything?'

'Of course not.'

'It will be thrown out then.'

'Bloody better be.'

'We'll meet with the solicitor and come back later. You'll need clothes to wear tomorrow,' Mary was very much in charge, 'I will pick up something new if necessary. And, Shane, phone your mother to let her know, and Conor too.'

'Don't tell Kate,' Dermot blurted, 'or Conor. I don't want anyone else to know.' He held his head in his hands.

'She cares about you.'

'She doesn't.'

'Of course she does. You don't appreciate her, never have. Now we must go,' Mary said.

'Don't leave me,' he blubbered.

'We'll get you out of here as soon as possible, don't worry.' She hugged him.

Shane patted his shoulder.

The following day, Mary, Kate, Conor and Shane were all in the body of the Court when Dermot was brought in flanked by two Gardai. He didn't look well, an exhausted pallor on his face, although he had shaved, and his new dark suit, white shirt and striped tie were smart. Kate had never been in a Court before and the whole procedure was like something in a TV drama. The evidence was presented by the prosecuting legal team and it was damning - Dermot accused of defrauding his clients of the property they had purchased in Spain through his company. It appeared that Manuel Pedrosa had given information to the Gardai about Dermot. And while Kate understood that the Spaniard had been the cause of Dermot's bankruptcy, she had never thought for one minute that they had been involved in something as fraudulent as this.

The proceedings didn't last very long and wound up with a discussion about bail. The Judge finally set the figure at twenty-thousand euro, and ordered that he would have to surrender his passport and sign on at a Garda station once a week. When she heard this, Kate's heart sank. She almost didn't even have the strength to stand up when the case was over, very much aware of Dermot's pathetic looks towards them as he was hustled away to jail.

'I haven't got any money to spare, we're saving for a deposit on a house,' Conor said bluntly.

'Surely you could manage something?' Shane asked.

'Conor, Shane, enough, wait until we can talk this through. We'll go somewhere for a cup of coffee.'

'It's a drink I need,' Conor muttered.

'There's a place down the street,' Mary suggested.

In the pub, they ordered what they wanted, and sat silently for a while.

'It's a desperate situation, we can't leave him in there,' Kate said.

'But who's got that sort of money under the mattress?' Shane swallowed his beer.

'It will never be needed. The bail is only if he doesn't appear on the day.'

'But you still have to possess the money,' Conor persisted.

Mary had been very quiet, so Kate tried to bring her into the conversation. 'What do you think?'

'I don't know.'

'Can you help?'

'I'll have to ask Des, but I don't think so, we're very strapped for cash at the moment.' She glanced towards Shane.

'Maybe some of his friends?' Conor wondered.

'I don't think he's any left, most of them lent him money and haven't been paid back,' Shane supplied that bit of information.

'We'll have to try and come up with something between us,' Kate said firmly, 'I will have a look at my bank account.'

'But he'll be in there for a second night if we can't decide now,' Shane was upset.

'It will have to wait until tomorrow.'

Kate spent some time working on her bank statement as soon as she arrived home. While the business was going well at the moment, there wasn't anything like the amount of money needed. She told Pat and Susie about it, hoping that they might help, but there was nothing forthcoming. Then, she phoned Dermot's two brothers in London, but apparently, he had borrowed a lot of money from them too and neither were prepared to offer anything. She phoned Jack after that, just needing to talk, but his phones were both on answering machines and she left messages, frantic by now. Whatever Dermot's faults, to leave him in jail would be terrible. But between herself, Shane and Conor, all they could raise was seven thousand. Mary and Des wouldn't contribute anything.

Chapter Thirty

Jack drove Margaret back to her home in Kimmage, very disturbed by his experience at The Hospice. Mia was obviously close to death and her little Marie Elaine would be left without a mother and a totally inadequate stranger as a father.

As they stopped outside the block of apartments, Margaret turned to him with a smile. 'Thanks so much for bringing me home, would you like to come in and have a cup of tea? Then you could meet Marie Elaine. My daughter Karen has been looking after her today.'

He nodded his agreement, but was scared stiff at the prospect.

'While I've mentioned the fact that she will be going to see her Daddy soon, I don't think we'll say anything this evening. Just see how it goes.' She ushered him into the living-room and introduced him to her daughter. But he didn't really see the teenager, as immediately his eyes strayed to the small girl who sat in front of the television. She was dressed in a pink pinafore with a lime-green T-shirt underneath. Her dark curly hair was pulled back into two bunches tied with pink ribbons.

Margaret went over. 'Marie Elaine, this is Jack. Won't you say hello?'

He went down on his hunkers to be closer to her, but she wouldn't look at him.

'We're just a bit shy today, I think.'

He stood up, feeling awkward.

'Karen, will you put on the kettle please?'

'Will I make tea?'

'Yes, love, or maybe Jack would like coffee?'

'Tea's fine, thank you.'

Margaret took the little girl on to the couch beside her. Jack watched from where he sat, amazed at the beauty of his daughter. With sallow skin and slanted dark eyes she looked very much like his mother when she was young, and his sister Rose too. It was extraordinary and he was captivated.

Karen returned with tea and biscuits and Margaret handed him a cup.

'She's a happy child, and quite clever too. She can read and write already and will be starting school in September.' She glanced fondly at the little girl who was sipping milk and munching on a biscuit. But she ignored him and he was disappointed.

Kate called later and he had to put his own problems aside when she told him what had happened to Dermot, and the urgency to find the bail money.

'I just don't know where to turn now. Even Mary and Des wouldn't help. And myself, Conor and Shane can only gather a few thousand.' Tears glimmered in her eyes. 'I hope you understand that it's not because of any fondness between Dermot and myself, I just feel I have to try to help him for the lads' sake.'

'Don't worry so, it's only money,' he was aware it sounded flippant, but when he thought of Mia and Marie Elaine, it put any financial problem in its correct perspective.

'Only money?'

'Let me help.'

'I couldn't ask you.'

'I'll put up the balance you need. Anyway, it will never be used. Dermot isn't the type who would abscond. Phone the solicitor in the morning and find out how it's organised. I'll probably have to go into the Court.'

'Thank you so much, I love you.' She threw her arms around him.

'It's nothing. If I can manage to make you smile then that's all I want.'

Chapter Thirty-one

Dermot closed his eyes and tried to sleep, but the ceiling of the prison cell hovered just above him with its yellowed watermarks and graffiti. He felt claustrophobic as he thought about the awful events of the last couple of hours and found it impossible to shut out the images. The humiliation of the procedures he was forced to endure, the fear which had flooded through him when he was brought into the cell, and met the eyes of its other two occupants, who were suspicious of him to say the least.

The younger was Len, and the older, Larry. Both of them were watching a match on television and seemed in no mood to make conversation, so he had climbed up on the top bunk and lay there. Feeling so alone, he had to fight hard not to burst into tears. Later he wanted to go to the toilet and had to ask Larry who indicated an area in the corner which in this extremity he was forced to use. Hours later, sleep finally took over, but it was broken by nightmares out of which he awoke sweating more than once to stare into the dimness, wondering where he was.

The following morning there was slop-out, which was another difficult part of prison life. In the large cafeteria he had to join a long line of men and then bring his cornflakes, toast and tea back to the cell, where he sat staring around him at the photos of Page Three girls and footballers which adorned the walls. The day dragged interminably. At lunch, Dermot ate the egg and chips which were slid on to his tray, the only dish on the menu that appealed to him. With a shake of salt and some bread, it wasn't the worst meal and he felt slightly better afterwards. But returning to the cell with the others after a break for exercise in an open area, the feeling of being incarcerated got to him and now he really regretted the things he had done, particularly his treatment of innocent clients who had paid him their hard-earned cash to buy a place in the sun. The solicitor had told him that there was a possibility of a civil suit being taken against him by one person and others could follow. He had a cramp in his stomach as his ulcer reacted to the combination of stress and greasy food, and he was aware that the day was passing and there was no sign of anyone coming to tell him to go home. Surely they would have raised the money by now?

'Do you want to read the paper?' The older man proffered it to him.

'Thanks very much.' Dermot leafed through it, spending an inordinate amount of time on every article.

'What are you in for?' Len asked suddenly.

'Eh, it's all a mistake,' Dermot stuttered.

'I asked you what you were in for?'

'It's a financial thing, it wasn't murder or GBH or any of those crimes you see on television.' Dermot noticed that the man had extremely bad teeth. Is that what happens to you when you've been in jail for a while? He remembered then that he should go to the dentist soon, they had sent him a note the other day.

'This isn't television; here you got the real thing.'

'I'm sure, sometimes.'

'Not sometimes, all the time.'

Dermot tried to swallow the lump in his throat.

'We're both murderers.' He sat back on his chair, crossed one leg over the other and folded his arms which were covered with tattoos. Hearts. Cupids. And the names of various women.

Dermot stared at him, speechless.

'You don't believe me?' He stood up swiftly and his hands encircled Dermot's neck.

What have I got myself into here? He thought frantically.

'Do I hear an answer?' Len grinned.

'No!' He could feel his throat constrict.

'That's not the right one.'

'Please stop, please?' Dermot struggled. His hands gripped the attacker's wrists, and he tried to pull them away from his neck. He didn't know what he was expected to say now.

'Give me the right answer,' he demanded roughly.

'Len, that's enough,' the older man intervened.

Dermot was dizzy. He couldn't breathe very well and was afraid he would pass out. 'Please?' he croaked.

'Ask me nicely,' the man sneered.

'Len!' Larry stood up. 'For God's sake, leave the geezer be.'

Immediately the hands were released from around Dermot's neck. 'I was only showing him how it's done,' he laughed.

'He doesn't need a lesson.'

Dermot was coughing and spluttering.

'Come on, let's talk about the game yesterday,' Larry suggested, 'what did they say in the paper?'

'They all get it wrong.'

Dermot began to breathe again, but he kept his eyes on the man, terrified that he would suddenly attack him again.

A key rattled in the lock, and a prison officer appeared. 'Dermot Mason?'

Shane drew up alongside in the van. 'Dad, get in!' He flung open the door and Dermot climbed up.

'What kept you?'

'I was with the solicitor and they couldn't give us an exact time.'

'While you were dawdling I was almost murdered.'

'What do you mean?'

'Strangled. I'm going to take a case against the State.' He turned around to Shane. 'Can you see any marks on my neck?'

'Dad I'm driving.'

'Look when we stop at the lights.'

'Where?'

'My neck.'

He looked quickly and then away again as the lights turned green. 'It's a bit red.'

'A bit?' Dermot pulled down the mirror and peered at his

reflection.

'What happened?'

'A maniac in the cell tried to kill me.'

'Dad!' Shane laughed.

'It might seem funny to you but it wasn't funny at the time.'

'You can't be serious.'

'Believe me, it happened.' He rubbed his neck. 'Where are we going?'

'Mary said to bring you over to Donnybrook.'

'Did she put up the bail money?' he asked as they stopped outside the house.

'We managed some of it, but Mum's friend, Jack, covered the rest.'

'What?'

'He was very generous.'

'Surely Mary and Des could have found that amount?'

'Apparently not.'

'Bloody hell, it had to be him. Shit!' he muttered.

'You were very lucky he offered, otherwise you'd still be inside.'

Mary threw her arms around Dermot. 'You poor thing, what an awful experience. Sit down, what can I get you?'

'A good stiff double-whiskey.' He flopped into an armchair.

'Shane?'

'A beer, thanks.'

She fluttered off in a nervous fashion and was back in a couple of minutes with their drinks and a vodka for herself.

'Why did a complete stranger have to put up the bail money?' Dermot demanded.

'We were all a bit strapped.'

'You couldn't manage that much?' he bellowed, 'it's an insult. Something like that should be kept within the family!'

'Be grateful to the man.'

'I need another of these!' He held out his glass.

'Relax will you, for God's sake. Drink won't solve this.' She poured a little whiskey into his glass. 'We have to discuss your

159

situation. It's more serious than you realise.'

He swallowed it.

'And don't drink so fast, you'll be unable to string two words together in a minute,' Mary warned.

He grimaced.

'Now, firstly, about working at the pub.'

'You can't have a jailbird there, is that it?'

'No, Dermot, it isn't that at all,' she hesitated for a few seconds, 'this is difficult for me.'

He said nothing.

'We've discovered that you have been eh … taking cash … ' She gulped some of her vodka.

Suddenly he was overcome by a dreadful sense of shame. Caught in the act like a little boy by his sister.

'We noticed the losses some time back, but when you were in hospital, the balances tallied with the tills, and when you returned … '

'That's not enough to point the finger at me.' His voice was slightly slurred now.

'Des decided to put in a CCTV camera in the office.'

Shane bent his head, and shifted in his chair.

'I'll pay you back,' Dermot muttered after a moment.

'When? And with what?'

'I'll get it as soon as I can.'

'Some hope of that.'

'I'll do my best.'

'I don't know if that will be good enough for Des, in fact I know it won't. He wanted to go to the Gardai, but as you're in so much trouble already, I persuaded him not to do anything yet.'

Dermot sagged back in the chair.

Chapter Thirty-two

'I can't thank you enough for helping Dermot.' Kate held Jack close.

'It's nothing,' he said.

'My God, nothing!'

'The next thing to consider is the Court case itself, that's going to be expensive.'

'He'll have to try for legal aid, none of us can cover the fees, there could be thousands involved.'

'Would he get it?'

'I don't know how that works.' Kate was suddenly worried again.

'Dermot's not your responsibility.'

'I know, but somehow it's hard not to be dragged into it.'

'I understand.'

'But tonight I'm going to forget about the whole thing. We'll go out and have a nice meal, my treat.'

'Sorry, I can't this evening.' He shook his head.

'You look a bit gloomy. Is there something wrong?'

'Do you remember that woman, Mia, the one who left the message on the phone?'

She nodded, very curious now.

'I only found out a few days ago that she is in The Hospice.'

'How awful!'

'It's very tragic, she's only thirty-five.'

'Cancer?'

'Yes.'

'Why didn't you tell me before?'

'I suppose I was a bit reluctant to mention it; we knew each other for a short time some years back. It was a whirlwind thing, not like us,' he smiled at her.

'I must admit I was slightly jealous of this mysterious woman. She was the one who would always pop into my mind when you seemed a bit down, which you have been lately, my love.'

'You never have to be jealous, Kate.'

'What about her family?'

'Her parents are dead unfortunately, although she has one close friend here.'

'Is there a husband or partner? And what about children?'

'No.'

'Do you want me to come with you this evening?'

'No thanks. They only allow two people in, or sometimes one, depending on how well she is.'

Kate said no more. But when she was back into the swing of work, she couldn't get the thoughts of this woman out of her head. It wasn't a suspicion there had been something going on all the time, it was more the fact that he hadn't shared it with her, and their supposedly open honest relationship wasn't quite as open as she had thought.

*

Jack was very much aware of Mia's struggle to live, but he wondered about his own relevance in this place of death where at any moment a breath might be held just a second too long and her heart would give up the fight. Suddenly worried, he touched her face, but the soft skin was still warm, and he sighed with relief. He knew there was no hope, but he didn't want her to go. He stared fixedly at the photo of Marie Elaine which stood on the locker, and only then became aware of a movement in the bed. He looked up to Mia's large eyes watching him.

He took her hand.

She smiled.

He kissed her fingers.

'Look after my baby for me,' she whispered softly. In the hushed air, it seemed to be the clearest thing Jack had ever heard. So much love in those words.

'I will, of course, Mia, you don't have to worry.' He took one of the cotton buds which lay on a chrome tray and dipped it into a glass of water. Then he gently passed the cotton along her lips moistening the cracked surface. She made a sipping gesture grasping the bud as if to squeeze every last drop of water from it. 'Is that better?' he asked. The slight inclination of her head gave him such gladness he wanted to hug her tight, but all he did was apply a gentle pressure on her hand. It was the last time he would see those eyes look at him with any recognition.

Mia's friend Margaret arrived a little later and they talked in low tones outside the room.

'How is Marie Elaine?' he asked.

'All excited about going to school. We've been buying the uniform and the books, so many things even for a small girl,' she confided.

'Let me reimburse you for that, I'm so sorry, I hadn't realised; and I must give you the money for her care as well.' He took three fifty euro notes from his back pocket, it was all he had on him. 'I hope this will keep you going, I'll give you more tomorrow, and we can arrange something more structured.'

'No, not at all, there's no need.' She shook her head. 'Mia has dealt with everything.'

He pressed the notes into her hand. 'She's my daughter,' he insisted.

'I didn't mean ... '

'Just look on this as a present.'

'Thank you,' she smiled.

'Can you continue to look after her?'

'Of course I can. I love her like she was my own and I don't relish the thought of losing her.' Tears filled her eyes. 'It's bad enough that Mia is so ... '

'You spend some time with her now.' He gave her a light kiss on the cheek and left, unable to talk any longer. His emotions were

163

jangled and raw and he found it almost impossible to focus on anything else.

But when he arrived home, he wandered upstairs to the studio. He hadn't done any work for days and now suddenly he picked up a brush, squirted paint and pulled out a new canvas. The image came out of this evening, and the whispered words of a dying woman. He worked fast. The picture which emerged reflected the light-filled room, a bright lemon-lilac dawn streaming in from the window and onto the bed where the woman lay. Her large green eyes were bright and intelligent and there was happiness in the gentle smile.

Chapter Thirty-three

'We've our first fitting arranged for Tuesday afternoon!' Irene put her head around the door of the workroom.

Kate looked up, surprised. She was examining some swatches of fabric, trying to decide between two shades of cream.

'Susie let me in,' Irene put her handbag down on the delicate embroidered silk curtains which were in the process of being made.

'Be careful!' Kate warned, 'your bag...'

'Sorry.' She took it up. 'Which fabric is this?'

'Christian Fischbacher.'

'It's gorgeous. I'll renovate the apartment after we get married so maybe I might use some of these fabrics.' She wandered around the room. 'Who supplies this one?' She ran her hand down the soft pile.

'Designs with Style.'

'And this?'

'Prestigious.'

'Watch that iron!' May cautioned this time.

'My God, I'm afraid to move in this place,' she grimaced.

'Come into the kitchen for a minute, we can talk there,' Kate suggested, 'although I don't have much time.'

'We've arranged to meet at Natasha's salon at two-thirty, and I was wondering if you could pick me up, I hate taking the car into town these days, parking is so difficult.'

Kate went into the office to look at the diary. 'I know I've an appointment with a client at twelve and there's something else on after that.'

'Irish Rollashades and Power Home Products holding for you,

165

Dave of Venice wants you to return his call asap and Coopers were on as well.' Debbie pushed a notepad across the desk.

'Sorry, Irene, I'm booked up.'

'But it's the only time Natasha is free,' Irene wailed.

'Maybe a little later, about four?'

'I'll have to ask.'

'Do that and let me know. Now I have to take those calls. Sorry, would you mind letting yourself out?'

Kate smiled to herself after her stepmother had left. Was she finally learning how to manage Irene?

Shane came over for dinner and she took an hour out of her busy evening glad of the chance to talk to him. But she wasn't so happy with his admission that he had been taking money for Dermot out of the takings from the gigs.

'Shane, how could you?' she shouted.

'He persuaded me, you know how he can be. I've managed to put most of it back, although there's still about five hundred owing. I borrowed that, but I don't know if I'll get a chance to replace it as they might not keep me on. I think their trust in both of us has been shaken.'

'You were very foolish to take money in the first place, no matter what your Dad said.' She was shocked and very angry.

'I've been up the walls about it, particularly since the whole gig promotion is going so well.'

'You'll have to be honest with Mary and Des. They may let you go anyway, but I think the only way to deal with it is to come clean,' she rapped, slipping into her mother role of old.

'Would you come over with me?' he asked with a sheepish look.

'You don't need me, surely?' She stared at him, surprised.

'How will I explain?'

'There's only one way to do that and you know what it is.' She was very disappointed that now another person whom she thought was above suspicion, honest to the last cent, was anything but that.

Pat burst into the kitchen. 'Hi there, great news! The lads won singles and doubles at the tennis tournament.'

'Congratulations,' Kate just about managed a smile.

Susie appeared. 'Howdy?'

There were footsteps in the hall above and loud voices.

'Who's upstairs?' Kate asked.

'The boys have brought back a few friends, do you think you could make some sandwiches? We'll take them out somewhere later.'

'I'm afraid I haven't got the time.'

Susie peered into the fridge. 'There's some cheese there, ham, salad, and bread.' She looked at Kate in a quizzical manner, and then at Pat. 'I suppose I'd better make them myself. Honey, help me please?' she appealed to him.

'Let's change and head out as soon as we can, Susie, forget about the sandwiches,' he said and they left the room. Kate followed upstairs to see at least a dozen boys of varying ages crowded into the sitting-room. Two of them were rolling on the floor pummelling. Another stood on the couch doing an imitation of something or other. Donal and Rob were in the middle of it all.

'Now boys, enough of that,' Pat warned, as he passed the open doorway. But none of them took the slightest notice and he hurried after Susie.

Kate stood at the doorway and yelled, 'stop!' They stared at her, faces suddenly scared. 'You there, get up off the floor, and you...' She pointed at the boy standing on the couch. 'Sit down,' she ordered, 'and stay quiet. Donal and Rob, if you and your friends can't behave, then you can all leave. Do you understand me?' She went back downstairs.

'They're very noisy,' Shane commented.

'Yea.'

'When are they getting their own place?'

'God knows,' she sighed.

Chapter Thirty-four

Shane called to the pub the following morning. Mary was usually to be found there around twelve and he would have an opportunity to talk to her in private. Nervously, he knocked on the office door and pushed it open to find her sitting at the desk, surrounded with paper.

'I miss Dermot already, he wasn't bad at the admin. Idiot! I'd have preferred to give him the money rather than have him take it.'

'Yea, it was stupid,' Shane said hesitantly, dreading the thought of owning up.

She looked at him. 'What are you doing here at this hour?'

'I have a confession to make,' he muttered, shamefaced. In his pocket, taut fingers gripped the bundle of notes.

She gave him her full attention.

'I took money from the takings of the gigs for Dad. This is the last of it – five hundred - I've already put the rest back.' He pushed a wad of twenties across the desk.

She stared at it, silent.

'I'm very sorry, but he was in such a state for money, I couldn't refuse.'

'How could you be so stupid?' she glared at him.

'I dunno.' He looked away.

'He's a right bastard, pushing you into a situation which could ruin your life,' she rapped.

'It was only supposed to be a loan which would be repaid as quickly as possible, but when it looked like that wasn't going to happen, I began to replace it myself.'

'I don't know what Des is going to say to this, he'll turf you out.'

'I know.'

She fiddled with a pen and moved some papers about on the desk. 'Of course you didn't have to tell me at all.' There was a sudden softness in her voice.

'I talked to Mum and she felt it would be better to be straight up about it, rather than just put back the money and say nothing.'

'I have to commend you for that.' She stared across the room to the window through which the sun shone, angular shadows thrown on the floor from the security bars which crisscrossed the glass.

Following her gaze, Shane had a sudden impression of a prison cell.

'Of course, I suppose we needn't tell Des.' She unrolled the notes.

He felt a tremendous sense of relief.

'You are certain that this is all of it?'

'Yes, absolutely. I kept a note.'

She put it into the drawer and then leaned forward on the desk.

'Sit down, please, Shane.'

He did as she asked.

'I hope I don't live to regret this, but I've decided to give you a second chance. However, perhaps it would be better if the manager handled the money at the gigs in future. It's always possible Dermot will get around you again.'

'That's OK, Mary, I don't mind.' It was true, he was just glad to have his job back.

'I must call around to see Kate one of these days, we don't see enough of each other.'

'She'd like that.'

'Dermot was lucky that Jack agreed to raise bail for him.'

'Yes, he was.'

'It's a very odd situation. The new boyfriend goes bail for the ex-husband.'

Shane didn't say any more. He wasn't sure whether he was happy about Jack and his mother. And he knew that Conor wasn't too pushed about him either. He felt sorry for his Dad, who could have done with the support of his mother now. As it was, he didn't have anyone to rely on except himself and Conor.

Kate received a text from Shane, and could have jumped around the place with delight, immediately phoning Mary to thank her for giving him a second chance. 'I know it looks bad, but I believe him, truly I do,' she said.

'I suppose I'd feel the same way if it was my son.'

'We're all like that, Mary.'

'What's going to happen to Dermot?'

'God alone knows.'

'I was sorry you two split up, but I wasn't surprised.'

'It was difficult to leave, to be honest, but finally I felt I had no choice.'

'You've been liberated,' Mary laughed.

'The liberated woman, that's me!' Kate joined in.

'You're a strong person, capable of standing on your own feet, and I admire that.'

'I'm trying.'

'Keep it up and don't be worrying about Shane. He's a great young man, and has a successful future ahead of him. I know he took the money for Dermot, but I can understand how persuasive my brother can be.'

Chapter Thirty-five

'I'm worried about you.' Kate stared at Jack's pale and rather drawn features.

'Once I have you, I'll be all right.' He pulled her close.

'How is Mia?'

'She's fading.'

'I'm sorry.'

'It's very difficult to watch someone die, I've never experienced anything like it before.' He led the way into the kitchen and she was met by the dog, who immediately jumped up on her

'Down, Chancer, down!' Jack ordered, but the dog took no notice at all.

She laughed, picked up the black furry bundle, and cuddled him.

'He's a brat, completely out of control,' Jack seemed exasperated, 'I just haven't had time to go up to the pound.'

'Don't bring him up there, poor little thing!'

'You try and look after him then. Peeing and pooing everywhere but on the sheet of newspaper where he should do it,' he grumbled, very much out of sorts.

'When he's bigger you can get a hut for him in the garden.'

'Sounds so easy.'

'Isn't he company for you?' Kate almost wanted to laugh at the expression on Jack's face.

'You're the only company I want, a dog was never part of the plan.'

'He adopted you.'

'I need someone to adopt me,' he managed a half-smile, 'but the person I want doesn't seem to want me.'

'Jack, you have to be joking,' Kate tried to introduce some levity into the situation.

'It's no joke. I feel you don't want to make a commitment to us.'

Kate was taken aback. 'Jack, I have committed myself. But to tell you the truth, there have been times lately when I wondered were you losing interest in me?' she grinned, not really serious.

'Don't even say such a thing,' he snapped, 'you're the only person that keeps me going, what with Mia and ... '

'I'm very sorry about that, love. It must be tough on you. We both seem to be at sixes and sevens lately. I have to deal with Pat and Susie and now Dermot as well,' but as she mentioned his name, she realised that perhaps it was a mistake.

'I'm fed up hearing about his problems.'

'I'm sorry, and you were so generous to put up the bail.'

'I only did it for you, because you couldn't bear the thought of him being in prison.'

'And I appreciate that, you've no idea how much,' she spoke gently, unsure how to handle this unexpected burst of hostility from Jack. Her hand smoothed the black curly hair of the puppy in her arms which gave her something to do in the silence which followed. But it didn't last, as Jack's phone rang, and he listened to whoever was on the line, the colour in his face draining to a gaunt white.

'I must go over to The Hospice, Mia's taken a bad turn.'

'Will I go with you?'

'No, it's all right, thanks.' He kissed her. 'I'm sorry, forgive me for being so moody, I shouldn't have taken the head off you.' He kissed her again. 'Maybe you might wait until I get back ... I'd like to talk. If it's too late, could you call around in the morning?'

'I'll stay for a while, but tomorrow is out, I'm sorry, I'm giving a lecture to some interior design students.'

'Doesn't matter.'

She took the dog outside and let him run in the back garden. Then she wandered back inside. It was rather strange to be here alone and she felt like an interloper even though she might one day live in this

172

house. Everything was spotless, kept that way by Bernie who came in every morning. She ran her finger along the door frame. Not a hint of dust. In the sitting-room she looked at the titles of books on the shelving which covered one wall. There were a lot of Irish authors, among them McGahern, Colm Tóibín, John Banville, Roddy Doyle and a mixed bag of thrillers, biographies, and books on art. There was poetry too - the volumes by Yeats, Áine Miller and Brendan Kennelly were well-thumbed.

His guitar stood up against the wall and she ran her fingers over the strings. The melodic sound echoed into the silence and she picked up a CD by Carlos del Rio. Looking down the list of pieces noted on the back, she was delighted to find a track entitled "Recuerdos de la Alhambra", and was reminded of those wonderful days spent in Granada when they had first met. She put it on and the resonance of guitars strumming echoed. Slowly she climbed the stairs and went into his bedroom, suddenly needing to draw him back from where he had gone. Into another world in which she didn't figure. She pulled back the corner of the white duvet and smoothed the pillows, pressing her face into the softness of cotton, breathing in the aroma of his body. That dear sweet scent that made her want to roll up in the bed and wait for him to return.

Suddenly aware that she was prying into his private space, she quickly replaced the pillow and settled the duvet again. The bright green readout on the radio clock told her that it was ten-thirty. Should she wait or go home? Her eyes strayed to the framed photograph of them together taken in Spain after Christmas, smiling and happy. A tinge of regret filtered through her and she wished that their lives were as joyful now as they had been during those few days.

Lastly, she went into the studio and held her breath as she saw the large canvas. The woman lay sleeping on a low bed covered with a blue quilt. Kate stared at it emotionally, reminded of the series of paintings Jack had done of her and which, unfortunately, had been sold. Questions shot through her mind. Questions to which she had no answers. And they were all about Mia.

It was the official opening of the new club, El Noches, and the place was buzzing when they arrived. Kate had been invited by Paul and brought along Carol, and Mags who had just returned from LA. She had asked Jack too, but he had to visit Mia.

'Wow, this is something else!' Mags exclaimed.

'It's super, isn't it,' Carol grinned as they accepted glasses of champagne from a waiter and pushed through the crowd, immediately spotting people they knew.

'What's this?' a previous client asked, 'all together again?'

'I'm working with Kate,' Carol explained.

'I'm just back from the States and bursting with new ideas,' Mags grinned.

'Crawford Design.' Kate handed her a card.

'Thanks, I'll be looking for you soon, we're renovating again so I'll send you an email.'

'I love the décor, black and red are so dramatic.' Kate stared around her. 'And the lighting is unusual, those spots which keep changing colour create a wonderfully subtle ambience.'

'It's not bad for Dublin, but you should see some of the places in LA.' Mags sipped her drink.

'What are you doing back here then?' Carol laughed.

'I missed old dirty Dublin.' Mags looked as stunning as ever in a lilac outfit.

'You missed us, cheapskate, admit it!'

'You know, I actually got tired of being on holiday and was thinking of getting a job, but it was really the place which had become a bore.'

'Will you go back?' Kate asked.

'No, I'll probably head off somewhere else one of these days.'

'Can't do that if you're holding down a job.'

'How about the three of us getting together again? We were a strong force in the interior design scene here and could easily pick up where we left off.'

Kate glanced at Carol. She enjoyed working with her, but to join up again with Mags would be an entirely different thing. Her immediate reaction was a definite no.

'And I've seen some fabulous designs, girls, wonderful homes, and offices. I'll have to show you the photographs I've taken. And with plenty of money Kate, we can set ourselves up in really swish offices. We'll make such a bang on the design scene, it will be knocked on its head!' Her eyes were wide with excitement.

'I'm sorry, Mags, but I'm happy with the way my company is organised at the moment, it suits me.'

'Kate, if Carol is working with you, why not me?' Mags asked peevishly.

'I'm only the nipper, Kate's the boss,' Carol laughed.

'That's some role reversal.'

Carol sipped her champagne and picked a chocolate-covered strawberry from a silver tray. 'Mmm these are gorgeous, try some.' They helped themselves. 'Come on, let's check out the rest of this joint. I wouldn't mind something decent to eat.' She led the way through the crowd to the restaurant and the contentious mood between Mags and Kate dissipated somewhat.

'The food is delicious. I'll be back here again.' Carol forked a prawn on to her plate.

'Mouth-watering,' added Kate, munching little pieces of chicken on a skewer.

'Kate!' Paul appeared beside them. 'I'd like you to meet Massimo, who designed the club.' They shook hands with the good-looking Italian.

'You've done a wonderful job, the place is fantastic,' Mags smiled.

'*Grazie*, I am pleased that you like it.' He bowed slightly.

'Kate is a very successful designer on the Irish scene,' Paul said.

'And we sold our company some months ago to an American group,' Mags explained with just a hint of pride in her voice.

'And she's been on a permanent holiday since.'

'So much I would wish also to be on holiday, but I have no opportunity, there is just so much work,' he sighed dramatically.

'Where are you based?' Carol asked.

'Rome.'

'Do you specialise in clubs?' Kate asked.

175

'Excuse me, there's someone I need to see,' Paul said, 'look after Massimo.'

'Bars and restaurants, similar to this, also hotels and private homes too.'

'It's a credit to you.' Carol finished her glass of champagne.

'I'm sorry?'

'She's trying to tell you this place is really great,' Mags laughed.

'*Grazie, grazie!*' he smiled.

'I'll have to refresh my Italian.' She moved a little closer to him.

'*Parliamo Italiano?*'

'I used to, years ago, but I've forgotten most of it now.'

'Perhaps I can help?'

'I wouldn't say no to a few lessons,' Mags simpered shyly. An unusual attitude for her.

'Perhaps we will arrange it. Now, let me show you around. More champagne!' He clicked his fingers and a waiter carrying a tray of glasses materialised beside them. Kate smiled to herself. Mags was up to her old tricks again and grabbed the first good-looking guy who came along. She never considered that Carol was single as well.

Music pounded and the noise almost burst their eardrums, but Massimo walked past the dance-floor, which was full to capacity of moving bodies, and through to a softly-lit area at the back with comfortable leather couches and low glass-topped tables. There he introduced the girls to the directors of the club, which was one of a chain of similar operations all over the world. They spent quite a while chatting with them and it was late when they finally excused themselves.

'We made some good contacts tonight!' Carol said, 'never know where we might end up working.'

'There's Mags over there with Massimo. Do you want to tell her we're going?' Kate asked.

'At this stage, she won't even notice we're gone.'

Chapter Thirty-six

'It's a marvellous opportunity, you have to take it. To be involved in the refurbishment of a palace in Rome is fantastic. Even to pitch for it will raise your profile!' Carol was excited.

'He must have got my email address from Paul. But why not Mags?'

'He has other ideas for her!'

'She's already gone out to Italy?' Kate asked.

'Yes, and I don't know when she's coming back, if ever.'

'I'm not sure if I can work with Mags again, you know I prefer to do my own thing.'

'Don't be such a stick in the mud, take a chance, be adventurous.'

'Things have never been quite the same since she moved in on Jack.'

'I thought you had kissed and made up and put all that behind you?'

'We did.'

'Well then, what's the issue?' Carol laughed.

'Perhaps I don't have the confidence to tackle such a job, maybe that's it.'

'Nonsense. It could be the making of you. And I can hold the fort here.'

'OK, Mammy.'

'So go ahead and book your flight.'

'Massimo is arranging it and the accommodation also.'

'And you're thinking twice about going? That's nuts!' Carol exploded with laughter again, 'how long will you be away?'

'A few days, I suppose.'

'What a delicious prospect.'

'It will be all work I'm sure.'

'But you'll switch off at some stage no doubt, maybe even have a chance to wander around the shops, pick up a couple of designer outfits. A smart little Versace number perhaps?'

'I wish I could go with you.'

'So do I.' Kate kissed Jack. A long slow sensual meeting of lips.

'My love.' He ran his hands over her body, slim in slinky jeans and clinging top. She giggled and responded by opening his belt. With heightened senses, their movements became more urgent and he drew her down on the couch.

'Don't go off with some Italian!' Jack murmured softly in between kisses, 'then I'll definitely have to follow you.'

'Those smoothies are exactly my type,' she giggled.

'The romance of Rome, the vino, never know what that might do.'

'Speak some Italian then, pour that wine and we can imagine.'

'*Si, si Caro ... ti amo.*'

'Sounds so romantic,' Kate sighed.

'I'm going to take you there as soon as I can.' He pressed his lips on hers, and the outside world receded.

Kate was enthralled by the beauty of Rome as the taxi drove through the Centro Storico, crossing the Via del Corso, the old Via Lata of the ancient city, the knot of narrow side streets and alleyways packed with shops and galleries. The car jerked its way along the crowded streets with other traffic, surrounded by scooters which dodged this way and that with terrifying speed. She had been here many years ago and was thrilled to be back.

Hotel Palazzo Venezia was stunning. Her fifth-floor suite was exquisitely appointed, with a gold and white colour scheme, and terrazza which ran the whole length. Immediately she was enticed through the drifting white voile curtains. From here she could see the Vatican in the distance, the rooftops and domes of churches, and other ancient buildings. She clung to the wrought-iron balustrade and breathed in the aroma carried on the sluggish air and thought of Jack.

'Welcome, Kate,' Mags embraced her.

'It's great to see you.'

'Isn't it wonderful – *la bella Roma* – I love it!'

'I hope Mags loves me more than Rome,' Massimo looked particularly handsome in a white jacket, dark shirt and trousers.

'Of course I do!' She put her arm around him.

'Andiamo, let us go to eat.' He led the way outside to his car, a sleek black Maserati.

'Isn't this car something else!' Mags shouted in her ear as it roared down the street, but Kate's eyes were closed, heart pounding, hair flying in the breeze. 'Hey, open your eyes, you're missing everything. See the buildings all lit up, and the fantastic fountains!' She dug Kate with her elbow, but at that moment Massimo applied the brakes and they came to an abrupt halt in a parking spot which seemed just made for the car, not an inch to spare. They climbed out and Massimo led the way to the Piazza de Campo dei Fiori.

'This is one of the most beautiful places in Rome.' Massimo turned to her. 'In the mornings, they sell flowers, and in the evening it is my favourite place to eat.'

Mags swung along in a green and pink dress, so short her suntanned legs seemed even longer than usual. Kate wore white linen and felt comfortable in high-heeled sandals.

'As we go I want to show you the historical places. Here is Palazzo Braschi, the Museo di Roma, you should visit if you have time. And Palazzo della Cancelleria, once the seat of the papal government.' They stared up at the elaborate buildings and then followed him down a narrow side street into the tiny Piazza del Biscione where he showed them the supposed site where Julius Caesar was murdered by Brutus. Over the centuries, he explained with a grin, the place was infamous as the site of public executions and burnings at the stake. At that Mags felt she had enough history for the night and they made their way to the restaurant. Sitting in the garden under a vine-covered pergola, the yellowing lamplight created a soft ambience, each group of people far enough away from their neighbours so as to ensure complete privacy. It was very romantic and Kate would have loved for Jack to be there with her, feeling rather like a gooseberry with Mags and Massimo who were obviously very much in love. But they were joined a little later by a number of other business associates, and the night turned out to be really enjoyable.

The following day he took them to the Palazzo Gabriele in the Piazza Spagna which was presently being restored. It was magnificent. In particular the frescoed ceilings by Pietro da Cortona, the building itself designed by one of the most famous architects of the time, Bernini. The ballroom was on the first floor and this was where Massimo was anxious to have Kate's input on the design of the drapes which he planned to install. He had a cutting of a previous fabric used, faded and worn now and wanted the pattern of flowers, vines and cherubs to be recreated.

'We have used a company in Paris who manufactured some silk similar to this on a previous job. I'm sure they would be delighted to work on it,' Kate told him confidently.

'They were very good,' added Mags.

'Can I take some photographs?' Kate asked.

'Certainly. As you can see, the colours are those which Cortona used in the ceiling, the blues, golds and maroons are dominant in the fabric.'

The walls were hung with mirrored sections, hand-painted with woodland scenes. These reflected wonderful crystal chandeliers, the thousands of sparkling shards creating a most amazing light. Kate used her video camera to record, and photograph, putting all details on to the lap-top.

'And I want to take you to see some other work-in-progress, Kate, perhaps you might be interested in becoming involved?'

She nodded, excited at this promise of a new dimension in her career.

'I'll be liaising with you Kate, Massimo wants me to stay here and work with him, well, more than that really!' Mags confided later.

'It's fantastic, he's a nice guy.' Kate was genuinely glad. And relieved too that she no longer showed any interest in Jack.

'I can't believe my luck, and all in a matter of weeks.'

'We told you Mr. Right was just waiting around the corner.'

'And I was so jealous of you.'

'I suppose I felt the same.'

'A right pair of twits,' Mags laughed.

They spent the last morning in the shops, a glorious whirl of wonderful clothes, shoes, bags, jewellery and Kate did buy something, not Versace, but just as gorgeous.

Chapter Thirty-seven

Jack walked along the corridor in an aimless manner, hands clenched in his pockets. Reaching the end he turned back, and went in the opposite direction, knowing every inch of The Hospice by now. At the front door he stood almost counting the seconds, able to gauge the length the time the staff usually spent with Mia as they made her comfortable. In these last days, while she had gradually fallen into a coma and was no longer able to communicate with them, he had become very attached to her. An unexpected emotion as he hadn't really felt much more than a temporary attraction when they had met originally.

Suddenly someone called his name and he hurried back quickly. The nurse ushered him into the room and he moved towards Mia with a dreadful sense of foreboding. He sat in the chair by the bed and knew instantly that there had been a change. A softening in her features, a luminosity.

'I will phone Margaret,' she murmured and left him alone.

He clasped Mia's hand, aware that her breathing had altered too, the almost imperceptible wheeze only occurring occasionally now, a warning that soon the length of time between each would stretch into infinity.

Some time later, Margaret arrived with her husband, daughters, and to his surprise, Marie Elaine.

'We came to see Mummy, didn't we, Marie Elaine,' Margaret said to the little girl, 'she isn't well, and the doctors have been looking after her here.' She brought her close to Mia.

'When is she going to wake up?' Marie Elaine asked, her large brown eyes staring wide.

'She's having a really long sleep. Why don't you hold her hand?'

But she flung herself on Mia, chubby arms curling around the wasted body. 'Wake up, Mummy, wake up.'

Jack's throat was tight as he watched from the end of the bed.

'Why won't she speak to me?' Tears filled her eyes.

'Give her a big kiss.' Margaret lifted her closer, and the childish lips pursed and pressed on to the pale cheek. 'That's a good girl. Now, we'll go and leave Mummy to have her nap.'

He wasn't sure when she died, but it was some time during the few minutes which followed, according to the nurse. A gentle end to a young life. But so unfair, and far too soon to leave a daughter whose memories of her mother would inevitably fade over time. They left the room and sat in the restaurant sipping tea, nobody saying very much. Marie Elaine the only one who was unaware of what had happened.

Jack watched her eat a biscuit and sip a glass of milk, and was amused to see how concerned she was if a crumb fell on the pretty blue top she wore. He smiled at her, but she immediately lowered her eyes. It disappointed him, but he knew it was far too soon to expect anything else. He was still a stranger.

Afterwards, they were brought back into the room where Mia lay. The curtains were drawn; in the dimness scented candles burned and there was a handful of flower petals arranged on the quilt. Marie Elaine had been taken out by one of Margaret's daughters and they knelt to say a decade of the Rosary. It took Jack back to his childhood, when all the family had prayed together each evening, something which most of them had resisted as they grew older. He wondered now would he be in the same position soon with his Mam or Dad. In particular, his father, who had this heart complaint no-one spoke about, and memory loss too. Jack determined to be more generous with his time in future.

Margaret invited him back to their house for something to eat and he was glad to accept, anxious to spend as much time in Marie

Elaine's company as he could. But she had fallen asleep in the car and was put to bed immediately so there was no chance. After a simple dinner, they sat together in the sitting-room with Margaret's husband, Kevin.

'Mia fought hard,' Kevin was morose.

'She wanted to live for Marie Elaine. Didn't want her to be alone, a child without a mother.' Tears welled up in Margaret's eyes. 'Or a father ... that is until she found you.'

'If I'd known beforehand, I could have helped perhaps, but Mia only told me about Marie Elaine a short time ago.'

'I encouraged her.'

'He smiled, 'I owe you a lot then.'

'You've surprised me. Most men wouldn't want to know.'

'I've no children, so it was quite a shock.'

'What will you do about Marie Elaine now?' Margaret asked slowly, a rather anxious look on her pleasant features.

'I'd like to take her to live with me, but I don't know how she'll respond,' he admitted.

'She's slow to make friends. There was just herself and Mia in the last couple of years, the two of them alone. When Mia was in and out of hospital, she didn't even want to stay with us here. I had to win her around.'

'I think it's different with a man.'

'She never took to me,' Kevin grinned, 'still looks at me with those great big eyes and such a serious little face.'

'Mia didn't have any men friends then?'

'She did have a partner, but they broke up. After that she kept to herself, doing her sculptures.'

'I'm not sure what to do. To be honest, I don't know anything at all about children.'

'What about your partner?'

'We're not living together yet, and she doesn't know about Marie Elaine.'

Margaret nodded, seeming to grasp the situation immediately.

'But I want to have her with me, she's my daughter,' he said adamantly.

'And that's the way it should be,' Kevin responded.

'I'll miss her a lot.' Margaret looked sad.

'It's good timing,' Kevin said, 'I've taken early retirement with a nice little redundancy package and we're planning to go out to Australia to see Margaret's sister.'

Jack was suddenly worried. If Margaret couldn't look after Marie Elaine what would he do? 'When are you going?'

'As soon as we can arrange it.'

'Could you look after her until then? I'll pay whatever you ask. Maybe we can do things together in the meantime so that she might get more used to me.'

'Of course I can, it'll be easier for me too,' Margaret smiled.

Driving home, the thought of telling Kate about Marie Elaine instilled a level of fear and uncertainty within him which had never happened before. While he couldn't abandon his child, accepting her into his life might mean that he would lose Kate. His heart twisted at the thought. And then another aspect of it all struck him. If he told her Mia had died, then how would he explain away the time spent with Marie Elaine? He was being sucked even deeper into the deceit, and wondered would he ever extricate himself.

The funeral was simple and Mia was buried in Bohernabreena Cemetary which overlooked the city. The handful of people stood with bowed heads around the grave, and each threw a red rose on to the coffin. Marie Elaine held on to Margaret, her little white face pinched and scared. Jack had insisted that she should be there. It was important for her memories. For the future.

The following day Margaret asked him to come over and go through Mia's things, a prospect which he didn't relish.

'The landlord wants possession, the rent was just paid up to the end of this month,' she explained, turning the key in the lock.

The living-room was sparse and simply furnished, with shelving around the wall which held some of her sculpture - beautiful abstract pieces in bronze.

'She's such a loss,' he murmured.

'This suitcase holds all of her private papers, birth certs, that sort of thing.' She lifted it out of the wardrobe. 'I know everything she had is left to Marie Elaine, and there is a small insurance policy.'

He stared around the room sadly.

'I might arrange an exhibition of the work, in memory.' He ran his hands over one of the pieces, almost able to feel her touch on the rhythmical cuts.

'That would be lovely.'

'Do you know if there is anything Marie Elaine would particularly like? Perhaps things she might have used, a mug, or dishes, which would be a reminder and help her feel more at home in my place?'

'I think she had a favourite mug,' She looked in one of the kitchen presses and found the white mug with a puppy painted on it.

He took the mug, and some other dishes, and Margaret offered to bring Mia's clothes to the charity shop.

He didn't sleep very much that night, as thoughts of what it would mean to be a father took him into a new world of little girls. How would he look after her. Know what she liked to eat. Buy clothes, and anything else she might need. Would he be able to talk to her. Be aware if she wasn't feeling well. The questions shot in and out of his head with speed and when he finally fell asleep in the small hours, his dreams took him somewhere he didn't belong, a place which scared him stiff.

He rose early and wandered around the house carrying a cup of black coffee, wondering should he redecorate the spare bedroom. Presently, some of his paintings were stored there, but he could put them in the studio without difficulty. He hoped the room wouldn't be too large for a small girl, but apart from his own, the studio took up the rest of the space at the top of the house. There was a craftsman nearby who created wonderful designs in natural wood furniture and the walls could be painted a warm sunshiny shade of yellow perhaps. He was staring into the room with a mixture of excitement and terror when the doorbell rang, one long and two short.

'Kate, what are you doing here so early?'

'I decided to pop down for breakfast. I've missed you the last few days, I'm so tired of travelling.' She kissed him.

The aroma of her perfume was intoxicating and he told himself that this was his chance to tell her that Mia has died and about Marie Elaine. But he backed away from it again.

'What would you like to eat?' he smiled down at her.

'You.'

He bent his head and covered her mouth with his, wanting to give her every part of him, but hating the fact that there was a side about which she knew nothing. 'Come upstairs,' he whispered.

They ran quickly, giggling as they took off their clothes and tumbled on to the bed.

'I love you.' He lay on top of her, kissing wildly. 'I love you, love you, love, love, love ... ' he breathed, 'tell me you love me too, show me how much!'

'I adore you. If I ever lose you again I don't know what I'd do.'

'That will never happen, never.' Their lips came close again and they rose together as passion surged. When that moment had exhausted itself, he smiled. 'You're something else, do you know that?'

'We're good together,' she giggled.

'That's an understatement, we're marvellous together,' he smiled.

'I'd love to stay here for the day.' She ruffled his short hair.

'Then do, please? But I want you here all the time, not only today.'

'It's what I want too,' she hesitated, 'and it will happen.'

Into Jack's head came a vision of a little heart-shaped face and large brown eyes. 'But there are always too many obstacles in our way.' There was a shadow on his face. 'If I told you I ... ' For one crazy second he was about to say what was in his heart, but changed his mind. 'If I said you had a beautiful body, would you hold it against me?'

She moved closer and cuddled into him. 'Is this what you want?'

He wound his arms tighter around her. 'Yes my love,' he

murmured, but his eyes were full of anxiety.

Finally, as he left her to the car, he blurted out the fact that Mia had died.

'I'm so sorry.' She put her arms around him. 'When is the funeral?'

'It was yesterday.'

'But you should have told me.'

'You were away.'

'I could have come back. Nothing is set in stone, Jack.'

'Thanks for saying that.'

'I would have liked to be there.'

'I know, but it was a very small group of people, and you didn't know her.'

'Still … '

He kissed her. Cursing himself for his cowardice.

Margaret brought Marie Elaine over to Harrington Place on Saturday afternoon. It was the first time she had been here and Jack hoped that today would be an improvement on the previous Friday when they had visited the zoo. Today Margaret introduced him as "Daddy", but as usual, Marie Elaine made no response to him at all. He brought them through into the back garden, the day fine and sunny and the puppy immediately ran towards them, jumping up on Marie Elaine with excitement.

'Chancer! Down!' Jack bent to pick him up, suddenly afraid that he would bite her.

'No, leave him, Jack,' Margaret said with a smile, as Marie Elaine cuddled the black furry bundle, and they watched in amazement at her immediate response. She knelt on the grass and played with him, laughing out loud with excitement. Then she was up and running around the garden, and along the gravel paths, Chancer chasing after her.

'Look at the little dog, look, he likes me!' She rushed up to Margaret, who rubbed his head.

'He's lovely.' He licked her hands.

'Can I take him home?'

'I don't think so, he lives here with Jack.'

She looked around at Jack, her large eyes questioning.

'You can come and visit him if you like,' he said.

'Can I?'

That was the beginning. The breakthrough. And all because of a little puppy he had wanted to bring to the pound. He couldn't believe it. After that, every day they came to see Chancer. Marie Elaine spent her time pulling and dragging him by the ears, or his tail, and anywhere else she could grasp. Finally exhausted by the end of the visit, she sat and cuddled him. The two completely in tune with each other. To Jack's surprise she spoke Swedish to him.

'*Kom-hit*, Chancer,' she said, and he immediately ran towards her.

'*Sitt!*' She pushed him down, but he hadn't quite grasped exactly what she wanted just yet.

'*Hämta!*' She threw a stick and the puppy ran after it, searching in every direction, his ears pricked up, but never finding it, although it usually lay somewhere that was quite obvious to them.

'*Ga-och lägg dig!*' Was another order he was given, but he failed miserably to understand what that meant when he was outside. Inside the house, it was different. He knew it meant to go to bed as she usually put him in the basket herself. But he never wanted to stay there and always climbed out again immediately, much to her annoyance - a mammy act which was played out religiously, and amusing to watch.

It was then Jack made a decision to learn Swedish. If he had some knowledge of the language it might help to win her over.

Chapter Thirty-eight

'Kate, we're going to have to do something about the house. The president of the company and some of the directors are coming over from the US in a few weeks and I want to entertain them here. We've always done it in our home,' Susie announced.

'What do you mean?'

'It's shabby Kate, we need new furniture and other things,' Pat added.

'Window shades also, I've made a list.' Susie pulled a sheet of paper from her capacious handbag.

'I told you before, I'm not in a position to make improvements to the house now.'

'But the directors of our company are used to far higher standards.'

'Hey Pop, catch!' Rob shot through the door and flung a baseball at Pat, who just managed to get his hands around it.

'Ready?' He sent it back to Rob who caught it neatly in the glove he wore on his right hand.

'Fancy a few balls?' he asked.

'Not now, maybe later. Where's Donal, can't he play?'

'He's out somewhere.'

'Where?' Susie enquired sharply.

'Probably at the tennis club.'

'Make sure you keep your eye on him,' Pat warned.

'Come on, Pop, he's only a kid, I can't be hanging around with him.'

'That was part of the deal, if you joined the club, you had to watch out for each other. Go and locate him.' Pat was angry and Rob slunk out of the room. 'Now back to the subject of the house.' He sat down on the arm of Susie's chair.

The ball-playing drove Kate spare. She didn't know when the ball would go through the window and shatter something and wanted to tell them to give it up altogether. But then she would remember her own boys and the things they did and tried to have more tolerance.

'We only have a short time, so decisions will have to be made quickly.' Susie took a pen out of her bag.

'I said I don't want to do anything with the house,' Kate said, striving for patience.

'But it badly needs it, can't you see that?' Pat walked around the room.

'First, throw out the drapes.' Susie joined him and lifted one of the old floral ones, which even Kate had to admit were a little the worse for wear. She planned to change the furniture and the curtains at the same time, re-do the whole room, but there seemed little point in doing it piecemeal.

'I said that the very first day I got here, but you've done nothing since and it's getting to me. I have to live here too.' Susie put a hand on her chest and looked at Kate tearfully.

'It will cost too much money,' she said bluntly.

'We'll share the cost,' Pat smiled broadly.

'No, I'm not ready to do it just yet.'

'Kate.' Pat sat down beside her on the couch. 'Come on, I'm sure you can manage to scrape half the money, and sure window shades are your business, they'll cost nothing at all.'

'I thought perhaps a nice rose colour might look well in here, and the couches could be floral - something bright, what dya say?' Susie smiled.

'I'll have to think about it,' Kate insisted. Angry that they simply wouldn't listen. And as for pink. That was definitely out. And floral on the couches! She had ideas of creams with perhaps a little blue, something classy.

'And I want to put lots more plants in the garden. We'll buy in and arrange them around the place,' Susie said happily, 'and maybe install decking?'

'There are enough flowers in the garden; it's the way Uncle Bill liked it, and I'm making no changes, especially decking.'

Susie looked crestfallen.

'I'm sorry, but it's my house. You're only staying here temporarily,' her heart thumped as she uttered the brusque words.

'And it's also the family home,' Pat growled.

'It was willed to me.'

'Dad was born here. It's our home.'

'You said that before, Pat, and I let it go, but now you'll have to accept that it isn't the case.' She looked directly at him.

'It's unfair to us,' he was sullen.

'I thought you were going to get your own place?'

'We changed our minds. We love living here, don't we, Susie?'

'Yea, but there has to be a major restoration job done, new kitchen, living areas, bathrooms, the mews.'

'That won't happen in the near future.'

'If we're to live here, then it has to be done.' Susie tossed her head.

'But I just said ... '

'Come on, Kate, you're hardly going to throw us out?' Pat laughed.

'Well ... ' She was cornered again.

'I certainly hope not,' he grinned.

'But you'll have to pay your way, I've a large mortgage on the house and there's electricity, heating and charges as well. It takes a lot of money to run,' Kate tried to be firm.

'I'm sure we have no problem with that,' Susie said in a high-pitched tone.

'Let's examine the bills. As it is, we supply all our own food and I pay for the cleaning woman, and you benefit from that too, Kate.'

'I'll get them out later,' she said, but still had that feeling of being manipulated.

'And I'll have another look at some couches I saw in a shop in town, they're exactly what we want,' Susie was excited again.

'I didn't agree to do anything at all yet,' Kate stalled.

'But you will, won't you?' Pat put his arm around her. 'You'll do

192

a wonderful job.'

Chapter Thirty-nine

'It's fabulous!' Irene screeched when she saw Kate walk out of the fitting-room in the pale gold silk suit, 'you look a million dollars!'

'Perfect!' Pru, the wedding planner, pronounced. She flitted about the place wearing what seemed to be a collection of colourful scarves in shades of pink, chattering all the time.

They were in the salon of the designer, Natasha. An enormous room on the first- floor of a Georgian house, furnished in an ornate Louis XVI style. Carefully positioned groups of chairs and tables were separated from each other by high screens covered in beautiful embroidered fabrics. Around the room pieces of sculpture were positioned, and the walls were hung with paintings. The lighting was soft and glowed from shaded lamps in various hues. Heavy ivory satin drapes hung from thick gold poles, ruched up with tasselled ropes.

Kate twirled in front of the huge mirror and smiled. The full-length dress and jacket really did suit her colouring and hugged her figure. Although she had tried to keep up the diet, she noticed lately that a few pounds had slowly crept on again and she was determined that by the time of Irene's wedding the outfit would fit perfectly, nothing huggy about it at all.

'And the hat,' Irene giggled.

'The headdress!' Pru corrected.

One of Natasha's staff, a good-looking young man, brought it over on a stand and asked Kate to sit down in front of the mirror. It could hardly have been called a hat, it was more a creation out of Natasha's imagination. He arranged it, tilting it ever so slightly to the left, the soft gold feathers floating into exactly the right position.

'I love it.' Irene stood behind her.

'Let me just move one a little to the right.' With her long forefinger Pru raised the offending feather just a centimetre above the rest. 'There,' she said softly, 'Natasha has done a wonderful job.'

Kate turned her head left and right, thinking that Natasha was very good indeed, but that she would be unlikely ever to ask her to design an outfit. The prices were exorbitant and way out of her league.

'Now for me, have they made the adjustments?' Irene asked excitedly.

'Yes. It should be perfect now. I get very frustrated when we must endure fitting after fitting,' Pru's smile didn't match her worried tone.

'I'm sure it will be all right this time,' Kate reassured. The alterations were miniscule and she was beginning to feel the same way as Pru. The ivory silk dress was magnificent. The edge of the square neckline was beaded in diamante and pearls and there was a treble row down the front of the bodice which continued around the waistline. The skirt was straight, with long narrow sleeves finished in a pearled point. When the tiara was delicately placed on Irene's head, she simpered like a child.

'*Ah, fantastique!*' Natasha made a dramatic entrance into the salon at exactly the right moment. She was an extremely tall beautiful woman with shining black hair, and today she was dressed in a full-length black tulle skirt, an almost completely see-through top, and wore nothing else underneath as far as Kate could see.

'It's beautiful, Natasha, I'm really happy,' Irene gushed.

'It is one of my most exquisite designs, *n'est pas?*' She walked around, examining the dress. 'Now for the coat.' She clicked her fingers.

'A coat?'

'It is something I decided to make as a surprise for you, Irene.'

The garment was carried in by two of the young men, and they helped Irene put it on. For once, she was lost for words.

'Somewhere in the middle of the night, I had a flash of inspiration and decided to get up immediately to put my ideas on paper. This is the result.'

'It's out of this world,' Irene whispered.

'Move slowly around the salon, let me see how it flows,' Natasha ordered, waving her long-fingered hands in a dramatic fashion.

Irene did as she was told and the coat spread out on the floor behind her. The sleeves billowed wide and sparkled with the same beading as the dress.

'I can't believe this is me,' Irene gushed, 'is it me, Kate? Is it really me?' She clapped her hands.

'Yes, it certainly is, and I've never seen you look better.'

'Walk with me, I want to see how well we complement each other.' She took her hand and they moved along the length of the mirror.

'I have the going-away suit and some of the evening wear for the honeymoon also.' Natasha clicked her fingers again and two more underlings appeared.

'I'm sorry, but I really have to go, I must get back to the office.' Kate moved towards the fitting-rooms.

'No! You cannot leave.' Natasha wagged an imperious finger, her voice sharp.

'Why not?'

'Because we are not finished. You are the matron-of-honour - part of everything.'

'Kate, you must stay.' Pru whirled around and pierced Kate with her large green-shadowed eyes.

'But I'm running late.'

'Nothing is more important, I have spent all this time working on Irene's trousseau, and you cannot walk away before we are finished.'

Her rather high-pitched foreign accent slipped slightly, and Kate wondered what country she really hailed from. While she claimed to be French Russian, was it in truth Manchester or Birmingham or somewhere like that. Kate glanced at her watch and moved slowly back to where she had been standing a moment before. 'OK, I'll wait a little longer.'

'What do you think, Kate?' Irene squealed, as she fitted on one outfit after another.

'They're all fabulous, Irene, Ted won't know what hit him.'

'I'm so grateful to you, Natasha.' She kissed her on both cheeks. '*Moi! Moi!*'

'It is my pleasure.' She clicked her fingers and the clothes were removed. 'Now, you will come back tomorrow. I do not like to show everything at one time, one's mind becomes jaded and it is not possible to appreciate the beauty.' Natasha struck a pose as she spoke, one hand on the marble mantel, her tall elegant figure stark.

'You're right, of course, you're always so right, Natasha.'

'I've approached Hello Magazine to cover your wedding, Irene, would you have any objection?' Pru asked.

'No, of course not, I'd love it,' Irene smiled, 'imagine that, Kate!'

'I thought they were only interested in celebrities,' Kate couldn't resist throwing some cold water on the proceedings.

'We'll all be celebrities after this wedding. I could go Stateside, now wouldn't that be something?' Pru whooped.

'I'd rather not,' Kate said flatly.

'But you must,' Irene wailed.

'No, I don't.'

'Think of the publicity?'

'I don't care about that, you'll have to do without me. I'm going to change.' She disappeared into a fitting-room, pulled off the outfit, not even caring when it slid on to the ground. Quickly she changed, carried it out and handed it to a young man who hovered nearby. 'There you are, I think it might need to be pressed again.'

'*Bien sûr, Madame.*' He bowed.

Chapter Forty

Shane searched through the pile of newspapers on the kitchen table looking for an old edition. Then he noticed a bundle of letters which didn't appear to have been opened and picked one up, sliding his thumb under the flap. The letter was from a bank. According to the terse words it appeared that the mortgage hadn't been paid in quite a long time, and they were threatening repossession. He was shocked and angry too with Dermot for not bothering to open the post.

'Dad, have you seen this letter?' He waved it at him.

'I'm sure I have. I've looked at them all.'

'But you never opened it.'

'What's the point? I can't do what they want, so I just don't bother any more.'

'But we could lose the house, do you realise that?'

'They're only sabre-rattling.' Dermot threw down the paper.

'Not by the tone of this.'

'Don't get your knickers in a knot, Shane, you're like a nagging wife.' He stood up.

'Do you think I should put on my apron, Dad, start making the supper?' Shane asked.

'I wouldn't say no to something to eat, but I don't think there's much there.'

The irritation Shane felt went completely over Dermot's head. He sighed with frustration and went into his bedroom/studio. He picked up his guitar and idly plucked the strings, but after a few minutes, put it down again as suddenly the urge to play disappeared.

He lit a cigarette and sat there pensively just staring into space, until the doorbell rang and he looked out through the Venetian blind to see Irene's car outside.

'Shane!' She enveloped him in the heady pong of some expensive perfume. 'This is Pru.' He shook hands with the woman, who wore the brightest colours he'd ever seen. It was a weird-looking outfit but appealed to his obscure taste. They shook hands and she gave him a rather teasing look.

'I've heard all about you.'

'Where's your Dad?' Irene swept down the hall into the kitchen.

'Should be there, I think.'

'Dermot!' Irene stood in the doorway, but he didn't even look around from where he sat at the table, reading the racing pages. 'I've brought Pru to meet you.'

'Who?' He glanced up, looking like he had just got up out of bed. Tired, pale, with stubble on his chin, and hair standing on end.

'My wedding planner, the best there is.'

Pru held her hand out, but he ignored her, and she drew it back slowly.

'We're here to discuss a few details,' Irene said.

'I've been looking forward to meeting the man who will give Irene away,' Pru smiled widely.

'Now you've met him.' He turned back to his paper.

'I've such plans for you.'

He looked up suspiciously.

'We'll have you all togged out. Top hat and tails, the lot.'

'I'm not wearing that sort of garb. I didn't want to give you away in the first place. You'd think I was an old man.'

Irene ignored his whining. 'The suit has been made to match the size of the one I borrowed a couple of weeks ago, but there may have to be small adjustments, so you'll have to come over to Natasha's.'

'Just make it the same as the other one. It will be fine.'

'Detail is very important. What if you lost some weight, or put on a few pounds?'

'Why don't we all discuss this in a sensible manner instead of taking the heads off each other?' Pru interrupted.

'I'm sorry,' Irene looked dejected.

'Don't worry, I've seen this sort of thing before. Everything will be sorted out, and I'm sure Dermot will do as we ask.' Pru patted her shoulder gently.

'Well, all right, I'll come over,' Dermot gave in.

'The beige with gold accessories will suit your colouring very well.'

'For God's sake, I'll look like a ponce.' His face flushed.

'You'll look so handsome you won't know yourself. Are you going to let me down?'

He leaned his elbows on the table and sighed deeply. 'No.'

'Thank you, Dermot, thank you.' Irene reached to kiss him, but he pulled away.

'Why can't I just wear something plain, maybe a tux, wouldn't that do?'

'Dermot, it would spoil everything. You've no idea how much work has gone into this.' She put her arm around him. 'Please please?'

'OK, I'll do it, don't lose your cool.'

'Thank you, Dermot, thank you.' She managed to plant a lipsticked kiss on his forehead.

'Right, how about tomorrow?' Pru asked.

'I'll have to check my diary,' he grinned for the first time, 'you're not the only people looking for my company.'

'I'm surprised you're so busy all of a sudden.'

'Eleven?' Pru asked.

'I've an appointment at nine, and lunch with some business colleagues at one, so I can just about fit you in.'

'Does it give us enough time?' Irene stared at Pru worriedly.

'Just about.'

'Good. Make a note of the address,' Irene smiled widely now.

Pru scribbled, pulled a page from her notebook, and handed it to Dermot.

'Pick me up here, or send a taxi. I'll be back by ten-thirty,' he growled.

The bank manager shook hands with Shane, and asked him to sit down.

'How can I help you?'

Shane didn't know what to say and simply pushed the letter across the desk.

He picked it up and looked at it. 'This is addressed to Dermot Mason,' he said.

'Yes, he's my father.'

'I haven't seen him in a while, so I don't know that I should discuss this matter with you.'

'Dad is ill. I'm going to sort it out.'

'We've been trying to contact him for some time now and the arrears are mounting.'

'I know that, but I just want a chance to pay it off. We can't lose the house.'

'Have you the ability to pay the mortgage?'

'I'll do my best. I'm earning good money at the moment. Maybe you might be able to extend the number of years since I'm that much younger, so the repayments won't be too high.'

'No, it wouldn't be possible, the mortgage was taken out by your father.'

'But it doesn't matter who pays it every month,' Shane pressed him.

'No, once the money comes in. But the terms cannot change without discussing it with him.'

'But couldn't you reduce it a little, so that I can get on top of it?'

The manager looked at the letter again and then flicked the computer keyboard.

'If you were to continue paying it then the arrears could be added on at the end of the term.' He noted a figure on a piece of paper and handed it to him.

Shane stared at the amount and nodded. It wouldn't be easy to find the money each month but then he was the only one still at home and had nowhere else to live. It was his responsibility.

Chapter Forty-one

'Guess what?' Jack just about managed a smile.

'What?' she giggled.

'I've been asked to do some babysitting, well, child-minding would be more accurate,' he hesitated, 'my grand-niece, Marie Elaine, who is almost five years old.'

Her laughter changed to amazement. 'You're going to look after a little girl?'

'I know it seems very unlikely anyone would entrust their child to me.'

'For how long?'

'A couple of weeks. Her mother ...' he suddenly had to think of a name. 'Eh ... Georgina ... is going on holiday and couldn't get anyone to look after her.'

'That's going to be a new experience for you. Do you think you'll be up to it?' she laughed.

'I thought you might be able to give me a few pointers.'

'Five-year-olds are very demanding.'

'I'm well aware. She was here today.'

'Don't worry, I'll give you a hand, Uncle Jack.' She kissed him.

'Thanks!'

'You're going to be exhausted! Work will have to take a back seat.'

Which it did from the very first moment she arrived. Crying piteously when Margaret left, banging on the window as the car disappeared down the road, and refusing to be comforted even when he put Chancer into her arms. As the time lengthened and she still sobbed into the puppy's black fur, Jack phoned Kate. 'I've a child here who won't stop crying. And every time I go near her she screams even louder. What am I going to do?'

'Have you any sweets, or biscuits?'

'Yes.'

'Try that, it might take her mind off the fact that her Mum has gone. I'll hold on.'

He offered her chocolate buttons, crisps, a lollipop, ice cream, various bars he had bought, but nothing worked.

Jack took Kate into the lounge where Marie Elaine still huddled on the couch with Chancer, and a rather threadbare yellow teddy bear. The last couple of hours had been a nightmare. For the first time in his life he had been completely at a loss. Useless.

Kate sat on the couch beside her and began to chat. 'When I was little, I didn't have a dog, but I had a cat. His name was Whiskers and he had black fur, white ears, and white paws. He wore a red collar around his neck, with a little silver bell. He was a very clever little pussycat. And we had two furry rabbits ... '

It had been the worst possible way to have Marie Elaine move into his home, her home now. He should have given it more time. Had her over to stay for an occasional night, but once Mia had died, Margaret's husband had been quite adamant about her needing a break, and obviously they didn't want the responsibility of looking after a child any longer. In the middle, the little girl was unable to understand what was happening.

Suddenly Marie Elaine spoke. 'What are their names?'

'Em ... Prissy and ... Roger.'

'Do they live with you?'

'They're down the country.'

'Are they coming home soon?'

'No, they like living there.'

Big dark tearful eyes stared into hers. 'Is it a nice place?'

'Yes, very nice.'

She seemed satisfied with that, and Kate smiled at Jack who sat

203

opposite. 'That summer my Daddy built a little house for the birds. We put seed in it and every day they would fly down from the trees and have their dinner. Would you like to come out into the garden to see if there are any birds?' She stood up and held out her hand. Marie Elaine took it and climbed down, still trying to keep hold of the puppy. But he wriggled out of her grasp and ran to the door with a squeaky bark of excitement.

They had fun then, pointing to the birds whenever she spotted one.

'That's a thrush. There's a robin and a magpie!'

Jack watched from just outside the patio door, feeling like an evil old man, afraid to go near.

'Have you got a ball?' Kate asked loudly.

He went in and a few seconds later came out and threw a rather chewed up rubber ball to her. After that things perked up as they played between them. And then it was hide-and-seek which she seemed to enjoy the most. After an hour, Kate was exhausted.

'You certainly made some impression on Marie Elaine.' He poured her another glass of wine, after they finished the Chinese meal which he had ordered in. 'And you were amazingly energetic playing in the garden, I don't think I could have kept up with you.'

'Has she ever spent time here before?' Kate asked.

'No, but eh, Georgina wanted to go off with her girlfriends so it didn't really matter to her who was looking after Marie Elaine, once she could get away. If I hadn't stepped in, she would have had to cancel.' He felt guilty at the glib explanation.

'Typical.'

'Do you think she'll sleep right through the night?' he asked worriedly. Kate had done everything. Ran the bath. Tucked her up and, finally, lay on the bed and told her another story.

'She seemed tired enough.'

'If she wakes and starts crying again, I don't know what I'll do. Stay, will you?' he begged.

'Now you want me to look after your niece's child. Big change from Kate, I really need you, please stay, please, please,' she giggled.

'Maybe I'm using Marie Elaine as an excuse. I can't get through to you any other way, so I've gone on a different tack?' he laughed.

'Chancer!'

'Where is that dog?' Jack looked around. 'Did we leave him outside? Can't afford to lose him now, the little tyke, it would break her heart.'

'He's upstairs.'

'In the bedroom?'

'Yes, I thought it was the best way to get her asleep.'

'Is he on the bed?' he was concerned.

'Probably, but it's the lesser of two evils. I don't think you'll be able to separate them anyway, so unless you want more tears, I'd leave him.'

Kate stayed in the end, it was Saturday night and she didn't intend to work on Sunday. There wasn't a stir from Marie Elaine and they relaxed in the lounge with the door open.

'She's very like you, the same dark eyes, and hair, amazing really,' Kate murmured.

'It's the Linley genes, you must have noticed the likeness to the family, surely?'

'I've only met them all once, but I suppose she has a look of your sister Rose.'

'Would you like to be back there again, with a child as young as Marie Elaine,' he asked.

'I wouldn't mind, I suppose. I've always wanted a daughter. I miscarried twice after the boys and then I had the hysterectomy so there was no chance after that. At one point, I used to dream about dressing a little girl in pretty clothes, buying her dolls, and teddies … but then I went back to work and put it out of my head. If I had a chance to start over at my age, I don't think I could cope at all. Don't forget, I'll be a grandmother soon. When they are small it's not too bad, but can you imagine having teenagers in your late fifties!'

'I would love to have had a child with you,' he said slowly, threading his fingers through hers.

'And I remember thinking the same when you told me about the baby you lost.'

'Yea ...' he sighed.

'But being responsible for a modern-day child until you're getting the pension? That's something else,' she laughed, 'and think how your freedom would be curtailed. You can't head off to Spain whenever you feel like it, or even go out for a night without arranging a babysitter, and a good one is not easy to come by, except you have an uncle like you!'

He smiled.

'And then the worry when they're a bit older and heading out on the town. Wondering what they're up to. Drinking. Doing drugs. Sex. I can tell you it's wearing. Have I persuaded you that it isn't such a good idea?'

Chapter Forty-two

'Sorry we're late, the traffic held us up, there was an accident.' Irene arrived at Natasha's salon with a disgruntled Dermot in tow.

'Irene, get in here, I haven't got much time left, I have a lunch appointment.' Ted snapped. He was already dressed in his beige suit, with the gold cravat and waistcoat. The best man Michael, a close friend of Ted's, stood beside him, dressed similarly.

'Don't they look wonderful!' Pru squealed.

'Yes my love, you are so handsome.' Irene reached forward to kiss him, but he had already turned away, and she was left with pursed lips, eyes closed for a few seconds, before realising he wasn't there any longer.

'Dermot darling, change into your suit quickly and let's have a look at it.' Pru ushered him into the fitting-room and waited impatiently outside until he reappeared. 'Right, we're all ready, now I will get Natasha.' She hurried away, while Irene fluttered around the three men, adjusting a collar here and a shoulder there, like a mother hen with her chicks.

'You are tardy!' Natasha swept in, dressed in cerise today, her dark hair pulled into a smooth chignon.

'It's all my fault, Natasha,' Irene immediately apologised, although the truth was that Dermot had still been in bed when she called, and had been in no mood to come with her, his supposed meeting cancelled.

'*Oui, oui!*' Now let me look at my designs.' She circled the three men. 'Walk towards the mirror.' She pointed a long finger at Ted who did as he was told, although he didn't look too happy about it. 'And back again! Now turn slowly, I want to see the flow of the coat tails.' She followed him, lifted the shoulders a fraction, and refolded the cravat. *'Va bien!'*

Michael was a thin awkward-looking man and the suit hung limply on his slight frame. Natasha clucked loudly as she tried to pull it into some sort of shape. After a few minutes, she rushed over to Irene. 'It is possible to find a new man?' she whispered.

'What?' Irene stared at her in horror.

'My clothes do not look good on this stick.' She raised painted eyebrows.

'There's nothing I can do,' Irene glanced fearfully at Ted.

Natasha heaved a long dramatic sigh.

'I suppose he can't help his shape,' Pru giggled.

'My standards are very high!' Natasha sniffed, and walked back to where Michael stood. 'Go, go.' She ordered imperiously. Then she turned her attention to Dermot.

'Tournez s'il vous plaît!' She waved her arm.

'I'm not going to twirl around in front of you like a ballet dancer,' he grunted.

'It is necessary to see all sides of you,' she retorted.

'This is the front,' he said abruptly and then turned around. 'This is the back.' He moved to face her again. 'That should be enough.'

She stared at him, her eyes shocked.

'Dermot, do as Natasha asks,' Irene ordered.

'I'm not an electronic toy,' he compressed his lips.

'You are very stubborn, no?' The tone of Natasha's voice changed. Suddenly there was a slight teasing quality about it.

'Yes,' he said abruptly.

'Dermot, please?' Pru moved closer. 'See how easy it is.' She tried to move him, but his feet were planted firmly on the floor.

'The trousers need to be taken up a little,' Natasha murmured. One of her staff rushed over with a box of pins and bent down to make the adjustments. 'The sleeves are at the right level, and the shoulders, *oui,* you have good shoulders, well-built.' She wandered around Dermot now.

'Right, are we finished,' he demanded.

'*Non, non, attendez un moment, s'il vous plaît?*' She tucked her finger under the collar.

'It's all right.' He shrugged her off, marched into the fitting-room and closed the door.

Natasha looked after him, a rather bemused expression on her beautiful face.

'We're all done then?' Ted asked.

'*Oui oui ...* ' she said with an abstracted air.

'I think she fancies Dermot!' Pru grinned at Irene, 'he's not a bad looker when he cleans up. I almost fancy him myself.'

'Ridiculous! Natasha and Dermot,' Irene snorted in a rather unladylike way.

*

'I'll meet you in the Four Courts at ten tomorrow morning,' Dermot said to the solicitor and put down the phone, dreading the thought of standing up in front of that Judge again and suffering the solicitors' interrogation. It was enough to make him want to end it all. Go to sleep and never wake up. He had actually looked into the bathroom cabinet earlier and noted what was there. Panadol. Lemsip. A flu remedy. Cough bottle. However, five tablets didn't seem adequate, and even when added to the flu capsules he doubted that amount of medication would have very much affect. Anyway, the thought of trying to swallow it all at once turned his stomach and was suddenly less appealing.

He left the house, checked his back pocket for money, and pulled out the few crumpled twenty euro notes he had borrowed from Shane. Asking his son for money stuck in his craw. Would things ever improve? Or would it require the miracle of a Lotto win to revitalise his life? He caught a bus into town, but it was only as it sailed past the Yellow House that he remembered he had to sign on. So he rushed for the door at the next stop and dragged himself back to Rathfarnham Garda Station feeling like the worst kind of criminal.

That put him in a particularly bad humour and when finally he

209

arrived in town, he just wanted to drink enough to blot out the thoughts of tomorrow morning. He ordered a whiskey and knocked it back quickly and then had a second, which sent a glow through him and eased the anxiety a little. This evening there was a good crowd in the pub, a noisy group of people who made him feel isolated and lonely as they talked and laughed together. Eventually on impulse he offered a drink to the man sitting next to him. He had to talk to someone, he couldn't bear to be on his own any longer.

'Yea, sure, thanks,' the man grinned.

'And your mate?' Dermot asked. The other nodded, and he waved to the barman to serve up another round. They seemed to be in their thirties, burly, dressed in casual clothes.

'What do you do?' he asked.

'Both of us are carpenters.'

'I'm involved in property.' Dermot grinned, delighted to find they had something in common.

'We're working on a complex in Ringsend.'

'Who's the developer?' Dermot asked eagerly.

'Grant Properties.'

'I've interests in Spain, the market is very vibrant out there,' he spoke with enthusiasm, but he hadn't a clue who Grant Properties were. Out of the business for well over a year, he had lost touch with what was going on in the city.

'We've bought a couple of apartments ourselves out there.'

'You have?' Dermot gazed at them in astonishment.

'Marbella; we get a good rental and might invest again.'

'My property is mostly around Alicante.'

'We had a look there, but the quality of tenant is higher on the Costa del Sol.'

'Hi lads.' A slim arm appeared on the counter beside Dermot. He glanced around to see the owner, very pleased that it belonged to a tall, blonde girl, whose low-slung jeans revealed a curvy stomach with a sparkling cluster of rubies in her belly-button.

'What'll you have?' Dermot asked.

'Vodka straight on ice, thanks.' She moved closer to him.

'And one for me too.' Another woman appeared beside her,

equally attractive.

The evening really took off then, the girls adding that extra dimension which made Dermot feel it was going to be an enjoyable night. He ordered more drink, laughter and jokes flew between them, and all thoughts of tomorrow faded from his mind. Much later they ended up in a small flat somewhere in the north inner city. As he stumbled in with the others into the dark dimly-lit room, he could see a small group of people sitting around. But since he had been in the fresh air, all he wanted to do now was sleep; he plumped down on the carpet and leaned against the side of an armchair.

'Hi.' A woman looked down at him, features indistinct in the shadow of an old-fashioned brass standard-lamp, which stood crookedly. A cigarette was passed to him, and he took it automatically, pulling deeply.

'I'll have it back,' she said after a moment, her hand hovering in front of him, red fingernails poised to retrieve.

'I think I have a cigar here.' He searched in his pocket, amused at the idea of sharing a cigarette.

'No thanks. These are much nicer,' she laughed, pink lips shiny.

He took another drag on it, exhaled, and handed it to her, only now realising that he was smoking hash or some other stuff. Wow! It was something he had always avoided, preferring his whiskey, scared of the consequences. But suddenly he didn't care. They shared a couple more, and Dermot floated off to a place of pleasurable sensations where life was good, so good. The other people in the room seemed to drift and move indistinctly, appearing and disappearing as if in the yellowing light of a thick foggy evening. He remembered a joke, tried hard to think of the punch line and began to tell her. Laughing every few words and somehow never getting very far with it.

She flopped down on the floor beside him. 'What's your name?' She tossed back her long dark hair.

He grinned at her, 'my name is - God, I can't remember!'

'Mr. No-name, that you?'

'I'm Dermot ... Mason,' he managed to stutter at last.

'Linda.'

211

They laughed uproariously, tears streaming down their faces. He hadn't felt so good in years.

Chapter Forty-three

Kate couldn't stay on Sunday night, and although she bathed Marie Elaine and put her to bed, Jack lay with the door open, listening to every sound, afraid to go asleep at all. About five, he got up, having to remind himself to wear a dressing-gown and be careful not to ramble around the house as he usually did. Immediately he looked into her bedroom, lit softly by the glow of light through the pale lemon lampshade. It created an oasis in which she lay curled up in her own duvet, brought over by Margaret. Her long dark curly hair was spread out over the pink pillow, and Chancer stretched at the end of the bed. His heart contracted with love for her and he quietly continued on down the stairs to the kitchen where he made himself toast and coffee.

Later he showered, dressed and went into the studio staring at the half-finished painting on the easel. It was a family group, a man, woman and two children, hugging together against some unknown threat. Fear dimmed their features, they stared out at the watcher, pupils dark, and suddenly he saw Marie Elaine's eyes there too, and shivered. He removed the canvas, and replaced it with another. A plain white blank.

His movements were fluid, his first strokes with the long narrow-handled brush gentle and slow, coaxing the image to emerge and be. It was a likeness of Marie Elaine, just the way he had seen her a short time ago in bed. Her head lay sideways on the pillow, long lashes cast a crescent shadow on soft rounded cheeks, cupid bow lips were pink, and slightly open. Cuddled in the curve of her arm lay the yellow teddy bear. He took his time, anxious to achieve every nuance of total surrender, that closing down of the senses by the narcotic of sleep.

He looked into the bedroom again, wondering how he would manage to persuade her to go to school. The dog bounded towards him and dashed downstairs. He let him out and hurried back up to stand in the doorway, as his daughter gave him a serious measuring look. An I don't know you look.

'How are you this morning?' he smiled in what he hoped was a friendly unthreatening way, but stayed at the door, reluctant to startle her. 'Chancer has gone outside, but he'll be back in a minute. Are you going to get up for school?'

She made no response, but he crossed the room, slid open the wardrobe door and took out the tartan skirt, shirt and jumper. Then found underwear, socks and shoes. Kate had said she was quite well able to wash and dress herself, so he left everything out.

After a while, she appeared downstairs, and sat at the table, ate cornflakes and drank a glass of milk. He had put out the mug with the dog painted on it, and was really happy to see her fingers trace around the raised design. The jug, sugar bowl and the other dishes all belonged to Mia, and he hoped that seeing the familiar things would make her feel more at home.

'Do you like school?' he asked. She didn't look at him, but nodded. 'What do you like best?' There was no reply, her eyes on Chancer who sat on the floor nearby. He tried to think of something else to say, but gave up. She finished breakfast, brushed her teeth, put on a blue anorak, and picked up her schoolbag. Stubborn should be her middle name he thought wryly as his attempt to help her up into the jeep was rebuffed as she insisted on climbing up herself. Very relieved when she allowed him to clip the seat-belt into position. He drove to the school in Terenure, deciding that he must buy a special child seat, the adult belt didn't hold her in safely. As they walked towards the entrance gate, again she insisted on carrying her own schoolbag, and marched ahead of him independently. He would have liked to take her hand, worried that she would step off the path unexpectedly, but caught up and held on to the hood of the anorak ready to grab if anything happened.

Among the throng of mothers, fathers and children, he was brought back suddenly in time to his own childhood. It was a strange nostalgic feeling.

'There's Marie Elaine, Emma,' a voice said from behind. He turned sharply to see another little girl run forward to catch up with his daughter and the two of them immediately begin to chatter together.

'Friends already,' the woman laughed.

'She's your little girl?' he asked.

'My youngest,' she smiled, 'where's Margaret this morning?'

'She's gone away on an extended holiday,' he explained.

'She did mention something about that.'

The children arrived at the door and Emma looked back and waved. But Marie Elaine had already run in.

'Give her my best, will you?'

'Sure, I will.'

'I'm Angela.'

'Jack.' He shook her hand.

They walked back to the road and said goodbye. She was a pleasant woman, and he was glad that Marie Elaine had a friend in school. He collected her later, meeting Emma and Angela again, delighted to see that she was all smiles. But to his disappointment, she reverted to her usual sullen mood the moment they had gone.

Kate came over that evening again and brought a present of a little kitchen, with all the pots, pans, and dishes to go with it.

'That's your breakfast, Kate. We have cornflakes here,' Marie Elaine said with an air of importance and handed her a small bowl with a spoon in it.

'Thank you,' she smiled and began to eat the imaginary meal. And later it was dinner and tea for both Kate and Chancer, and she was so engrossed in this new game it was difficult to persuade her to go to bed until tiredness finally caught up, and she allowed Kate to bring her upstairs.

'Marie Elaine seems to be really attached to you,' Jack managed a crooked smile.

'She'll get used to it here soon, and you won't want to let her go by the time Georgina is back.' Kate dipped crunchy bread into the sauce on her plate.

'You're so good to help, this is proving much more difficult than I anticipated.'

'But she is very well able to look after herself for a child her age. Gets in and out of the bath, dries herself off, brushes her teeth, combs her hair. All you have to do is run it, and put out her pyjamas, and clothes for the morning.'

'It's probably a bit much to ask you to come over every night,' he said hesitantly.

'I can't do it tomorrow or the following night, I've a job to finish off and a client to see.'

'Don't worry,' he accepted it gracefully, but would have given anything to have Kate here permanently. Fatherhood was something for which he didn't seem suited, in spite of his longing for a child in the past. 'At least she eats anything I give her. We had pizza for lunch which she gobbled, and she even ate some of this dish I made for us.' He sipped his glass of red wine.

'She seems quite a solitary child, has she any sisters and brothers?'

'No.'

'And what about her father?'

He was taken aback. 'I ... don't know about him.' More lies, he thought with a pang. Deeply regretting his invention of this Georgina. He was worried. It could get very complicated if he wasn't careful.

'She seems quite advanced for her age, but came out with some weird words tonight, particularly when she talks to Chancer. I couldn't understand them at all.' Kate finished her dinner, and sank back on the couch.

Jack's stomach took a dive. 'Words?'

'Yea, but I made no comment. it might be a throwback to when she was younger and couldn't get her tongue around some phrases.'

'Probably,' he agreed.

Now his life had changed completely. Work crammed into the mornings, and after Marie Elaine had gone to bed at night. He spent time sketching her during the afternoon, grabbing a moment when she was engrossed in the toys, or with Chancer. Loving the look of delight on her face when she smiled at the puppy, or the slight frown of concentration when she played. But he hated the fear in her large brown eyes when he spoke, or came close at all. And she could stare him out until he looked away uncomfortably. Made to feel self-conscious, not knowing who or what he was in this new world, and all of this uncertainty by a small girl.

He ran the bath, left out a towel and pyjamas, and after Marie Elaine had gone in, waited anxiously, his ears straining for the sound of a fall or any other catastrophe. This was the worst part of it. The rejection. She had such an independent streak he wondered was it inherited from himself or Mia. Whomever, it was strong and she stood up to him like an adult, her little face frozen in cold resentment. He heard the bathroom door close and waited a moment before going in. She was climbing into bed and he made a move as if to cover her with the duvet, but immediately she slipped underneath and pulled it up under her chin staring balefully at him.

'Jag tycker inte om dig!'

He drew his hand back as if stung, hurt by the challenge in her voice. God knows what it meant, but he kept a smile on his face and went into the bathroom. He emptied the bath and cleaned it. Picked up her clothes and the towel from the floor. The toothpaste tube lay on the unit and had a long squiggle snaking out of it. The blue hairbrush was in the sink with the softening soap, half covered with water, and the loo paper was partially unwound and curled on the white tiled floor. He grinned, realising that this was going to be the norm from now on.

She was asleep when he came back into the bedroom, opened the window a little, and drew the blinds. He would have preferred to give Chancer a shove and force him off the bed, but resisted the impulse. God knows what she would do if he crossed her on that. 'Night, Marie Elaine, God bless,' he said softly and went out, leaving the door ajar. He had managed to finish her painting and was quite pleased with it, starting another yesterday morning composed of a woman and child. In the background, evening light darkened to the deeper shadows of the night. The woman had the look of a spiritual being. A ghostly grey spectre rushing back to some nether place and taking the laughing child with her. It was the way he felt. Mia had given her daughter to him when she died, but in some strange way she still possessed her. He had not intended the painting to turn out this way, but his work always had its own volition, guided by some unknown force.

His phone rang and he pulled it out of his pocket.

'I'm just around the corner, are you there?' It was Chris, and he was disappointed; he had expected a call from Kate this evening but so far there had been no contact.

'Yes.'

'Right, see you in two.'

'Marie Elaine has arrived already?' She turned to him with a laugh, when she saw the litter of toys in the lounge.

'Yes. Fancy a G & T, or a glass of wine?'

'Coffee will be fine, thanks. And this is your favourite television programme, I suppose?' She indicated the cartoon which was still on.

'I'm reduced to that.'

'You don't sound too happy about it.'

'It's not going well.'

'I'd love to meet her, but she's in bed, I suppose.'

'Yea.'

'Let me have a peep?' she asked.

They stood at the bedroom door together, and she turned to him with tears in her eyes. 'She's beautiful, and so like us, Rose in particular I'd say.'

'Isn't it amazing?' he grinned.

'Unbelievable.'

Downstairs again, she began to pick up the toys and put them away in a box in the corner. 'She winds you around her little finger I suppose?'

'You could say that, but she doesn't get any enjoyment out of it.'

They sat and sipped coffee as he told her what had been happening since Marie Elaine had arrived.

'Kate knows nothing?'

'It's lies upon lies, I hate myself. And I've created another niece for us – Georgina.'

'This could rebound on you, it might have serious consequences,' she warned.

'And what am I going to do about the family. Can you imagine telling Dad?' He looked at her morosely. 'He already makes caustic comments about the fact that I was once married to Paula.'

'Could be difficult.'

'Mam will be all right, I know that, but he's firmly embedded in the last century.'

'The parents still see us as kids.'

'I'd like to tell the others, but it's going to go around like wildfire and Dad's bound to hear about it. I really don't want a confrontation with him now, not in his condition.'

'What condition?'

He went on to tell her what had happened the last time he was at home.

'If I was here more often he'd take it easy, I can tell you,' she was angry.

'We can't force him to do things our way.'

'I'm going around there in the morning.'

'Don't say I told you.'

'No, I'll be diplomatic.'

Chapter Forty-four

He awoke late in the day, the light curling around the edges of the limp pink-hued curtains which hung on the window. He was cold and sat up in the bed, surprised to find that he was naked, and only half-covered by a rather washed-out sheet. Beside him lay a woman, dark hair streaming out across the pillow, pale face unfamiliar. He couldn't remember having met her before, or even how he had arrived in this place. There was a bad taste in his mouth, and his head pounded. Some mixture of a hangover this was, he thought, trying to recollect what had happened last night.

'Dermot?'

He looked at her, feeling embarrassed. 'Hi.'

'That was some night.' She leaned towards him.

'Yea.' A vague recollection of a dark shadowy room came into his mind.

'Fancy a drag?' She lit up.

'I feel I am a cigarette, dried up, reeking.' He leaned against the wooden headboard which wobbled with his weight.

'Here.' She handed it to him and he inhaled deeply. After a few minutes, the delicious affect of whatever this was began to take affect again and the world became a rainbow dream place where there were no problems of any sort at all.

*

'Where is he?' Kate looked around worriedly.

'He'll be here soon, I'm sure.' The solicitor glanced at his watch. 'I talked with him yesterday.'

'I'll have a look outside.' Shane walked out through the entrance-hall and disappeared.

'I hope he comes.' Her fingers curled around the strap of her handbag so tightly they were numb.

'Don't worry,' Jack reassured.

But as the minutes passed, she became more and more concerned.

The solicitor moved away from them and began talking to the barrister in hushed tones, then he came back and indicated that they should follow him.

'I'll get Shane.'

The public galleries were packed with people; Shane and Kate stood just inside the door, while Jack went with the solicitor. The main body of the Court was occupied by the legal teams. Solicitors and barristers discussed cases, heads bobbing like a flock of birds. They shuffled through their documents and hurried to and fro with an air of urgency. The Judge sat on the bench and conferred with the Clerk of the Court.

Kate watched events unfold with a distinct sense of dread. The barrister approached the Bench and spoke to the Clerk of the Court, who turned and called for the Bailsman. Her heart began to thump when she saw Jack take his place in the box.

'You are Jack Linley?' the Judge asked.

'Yes.' Jack nodded.

'Do you know where Dermot Mason is and why he has not appeared here today?'

'No, Your Honour.'

'Why did you put up the bail for him?'

'He is an … acquaintance.'

'And you trusted him?'

'Yes, Your Honour.'

'Is he still in the country?'

'I don't know. I presume so.'

'Did you contact him to make sure he complied with the bail terms?'

'No.'

'Has he been signing on?' the Judge asked the Garda.

He looked down at his notebook. 'Yes, Your Honour.'

The Judge stared at Jack for a moment over gold-rimmed glasses, brow furrowed, and then glanced down at the document in front of him. 'The bail amount is twenty thousand euro. Clerk of the Court take note.'

'I'll pay it all back, I promise,' Kate was distraught, 'when I see him I'll kill him. To do this to you is despicable after you were so generous.'

'I'll help as well,' Shane said.

'There's no need, it's only money.'

'Don't be ridiculous, you can't be out of pocket!' she was very angry.

'He was scared about going back to prison,' Shane said slowly.

'But there's a warrant out for him now.'

'He probably doesn't realise that.'

'Idiot.'

'Don't be so concerned, my love.' Jack put his arm around her.

'I'll call around this evening.' She kissed him.

'Thanks, I'm sorry we can't go out somewhere but with Marie Elaine it's impossible.'

'Now you know what being a parent is like,' Kate smiled.

*

Dermot sat in a comfortable cushioned chair and stared at the television. There was one of those old comedy films on and the antics of the actors sent him into peals of laughter.

'Are you enjoying it?' Linda came in from the kitchen with two bowls of soup.

'Yea.'

She put them down on the small table and handed him a fresh buttered roll.

'There you are, pet, eat up.'

'Thanks.'

'It's nice having you here, I haven't had a man around in ages, not since my last partner went back to Mountjoy.'

He stared at her, as suddenly the mention of that place rang a bell in his head, and he remembered the Court case.

'Why is he there?'

'Drugs.' She ate her soup, seemingly unconcerned.

Linda wasn't the type he normally went for. She was probably almost as old as himself, and it showed in her thin features. She didn't wear designer labels, or spend hours at the beauticians, but her eyes lit up when she saw him, and he liked that.

'Thanks for letting me stay here with you. Unfortunately, I've no money, I'm broke.'

'Don't worry, I've enough for both of us.' She kissed him. 'And you can wear my fella's clothes, he's about the same size as you. And they're all designer by the way so you can nick them; he probably did.'

Dermot didn't go home. And even though he must have got up each morning and gone to bed at night, the days passed in a haze and he didn't remember very much of anything. He ate, drank, showered, dressed, had sex, slept ... and smoked.

Chapter Forty-five

'I'm still up the walls about the money.' Kate hugged closer to Jack on the couch.

'I told you to forget about it,' he kissed her, and they slid down on the cushions.

'You are my love,' she whispered. There was so much happening lately that they had little time to themselves and frustration exploded now into passion.

It was just a slight movement at the door which drew Kate's attention. The child stood there, dressed in blue pyjamas, clutching the teddy in her arms. Hurriedly, Kate sat up straight, and she could hear Jack swear under his breath. 'Marie Elaine, are you all right?' She went across to her.

'I'm thirsty.'

'Would you like some milk?'

She nodded.

Kate took her hand and led her into the kitchen, very much aware of the soft warm grip of the little fingers around her own. She poured the milk into a glass, and handed it to her. After she had finished, they walked up the stairs to the bedroom, followed by Jack.

'Maybe we'll read a story before you go to sleep.' Kate picked up one of the books which were on the bedside table. 'Which one would you like?'

'The Flower Princess,' Marie Elaine smiled and cuddled up to Chancer.

'Right.' Kate glanced at Jack who stood in the doorway, a rather dejected look about him as he leaned against the door jamb with shoulders slumped. She opened the book and began to read slowly, holding it in front of the little girl and going through the pictures, until she noticed her eyes beginning to close.

'We'll read another page tomorrow.' She stood up, and tucked the duvet around her. 'Goodnight, sleep tight.'

'Will you be here?'

'I have to go to work, but Jack will be. Now, close your eyes, it's very late.'

'God natt.'

She kissed her on the forehead, stroked back the dark curls, and by the time she reached Jack and looked back she was asleep.

'I don't know how I let that happen.' Jack sat down on the couch, a worried look on his face.

'Me neither. I suppose we're not used to having anyone else here.'

'Do you think she'll have a bad reaction?' he asked.

'For goodness sake, we were only having a bit of a cuddle,' Kate laughed, 'I'll go up and check on her again.'

'Would you? I'll make coffee.'

Marie Elaine was asleep and Kate sat at the end of the bed thinking how lonely she looked lying there. She wondered about her mother. Was she missing her? Had she been on the phone? Two weeks seemed so long to leave such a young child. She couldn't have tolerated being parted from her own boys for that length of time when they were young.

'I'll have to head home soon, I've an early morning flight to London.'

'So you'd leave me alone?' he grinned.

'It's business.' Kate sipped her coffee.

'When will you be back?'

'Wednesday.'

'I hate it when you're away, then I can't send out an SOS if I have a problem with Marie Elaine.'

'Maybe it would be better if I wasn't here.'

'You haven't seen the way she looks at me. I feel like a pariah,' he grimaced.

'She'll do what you tell her?'

'Yes, but she only talks to the dog or her toys, I can't get a word out of her.'

'That doesn't really matter now, her mother will be back at the weekend.'

He jerked up and walked to the window, staring out, his arms tight across his chest. Into the second week now of Georgina's holiday, his nemesis loomed ever closer. 'Who are you meeting this time?'

'Travers - the architects.'

'Will this Massimo person be there?' He turned back to her.

'Probably.'

'I'm jealous.'

'I told you Mags is the woman in his life now.'

'God help him,' he laughed wryly, and kissed her.

Early on the morning after her return, Jack phoned.

'Kate, I need your help, Dad has collapsed and he's on his way into the hospital by ambulance. I want to get down there as quickly as I can, but I don't know what to do about Marie Elaine.'

She could hear the panic in his voice. 'I'll look after her, don't worry. How is your father? What happened exactly?'

'I'm not even sure yet.'

'Bring her over. And I suppose you'd better bring the dog as well, and some of her things in case you're held up at the hospital. Do you want me to take her to school?'

'Maybe we'll skip it for today, I'll phone them. And thanks, my love, I really appreciate this.'

Marie Elaine seemed delighted to see her, hugging and kissing her wetly with much enthusiasm, as the dog ran around excitedly.

'I can't thank you enough.' Jack brought in a bag.

'Get going, will you, and give my regards to your father, I'll say a prayer he'll be all right.'

226

'Thanks, I'll let you know.' He hurried away.

'Right, young lady, what are we going to do today?' Kate bent down and smiled at her. 'Let's go and meet the girls who work here.' She took her into the workroom.

'Well, who is this pretty girl?' May stopped sewing. 'What is your name?'

'Marie Elaine,' she whispered.

'It's lovely to see you. Now come and meet Sinead, who is on the machine, that big noisy thing over there.'

'Could I play on that?' Marie Elaine asked.

'When you're a big girl.'

She put both arms on the edge of the machine stand and swung her feet off the floor. 'Can't I do it today?'

'No, it's far too grumbly and loud, it might eat you up,' both May and Sinead laughed.

'No, it wouldn't,' Marie Elaine giggled.

'You never know,' Kate laughed too from where she stood watching this little scene being played out.

'Chancer would bark at it.' There was a sudden worry on her face. 'Where is he?'

'We can't let him in here, he's too hairy.'

'I'll have to get him.' She stood on tiptoe to reach the round brass door handle. 'He'll want water and his biscuits.'

'OK. Now say goodbye to May and Sinead,' Kate was amazed when she threw her arms around both of them. Then she was all anxious about the puppy, who was brought out to play in the garden, fed and watered.

'She's adorable.' May watched her play ball with the dog. 'I'd run away with her.'

'Catch!' The ball flew towards them and Sinead returned it.

'I don't think there will be much work done today at this rate,' May smiled.

'Where are we at the moment?' Kate asked.

'Well up-to-date.' She handed her the list.

'That's great, I don't know what I'd do without you two.'

'We're glad to be appreciated,' she laughed, 'but if we do nothing at all, that could change very quickly.'

Jack phoned later in the day to let her know that his father had had a heart attack, but that he was stable now. He wanted to stay there overnight just to be with him, and Kate assured him that she had no problem looking after Marie Elaine.

'I'm enjoying having her, she's such a pet.'

'Yes ... she is.'

'Are you all right?' she asked, suddenly worried.

'I'm OK.'

'You must be very upset about your father.'

'We hope that he'll pull through.'

'I'll get a Mass said for him, my love.'

That night Marie Elaine slept with Kate, as there were no spare beds in the house with Pat and his family staying. But they had gone to Connemara for a few days, and she was glad to have the house back to herself. To keep the little girl company, she read the story of Snow White, her own voice faltering before reaching the end, eyes closing not long after Marie Elaine fell asleep. She awoke only once in the night, loving the feeling of a child lying close to her; that special aroma reminding of when her own two boys were little. Although she had no feelings for Dermot now, there was a tinge of regret for those wonderfully happy days, all sunshine, and brightness.

At Jack's suggestion Kate didn't take her to school, and as the weather was quite warm for the time of year she was content to play in the garden with Chancer, occasionally coming inside to the workroom or the office to ask a question, or make a comment but, once they listened, she went off again, quite happy with the company of the puppy.

Jack still felt he needed to spend time with his Dad, and Kate agreed to look after Marie Elaine for as long as he wanted. Although a second early night wasn't possible for Kate, she took her to bed about nine. Then lay on the bed and told her the rest of the Snow White story until she closed her eyes.

'Sleep tight.' She leaned over and kissed her forehead.

'God natt. ' the little voice said.

'You're not asleep at all!' Kate laughed.

'Can I live here with you? It'll be my birthday soon.' The big eyes stared solemnly.

'How old are you going to be?'

'Five! And that's old enough to live with you.' She sat up.

'But your Mummy will be back at the weekend.'

'My Mummy's gone to Heaven.' Her lip trembled.

Kate was speechless for a moment.

'Margaret said I must go to live with ... ' she pressed her face into the teddy's soft fur.

'Live with?' Kate asked softly, very puzzled now.

'You know.' She pulled at the teddy's ear.

Kate simply didn't know what to say.

'Chancer would like to live here too.'

'I'd like that as well.'

'Then I can?' she smiled excitedly.

'Who's Margaret?' Kate avoided answering her question.

'Margaret looked after me when Mummy was sick.'

'Oh I see.'

'If you let me come here I'll be really good.' She put her two arms around Kate's neck and leaned closer.

'Let's go asleep now, it's late.'

'Tell me another story.' She snuggled down under the duvet.

'What would you like?'

'Winnie the Pooh and Rupert Bear,' she murmured the words sleepily. But Kate had only just started the first couple of lines when Marie Elaine's eyes slowly began to close, and within seconds she was fast asleep.

Kate left the room slowly, very puzzled. Who was Marie Elaine? She had been tempted to mention Georgina, but hesitated, unsure of the relationship between them. Had she adopted the little girl? A single mother? Unlikely, she decided. But then perhaps she had split with her husband? And those strange words were puzzling. Various scenarios drifted through her mind, and she wondered why Jack had not mentioned anything? She was disappointed with him then, feeling excluded.

Grace came around for dinner the following evening. She was particularly pleased to see Marie Elaine who looked very pretty in a new pink cotton dress which Kate had bought for her that afternoon.

'I was up in the attic the other day and brought down some of Uncle Bill's things, I thought you might like them,' Kate said as she took a casserole from the oven, and they sat down. Grace rewarded her with a grateful smile. 'We'll have a look through them later. Marie Elaine, sit up and have your dinner.' Obediently she climbed on to a chair, spread the napkin on her lap, and ate the small pieces of chicken with an air of concentration.

'This is delicious,' Grace complimented.

'It's nothing special and doesn't compare with your Japanese cooking.'

'I'm still a novice.'

'Well, anything you've cooked for me has been wonderful, I'll have to buy a cookery book.' Kate poured a glass of wine for them both.

'My Mummy had lots of cookery books.' Marie Elaine sipped her orange juice.

Kate smiled but said nothing.

'Does she cook special things for you?' Grace enquired.

She nodded.

'What are your favourites.'

'Cupcakes.'

'We'll have to make some for you,' Kate said.

'Yes please!' she grinned.

'I can see you're going to be kept busy.'

'If she was around all the time, I'd get nothing done,' Kate spoke in an undertone.

'I always regretted that I had no children.' Sadness fleetingly crossed Grace's face. 'A little girl like Marie Elaine would have been so ... if I had the time back again I think I would do things quite

230

differently.'

'Bill was a hoarder, and kept everything. Letters. Lists. Christmas cards, birthday cards, so much stuff.' Kate and Grace stood looking at the collection of boxes on the bed. His full dress uniform, with its shiny brass buttons, hung on the outside of the wardrobe door. Grace walked over and reached out to touch it. Her thin fingers slowly trailed along the soft navy wool of the collar. Then she bent her head and leaned her forehead against it. Feeling self-conscious, Kate walked out of the room, and closed the door. There were tears in her eyes.

In the kitchen she cleared up, and took Marie Elaine out into the garden which was splashed with the last of the evening sunshine.

'Kate, catch!' Marie Elaine threw the ball and she caught it, lobbed it back, and had it returned again. It went back and forward until Kate collapsed on the garden seat.

'I'm too old for playing ball,' she complained.

The phone rang and she pulled it out of her pocket, glad to hear Jack on the line. Immediately, she wanted to quiz him about Marie Elaine, but couldn't quite find the words.

'How is your Dad?'

'He seems to be over the worst, the doctors are reasonably hopeful.'

'You must be so relieved, but it's tough on your mother.'

'You know Mam, she never seems to show stress, she just gets on with things.'

'Like most mothers.'

'How are you, my love? And Marie Elaine?'

'We're fine, thanks, although I'm a bit puffed, we've just been playing ball. Why don't I put her on?' Kate waved Marie Elaine over. 'Jack's on the phone, he wants to talk to you.'

But she stopped her headlong rush abruptly. A shadow crossed her face and then she turned and ran back to where the puppy lay on the grass. 'She's too engrossed in some game with Chancer, I can't get her attention.'

'It doesn't matter. Can I ask you a big favour?'

231

'Sure.'

'Could you look after Marie Elaine for one more night for me, I'm not sure if anyone's staying at the hospital tonight, or with my mother, the girls have taken it in turn.'

'Of course I can, I'm enjoying her and she seems to be happy, although she did say something a bit strange today, I wanted to ask you about it … but her mother's coming back tomorrow, isn't she?'

'Yes, I'd better go back in, thanks for looking after her for me.'

'Why didn't you want to talk to Jack?' she asked a little later as they picked up the toys which were thrown around the garden.

She didn't answer.

'Come on, Marie Elaine, you can tell me,' she persuaded.

'Jag tycker inte Jack.'

'What do you mean?' Kate asked, puzzled by the strange words.

But before she could explain, Grace walked out from the house and Kate embraced her. 'I was afraid that it was going to be too much, all at once.'

'It was good. A cleansing. Going through all his things, looking at his handwriting and then to see my own letters. That was strange, you know. I was so naive, I couldn't believe I was ever that young.'

'I read some of those letters just after he died.'

'Childish.'

'No, very loving. You don't mind, I hope?' Kate was suddenly worried.

'Not at all, you're welcome to look through them again whenever you want.'

'Thanks, but I wouldn't like to intrude. Anyway, you should take everything home, it's all yours.'

'No, I couldn't.' She shook her head, her thin lined hands gripped together.

'You must. You're the closest person to Uncle Bill that I know, please do?'

She smiled, 'you're so generous.'

'He would have wanted you to have everything, I know.'

'Did he ever mention me?'

232

'No,' Kate hated admitting that, 'I'm sorry.'

'Neither of us spoke about the other.'

'It was the same between Jack and myself. We had an affair while I was still married to Dermot, although by then we had grown apart, and I only stayed in the end because of his financial problems. Misguided loyalty. I almost lost Jack you know.'

'I'm glad you didn't, so glad.'

'I wish you and Bill could have been together.'

'Kate, it just wasn't meant to be. Karma.'

'Perhaps Jack and I … ' She picked up a baby doll from the grass and stared at it.

Chapter Forty-six

The main lights in the ward had been lowered and as Jack awoke from a brief doze the red and green pinpricks of light from the machines suddenly assumed enormous grotesque proportions. He jerked up in the chair. 'I'm sorry, Mam, I fell asleep for a few minutes.'

'You must be tired, staying here for the last couple of nights.'

'It was easier for me, and anyway, I want to be with him.'

'Dad's going to be all right, isn't he?' she asked anxiously.

'I hope so, he seems over the worst of it now,' he reassured. Although he didn't know whether it was the truth or not. It was all in the hands of God. He thought of that time spent at Mia's bedside as she waited for death – at least his father had a chance.

'Mam?' He took a deep breath.

'Yes?'

'There's something I have to tell you.'

She looked at him, a query in her dark eyes. So like Marie Elaine, he thought.

'This may come as a bit of a shock to you; I've wanted to tell you for ages, but couldn't find the right moment.'

'There's very little that shocks me these days, Jack,' she smiled.

He grinned and then told her about Marie Elaine and Mia, more than surprised at her calm acceptance of the news.

'Hi?' A soft voice interrupted their conversation and they turned to see two of his sisters tiptoeing around the curtains. 'How is he?' Rose asked.

'He seems fine.'

'We're staying tonight, so you can have a decent sleep,' Chris whispered.

He drove his mother home to Inchicore and went in with her, intending to make sure that all was well before heading on himself. But there was something about the dark empty house which made him decide to stay for a while to keep her company. He lit the gas fire, made tea, and they sat in the warmth, chatting.

'You must be happy to have found your daughter,' she said.

'It's been astonishing. A shock. To discover at my age that I had a daughter about whom I knew nothing is - there are no words to describe it.'

'I used to wonder why there were no babies when you were married to Paula.'

'It just didn't happen,' he said awkwardly, 'she didn't want any, at least at that time.'

'I understand,' she sipped the last of her tea. 'She was a very busy person.'

'It wasn't what I wanted, and one of the reasons why we broke up.'

'Every marriage is different, but you're happy now?'

He nodded.

'You go on home. I'm quite exhausted to tell you the truth. The hospital is so tiring.' She held on to the arm of the chair and pushed herself up.

'I'll stay with you tonight,' he offered, hating the thought of leaving her here alone.

'No, you won't; I'll be fine, go on home. Chris was here last night, and Kathleen the night before. I told them I didn't need a babysitter,' she laughed.

'I'll sleep in my bedroom, just for old times' sake.'

'You think I can't manage to stay a few nights on my own?' she asked with a spurt of defiance, and a shake of her grey head, 'I might be seventy-eight but I'm not ready for full-time care just yet.'

'I hope not!'

'Well then, you go home and sleep in your own bed,' she rapped, sounding so like the mother he remembered.

'Let me stay tonight, I want to. It's been so long,' he asked, somehow needing to sleep in this house just one more time.

'All right, if it's for you and not for me.' She led the way upstairs.

'Thanks,' he grinned.

'You'll have to make up the bed, get fresh linen from the hot press.'

'Yes Mammy.'

'Cheeky!'

He rang Kate and they had a brief chat. Then he lay down in the single bed, the mattress soft and yielding, curving around him in welcoming embrace. When he was young the bed had seemed far too big. Now it was the opposite and his feet dangled over the end. But it was comforting to lie here in the fuzzy sheets which his mother always used; to stare up at the undulations in the ceiling created by uneven plaster, which could be imagined into anything strange in a boy's head. The mahogany wardrobe was a dark shadow and the mirror on the dressing-table reflected the light from the lamp on the road outside. Now he was in a room which held the breathing of three of his brothers. The shuffling murmuring sounds of boys asleep in the darkness of the night. The suppressed laughter. The eruption of a row, one climbing on another to aim punches, the others dragging him off. The thump of the sweeping brush on the ceiling below when the noise got too much. The boys slept together for years, until one by one they grew up and moved out of the house, until Jack had the room to himself.

Suddenly it was Sunday and Jack still hadn't decided how he would explain to Kate that his niece Georgina didn't exist. He felt sick at the thought of it. After dropping his mother to the hospital and finding his father much brighter, he called around to Berwick Road.

'How are you, my love?' He put his arms around her as she stood in the doorway, looking surprised to see him.

'You're early, I didn't expect you until later.'

'Dad will have a lot of visitors today, so I took my chance to come

236

around.' He kissed her. 'It's so good to see you.'

'We're just having a late breakfast in the garden. Will you have something?'

'Just a coffee, thanks.' He followed her through into the kitchen. 'What time do you leave for the airport?'

'About three.'

'Kate, where are you?' A plaintive voice could be heard from outside.

'I'm here, pet, Jack's just arrived,' she called out, 'we'll be there in a minute.'

'Hello Marie Elaine, have you been a good girl?' He went over to his daughter who sat at the wooden table on the patio eating a bowl of cereal. But she didn't look up, a sulky expression on her face.

'We've had a lovely time, haven't we?' Kate hugged her. 'And she's all excited about her birthday.'

'The sixth of October.'

'Yes, it's the same day as Irene's wedding.'

'I'll be five!' she smiled up at Kate.

'I know my love, you're a big girl now.'

'What age is Chancer?'

'He's only a baby,' Kate smiled as Marie Elaine jumped down from the table and rushed to play with him. 'Have you got your tuxedo ready?' she asked Jack.

'Yes.'

'You'll look a million dollars. Far more handsome than the groom!' She kissed him.

'I'm so glad to be going with you, partners in public.' He had been looking forward to the wedding. But now ...

Kate smiled, 'why not come to Paris with me? You could fly out tomorrow morning, I'll finish up mid-afternoon and we could have a lovely romantic night together. I presume Georgina will collect Marie Elaine later this evening?'

He looked at the little girl playing in the garden, and a shadow crossed his heart.

'I don't think I could get away, my father ... '

'Oh, that's right, sorry. Oh, by the way, I didn't mention this to

237

you, Jack, because there's been so much happening, but Marie Elaine said a curious thing the other day, I couldn't quite understand it.'

'What was that?'

'She said her mother was in Heaven.'

Chapter Forty-seven

Linda pottered around the flat making a half-hearted effort to clean up. But Dermot wasn't too worried. Once she didn't expect him to take out the vacuum cleaner, cook, wash and iron his clothes, he was happy. It was such a change to be living with someone and they were fairly compatible, enjoying a jar, a few bets on the horses, a good steak. And because she was financing him, all the pressure had eased. He had escaped from the world, hidden away in this flat with Linda. Even the police wouldn't find him here.

'I love you.' Passing by, she kissed the top of his head.

'Come to bed,' he cajoled.

'Mmmm, you're teasing me!' She wound her arms around him. 'You know we're going out.'

'Let's stay home,' he persuaded, 'please?'

'It's Joe's fortieth.'

'Do we have to go? I'd much prefer to be here with you.'

'I've to get a few smokes, and they've had a delivery of cocaine so we could snort as well. Have you tried it?'

'No.'

'Well, the first time is always the best, and when we get home, making love will be even better than usual.' She went into the bathroom.

'Promise?' Dermot followed and watched as she stripped off. There was nothing soft or voluptuous about her body; it was extremely thin, boyish almost, pale skin stretched taut. But he had grown to like her, and was happier than he had been in a long time.

The celebration was loud, vociferous and there was plenty of gear.

'I'm not sure about this.' Dermot snorted up the powder through a rolled twenty euro note and grimaced.

'Wait until it takes affect and then you'll feel like the world is your oyster,' Linda grinned at him.

'If you say so.'

And she was right. As the evening progressed, he began to feel like he was young again. All the colours in that magic place were bright, every tone accentuated. Tonight he was a success. A millionaire many times over, living a luxurious life on his fantasy island where he reigned as king.

'Let's dance!' he grabbed Linda's hand and swung across the room, moving fast, twisting, turning and jumping like someone half his age. So carried away with the music, the shouts didn't impinge on him at first, and he continued on dancing, until Linda caught his hand and dragged him down the corridor into the bathroom, locking the door behind them.

'Why are you bringing me in here?' he laughed.

'Sssshhh, it's the cops, get out quick.' She opened the window.

'We can't climb down there, we'll kill ourselves.' He began to shake with fear.

'Go on, will you!'

He stared out into the darkness, and could immediately imagine his body splattered on the area below. 'No, I can't,' he whined.

She pushed past him and climbed over the sill.

He grabbed her striped top, but she swung herself over the edge and disappeared. 'Linda!'

Suddenly wood splintered with a loud crash and the door was kicked in.

Chapter Forty-eight

'Is Georgina her natural mother?' Kate asked in puzzlement.

'No.' Jack was in shock. He had hoped to break it gently to Kate. Now he had been thrown in at the deep end without warning and he floundered around like someone learning to swim.

'Then she's adopted?'

'There's no such person as Georgina.' He couldn't look into her eyes and stared down at the ground fixedly, very ashamed.

'Who's child is she?'

'Mia's ... and mine.' This was it. He had crossed the line, he knew it now.

'My God!' she whispered.

'I'm so sorry. I intended to tell you today anyway.'

'Today?'

'Marie Elaine is supposed to go home.'

'You lied to me!' she accused.

'I know, I'm so sorry.' He raised his head and looked at her.

'How could you do that to me?' she demanded, her blue eyes wide and full of fury.

'I've wanted to tell you so many times, but I hadn't the guts. I was afraid I'd lose you.'

Marie Elaine ran up and drank thirstily from her glass of orange which stood on the table under the umbrella. 'Kate, Chancer needs more water in his bowl.' She was out of breath.

'I'll fill it in a minute,' she said automatically, turning back to Jack. 'You kept this ... her ... a secret for all this time?'

'I didn't know until a few months ago.'

'You jest!'

'It's true. Remember that call on the answering machine the night we came back from Kilkenny.'

'So Mia wanted to catch up with you, the runaway father.'

'It wasn't like that.'

'How was it? Tell me!'

'She was ill.'

'I know, you told me that much at least.'

'She gave Marie Elaine to me when she died. To me, Kate, a man who hasn't a clue how to look after a child.'

'So you thought I'd come in useful, is that it? Good old Kate will help me look after her. She's had plenty of experience. Why didn't you tell me who she was? I don't know how I didn't cop on anyway, she's the spitting image of you!' She marched into the kitchen. Neither of them noticed that Marie Elaine stood watching with tear-filled eyes. He followed and stood beside her as she leaned on the counter. Arms taut, head down. 'Don't tell me you're sorry again, I simply couldn't bear it. Just get the hell out of here - and take her with you.' The last few words were whispered, but none the less vehement.

'Please Kate, don't do this,' he pleaded.

'Go up and take her things from my room, leave nothing behind.' She rushed through the door and closed it with a bang, the old wood frame rattling.

After a moment, Jack followed, but Kate wasn't in the bedroom and he stood on the landing and called her name. She didn't answer. It was all quiet. Deathly quiet. Then he heard the swish of water from the bathroom, and realising where she was, stood outside for a few minutes hoping that she would come out and he could at least talk to her. It was a catastrophe, and he had no idea how to handle it.

'Kate?' He banged on the door.

But as the minutes passed and the water continued to run, he went into the bedroom, and threw as much of Marie Elaine's things as he could see into the bag. He waited on the landing again for a few minutes, but now knew that Kate would wait until they had left before reappearing. He called Marie Elaine to him, but she wouldn't come, sitting on the grass, her arms around Chancer.

He stood in the doorway.

'You gave out to Kate,' she screamed, tears streaming down her cheeks, *'jag tycker inte om dig!'*

Distraught, he didn't know what to say. For the first time she was communicating with him, and it had to be in anger. 'It was just grown-up talk.'

'You shouted.'

'I'm sorry.'

'Jag hatar dig ... I hate you ... I hate you!'

'We have to go home now.'

'I want Kate,' she cried bitterly.

'We'll see her soon.'

'She tells me a story every night,' she flashed at him.

'I'll tell you a story.'

'Jag hatar dig.' Her lips trembled and she jumped up and ran down into the trees. Frantically, he stared up at the windows of the house as his life fell apart.

*

Kate stood under the shower, washed clean by now. Her head was splitting and she felt terribly upset, unable to believe that Jack had deliberately excluded her from what must be such an important part of his life. She turned off the water and wrapped herself in a white towel wondering had he left yet. But after a while she heard him call Marie Elaine in the garden and took her chance to leave the bathroom. She dressed quickly, took her overnight bag which she had already packed this morning and ran down the stairs, grabbed the keys and let herself out. There was no need to leave for the airport yet, but she just had to get out of the house. The fact that Jack had created another family altogether for the child, a complete fiction, horrified her.

Kate embraced Grace tightly and held on to her for a moment, just needing to feel the warmth of another human being.

'What's wrong?' Grace drew her inside, but it was two cups of strong tea later before she could explain.

Grace held Kate's hand.

'I can't really believe what's happened. It's like a nightmare.' Tears flooded her eyes, and she searched for a tissue unsuccessfully.

Grace handed her one.

'I'm sorry.'

'Don't worry, sniffles are allowed.'

'How could he keep the fact that he had a daughter from me for all this time?' Kate shook her head in disbelief.

'I thought he said he only found out about it some months ago?' Grace asked gently.

'A likely story!' Kate scoffed, wiping her eyes. 'Anyway, why didn't he tell me then?'

'Has he been untruthful on other occasions?'

'How would I know? I don't if anything he ever told me was true, it could all be fabrication.'

'Surely you're a better judge of character than that?'

'I thought I was.'

'It must have been a shock when the mother died and left a little girl for Jack to raise.'

'Well I suppose so, although I'm sure he must have maintained her since she was born, he's not mean with money usually.'

'You say the child doesn't get on very well with him?'

'No, she seems very suspicious of him.'

'That seems rather odd if he knew her from the day she was born,' Grace suggested.

'I don't know the exact circumstances.'

'It does seem to support his assertion that he only met her a short time ago.'

'I'm not sure what to think, all I know is that he lied to me.'

'Perhaps he was afraid you might not understand.'

'Bloody right! I'm tired of people taking me for granted,' Kate burst out.

'I think you should give it a little time. Go home and have a good night's sleep. In the morning your mind will be clearer. You'll know then what you have to do.'

'I've to fly out to Paris in a couple of hours, and I should be on my way to the airport now.' She glanced at her watch.

'Perhaps being away may help, and by the time you come back, the shock will have eased, believe me.'

Chapter Forty-nine

Dermot sat at the table, his shoulders slumped, feeling very low. The interrogation had continued since the early hours of this morning, during which he explained about the party and that he knew nothing about any drugs. But it didn't seem to satisfy them, and they threw question after question about distribution, ships, containers, ports. Was it Russia, Africa, Holland or the Far East? Who were his contacts? How much money had he been paid? On and on, until he couldn't think straight. Then they began all over again.

'Have you invested the money?' one asked sharply.

'Or stashed it away?' the other interjected.

'In a bank account?'

'Under a false name?'

He shook his head and mumbled no to all of those.

'Have you put it in bricks and mortar?'

'No!' He felt sick.

'But you've been involved in property scams before, haven't you? We have a warrant out for you.'

'What about those developments in Spain?'

They took it in turns to shoot the questions.

'That's all in the past.'

'And a lot of Irish people were taken to the cleaners.'

He badly needed a stiff drink now.

'Do you know Manuel Pedrosa?'

His heart sank. Nervously, he twisted hot sticky hands together.

'He gave us a lot of information about you.'

Dermot felt weak. So that's how they had found out about him.

'What were you smoking tonight?' They changed the subject again.

'Just hash.'

'That's all?'

'I think that's what it was.'

'And the cocaine?'

'I only tried it a couple of times.'

'Sub-machine guns, hand guns, ammunition?'

'What?' His face paled.

'Are you a good shot?'

'No, I never … never used a gun.'

'Where did you obtain the mixing agents, scales, everything you needed?'

'I know nothing about any of that stuff,' he stuttered apprehensively.

'What we need are names. If you give us some of your contacts, then we won't be so hard on you.'

'I have no contacts.' He wiped the sweat from his brow with his sleeve.

'None?'

'No.' Dermot couldn't get his breath. He felt like he was running a marathon and was just at the last few yards.

'What about your girlfriend, Linda?'

He coughed. 'Could I have a drink?'

'Yea sure.'

A Garda left the room.

'This woman, how long do you know her?'

'She's just someone I met recently.'

'Was it a date?'

'Not really.'

'Does she smoke?'

He nodded.

'Use heroin?'

'I don't think so, I never saw her inject or anything like that.'

The Garda came in and put a glass of water in front of Dermot. He swallowed it thirstily.

The other man suddenly produced a photograph of Linda in three different poses. 'Is this her?'

Taken by surprise, he nodded, only then realising perhaps that he shouldn't have identified her. Would these people have it in for him whenever he got out of here?

'She's told us a lot about you as well.'

'Gave us all the information we needed.'

His stomach cramped. 'She doesn't know anything about me.'

'No? Well, she's in the next room, and talking like there's no tomorrow.'

So Linda hadn't escaped after all.

'She listens very carefully to everything and then comes to us. We have a nice little arrangement.'

'You pay for information?'

'That's her job.'

Chapter Fifty

Paris was beautiful, the weather quite warm, but Kate was unaware of the atmosphere of the vibrant city, her mind no clearer this morning, still in the grip of a terrible feeling of loss. But as she showered and dressed, a numbness gradually imbued her, and strangely, there were times it seemed hard to believe that the events of the previous day had happened at all. Jack phoned a number of times but she had decided to let all calls ring through to the voicemail, and didn't respond to his soft-voiced entreaties.

The first appointment was with Moritz and she had been looking forward to seeing the samples of the fabric for the palace in Rome. But today it was just work; something to fill the hours of the day, to take her mind off the fact that Jack had deliberately pushed her out on to the periphery of his life. Into the position of a mere acquaintance.

Sales manager, André, took her around the production facility. Huge machines processed fabrics, a myriad of colours whizzing from roller to roller, the various stages computerised, controlled by only a handful of operatives. She tried to form intelligent questions and responses, feeling so fragile she would have given anything to lie down, and close her eyes. But when she saw the superb standard of the reproduction of the original silk, she managed to show genuine enthusiasm. After a meeting with the production team, they had lunch in a nearby restaurant, and with the help of a cool glass of white wine, she began to behave a little more like her normal self.

In the afternoon she kept the appointments arranged with other companies, busily going through the schedule and finally, absolutely worn out, was very glad to get back to the hotel. On that last visit to Paris, she had longed for Jack to be here with her, but now there was nothing. She lay down on the big bed, sinking into its crisp white cotton softness and tried to calm her racing heart.

*

Jack put down the phone and stared into the shadows. Unable to sleep, he pushed himself up into a sitting position and turned on the bedside lamp, staring at a photograph of Kate. He had lost her once and everything in his life had been affected, particularly the need to paint, the one thing which had sustained him. Now when he looked into the future it was dark.

*

'Kate, do you know where Dermot is? The wedding rehearsal is on Thursday night and I can't find him.' Irene screamed into her ear almost the minute Kate had switched on the phone again after landing at Dublin.

'I've just flown in from Paris.'

'Would you call up to Rathfarnham please, I'm afraid he might have gone on a bender and is out of it. And get back to me as soon as you can, will you? I'm at my wits end. Now, the final fittings will be tomorrow afternoon at three o'clock and I'll be going through all the details with Pru on Thursday. I need you there as well.'

'What time?' Kate asked with sinking heart as she saw her already shortened week being cut up into tiny pieces.

'First thing; and the rehearsal will be at six o'clock with dinner afterwards. Everybody has to be there, particularly Dermot.' Her voice rose dramatically.

Kate opened the car and sat in, but she didn't say anything for a few seconds.

'Are you there?'

'Yes, Irene.'

Kate phoned Shane first but he was down the country organising gigs; Conor and Michelle were anxiously awaiting the imminent birth of their baby. No-one knew where Dermot was.

Mount Asher Road was in an even worse state than earlier in the summer, the beautiful gardens wild and overgrown. She opened the door and walked down the hall with sharp businesslike strides, suppressing the treacherous wave of emotion which suddenly ambushed. Her footsteps boomed into the silence, and her erratic heartbeat echoed the sound. She was astonished that the downstairs rooms were almost devoid of furniture. The floors were thick with dust, and the place had a vacant feeling, as if it hadn't been lived in for a long time. Memories flooded back and reminded how different it used to be. Warm and atmospheric, with soft lamplight, flowers, comfortable furniture - a home. She walked slowly upstairs but hesitated for a moment at the door of the bedroom, before taking a deep breath and pressing down the handle. Dermot's usual mess greeted her, bed-linen dragging on the floor, clothes thrown around. However much she disliked the man Dermot had become, she was thankful not to find him lying unconscious in the bed. After that, she took a quick look around the other bedrooms, and sure that he wasn't there, left and turned her back on the past.

'Have you found him?' Irene's voice reached a hysterical pitch.

'No, he wasn't at the house.'

'I want him here for my wedding, he's playing a vital role.'

'I'm sure he'll turn up.'

'Sure isn't good enough.'

'He'll be there.'

'He'd better.'

'Don't worry, I'll try and find him,' Kate reassured, but really didn't have a clue where to look and certainly wasn't going on a pub crawl.

'What do you mean, don't worry? This is the biggest day in my life and it could be ruined.'

'That won't happen.'

'How do you know?'

Debbie put her head around the door and waved the other phone.

'It's urgent,' she mouthed.

'I've another call, Irene, I'll talk to you later.' She took the phone.

'Mum, it's a girl, it's a girl!'

'That's wonderful! Congratulations!' Kate could feel tears moisten her eyes.

'And it only took a couple of hours, she's eight pound two ounces and has got the thickest head of dark hair you ever saw! I couldn't believe it Mum, it was - incredible!' His voice began to break.

Tears overflowed. 'How is Michelle?'

'Thrilled, but a bit tired.'

'I'll bet.' She searched for a tissue.

'I wanted to say … '

'Yes?'

'Thanks.'

'For what?'

'For everything you've done for me, and which I didn't appreciate.'

'Massimo, the samples of fabric look superb and I'm certain you'll like them. They'll be picked up later today by Cyclone and should be with you tomorrow. I've emailed the quotation.' Kate fingered the silk.

'I will send a purchase order as soon as it is approved. What is the delivery time?'

'The factory in Paris is on standby. I just have to give them the quantity details.'

'*Bene*, now I would like you to look at a job in Florence, we are going over next week, can you be there?'

Kate looked at the diary, suggested Wednesday, and it was arranged. But putting down the phone, she sighed. There was almost too much hassle in travelling to Italy. But business opportunities like this couldn't be turned down, she reminded herself, and Carol was able to deal with everything here. In recent months, the business had taken an amazing leap forward. With the publicity, orders had come from the most unexpected quarters. Requests to speak at conferences. Also bookings to give workshops. An enjoyable, if exhausting, experience, since they usually occurred at weekends.

'This is the list of calls from yesterday, I've marked the urgent ones.' Debbie handed her a sheet of paper. 'And these were delivered this morning.' She handed her a bouquet of roses.

'Thanks.' Kate brought it into the kitchen where she left it on the counter. She didn't bother to open the card, or put the flowers in water, knowing very well who had sent them. She looked at the names and numbers on the list. Some were familiar, some not. Jack's name was at the top.

'Kate, can you have a look at this job?' Sinead asked and she went into the workroom to deal with what had looked like a problem but was easily solved between the three of them.

'She's just beautiful.' Kate touched the soft pink cheek of the baby, feeling very emotional.

'Do you want to hold her?' Michelle asked.

'I'd love to.'

Conor took the tiny baby out of the cot and gently put her into Kate's arms. The little one squinted and stretched her fingers, but seemed quite happy.

'It's so long since I held a baby this size, I'm almost afraid I might drop her,' she laughed.

'Can you imagine how I felt?' Conor grinned.

'I'm amazed at you.'

'I have talents you never suspected.'

She smiled down into the dark blue eyes of the child. 'Have you decided on a name yet?'

'Abigail,' Michelle said, and the proud parents smiled at each other.

'That's a lovely name, Abigail Mason.'

'This is your Gran, Abi, smile for your Gran,' Conor said.

'She's Abigail, Conor. You've been warned, haven't you?' Michelle laughed.

253

'Yes, ma'am,' he drawled.

'I don't mind, really, once she's OK, that's all that counts.' Michelle lay back on the pillows.

'Your parents must be really delighted?'

'Dad and Mum are both over the moon, she's their first grandchild.'

'It's the same for us,' Kate murmured.

'I haven't been able to contact Dad yet,' Conor said, 'I want to tell him about Abigail.' He curled his finger into the tiny fist.

She left the hospital and drove back to the office, reminded of those days when Conor and Shane had been born, and experienced again that wonderful feeling of love and emotion when she had held Abigail close, and smelled that special baby aroma. Remembering too how she felt when Marie Elaine slept with her, the warm body of the little girl hugging close, their hands curled together. How awful it must be for Jack to be rejected by his child. She thought unexpectedly.

Chapter Fifty-one

Dermot was taken to a holding cell after the interrogation. There were a number of other men there, slumped in sleep. He was exhausted, but his mind continued to go around in circles, re-hashing the events of the last forty-eight hours. He had been caught with cocaine in his blood and was connected with the large seizure of drugs in the house where the party was held. He could get twenty years.

If only he had appeared in Court on the property scam. The solicitor had said that he would probably get a couple of years with luck, and do half the time with good behaviour. Now he didn't even have a solicitor. The bills had come and they had simply been pushed under the pile of correspondence on the kitchen table. Everyone had been approached for money. Fleeced. Even Jack Linley probably got stuck for the bail. He had a sense of satisfaction at that thought. The cheek of the bastard to take his wife away from him. God, he was so blasé, so cool, you'd think butter wouldn't melt in his mouth.

The man beside him began to cough and sat up, mouthing a stream of obscenities. Dermot tensed, the rough loose chesty coughs sounded as if he might throw up any minute and he raised his head. 'Are you all right? Will I ask them for water?'

His reply was to push one finger up into the air.

Dermot reached out and thumped his back a couple of times. 'You're in a bad way, should do something about that, maybe go to the doctor and get a prescription for some antibiotics.'

He was about his own age, with tight-cut hair, and darkly-shadowed eyes. 'Yea, fifty a go, yea, I'll phone and make an appointment straight away.'

Dermot said no more, realising how stupid it was to make such a suggestion. The guy probably hadn't a cent in his pocket, no more than he had himself. 'What are you in for?'

'I was ... ' Dermot hesitated, afraid to even mention what the charges were, 'in the wrong place at the wrong time.'

'You'll do time for that.'

A Garda stood outside the bars and stared at them. 'Having a pleasant little chat?'

'Just passing the time,' The man remarked with heavy sarcasm.

'There'll be plenty of that for you. Keep quiet.' He turned away.

'Bloody hell, f-you!'

The Garda stopped and looked back. 'What did you say?'

Dermot's heart thumped in panic, wondering whether he would be blamed.

'Nothing.'

Dermot gripped the edge of the bench and sat rigid.

After a few seconds the Garda turned away again and disappeared out of sight.

'Wet behind the ears. Just out of Templemore. Couldn't punch his way out of a paper bag. Waste of space.'

Dermot closed his eyes again. Anxious now to keep his distance from this person who looked like he could cause any amount of trouble.

'For God's sake, don't join the rest of these snorers, I need company.' He grabbed Dermot's jacket. 'Nice bit of stuff.'

Dermot suddenly remembered that he was wearing an Armani jacket belonging to Linda's boyfriend. What if he bumped into him here?

'Got a cigarette?' the man asked.

'No.'

He stood up and shook the shoulder of one of the other men. 'Any smokes?'

Puzzled, the man stared at him for a few seconds and then pulled a butt from his pocket.

'That all?'

'Yea.'

'Fat lot of use, have you got a match?'

He scraped one along the wall and when it flared he lit the butt.

'This isn't going to keep me going for very long,' he grimaced.

Dermot didn't say anything, his eyes suddenly closing now of their own accord.

'Hey, stay awake, I don't like to be on my own, I told you that,' he dug him with his elbow, and flashed a look of contempt. 'You've never been in before, have you?'

'Eh ... '

'Then you'll need someone to look out for you.'

'I told you to keep quiet.' The Garda appeared outside again.

They both moved back on the bench and a terrified Dermot wondered how he was going to make it through the night. How could he ever survive a jail sentence, day after day, night after night, locked in with people like that man?

Chapter Fifty-two

Jack had left a number of messages during the week. Another bouquet arrived on Wednesday and Thursday and, now, Kate felt under so much pressure that she had to phone.

'Please stop ringing, and sending flowers!' she blurted, her heart beating rapidly.

'Kate, I need to talk to you. To see you. Even for a few minutes.'

'No.'

'Please?'

It was hard for her to resist his obvious upset.

'I want to say how sorry I am about this situation. I'd give anything to take back all the hurt, you know how much I love you.' His voice broke, but she pressed the off-button on her phone as tears spilled over, flopped down on the chair at the desk, and began to sob. For the first time she let go and all the pent-up emotion exploded.

*

'You can take your antiquated kitchen, your one bathroom, crummy heating, dust, rattles, draughts and ... '

'But Susie, we're intending to do a job on the house, you know that.'

'No sign of Kate doing anything. Ages ago I got some paint charts, samples of fabric, flooring, kinda put together a plan, but she wasn't remotely interested.'

'I'll get around her, don't worry.'

'But when?' the peevish whine echoed.

'It's not something which will happen overnight.'

'I'm not hanging around waiting for her to decide. The boys are fed up with it. They want their own bathrooms and hate playing with the computers in that freezing dining-room. There's nowhere to bring their friends, or to play pool or any of the other things they like to do. It's a pain in the ass!' she raised her voice a few decibels.

'Listen, Susie, you know I want this house, and I'm hoping to persuade Kate to split it between us. I guess she'll probably be going to live with that Jack fellow one of these days.'

'It's pie in the sky! You have no guarantee that she'll do that at all, or maybe he's going to come and live here?' Susie grew even more angry.

'I asked her about it ages ago, but she more or less denied it.'

'More or less?'

'Well, yea.'

'You're a goddamn idiot, Pat, I don't know how I put up with you. Dragging us all this way to a backwater, it's like somewhere in the mid-west. You should have stood up to the board, not let them sideline you. I've a good mind to go back with the boys.'

'No, Susie, please don't do that, what would I do without you?'

'Well, if you want us to stay you gotta sort things out. This place has to be made habitable; it's like living in a trailer.'

'But there's great potential here.'

'Which we might never realise. No, Pat, I've had it. The place is a mess. We can't even invite the directors over, it's humiliating.'

'Kate's changed, I'll admit that. In the old days she was easy-going, do anything for you. Now she might as well not be living here, all that travelling. Italy. Paris. London and God knows where else.'

*

Kate was worn out. The tears had dried up by now and as she sat there miserably the shouting match had gradually impinged on her desolation, until a sudden spurt of anger caused her to throw open the door and march into the kitchen. 'I've changed, have I?'

They both stared at her, Pat's face grew paler by the second, and a wave of bright red spread over Susie's cheeks. Neither said a word.

'I'm just going to explain exactly where I'm at. Uncle Bill willed me this house, and there's no way anyone's going to get half. I understood you were going to stay here temporarily until you bought a new place for yourselves.' She took a deep breath. Her anger with Jack had multiplied and unfortunately Pat and Susie were now receiving the brunt of it. But it was an opportunity to get them to move on and she couldn't let go of that. 'So I think you should make plans as soon as possible.'

'Kate, you can't push us out, we're family,' Pat protested.

'I want my home back to myself.'

'But why do you need a place this size?'

'That is beside the point.'

'I wanted to share this house with you; my ancestors lived and died here, I'm a Crawford and must continue the line. You're a Mason and so are Shane and Conor, so it will be the end of the family name.' He moved towards her suddenly, a slightly threatening figure.

'I've reverted back to my maiden name.'

'But after you, what then?'

'That's my business.' Kate shrugged.

'What about Bill's money?' Susie's question cut between them.

'There was no money as such, just a huge tax bill.'

'A likely story,' she sneered.

'Don't take any notice of her, Kate, I believe you, but … ' his earlier bluster began to fade, 'we don't have the money to put down a deposit on a house.'

'What?' Shock registered on Susie's face.

'I'm sorry, honey, but I couldn't tell you. I was hoping that Kate would agree to our plan, and then we'd only have to take out a loan for the renovation.'

'What happened to the money from the sale of our home in Boston?'

'I had borrowed against that, so there wasn't much equity left.' He sat down like a limp sack, all the puff driven out of him.

'You bastard!'

'I'm sorry, Susie.'

'You stupid goddamn jerk!' She raised her arm and slapped him hard across the face.

'I know I should have told you,' he mumbled.

'You lied to me.' She stood over him now, shaking with anger and hit him again. His reaction to her violence was to cower even lower, a pathetic figure.

'Stop.' Kate stepped between them.

'This is all your fault.' Susie grabbed Kate, and threw her up against the old black cooker, the sharp edge of which dug into her back painfully.

Kate tried to push her away, but she wrestled with her ferociously, thumping and scratching. Suddenly she felt her hair being dragged painfully.

'Bitch!' Susie shouted.

'Let go, stop!' Kate twisted and turned in an effort to escape her grasp and she could see a wildness in the blue eyes which suddenly sent fear through her.

'Get out of the way, Kate, I'll handle her. Go ... ' Pat yelled and grabbed Susie.

'I'm going to kill you,' she shouted at Kate, who now stood at the other side of the room, shaking.

'No, you're not, Susie, pull yourself together,' Pat spoke firmly.

'I am too, I'm going to tear her apart. Goddamn bitch. What are you interfering for, she's the cause of all our problems.'

'Susie, enough of this, enough.' He put his arms around her.

'Get off me,' she muttered.

'Not until you promise to be quiet.'

'All right, all right, I won't kill her today,' she glared at Kate and he slowly moved away. She flounced out, banging the door behind her.

'I'm really sorry, Kate.' Pat turned to her, shamefaced. 'I don't know how to apologise for Susie. She loses it sometimes, but it's just frustration. I can't give her everything and, oh my God, your arms?'

Kate looked down, surprised to see blood there. Sudden tears blurred her sight. He was solicitous, and pulled out his handkerchief. 'Here, let me ... '

'It's all right.' She dabbed her arms with a tissue.

'They look painful.'

'Leave me alone!'

'I could get some disinfectant?'

Feeling very vulnerable, she sank into a chair. For the first time in her life she had been attacked by someone, the physical assault sending her into such a state of shock that she couldn't stop shaking.

'I'm very sorry, Kate.' He poured a glass of water and handed it to her. Awkwardly he patted her shoulder.

Where had all this malice come from? Malice which bred such hostility. Pat and Susie had argued before. Often a row erupted out of nothing and Kate had ignored it, but this violent outburst against herself was something else.

'Pat?'

'What?'

'I meant what I said, you'll have to find somewhere else to live, and soon.'

'Kate, I still can't get in touch with Dermot, what am I going to do?' Irene said tearfully.

'I think you'd better consider someone else.'

'What?' Her screech echoed into Kate's ear like a whistle blown at full pitch.

'I'm sure one of your friends would oblige,' Kate said gently.

'But the clothes are made to fit Dermot - Natasha will have a heart attack.'

'If you don't want to walk up the aisle on your own, then that's the only alternative.' Kate was becoming a bit impatient with her. There was silence for a moment and she could hear the sobs. 'Irene, there's no point crying about it, get on to Pru, and between you come up with a substitute.'

'Come over, Kate, will you please? I can't bear this on my own. It's destroyed my wedding, destroyed it completely.'

'I'm sorry, Irene, but I'm up to my eyes.'

'But Kate, I must get this problem sorted, who will replace Dermot?' she wailed.

'Why don't you make a list? I'll see you this afternoon at Natasha's.' She put down the phone.

'Morning Kate!' Mary and Sinead came through the door, all sunshine and good humour.

She managed a smile and immediately got stuck into the day's work, putting Irene out of her head. Although that didn't last very long, as she rang back a short time later and read out the list of possible replacements for Dermot.

'What do you think?'

'Pick the best and ask him.'

'That's the problem, I don't know whether any of them will agree to do it.'

'Why bother? Just simply walk up the aisle after me, you're old enough.'

'I wanted someone to give me away.'

'That's usually because the bride's father is giving her to a husband, but you're a free woman, forget about it.'

'But I want all the old traditions.'

'Then you'd better choose someone quickly.'

It was one of those days, fractured with disturbances, and because of that, the call came through unexpectedly and sent her pulse racing.

'Kate!' The little voice was excited.

'Marie Elaine, how are you?'

'I'm just home from school.'

'Are you a good girl?' Kate tried to control her emotions. Over those few days she had grown very fond of the child and really missed her.

'Yes.'

'Where did you find my number?' Thinking that Jack certainly knew how to get around her.

'I asked Bernie. It was in the book. I'm having a party for my birthday.'

263

So it was Jack's cleaning lady.

'That's going to be great fun.'

'I've got a lovely party dress. It's pink! Will you come?'

'I'm very busy at the moment, but I'll send you a present.' Kate felt bad making the excuse. 'What day is the party on?'

She could hear the question repeated at the other end of the line. 'Saturday! And we'll have crisps, and sweets, and lemonade and a jumping castle and a man who makes a rabbit come out of his hat and wears funny clothes.'

'A magician?'

'Yes!' she giggled.

'I hope you have a lovely time.' Kate struggled to stay calm, as Debbie sat at the other desk and could hear everything.

'Will you come soon?'

'I'm not sure … '

'Please?'

'I have to do my work now, Marie Elaine, so Happy Birthday for Saturday.'

There was no more talk, just silence and the sound of her slightly husky breathing. She must have a cold Kate thought, and wondered had Jack taken her to the doctor.

'Hi Kate, it's Bernie, how are you? Marie Elaine pestered me to phone you, and insisted that I wrote your number down on a piece of paper for her; I hope you don't mind?'

'Not at all, Bernie.'

'She's always talking about you.'

'She is?'

'Yes, and Margaret, the lady who looked after her. I'd better go now, I've to get a bite of lunch and then we have to have our hair cut. She's not too keen on that. Bye.'

Kate's heart dropped down into the pit of her stomach.

She heard the door open and looked around to see Susie standing there. There was an awkward moment then and they stared at one another silently.

'Can I talk to you?'

Anger swept through Kate again and she had an immediate

264

impulse to give Susie a piece of her mind. 'In the kitchen,' she said, and walked through.

'I'm very sorry for losing my cool yesterday, Kate, I don't know what got into me.' She looked very contrite, fiddling with the gold chains around her neck. 'It will never happen again.'

'I hope not. It was an assault, Susie, I could call the Gardai you know,' she said that to frighten her.

'Oh please don't.' She grew pale, hands fluttering nervously.

'I'm still thinking about it.'

'Pat will be furious with me, the company, his reputation.' Tears trickled down her cheeks.

'And you'll have to make plans about finding your own place.'

'But how can we do that, we've no money.' She plonked down on a chair, the picture of despair.

'You can rent. He must be earning a decent salary.'

She nodded.

'I'll leave it with you, now I'm busy.' Abruptly she turned and went back into the workroom.

Chapter Fifty-three

Dermot was up before the Judge the following morning. He was silent when his name was called and very much ashamed when he was granted free legal aid, but refused bail. It was all over in minutes and then he was hustled into a van parked outside. The other occupants were a middle-aged man, and two pale-faced teenage boys. During the uncomfortable bumpy journey Dermot kept his eyes down. All he needed was to have a run-in with one of them and imagined being terrorised by a group in the jail, with an evil godfather character at its head. Perhaps beaten up in the showers so badly he would be afraid to tell one of the prison officers, or blackmailed into doing favours for them all. Maybe he would be raped? That scenario sent terror shooting through him, and he prayed to God. Don't let that happen to me. Please don't. Anything but that. Anything.

They arrived at the prison and were brought through to reception. Dermot was familiar with the procedure now. It wasn't quite as bad as that first time, and he hoped there would be no surprises ahead. After a shower, all his clothes and other possessions were put away in a locker, and he dressed in the regulation green shirt, grey cords and sweater, the same as everyone else. Then he was informed that he could make one phone call.

'Shane? It's me,' he muttered.

'Dad? Where have you been? Everyone's looking for you, and Irene's doing her nut altogether!'

Shane sounded so pleased to hear from him, Dermot felt a bit better. 'I'm sorry, but I'm inside again.'

'You're what?'

'I haven't much time, but tell Irene I'm really sorry for letting her down. It's not my choice to be here.'

'But what are you in for now?'

'Well, it's ... '

'Are you finished?' The prison officer stood beside him.

'Where are you?' Shane asked.

'Mountjoy.'

'For God's sake, Dad, what were you doing?'

Dermot could hear Shane's deep sigh, and then the phone was taken out of his hand before he had a chance to say any more.

The prison officer locked the heavy cell door and Dermot turned to face three pairs of eyes which stared back at him blankly.

He smiled.

One of them put out a hand and shook his. The other two just nodded.

'I'm Dermot.'

'Seamus.' The man who looked as if he was in his sixties was almost completely bald and his chubby face had a wide-open grin, reassuringly friendly.

'How are you?' Dermot felt like hugging him.

'We're as good as we could be stuck in a bloody place like this,' he replied.

The younger man was a slight individual, a cigarette held loosely between thin lips, dark eyes squinting through a pale blue smoke haze. The other was much around his own age, with a stocky muscular build and shoulders so developed they almost hugged his chin giving him a dwarf-like appearance.

'This is Bert.' The older man pointed. 'And that's Christy.'

Bert's firm grip squeezed painfully, but Christy didn't bother.

'Good to meet you,' Dermot said, with a forced grin, 'which is my bunk?' he asked, when at last able to extricate his hand.

'Last in is up top.'

'Thanks.' Dermot looked around for somewhere to sit. 'Do you have a spare chair?'

They looked around and shook their heads and he thought he saw Christy grin as he stubbed out a half-smoked cigarette and lit another.

'I'll get one later.' He climbed up on the bunk and lay down. It was even worse than before. The ceiling above pressed down, squeezing, squeezing, until he wanted to scream. Escape the heavy locked doors. The barred windows. The high walls.

For the second time in his life, he had no control over even the most basic of choices - none at all.

Chapter Fifty-four

'Did you see yourself in the supplement?' Carol rushed in waving it.

'No, let me have a look?' Kate stared at the colour photo of herself in the sitting-room of Berwick Road. The cream suede skirt she had bought in Rome looked good, and the matching boots were just visible under the bias-cut full skirt.

'The house looks surprisingly good.'

'It's amazing what photographers can achieve.'

'A double-page spread. That's what happens when you become a personality. Fame and fortune!'

'The person who's reading the article now will have forgotten it by the time they turn the page.'

'Some of it will definitely stick.'

'Like mud,' Kate laughed.

'You've no idea how good it is to be working with you. It became so tedious trying to drum up enthusiasm for the job with Brent. Thanks again for the chance,' Carol grinned at Kate.

'It's great to have you here. Makes such a difference.' She felt completely worn out. Really only dragging herself around. The loss of Jack and Marie Elaine in her life was heartbreaking, and she was still upset after the row with Susie. The last few days had been hectic with the pressure of work, and preparations for Irene's wedding.

'Well, did Barry fit the bill as father of the bride?' Carol asked, sipping a mug of herbal tea as they shared a sandwich.

'He was fine.'

'Irene was probably tearing her hair out when she heard about Dermot.'

'That's a mild description.'

'The whole thing's a bit over the top. Where are they going for the honeymoon?'

'Apparently it's a complete surprise. Irene gave Ted the money and he's to arrange it.'

'Is "Hello" covering it?'

'No, thanks be to God! It's the Irish magazine.'

'The publicity won't do us any harm, particularly now that you're going to be on television. When is the programme going to be screened?'

'Next week.' Kate was very nervous about the offer from a production company to take part in an interior design show.

'Cheers, you're going to be a TV star!' Carol raised her mug.

'I'm terrified.'

'It's a marvellous opportunity. We'll have a full order book for the next twenty years.' She finished the last of the tea with a sigh of pleasure. 'And there's the possibility of that job in Paris as well.'

'Yes, Massimo was on about that, and the Florence quote has been accepted, so that's next.'

'I think you should move abroad. Mags is definitely going to settle in Rome with Massimo. Maybe we'll all emigrate. What about Paris! So romantic.'

'Wouldn't mind getting away, after all that's happened,' Kate grimaced.

'You could buy a nice villa on the outskirts of Paris and set yourself up.'

'I don't know when I'll have enough money to do anything like that,' she laughed.

'I've been thinking about it. Mine is sitting in the bank and probably would be better invested in property. We could share an apartment and work from there. Imagine sauntering along the Left Bank in the evenings. The wonderful restaurants and bars, music, warm weather, atmosphere. And the men!'

'Maybe we'll go together next time and have a good look around.'

Chapter Fifty-five

Jack tried to get his tongue around the Swedish words. But his version *"Ät upp din frukost"* - "eat your breakfast" - didn't sound anything like the voice on the CD. Something about going to bed - *"Ga och lägga sig"* - was next, but it was just as bad. He was anxious to filter in a few words here and there to Marie Elaine, but was afraid to chance it yet. While obeying him in most things, her dark eyes continued to look at him coldly and he certainly couldn't attempt to come too close. It pained him, particularly when he saw how she behaved with Bernie. Happy, smiling, excited, all those things you would expect from an almost five-year-old. And that was another thing. The birthday party was on Saturday, and he was worried that her attitude to him would become apparent, and invite comment. Although when he had mentioned that she might have a party, her eyes brightened with excitement and she murmured something in Swedish that sounded like "jack." Later, when he had an opportunity to look at the dictionary he thought perhaps it might be thank you, or then maybe it was his own name which she had never uttered; whatever, it was positive.

He still missed Kate terribly, and had stopped sending flowers and leaving messages. He would have loved to share all of this with her, but his heart said to give it time. She wasn't the sort of person who would hold a grudge, he knew that, as was evidenced by her attitude to Dermot, who had been supposedly playing around with Irene. Why was it that she couldn't forgive him? Was his sin so much worse?

Bernie was a great help, suggesting the bouncing castle, the magician, balloons, and promising to be here to arrange things. The food he could deal with himself. He had already bought Marie Elaine's present, and the pink bicycle was locked away in the garden shed. He took her into town to buy some new clothes, and was surprised to find that she knew exactly what she wanted. Barbie and Bratz were the names. Pinks, purples and lilacs seemed to be the favourite colours and anything which sparkled. Matching shoes, boots and handbags had to be bought with everything. The shop assistant was very helpful, particularly with the sizes, and in choosing new underwear and nightwear. He was taken aback at the final bill, although he had no problem with paying that sort of money. Reminding himself that this was par for the course in future. Children were expensive. But she was thrilled with everything they chose, and as they left the store, she sang a little tune to herself, murmuring "Bratz, Bratz, Bratz" as she walked along, staring into the shop windows. He smiled down at her, delighted she seemed so happy. They passed one of those teddy shops. She stopped abruptly and peered through the glass at the wonderful display. He could see where he might be heading with this and didn't relish the thought. Would she be clever enough to play games with him? But to his surprise, even he couldn't resist the appeal of the vast range of soft animals, and a furry brown bear was purchased, and put in a bag, Marie Elaine insisting on carrying that one herself.

He went into the hospital every day to see his father. While his physical condition had improved, Jack found his memory loss becoming more noticeable. But today he seemed in good form and the grin he gave Jack was like old times.

'I told that doctor fellow this morning that I want to leave tomorrow, first thing in the morning.'

'You might stay a bit longer,' Jack was concerned, 'you don't want to have a relapse.'

'The food is awful, and the company!' He raised his eyes upwards.

Jack laughed. It was typical of both his mother and father.

Neither of whom considered themselves to be old, and hated to be around anyone over sixty.

'You have to get well first.'

'I am well.'

'I know you feel good, but the doctors don't want to let you home just yet. Mam can't look after you.'

'How long more will they keep me here?' He was worried now.

'It's hard to tell, the doctor will make the final decision when he sees how you are progressing.'

'For God's sake,' he groaned.

'Have patience, Dad.'

'They can't keep me here against my will,' he muttered angrily.

'There's no point in getting annoyed.'

'What do you know. You haven't a clue what it's like to be stuck in here day after day.'

'I know I don't, and I feel sorry for you, but ... '

'But what?' he barked.

Jack didn't say any more.

'But what?' he demanded, 'you didn't finish the sentence! Is there something you're not telling me? Are they keeping me here for another reason, is that it?'

'No, of course not, Dad,' he said gently.

'What's going on? All this pussyfooting around is driving me crazy. I'm going to talk to the doctors myself, and they'll have to tell me the truth.' He threw back the bedclothes, and began to climb out of the bed.

Jack held his arm. 'The doctors aren't here at the moment. Won't you wait until they come around and then you can ask them?'

'I don't believe anything you say, you're just trying to fool me, treating me like I was senile or something. Let go!' He pushed Jack off. 'Get away from me!' he roared. But at that moment a nurse appeared and took charge.

'Mr. Linley, what are you doing out of bed?'

'I want to see a doctor. They're not telling me the truth and I want to know what they're hiding.' His voice broke suddenly.

'They're not hiding anything, let me help you back in.'

'I don't want to.' He struggled against her.

'Dad?' Jack put his arm around his shoulders. 'Please do as the nurse says.'

'No! You're all part of a plot to keep me in here, get out!'

A second nurse joined the first, and Jack let them deal with the situation. Soon they had him back in bed, but he was still extremely agitated, and one of them hurried away to get a doctor.

The injection administered was effective, and he dozed off. Jack stayed sitting by the bed reading the paper, and hoped that by the time his mother arrived he would be back to normal.

Rose came in first, but Jack didn't go into the detail of his father's upset. She bent over him and kissed him lightly on his forehead. At her touch he opened his eyes.

'Who are you?' he muttered.

'It's Rose, Dad, are you still half-asleep?' she laughed.

'Rose?' He sounded puzzled.

'Yes! And that's Jack there.'

'I don't want to talk to him.' He looked away.

'Why not?'

'I told him to get the hell out of here,' he growled, 'whoever he is.'

'Dad?' Rose sounded surprised. 'What's all this about?' she asked Jack, who shrugged helplessly.

'I asked the nurse for another vase, I've a nice bunch of flowers for you.' Mrs. Linley came in and put it on the locker. 'Are you feeling better today?' She patted her husband's hand gently.

'Bloody awful.'

'What's wrong?' Her face paled.

'They won't let me go home,' he grumbled, and plucked at the buttons on his green pyjama top.

'You're not better yet.'

'Will you stay with me?' He gripped her hand tightly.

'Of course, love.'

'Tell those others to go away, I don't like them.' He flashed a belligerent glance towards Rose and Jack. 'Get out of here.'

'Dad sssshhh.'

'Get out!' he roared.

Jack put his arm around Rose and took her into the corridor.

'He didn't know me.' She dissolved into tears.

'I'm sure it's just a mood, Rose.'

They waited for a while and then they moved through the door again. Inside they were shocked to see their father in floods of tears, Mam standing with her arms around him, rocking him gently, as she would one of her children.

'Oh my God!' Rose was horrified. 'What's wrong with Dad?'

'I don't know, it's probably the medication,' Jack reassured. But he was worried. There had been incidents here and there lately, particularly that time he had been helping him in the garden. But this onset of confusion was the most severe yet.

Just after he arrived home, Bernie and Marie Elaine arrived back from school. She was silent as ever, clutching some pieces of folded paper.

'Are you going to show Daddy your drawings?' Bernie asked.

But Marie Elaine shook her head, and ran upstairs to her room.

'Take off your uniform,' she called.

'Thanks Bernie.'

'She's still a bit strange with you, it's a pity.'

'Yea.'

When Bernie had heard that Marie Elaine was his child, she had been thrilled, and was only too glad to help. As it was, she did all the housework, and laundry, and now had no problem giving him an extra few hours in the afternoons to look after his daughter. She washed her hair, cut her nails and took care of all those other little things he wouldn't dare do.

Life was difficult, and all the time his mind went around and around trying to think of ways in which he might persuade Kate back. But he always felt that anything he might say or do held a taint that he might need her to help him look after Marie Elaine. Kate had had her own family and he knew she didn't have any interest in starting all over again with a five-year old. She wanted to enjoy her career and have a good life. They had talked about taking off for weekends at the drop of a hat, or interesting holidays, things which couldn't be done with a young child. Now it looked as if that would never happen. He had decided to write to Kate, to try and explain exactly how he felt, but the scribbled notes he had made already made very little sense and, frustrated, he had torn them up.

It happened one evening after he had cleared up after their evening meal. Marie Elaine was watching a Noddy video, one of her favourites, and he went upstairs into the studio. But the place was in a much worse state than he remembered leaving it earlier. His brushes was strewn across the workbench, large sheets of sketching paper were on the floor, and prepared canvases had toppled down into an untidy heap. He was puzzled, immediately wondering if the dog had got in here. But he couldn't have reached the workbench, so that explanation was eliminated. It certainly wasn't Bernie – and that left Marie Elaine. Now he was angry, and went downstairs determined to have it out with her. He couldn't ignore this.

'Marie Elaine, have you been in my studio?' he asked heatedly.

She ignored him, and continued to stare at the television.

'Marie Elaine?'

She tightened her grip on Chancer.

'Answer me!'

Her face puckered up.

'Someone has been in the studio and thrown things around. That isn't allowed.'

He switched off the television. 'Now tell me if you were in there today?' His voice sounded very loud in the silence. There was no response. He wanted to control the situation, but didn't know how. He switched on the television again. Once again, the room was filled with the childish voices of the characters.

He was excluded.

Chapter Fifty-six

Friday night began the celebrations for Irene's wedding at the hotel in Wicklow. Cocktails, dinner, with entertainment by a music group, and comedians. Irene and the others there threw themselves into it with wild enthusiasm, but Kate found the whole thing just too exhausting and couldn't wait to leave. Which she did eventually, sure that no-one would even notice her absence.

The following morning she was swept up into the excitement of the wedding. Manipulated by Pru and Natasha, she did everything that was expected with a smile on her face. But it was very difficult to play at being happy.

'This is the most wonderful day of my life.' Tears glimmered in Irene's eyes and she fingered the diamond choker she wore.

'Irene, no tears please, no, no, no!' Pru pulled a tissue from her generous cleavage.

'Sorry.' Irene blinked a couple of times. 'I'm all right, don't worry.'

'Let me look, have you spoiled your make-up?' Pru peered into Irene's face and touched the corner of her eye with the tissue. 'You simply cannot cry. You are not allowed to show any emotion today.'

'Oh Pru, how is that possible?'

'Make it possible! You can't have smudged mascara wrecking the photos, just remember that.'

'My designs look *magnifique, n'est pas?*' Natasha was dressed in purple, the full-length gown with a sweeping high collar framed her dark hair which was elaborately arranged with matching feathers.

She had that dramatic look of the witch in Snow White and The Seven Dwarfs, Kate thought, almost laughing. *"Mirror Mirror on the wall, who is the fairest of us all?"* This whole thing was the stuff of fairytales.

'I can't thank you enough, Natasha,' Irene gushed.

'I am proud of my work, I should receive much publicity.'

Kate stood there, her back aching. She would have loved to sit down but didn't dare attempt it in case the skirt became creased. She thought about the long day ahead, thinking how much she had been looking forward to spending it with Jack. But now loving him seemed to be something dreamed up. A fleeting moment of happiness which couldn't be recaptured. She stared out the window fixedly, very much aware of Pru's warning. No tears today.

'It's almost time!' Pru announced, 'it will take fifteen minutes to get to the church and as Ted should already have arrived, we will be there just late enough to keep him wondering. The carriages are waiting for us downstairs.' She glanced out the window. 'I put the Child of Prague in the garden last night, so our prayers are answered, no rain so far.'

'I'll die if it rains!' Irene adjusted the position of the tiara a fraction.

'Do not touch, do not touch!' Natasha screamed, 'you could ruin the overall look.'

Irene fingers stopped mid-air. 'I was just … '

'You cannot see yourself as we do, you have not the objective eye.' She reached down and rearranged the fabric of the coat, which trailed out, the silk floating like surf at the edge of the sea. Then she clicked her fingers. 'Pierre, Pierre, the camera. I need photographs for myself. Positions, please.'

'Girls, get those smiles on again,' Pru ordered, 'and don't forget your flowers.'

When the shots were taken, they were carefully ushered out of the room and down the long staircase, to a polite round of applause from some staff and guests who were in reception. Irene bowed her head like a queen, but Kate felt self-conscious, dreading the day ahead.

Chapter Fifty-seven

The incident of the mess in the studio was not mentioned again. It was the first time such a thing had happened and Jack really regretted his mishandling of the situation. How was he going to deal with the everyday incidents which would undoubtedly crop up in the future? Fear settled like a heavy weight on his shoulders, but he had to rise above that and get on with the organisation of the party. Take each day at a time he advised himself. Try to be a good father. The sort of person Marie Elaine wanted. Whatever that was. He felt quite unable to deal with the exigencies of his life alone and longed for Kate.

The birthday was a great success. Marie Elaine seemed excited when he surprised her with the pink bicycle, and spent the morning cycling around the garden followed by Chancer, who barked at it constantly. When the crowd arrived later in the day, the little girls spent most of their time playing in the bouncing castle and he had never seen Marie Elaine so animated. He had invited everyone in the family, since the news of his daughter was common knowledge by now, and was delighted to see Kathleen, Rose, Chris, Gerry and his mother, who was quite taken by her new granddaughter.

He joined in the festivities and even made an attempt to bounce on the castle for a laugh with the rest of the adults who tried to keep their footing on the unsteady surface, much to the delight of the kids. The magician went down really well with everyone, doing his tricks and organising games with the kids. But the best part of the day was when Marie Elaine blew out the five candles on her cake and everyone sang Happy Birthday. And of course there were lots of presents, far too much he thought, she had so many toys there wouldn't be any space left in the bedroom. He might have to consider converting the attic or building on an extension yet.

A large box was delivered mid-afternoon by Cyclone, and Jack carried it out into the garden. With shining eyes Marie Elaine watched as he opened it and screamed with excitement when a beautiful doll's house was revealed.

'Who sent this lovely present?' he asked, 'look at the card there on the roof.' Marie Elaine picked it up and opened it. 'Now tell us who wrote it?'

'Kate,' Marie Elaine whispered. Then she bent down and stared inside, surrounded by all the other children, who suddenly seemed to have forgotten the castle and were now much more interested in this new toy.

Jack was taken aback. It was so typical of Kate's generous nature to remember Marie Elaine's birthday, in spite of their own disagreement.

'Where is your other half? I was hoping to see her,' Rose asked.

Jack didn't know what to say. Regret choked him and he had to make a hell of an effort to hide his feelings. There was an uncomfortable silence.

'You've certainly given your daughter a great birthday party,' Chris commented after a moment, tucking into a large piece of chocolate cake.

'And you've slipped into the Daddy role very easily; painting is obviously going to take second place from now on.'

He remembered Rose's words later, and they reminded that there was still a lot of work to do on his collection for the exhibition. He went up to the studio when everyone had gone home and tried to put some shape on the place to begin work in the morning. That was when he noticed the boxes containing Mia's pieces of sculpture. They were exquisite abstract shapes in bronze, with obscure meanings which even he couldn't fathom. He intended to show them in his exhibition, but they wouldn't be for sale. They were Mia's legacy to her daughter. Engrossed, he didn't hear the dog pad up the stairs and come into the studio until he was beside him.

'Chancer! You shouldn't be up here. Go downstairs,' he hunted him out, but then saw Marie Elaine peering around the door and his immediate response was to shut-up. She never ventured in here, even when he encouraged her. But now she continued to walk across the studio, her eyes riveted on Mia's sculpture.

'They're your Mummy's.' He stood back. 'She made them for you.'

Quickly then she was beside the bench and reached upwards to touch one. Her small fingers softly ran down the cuts in the nearest piece she could grasp, and he shifted the others nearer, praying that they wouldn't fall and be damaged. Still, they belonged to her, and if that did happen then so be it.

'I think they're beautiful, don't you?'

She clasped her hands around one and tried to lift it off the bench.

'It might be a bit heavy for you.' He steadied it.

'Give it to me!' she demanded angrily, *'jag vill ha den.'*

'It's not something to play with.'

'I want it.' Her arms were wrapped around it in a loving possessive way. 'In my room!'

'There wouldn't be any space.'

'They can go on my bed.' She reached to drag it down.

'You have to sleep there.'

She glared at him, eyes full of fury and resentment.

'All right, we'll try and find somewhere.'

At that she let go. He picked it up and they walked down the corridor. She opened the front of the doll's house which she had insisted he put in her bedroom, and pointed inside. 'Into Kate's house.'

He bent down on his knees and inched the bronze into what was supposed to be the sitting-room of the house, luckily managing to position it in such a way so as to avoid the tiny wooden furniture. When he stood up again, she took hold of the door and closed it firmly.

Suddenly, he knew that she could make him do anything.

Chapter Fifty-eight

The horses clip-clopped along the road leading to the small church among the trees, drawing the carriage in which Kate rode. She felt like someone living in the last century on her way to Mass on Sunday, and gazed out at the landscape thinking how beautiful it was even on this misty day. The grey stone spire appeared up ahead and she gripped the holder of her spray of lilies, suddenly nervous. A little pulse began to thump at the nape of her neck when the church appeared, and the carriage drew up. A group of photographers trained cameras on her. She forced a smile and prepared to step down, but to her surprise Shane hurried through the gates. He was dressed in a strange mixture of black clothes, like one of those preachers from the wild west, a white shirt with a wing-collar, string tie and cowboy boots.

'Mum, I hate to tell you this, but neither Ted or his best man Michael have arrived yet. When I saw the carriage, I was sure it was them,' he whispered nervously.

'What?' Kate exclaimed, 'give me your phone please, I'll have to delay Irene although I know she's not far behind me.'

She rang Pru, following in a car with Natasha, and told her. What could have happened to a carriage being drawn by six horses? It wasn't a mechanical vehicle, it couldn't break down. But maybe a wheel had come off, or the horses had bolted, or - Shane's phone rang.

'I can't get a reply from either phone, they're just on voicemail. I'm heading over to the hotel now,' Pru sounded panic-stricken. 'We've stopped Irene, but we just said something about the photographer from VIP being late. Natasha has sat in with her and Barry.' Kate was very worried. Surely Ted wouldn't? He seemed such a nice man. Not at all. That absurd thought was dismissed. Something must have happened.

It was cold sitting in the carriage, and she shivered.

'Mum, why don't you come into the church?' Shane asked.

'I couldn't, Shane, not without the bridegroom being there. Will you go in and check on the guests, I'm sure they're all getting very impatient. And let me keep your phone, I'm sure Pru will be on any minute to tell us that there has been some mix-up.'

She watched him walk to the door of the church, and disappear inside, and then her eyes strayed to the photographers who were in deep conversation at the gateway. She sat there, willing the phone to ring with good news. But when it did, it wasn't what she hoped for.

'Kate, it seems that Ted and Michael checked out after all the other guests had left for the church.' Pru was in tears.

She listened. Speechless.

'Kate, are you there?'

'Yes.'

'What are we going to do?'

'I don't know.'

'I could kill the two of them, my reputation will be absolutely ruined. All my work gone for nothing, I'll be a laughing stock,' she snuffled.

'What about Irene?' Kate whispered.

'Someone else will have to tell her, I'm in bits.'

'Couldn't we do it together, it might be easier?'

'I'm going straight back to town, I'm not hanging around here.' The phone cut off.

Kate was shocked, and couldn't think what to do.

Shane reappeared. 'Mum they're all getting a bit uncomfortable. And so is the priest.'

'Ted and Michael have left the hotel, but they're not coming here,' she said slowly.

'What do you mean?'

'They've done a bunk! The bastards!'

'What?'

'I'll have to tell Irene myself, Pru's gone as well.'

'Ted and Pru? Together?'

'No, I didn't mean that, but she can't face everybody, stupid useless biddy! Will you get the driver to turn these horses around, and take me back.'

He talked to the driver. 'There isn't room, the road is too narrow.'

'For God's sake! Help me out then, will you please?' She pushed open the door, climbed down and together they hurried to where Irene's carriage was waiting. It only took a few minutes, but the high-heeled shoes she wore prevented her from walking very fast and she almost fell over more than once.

The minute she drew abreast of the carriage, she heard a wail from inside, and knew instantly that Irene must have some idea of what had happened.

'Stop crying, *ma petite* Irene, your face is a complete mess,' Natasha warned.

'Irene, I'm sure there is a rational explanation,' Barry said.

'I don't care about my face; what's going on? That's all I want to know.'

Kate opened the door and faced the three of them.

Irene grabbed hold of her hand and squeezed it tight. 'Kate, why is there such a delay?'

'Well ... '

'Has there been an accident? Tell me!'

'No, nothing like that.' She squeezed in beside her.

'Then why are we still sitting here?' Irene howled.

'Ted and Michael are not at the church. They have left the hotel,' Kate blurted it out quickly.

Irene's mouth fell open, and a rather strange gurgling sound could be heard.

'Have you got a phone?' She found her voice again.

Barry handed his to her and she pressed the digits. 'I refuse to believe it. He would never do this to me. Not after all we've been to each other.' More tears coursed down her cheeks, creating rivulets through her honey make-up. Her mascara was smudged, layers of

284

turquoise eye shadow had merged, and the pink lipstick was almost gone altogether. She dialled again, and again. 'Bastard, bastard, bastard! I'll strangle him; hang him out to dry!' She snuffled into a tissue, and wailed dismally, 'and I loved him so much.'

'Perhaps something has happened?' Kate ventured.

'He might have got in touch, or asked someone else; not left me here like this. My dress is out of this world. The castle is so romantic, the carriages, the flowers, and my honeymoon ... ' she began to blubber again. 'I didn't even know where he was taking me and now I'll never know. He's probably on his way there now with Michael. They're going to have a great time on my money. My thirty-thousand euro,' she screamed.

'Listen, Irene, listen to me,' Kate said urgently.

She raised her blue eyes, which were dark-shadowed pools of tragedy.

'Look, we have to try and sort out something now. The guests have all arrived, and they don't know what's happening. The piper, the man with the doves, and the photographers are here. There are amazing chefs and waiters ready to serve food at the castle, musicians, and entertainers. Are you going to disappoint these people?'

'I've been disappointed.'

'Don't let this beat you. March up the aisle and say it like it is. Most of the people are friends of yours and will be delighted to see you stand up to Ted. He's a low-life. Now dry those eyes and ask everyone to one hell of a party. You're good at that sort of thing. You always were!'

'*Oui, oui, si, si,* Irene, it is good what Kate says, let us have one 'ell of a party,' Natasha nodded.

'A party?' She took a gulp.

'Yes! Are you going to let them throw all that delicious food into the bins? And the band go home without playing a note? You can't let that amount of money go down the drain!'

It was her last remark which drew the first positive response from Irene. 'Yes, that's true, I've paid for it all, haven't I?'

285

The carriage moved towards the gates and stopped slowly. Ironically, just at that moment, the sun came out from behind the clouds and cast a brilliant pool of brightness over the church. First to alight was Kate on the arm of Shane; Natasha came next, feathers floating in the breeze as she posed for the cameras, followed by Barry with Irene. Her make-up had been quickly repaired by Natasha, who seemed to carry everything needed in her little bag. The signs of distress had almost disappeared. The kilted piper led the way under the flower-covered pergola, stopping for the photographers and video cameras, as a flock of white doves wheeled above. In the vestibule, Kate had a quick word with the priest; then Shane and herself continued on up the aisle to the tune of something from Mozart which the orchestra were still playing. It was far worse than she had expected, every eye on her with curiosity, the loud rumble of voices quickly diminishing to low whispering. And then silence. At the altar, they stood on the steps to one side of that flower-trimmed bower under which Ted and Irene had been supposed to sit on their gold thrones, looked at one another, and slowly turned around to face the sea of expectant faces.

'Ladies and gentlemen,' Shane began, and then turned to the orchestra and indicted that they should stop playing. 'We are sorry for the delay, but there have been some unfortunate developments.' He twisted the stringy tie around his fingers nervously, coughed, and continued. 'Ted is not coming. He seems to have dropped out of sight without a word of explanation to Irene. But she isn't going to let this small unimportant fact spoil your weekend,' he grinned and raised his arm. 'I give you – Irene!'

She flounced up the aisle, and immediately the strains of *"Here comes the bride"* echoed out. At the altar steps, she whirled around, tossed her head, striking a pose with one hand on her hip. 'Hi everyone. Sorry to have kept you waiting, but it really won't make any difference in the long run. The champagne is on ice and the timing is perfect. So follow us, the party is just beginning!' She lifted her flowing coat, slung it over her arm and sauntered down the aisle as the orchestra struck up a triumphant marching tune.

Chapter Fifty-nine

'I think we should write a note to Kate to thank her for the lovely doll's house. I'll help you,' Jack suggested to Marie Elaine, picking up a sheet of writing paper and a pen. But she shook her head, slid off the chair, and disappeared out of the door. Returning a moment later, shyly holding something behind her back.

'What's this?' he asked with a smile.

She handed him a piece of paper.

It was just a page torn out of a copybook, and all around the edge were carefully drawn flowers in red and blue marker. In the middle she had written a message, and he read out the words. *"der kat tank yu for the dols hoos I luv yu Marie Elaine"*. For a moment he couldn't say anything, desperately touched by the childish love expressed there.

'That's a really nice letter. I think we'll have to send it to her straight away.' He found an envelope, and addressed it. Then she folded the sheet, pushed it in, peeling a stamp off the strip and pressing that on carefully. 'Would you like to post it now?'

She insisted on riding on her bicycle, and he held the dog on the lead.

'When will it be there at Kate's?' she asked, her voice soft, after she had reached on tip-toe to push the letter into the box.

'Tomorrow.' He thought of his own attempt to write to Kate. The page still lying in the drawer of the bedside locker, a mess of crossed out words. Somehow, he couldn't get it right, his heart grieving for her. They went back home and he bought Marie Elaine an ice cream on the way. It was strange. For the first time she had let him come a little closer to her and it was all because of Kate.

But when he went upstairs that evening to his room for something, he was thrown into confusion again. Most of his trousers and jackets had been pulled off the hangers and were now heaped untidily at the bottom of the wardrobe.

Chapter Sixty

Irene's big day was an amazing event. When they arrived at the castle, the pipers played the wedding party into the Great Hall where trays of hot punch, champagne and a wide variety of tasty finger food were served. Fires had been lit in the huge rooms and the leaping flames threw out great heat. As the guests gathered, a jazz group played from the gallery above, and the music really added to the festive atmosphere. Irene smiled and nodded as she wandered through the crowd. Plenty of sympathetic hugs and kisses were exchanged, the general view being that Irene had been fantastic to be able to recover so quickly from such a blow, which she seemed to have done with astounding aplomb. Her wedding dress was much admired and she sparkled and preened as if nothing had happened. They sent the press away and the only shots were taken by the private photographer. Although Kate was sure that the story would be carried by some of the dailies, it was too good a headline to turn down - *"Bridegroom leaves bride at the altar."*

The meal was delicious, the entertainment top-class, and when the band began to play, Irene took Shane out on the floor for the first dance. But as time passed, and the amount of champagne she consumed began to take affect, the strain began to show. 'I don't know how I'm going to manage without Ted.' Tears filled her eyes.

Kate patted her hand. 'I know it's going to be difficult, but in time someone else will come on the scene. You can attract them like bees to a honey pot!'

'But what about tomorrow and the next day?'

'Why don't you head off somewhere? New York, or Rio?'

'I'm not in the mood. I need someone to take care of me.' She snuffled into a tissue.

'Or Dubai? Gorgeous sunshine, and all those amazing hotels? You could enjoy the luxury, be pampered and have a chance to wear that fabulous wardrobe Natasha designed.'

'Can I come and stay with you?'

'But I've no room.' It was the first excuse Kate could think up.

'Just for a few days? I can't bear the thought of being alone. And you've always looked after me so well.'

'I don't know, Irene, the house is bedlam with Pat and his crowd and we're working there as well.'

But in the end Kate couldn't refuse and brought her back to Berwick Road. Arriving in the afternoon, they walked in on another argument between Pat and Susie.

'What's going on?' Irene asked.

'Just a tiff, I presume.'

'I'm exhausted. I'm going to take a shower and go to bed. If I don't wake up for a week it will be too soon for me.'

Kate silently led the way upstairs.

'Oh, it's a double-bed,' Irene remarked.

'Yes. But you can have it to yourself, I've a camp-bed which I'll use in the workroom.'

'You are so sweet. I love you for it.' Irene hugged her.

'Here is some clean bed-linen.' She took a white cotton duvet-cover, pillow-cases, and sheets from a drawer in the tallboy.

'Thanks.'

Downstairs the voices had stopped, and there was silence. Kate pushed open the door of the kitchen to find them sitting at the table.

'How is Irene?' Susie immediately asked. They hadn't stayed over in the hotel and returned the night before.

'In reasonable form. She's going to stay here for a few days.'

'That was a terrible thing to do to her,' Pat said, 'but she coped really well, I couldn't believe it.'

'Coffee?' Susie reached for the pot.

'No thanks, but I'm sure Irene might.' She poured it into a china cup, put some cream in a jug, a few biscuits on a plate, and took a tray upstairs, automatically knocking on the door before she went in.

'Thought you might like a cuppa.'

'Oh thanks, you're so good.' Irene wiped her eyes.

'Susie made it actually.' Kate put the tray down on the bedside table. 'I'll give you a shout when dinner is ready.'

'Couldn't eat.'

'I'll cook up something tasty. You won't be able to resist. Now sit on the armchair, drink your coffee, and I'll change the bed.' She made her comfortable and then left, not a bit enamoured of the idea of bunking in the workroom. Coming out on to the landing, she could hear the sounds of the row which had obviously erupted again, and decided to go out and do some shopping rather than have to listen. But returning home after picking up some fillet steak, and a few other bits and pieces, it was still in full spate. Where could she go in her own home for some peace and quiet?

'Well, have you two made any plans?' Kate asked, cutting across the shouting match.

They looked at each other, their voices stilled abruptly.

'Plans?' Pat face flushed a little.

'I presume you're going to rent a house, we discussed it,' she avoided saying I told you to do it. Since the night Susie had attacked her, she had been very careful not to antagonise her sister-in-law. It was like walking on eggshells, and made everyday life uncomfortable.

'We ... ' He cleared his throat.

'We were hoping to persuade you to let us stay,' Susie said, 'if we make it worth your while. Perhaps pay rent? You know, a formal contract between us?'

'We love it here, Kate, you can't throw us out.'

'I've explained how I feel.'

'It's like being evicted on to the side of the road.'

'I'd prefer to have my house to myself, working here as well isn't ideal.' Kate felt she was being cornered as usual. 'And now with

291

Irene staying ... '

'All the more reason for moving over to Jack's place. You're both mature people, and should be living together.'

'That's none of your business!' she retorted angrily.

'Sorry.' He looked embarrassed.

'But, I may as well tell you my relationship with him is finished. And now I want my own space.' She looked vaguely somewhere over their heads, unable to make eye contact, particularly with Pat.

'Is there a chance that you and Dermot might get together again?' Pat asked.

'No.'

'Then that's where we come in, Kate, don't you see? We've talked about extending the place and renovating the mews, which would be an ideal working space for your business. We're prepared to borrow money to do that, share the cost, and both of us would benefit,' Pat's tone suddenly became very reasonable.

'I don't think you understand my position,' Kate said carefully.

'Of course we do, but you have to see ours as well.'

'I want to live alone, that's the bottom line.'

'But surely it would be lonely here?' Susie sounded sympathetic.

'It's the way I like it.'

'You're so selfish, Kate, I can't believe it.' Pat shook his head. 'You'd throw your brother and his family out on the side of the street just because you must have your own way?'

Kate didn't say anything. He was right. She probably was selfish.

'You can't do this to us,' he said, his expression gloomy.

'There are too many of us living here. I want my house back to myself in two weeks.'

'But it's the Fall now and soon it will be Christmas.'

'There's plenty of houses out there. I'll have a look for you.' She was giving herself work, but didn't care.

'It might be very difficult to get us to leave,' Susie's tone changed, 'do you intend to carry us out?'

'I hope that won't be necessary.'

'You can't make us walk out that door unless we want to go. And we haven't signed a lease for a specific length of time, so you can't put any legal pressure on us.' Her words hung in the air between them with all their implications.

'I've told you what I want, legal or otherwise, two weeks.' She left the room.

Chapter Sixty-one

Dermot slowly became used to prison routine. He now expected to be in here for some time as the young solicitor assigned to him hadn't been very hopeful of an early trial. In an effort to get fit, he joined the queue of men going into the gym, where he lifted weights, and worked the treadmill. In the library he picked up books, thrillers mostly, but, unable to concentrate, he never got past the first few pages.

The other men in the cell knew by now that he was in here on a drugs charge, but he dreaded the day when they would offer to sell him hash or cocaine or, God forbid, heroin, as they all seemed to be on something or other, with glazed eyes and a permanent head cold. Luckily, he hadn't taken enough to become addicted, and had got such a shock when he was arrested that he vowed never to touch the stuff again. Labelled a drug dealer, he felt ashamed, even in this place of criminals. To sell the stuff was far worse than using. Each day the same questions bombarded his mind. Would the judge believe him about Linda? Was she in the women's prison now? Or still doing her job as a paid informer?

In the exercise yard he ambled alone, glad of the chance to breath fresh air into his lungs and get rid of that recycled stuff which passed as oxygen inside the building. A lonely man who wasn't accepted into the group who gathered to play football, or those who huddled in corners to talk about sport, or whatever else was going down in their narrow lives. The bleakness got to him. And at his lowest, regretted he hadn't had the guts to end it all that day before the Court case.

To his surprise Kate came to visit him one day. She made small talk for a while, and then commented on how tired he seemed.

'What do you expect in this place?' he snapped.

'I'm sorry.'

'You haven't a clue what it's like here,' he barked, jealous of how well she looked. With soft blonde hair curving around her face, and lips outlined in a peachy gloss, so much like the girl he had once known, the Kate with whom he had fallen in love all those years ago. He could even smell the aroma of her perfume.

'I talked to your solicitor.'

'What did he say to you?'

'It's a serious charge.'

'And what else?'

'Nothing else.'

She seemed guarded and he sensed that. 'Whatever he said, I know it already.'

'What's it like for you here?'

'Terrible.'

'And the food?'

'Sludge.'

'I've left some money with the prison officer, that's the form apparently.'

'Thanks, I hope it's delivered.'

'It's addressed to you.'

'That doesn't mean anything in here.'

'What are the other men like, the ones in your cell?'

'Scary.'

'What do you mean?'

'They're all high on something, and I'm afraid of them.' His eyes darted around nervously.

'Do you need me to do anything for you,' she offered.

'What can you do, other than arranging for your boyfriend to cough up another few euro to pay someone to drop down in a helicopter and winch me up.' His greyish-complexioned features twisted bitterly.

'As a matter of fact, he's no longer my boyfriend, and he lost all of the bail money because you didn't turn up in Court. Shane, Conor and I lost what we put up as well.'

There was a sharpness in her voice now, and he was suddenly aware that perhaps he had gone too far. 'I'm sorry, it's hard to be cheerful and good-humoured in here.' He shrugged, and lowered his head.

'I can understand that.'

'Why did you come in?' He suddenly needed to know. Was there any hope that she had changed her feelings towards him?

'I hate to think of you in here.'

'You're very forgiving, Kate.'

'I'm trying to put the past out of my head for now. I decided that there's no point letting it corrode my thinking. That's all Grace's influence, you know.'

'Grace?'

Kate went on to explain who she was exactly, and it gave them something to talk about for a while until silence yawned again.

'Has Conor been in.'

'No.'

'They're very busy now with the new baby.' She took a small wallet from her pocket and opened it. 'Here's a photo of Abigail, isn't she beautiful?'

'Yea.' He looked once and then away.

'How does it feel to be a grandfather?'

'It doesn't make any difference to me, she'll be grown up before I see her.'

'Hopefully, not that long.'

'I won't hold my breath.'

He watched her put away the wallet, noticing how, afterwards, she twisted her hands together tightly, the skin creamy, fingernails polished, tips white.

'I'd better go.' She stood up.

He nodded, suddenly sorry that she was leaving. He wanted her to stay, but he didn't know how to ask. 'Thanks for taking the time.'

'I'll come in again,' she said.

'Yea, please do.' He watched her turn away, and his heart did something when she looked back at him with a little smile and murmured goodbye.

Her visit had an amazing affect on him. As he walked back to the cell, he held his head up and shoulders straight. All thoughts of suicide were banished from his mind, and instead, all he could think of was Kate, and how soon she would come back to see him.

Chapter Sixty-two

Kate awoke even earlier than usual. Although she worked right through until twelve most nights in an effort to exhaust herself, it didn't seem to have any affect, and she often lay there staring into the darkness, wondering why all of the men she loved had let her down? Even her darling father had sold the family home when he met Irene, throwing out all those things which meant so much to Kate. Memories of her mother just dumped without a thought. Then Dermot's cheating. Pat's efforts to push his way into Berwick Road. And, worst of all, Jack. Maybe she should take Carol's advice to move abroad and make a new start? The idea suddenly seemed very attractive.

Today was her television debut, and she was so nervous she would have gladly opted out. But to her surprise in the post was a letter from Marie Elaine. The carefully written words brought tears to her eyes, and she pinned it up on the notice board in the workroom, reminded of how she used to do the same with the drawings of the boys when they were young. It unsettled her so much she left the house feeling even more edgy than before. But there was no turning back. The new independent businesswoman could see that this was an opportunity which mustn't be missed. Carol came along to the television studios for moral support, and bolstered her confidence somewhat before she was ushered into make-up, thinking that she looked awful with the heavy layer of foundation they used on her face. Brighter than normal lipstick and eye make-up didn't improve the reflected view in the mirror, although she was happy enough with the blue silk jacket and full-length skirt she had chosen to wear.

Next she was ushered into the studio and met with the floor manager, Tom. Bright lights were switched on, cameras swung across the floor, and the director communicated with the engineers in the box above going through a test run of the videos. They had filmed a number of interiors which Kate had designed and would use a selection in this programme.

The researcher, Tara, brought her along to the Green Room, and she met the architect, Damien, a builder, Fergal, and Vivienne, a woman who had been invited to talk about her own home which she had just renovated. It was all very friendly, and Kate's heart eased its mad gallop as she sipped a cup of tea, reluctantly refusing a drink. Damien and Fergal had been involved before, but for Kate and Vivienne it was their first time and they chatted together sharing feelings of terror at the thoughts of imminent exposure to the whole country.

All too soon it was time to go on, and she was back in the studio. The set was designed with a skyline of buildings in vibrant colours, draped muslins, and plasma screens. The audience was part of the plot, the seating arranged in the round for greater intimacy. Kate and the other panellists each had a laptop which could be used to bring up any images which might suit a particular query. They had already been shown a list, so there was control from that point of view, but a level of uncertainty too, as the audience could chip in with their own comments if they wished.

'Ladies and gentlemen, we'll be going on air in a few minutes, so we want everyone to settle down. Do you need anything, glass of water for a cough, or sucky sweets?' Tom laughed. 'You've already met the people who will be answering your questions, but we'll just ask them to stand up again so that we know where they are. Now join your hands together!' The audience obliged enthusiastically.

He looked up at the control box and then made a sign to Dee who stood off-set. 'Twenty seconds.'

Kate could feel the heat from the lights now.

'Ten seconds.'

The cameramen shifted position. The signature tune sounded as the intro flashed on to the large screen. The opening titles rolled and Dee walked on.

After that, the programme swung along at a fast pace.

'I've been doing up my home and now that I'm almost finished I find that it is very bland. My bedroom is all cream and beige and too boring for words.' It was one of the first questions from the audience.

'Kate, that's definitely in your area, what ideas have you got for Breda?'

A picture flashed across her mind. Bed. Wardrobe. Bedside lockers. Chair. For a few seconds her mind went blank, but then she managed to pull herself together. 'It sounds very fashionable, but perhaps it needs colour to dramatise it, or maybe an item of furniture. So I suggest a padded headboard, some cushions, and a throw which might incorporate a contrasting colour, maybe burnt orange or terracotta, or both. The headboard could have vertical or rectangular contrast sections and the size can vary, perhaps even being as large as the wall behind the bed.' She clicked the keys on the laptop and an image appeared on the screen. The audience applauded and suddenly she was on a high. This was followed by a query about a conservatory, a theme for a modern penthouse and ideas for an eco-friendly home in between various other subjects to which she contributed confidently. There were a lot of laughs, the light-hearted tone defining the programme, and, almost before Kate knew it, Dee was thanking the audience and the experts. They received a loud round of applause. It was over.

They went back to the Green Room again, where Carol waited. 'You were great! I really enjoyed the show.'

'What did I sound like? Look like? Go on, please tell me. I want it all.'

'As usual you had plenty to say and looked a million dollars in that outfit.'

'I was terrified.'

'I loved the audience participation, tell us your problems and we'll sort them out.'

'Yea, but you have to perform, and be able to pull out the ideas at the drop of a hat.'

'I have green walls, purple carpet, pink suite, but I'm being driven crazy with all these colours. It's a mess!' Carol giggled, 'sort that out and you'll be made. Give up the day job, and turn into a TV personality.'

'What a prospect!' Kate laughed.

'If it takes off, go with it.'

Back at the workroom, the girls stopped what they were doing and screamed congratulations.

'It is wonderful. I can touch your hand, a TV star,' Olga said.

'I can't wait to see the programme,' May said breathlessly, 'will you be on again?'

'When they see the ratings for this one.'

'It will be like a reality show with someone voted out each week.'

'We'll go around and promote you,' Debbie laughed.

'A politician before an election.'

'What will you wear next time?'

'If I'm asked.'

'You'll have to be prepared, so I'm booking you for next Saturday, we'll have a pleasant amble around town before we watch your programme,' Carol grinned.

'Kate!' Irene put her head around the door.

'Congratulate the TV star!' the girls chorused.

'What?'

'She'll be on the show on Saturday night.'

'The show?'

'You don't know?'

'I've other things on my mind.' She stepped in and pulled a white lacy wrap around her, looking rather dishevelled. Obviously no visits had been made to the hairdresser or the beautician in a while.

They fell silent.

'Everyone's very sorry about what happened, Irene,' Carol said.

'I'm heartbroken.' She pushed her lank hair back, looking very unlike the beautiful woman everyone knew.

'It's tough,' May murmured.

'I don't know how I'll keep going.' Her shoulders slumped.

'Irene, you just have to make a huge effort to face up to life. Get back with your friends at the golf club, they'll all rally around, and there will be a new man on the scene before you know it,' Kate tried to sound encouraging. Thinking that if someone gave her that advice it certainly wouldn't help the deep feeling of loss which dragged her down, day after day, making it so difficult to give the impression that she was happy.

'Never.' Irene shook her head.

'He's waiting around the corner.' Carol hugged her.

'Can I get you something?' Kate asked.

'I'm feeling a bit peckish.'

'I'm just in the door - why don't you have a look in the fridge and see what appeals to you?' She glanced down at the list of calls which had come in during the day.

'Did you get a newspaper?'

'I've done no shopping yet.'

'Maybe you could pick one up for me?'

'Yea, sure, soon as I can.'

'Thanks.' She disappeared through the door.

The girls looked at one another.

'Get your skids on,' Carol said, as the others went back to work.

But to her delight, Kate received a call from Tara the following morning and was offered a contract for three more programmes.

As she had promised, Carol insisted on meeting her in town on Saturday, and in a matter of minutes they found a wonderful black velvet skirt and jacket by the Spanish Tintoretto label. Next was a pair of high tight-fitting suede boots which could just be seen under the unevenly cut line of the skirt, and some glittering costume jewellery, which was Carol's choice really.

'The outfit needs something dramatic. Go for it!'

Kate laughed and did as she was bid. They went on a spree after that, and the plan to work later was dropped.

'I'm delighted I persuaded you to climb out of your lair, you need to get out more.' Carol topped up their glasses of white wine as they enjoyed a delicious meal at the Turban Restaurant. 'I'm looking forward to seeing the programme.'

'Don't keep filling up my glass, I have to keep my wits about me,' Kate warned.

'For God's sakes, you should be celebrating! I know you're scared stiff to watch yourself on television, but it will be easier after a few jars. And I'm going to bring you out some night next week. We'll go on the town. You can't work your life away! Think of the advice you gave Irene, maybe you should take a bit of that yourself.'

'Yea.' Kate looked sheepish.

'You do a good job of hiding your feelings, but don't think you're fooling me.' Carol looked at her with a serious expression. 'You never open your mouth about him now, has he been in contact?'

'Messages on the phone, and texts, but I wish he would leave me alone,' Kate murmured.

'But ... you still love him?'

'No!'

'It's such a pity, you two were good together.'

Kate took a gulp of wine.

'Sorry, I shouldn't have mentioned him, I don't want to spoil the evening.'

But it was spoiled, and Kate tried hard to hide the wave of unhappiness which swept over her.

'If you open up your heart to someone it can really hurt if it all goes pear-shaped,' Carol said softly, 'I think it's what keeps me on the edge of never taking a step towards commitment with anyone.'

'I'm dreading it,' Kate confided to Carol when they arrived at her house later.

'Don't be silly, you'll be great!' She switched on the television, pressed play on the video and almost immediately the signature tune echoed and Dee appeared on the screen.

Kate closed her eyes.

'There you are!' Carol screeched.

Kate trusted one look and found that it wasn't as bad as she expected, and by the end of the programme she was just as excited.

It was Sunday, and unaccustomed to drinking these days, she had awoken with a splitting headache. Regretting her over-indulgence, she lay there, eyes closed, trying not to listen to the racket which was going on in the kitchen. Pat and Susie were arguing again. Reluctant to get involved, she tried to drift off to sleep, but it was impossible and finally she got up at about eleven, the row having died down by now.

After sipping a welcome cup of tea, she prepared toast, eggs and coffee, for Irene and took it up.

'Have some breakfast.' Kate put the tray down on the locker.

'I don't want anything.' She lay propped up on the pillows, the bedclothes in disarray.

'You must, otherwise you'll be ill.'

'I feel so bad, Kate, you've no idea.' She closed her eyes and a tear trickled down her cheek.

'I understand how you feel, Irene, but you have to try and put it behind you.'

'It's all very well for you,' she grimaced.

'Come on, try the coffee at least.' She helped her to sit up. 'After breakfast, why don't you have a shower and dress and then come downstairs. Maybe you might like to go out? We could have lunch somewhere.' It was the last thing Kate wanted, but she was worried about Irene, and wondered if she would ever get back to normal and go home.

'No, I couldn't face the world in the state I'm in. Just turn on the television for me, and when you go out bring back the papers, and some chocolates, I feel like something sweet. I need to pamper myself.'

Kate nodded and did as she asked, retreating finally into the workroom and trying to concentrate on her accounts, a sudden impulse to hide from the world also. But there was no peace in the house with the noise of Rob, Donal and a gang of friends who were all crowded into the dining-room playing games on the computers, and when Grace phoned later she was glad to go over, her home an oasis by comparison.

Today the trees and plants were almost bare, although there was still a beauty about the garden where they walked for a short time before it began to rain.

'You're rather preoccupied,' Grace observed when they went back inside.

'I'm hung over, too much wine last night,' Kate explained with a rueful smile, 'Carol persuaded me to join her on a shopping spree and one thing led to another.'

'I watched your programme. It was really good. You came over so well, very knowledgeable and confident too.'

'Thanks.'

'This new aspect to your life is going to take up a lot of time, I presume?'

'I know.'

'Perhaps you should try and cut back in other areas?'

'Carol gave me a roasting.'

'Did you deserve it?'

'Probably.'

'Let us take tea, I have Kukicha today.'

They knelt on the mats while she brewed it carefully. Kate watched her silently, letting the artistry of the older woman's movements take her mind into another world. To live in the moment, the ties to everyday things gently broken, tension easing. Even Jack temporarily pushed further into her subconscious.

'I feel much better, thank you.' Kate kissed her.

'I'm so glad. That strained look in your eyes has disappeared. But you need to have a good look at yourself. Just remember, Kate, life is today. Yesterday has gone, and tomorrow doesn't exist yet. The now is all that matters. And to be truly spiritual, we must not let materialism dominate our lives.'

'But for the first time in my life I feel on top of things. I'm independent. Successful. I can't believe it really!'

'Success is very fragile, Kate; it can collapse overnight.'

'Everyone seems to think they know what's best for me. I don't

305

need anyone telling me what I should do!' The words popped out before she had thought how Grace might react. 'Sorry, I shouldn't have said that.'

'Don't worry,' she smiled.

Kate felt guilty. She would have hated to hurt her intentionally. But it was the mantra which kept her going from crisis to crisis. The words she used to lash herself when she weakened. I don't need anyone … don't need … don't need.

Chapter Sixty-three

There was an excited babble of voices coming from the sitting-room as Jack brought Marie Elaine into Tyrconnell Park, so glad to see Dad sitting in his usual chair by the fireside, surrounded by most of the family. After weeks in hospital he was home at last. But he was very depressed, a condition which had troubled him since that day of the outburst at the hospital. And he had become much more confused. Sometimes he didn't recognise his children, as was the case with Rose and Jack; or he simply forgot their names, and even his own on occasion. But thankfully he knew their mother, who was the only one who could handle him.

Everyone welcomed them effusively, and it seemed that they were glad to have some new faces among them, particularly Marie Elaine.

'It's good to see you home, Dad.' He walked over and patted him on the shoulder. But the bent figure grimaced and shook him off. Each time that happened, Jack could feel a thump of disappointment in his stomach. Since that day in the hospital, he hadn't changed his attitude towards his youngest son. Any time he had gone in to see him, his father had turned away, or told him to get out. But he hadn't left, and walked up and down the corridor outside, always hoping that next time he went in his father would be the way he always knew him. But so far that hadn't happened. It was very distressing and he found it hard to deal with the situation. So similar in ways to Marie Elaine, and Kate too. It seemed he was rejected by those people he cared about the most.

'Marie Elaine, my little pet.' Mrs. Linley came in and kissed her. 'You're looking really pretty today; that lilac skirt is so nice. Did

Daddy buy it for you?'

Marie Elaine smiled and pointed to the matching fur-trimmed boots.

'I'd love a pair of boots like that.'

'They wouldn't fit you.'

'No, my feet are much too big.'

Marie Elaine giggled.

'Now let's say hello to your Grandad.' Mrs. Linley brought her over to the hunched figure. Shyly, she stared up at him, and, to Jack's surprise, made no move to back away as he looked up, smiled, and raised his hand to pat her cheek. 'My little Rosie.'

Jack stood watching, amazed at his daughter's reaction to her grandparents, and envious too, wishing she would look at him in the same way. He was astonished that his Dad obviously thought she was his own daughter, Rose, when she had been a child. He was so grateful to his mother; what would he do without her? But then he noticed that Rose had rushed out through the door, and he followed, to find her crouched at the top of the stairs, in tears. He sat beside her and hugged tight.

'I can't understand. Dad doesn't know me any more, but he thinks Marie Elaine is ... ' She sobbed into a disintegrating tissue, and Jack gave her his own handkerchief.

'I'm sorry.'

'He doesn't know you either,' she said mournfully.

'I'm not sure whether he does or not.'

'What are we going to do?'

'We'll just have to live with it, and hope that his condition doesn't get any worse, it's Alzheimers, you know.'

'Who told you that?' Her head snapped up.

'I talked to the doctor a few days ago. Mam knows too but she doesn't want it known generally yet. I think she's afraid we'll say she can't look after him.'

'Poor thing.'

'We'll have to be there for her, and help as much as we can. Although that's going to be difficult for you and I.'

She sighed deeply.

'Come inside again, Mam will be wondering where we are.'

'Did any of you see Kate on the television, I couldn't believe it was her,' Kathleen asked after they had finished lunch.

'I was talking to a couple of my friends and we were thinking of getting audience tickets, particularly since we know her. I could certainly do with a bit of advice about our front room, it needs a radical make-over!' Gay laughed.

'We've got somebody famous in the family at last.'

'What about Jack, he's famous.' Chris poured more tea.

'But he isn't a TV personality. She'll be a household name before long. If you want her to design your house you'll have to join a long queue no doubt.'

'She must be thrilled.'

'Yes, she is,' Jack said awkwardly. He felt such an idiot. Imagine he didn't even know about it. He should have told them it was over there and then, but really couldn't have said anything now. Obviously his loss was having no detrimental affect on Kate. He looked over at Chris, but to his relief she said nothing.

Later in the day when his Dad had gone to bed to rest, Jack said goodbye and headed over to see Margaret. She was just back from Australia, so he thought it would be good for Marie Elaine to see her again, which it proved to be. When the eldest daughter, Karen, brought her out to the patio to play on the old rocking-horse, he took his opportunity to talk seriously with Margaret.

'She still hasn't taken to me,' he said morosely.

'I noticed that.'

'Yet I brought her over to see my family today and there seemed to be no problem, even with my father. I keep thinking that perhaps the man who was living with Mia might have done something to her, although I dread the thought of such a thing.' He hesitated for a few seconds, but then continued. 'I was hoping that you might be able to give me some help on that. How much do you know about him?'

'Look at me, look at me!' Marie Elaine screamed.

Margaret smiled and waved, as did Jack.

'It wasn't a good relationship, he was quite violent.'

Jack was shocked.

'On numerous occasions Mia had to run in here with Marie Elaine to get away from him. Sometimes, they bunked down on the settee for the night and would go home in the morning when he was sober.'

'My God!'

'Mia was a very gentle person and couldn't deal with someone like him. She often had to try and cover up the bruises with make-up.'

'How did Marie Elaine respond to all of that?'

'She was terrified.'

'What age was she then?'

'He was there for a couple of years, up to the time she was about three, I think.'

'So impressionable.' He couldn't believe what he was hearing.

'He was a nice man most of the time, but changed when he hit the bottle.'

'What did he look like?'

'Tall. Dark. Very like you actually.'

'Perhaps that's where all of this comes from. I remind her of him.'

She nodded.

Jack stared at Marie Elaine who was laughing out loud in huge enjoyment, thinking that he might buy her a rocking-horse. But even if he bought every material thing her heart desired, would she ever be his daughter in truth, or always see that other bastard when she looked at him?

Chapter Sixty-four

Mountjoy Prison was bleak on that December day. The procedures were frightening. Heavy keys rattled, doors were locked and unlocked, banged open and closed. For Kate it was claustrophobic. She felt as if her freedom was taken away. And the horrible thought that by some mistake she would be kept here against her will was even stronger than that first day she had visited Dermot. She couldn't get out quick enough.

The package which she had brought was handed over to the prison officer and finally she followed the group of other people into the visiting room.

She leaned across the counter towards Dermot, hating the space between them. Not that she particularly wanted to be any closer, but it was just the physical barrier which bugged her.

'I've been counting the days,' he smiled.

She drew back a little, wondering if he had misconstrued the reason for her visit.

'Conor said he had been in to see you.'

'Yes, last week. He was telling me all about his little baby.'

'They're very happy.'

'And Shane was in as well. He mentioned that you're on a TV show now.'

'Yes.'

'That's good for business. Although the lads here would never look at a show like that.'

'I suppose not,' Kate murmured. There was a silence between

311

them then and she didn't know what to say next, very aware of all the other people in the large grey room. The murmurs of a dozen conversations, the squeals, cries and shouts of children.

'How are you getting on with the men you share with now?'

'Better, I suppose. But it's hard when you live so closely with people,' he whispered, 'I'm last in so I have no say in anything. They look at what they want on television, and don't give a damn about me. Most of the time I just lie on my bunk and read the paper.'

There was another silence.

'Have you met my solicitor?' he asked anxiously.

'Yes, I had a meeting the other day, but he doesn't know when the trial will be.'

'Could I go to the judge and ask if he will give me bail?'

'I talked about that, but he said no.'

Dermot grimaced.

'No-one will go bail for you now anyway; the amount of money would probably be even higher than before, and none of us have enough.'

'Couldn't you borrow it?'

'I don't think there's much point, the solicitor was quite adamant.'

'Bastard.'

'I think you're going to have to get used to being in here, Dermot. I know it's awful, but I hope it won't be for too long.'

'I'll go mad, they'll have to certify me.'

'Try not to let it get to you,' she made these futile remarks with no confidence at all that he would manage to handle his incarceration without breaking down.

'Will you be there for me when I get out, Kate? It would make such a difference to me if I could be sure of that.' His hand reached out to hers, but she moved back a little.

'As a friend, perhaps.'

He stared at her, disappointment flooding his face. 'Why are you here then?'

'To see how you're getting on.'

'If I tried hard to be what you want, would that change your

312

mind?'

'Dermot, there's no point talking about it now,' she put him off, reluctant to upset him by telling him the truth.

'I suppose there's another man in your life now?' he asked with heavy sarcasm.

'No, Dermot.'

'So there might still be a chance for you and me?' he smiled.

'No, I'm sorry.' She began to feel this might get very awkward. 'Now, I'd better go.' She stood up. 'I mightn't have a chance to get in again before Christmas, we're terribly busy, but I hope it's not too bad for you.'

'No, it won't be, now that I know … ' he smiled broadly.

Driving home, Kate's morbid thoughts brought her back to her own situation. She would have given anything to lift the phone and talk with Jack, remembering how he was always there for her. She climbed out of the car and went up the steps and even at that distance, could hear the sound of voices reverberating from the sitting-room. Her heart sank. She pushed open the front door and put down her briefcase. Weeks had passed since she had asked Pat and Susie to get their own place. But nothing had happened. They had ignored her completely.

'Kate!' Irene hurried down the stairs, wrapped in a pale cream velvet dressing-gown. 'I was watching out for you, I'm going crazy with the noise here since they've all come in. On and on! Can you tell them to shut it please?'

'Irene, they live here,' she said wearily.

'I thought I was going to have a bit of peace and quiet, but it's bedlam, and you're hardly ever at home; if I need something I have to get it myself; and I can never get into the bathroom, you'd need a ticket!' she pouted childishly, 'you asked me to come and stay here, but what was the point if you're out all the time? Lecturing, meetings, television, flying to Italy, France and God knows where!'

'I've told you that I can't manage on that amount of money!' Susie burst out of the sitting-room.

'I'm trying Susie, I'm trying to save, you know that.' Pat followed.

'You're a twit, a stupid useless twit, and I'm sorry I ever married you,' she yelled, 'and as for having to live here in this old shack with your dumb sister ...'

'Susie!' Pat touched her on the shoulder and she turned, glared at Kate, then rushed down the hall.

'Bloody noise, always bloody noise, it drives me crazy,' Irene muttered and flounced back upstairs.

'Pat, we have to talk.' Kate motioned Pat back into the sitting-room and he followed meekly. She closed the door. 'This is it, Pat. You'll have to go. I've had it.'

'But ... '

'No buts. If you don't find a place immediately, then I'm going to change the locks. And I will do it, believe me. Tomorrow morning, phone an estate agent and find out what rented properties are available. I'll give you a couple of days,' the speech spewed out without hesitation.

'Kate, you can't do this.'

'I can, Pat, and I think we'll have a far better relationship if you're living in your own place, in fact I'm sure of it. Let's not fall out.'

He nodded.

Then she went upstairs, and knocked on the door of her own bedroom. She was very tired of sleeping on the camp-bed in the workroom by now. It wasn't the most comfortable even for the few hours she spent in it. And it was awkward having her clothes in the wardrobe in what was now Irene's room. When she chose the next day's outfit in the evening, sometimes she forgot an item, and then had to make do until Irene surfaced.

'Come.'

She went in to see Irene sitting in the armchair smoking a cigarette, a glass of what looked like vodka in her hand. Some quiz show was on the television.

'Irene.' Kate sat on the end of the bed.

'What?' she snapped.

'I'm going to have to ask you to move back to your own place. There are too many people in this house.'

314

'How can you do that to me?' Tears sprang into her eyes.

'It will be the best thing for you. Get back to normal life. Book into the hairdressers. Have a session with the beautician. Meet some of your friends.'

'You haven't a clue what it's like to be in my position, I've lost the only man I ever loved.'

'You're better off without him,' Kate said gently.

'Fat lot you know.' She tossed her head. 'Something might have happened to him. He could have been murdered, or had an accident. I'm still trying his phone but I can't get through. Any moment he might ring. I'm never going to give up hope.'

'I'm sorry Irene.'

'Please Kate, don't make me go, I can't survive on my own.' She wiped the tears away with her hand.

'I know I sound harsh, but I do think it's the best thing for you. It will be far more peaceful to be at home again.'

She snivelled.

'Perhaps tomorrow would be best. I'll drive you over.'

'Do you think you can find the time out of your busy schedule?'

'Yes, Irene.' Kate took a deep breath, reluctant to show the irritation she felt at her sarcasm. 'Now I'll cook something nice for you this evening, perhaps you might dress and come down. We could open a bottle of wine.'

She shook her head and stared at the television.

The following morning just after nine, Irene opened the door of the workroom, wearing a casual sweater, and jeans. 'I'm off,' she announced. For the first time she was going outside without being dressed in a chic outfit and full make-up. Today she looked every year her age, probably nearer fifty than forty.

'Just give me a minute and I'll take you,' Kate offered.

'There's no need, I've booked a taxi.'

Kate followed her up to the hall. 'Let me help you with your bags.'

'I can manage myself, I don't need any assistance.' She lifted two heavy suitcases and tottered down the front steps still wearing her slippers.

Chapter Sixty-five

'I don't know what to do. I've given Pat and Susie an ultimatum and now I must carry it out.' Kate was morose. She hated being forced into such a contentious position. It wasn't in her nature to fall out with people. It affected her appetite, sleep, concentration, all those vital things necessary for a good life. She felt bad enough about Jack and Marie Elaine - now this was just too much.

'It's a heavy burden. Try not to let ill-feeling come between you, the affects can last a long time,' Grace said gently.

'I don't want to, but it's ... ' Tears welled up in Kate's eyes.

'Then perhaps you should look for another way?' She poked the fire and the flames flared.

Kate shook her head and stared into the red-hot embers. She couldn't think of an alternative, other than letting Pat and Susie reside permanently in the house.

'Maybe I'm too selfish.'

'Perhaps you let people take advantage.' Grace picked up a lump of coal with the tongs, placing it carefully into the middle of the fire. It was the way she did everything, Kate thought suddenly. So measured.

'I wish I was like you.'

Grace laughed, 'you don't know what you're saying, sometimes I don't want to be me.'

'It seems you have it all worked out, while I don't know where I'm going.'

'We're never satisfied with ourselves. That's human nature. We have to make the most of the hand God has dealt. While we think we have control over everything, perhaps that's all in our imagination.' Grace topped up their glasses of white wine.

'It's fate then?' Kate smiled.

'Yes.' She raised her glass. 'To destiny. You have a long way to go, Kate, and there will be many twists and turns in your life. I'm nearly eighty years old, and any one of these days could be my last.'

'Not at all.' Kate didn't want to hear this. 'You're in great shape.'

'We can't choose the time we go.'

'I suppose the same applies to me.'

'Let's make a toast to the future whatever length of time is left.'

They clinked glasses and smiled.

On Thursday when Kate was taking her fabric swatches out of the car, the front door opened, and she looked up to see Pat carrying a suitcase down the steps.

'We've found a house, Kate!'

'Oh ... where?'

'Terenure.'

She was astonished to find that they were really going.

'You were right, it will be much better for all of us, particular the boys, they have been a bit cramped. And I'm hoping to be able to get a mortgage soon, so we'll have our own place eventually,' he smiled.

'Honey, can you lift this one for me, it's a bit heavy?' Susie asked from the front door.

'Yea, sure, darling!' He bounded up again, as a taxi pulled up outside.

'Don't forget the tennis gear.'

'I've got it.' Donal thumped down carrying the rackets, followed by Rob.

'We'll probably have to do another run, so see you later.' Pat waved and got into his car, while the others crowded into the taxi, shouting goodbye.

Slowly, Kate walked into the house. It was very quiet. Her heels echoed on the wooden floors as she went down into the kitchen and eased herself wearily into Uncle Bill's armchair and closed her eyes. It was some time later before she could motivate herself to get up and flick on the kettle. Only then she noticed the bouquet of roses on the dresser, and immediately assumed they were from Pat and Susie, experiencing a warm glow at their unexpected thoughtfulness. Beside it, there was a large white envelope, and she opened it, surprised to see the catalogue for Jack's exhibition at the Nestor, a beautiful painting of a woman and child on the cover. She turned the first page to find a sheet of paper in Jack's handwriting tucked inside, and wondered for a few seconds whether she wanted to read it or not.

Suddenly she was startled out of her reverie by the thump of footsteps in the hall above, but her heart slowed down its irregular beat as she heard Pat call her name, and ran up to meet him.

'I just came back to get the rest of our things.'

'Can I help?'

'No thanks, I have enough space in the car.'

'Thank you for the bouquet, the roses are beautiful.'

'They're not from us; probably from one of your admirers!' he laughed.

She was silenced for a few seconds. 'Is the house nice?'

'Great! Like you wouldn't believe.' He hurried up the stairs and brought down the last of the boxes.

'I'm going to miss you now,' she admitted.

'You'll see plenty of us,' he laughed.

'I'm sorry about everything, but I found it quite difficult with so many people in the house.'

'Don't worry, we probably overstayed our welcome. Anyhow, we're delighted with the new place, and Susie is happy, which is all that matters to me. I know that I hoped to live here because of the family, but what are bricks and mortar when I almost lost her? It took me a long time to realise that.'

'I'm glad.' She hugged him, amazed that all the aggro between them had fizzled into nothing.

After he had gone, she closed the door and went back into the kitchen. She picked up Jack's letter again. But sudden anger surged.

She tore the page in two. Then in four, eight, and binned it.

It was hectic in the lead-up to Christmas, and the girls had all pitched in, working late each night to complete the orders. Kate was glad she was this busy, but she still found herself wondering about Jack's letter. When her anger had died down, guilt took its place. Should she have given him the courtesy of at least reading it? But the bins had been collected by now so it was impossible.

Now it was even more difficult to get him out of her head. As she waited for someone on the phone, or even when having a conversation, her treacherous mind could suddenly take her attention away. Romantic songs were particularly difficult. She never turned on the radio these days, but in the workroom, it was wall-to-wall music and she was forced to listen.

'I hate this mad Christmas rush. What is it that makes people insist on having everything for that one day,' Carol sighed, as curtains were pressed, folded, and packed for the fitter who would hang them the following day.

'Have to get the place tarted up for the relations,' Kate laughed.

'Which is something I should do myself, but the chances of that are more like next year or the year after. Mind you, if I buy the apartment in Paris, then it won't be necessary. I'm serious about that, you know. I talked to an estate agent who has a branch in France and he's sending me some brochures.' Carol glanced at her watch. 'Right, I'm off, I'm going over to Jack's exhib ... ' she stopped speaking mid-sentence, and said nothing else for a few seconds. But then she put an arm around Kate. 'Thanks for inviting my Mam and Dad over for Christmas dinner, they're really looking forward to it.'

'I'm glad they can come. Shane will be here, Conor, Michelle, the baby, the American contingent and Grace as well.' Kate was grateful for Carol's effort to change the subject, but it didn't make any difference. Because she could imagine Jack so clearly at the Nestor, that place where they had first met, she felt she was there beside him. His warm touch, sensual whisper, and dark eyes swept her back in time and she had to fight hard to escape the power of the love which had once possessed her.

Chapter Sixty-six

Dermot came into the visiting area. He was exited, hoping that it was Kate who waited for him.

'Dermo!'

'Irene?' He was stunned.

She sat into the chair on the other side of the counter, and leaned towards him. The deep blue low-cut jacket was revealing, the heavy sapphire and gold pendant sinking into her golden brown cleavage.

'What are you doing here?'

'What do you think?' she smiled.

'I'm amazed, after all that business about giving you away.' He had never expected to see Irene again.

'Perhaps it was all for the best.'

'What do you mean?'

'Ted and I ... we weren't really suited. It was all a mistake.'

'My poor Rene, I'm so sorry for you.'

'No need for sympathy, Dermo, you know I never let things get me down.' She slid her hand over the counter.

'You think maybe when I get out of here?' he whispered, his heart thudding, 'if that ever happens.'

'Dermot, you'll have the best barrister in town; just leave it to me.' She pursed her lips, and reached forward to kiss him.

A prison officer stepped forward. 'No touching!' he barked, and they slowly drew apart.

Chapter Sixty-seven

Jack stood outside Marie Elaine's bedroom door, hoping that she wouldn't be much longer. He sighed. She took as long as any woman to get ready, although she always managed to dress herself perfectly, amazing really for a child of her age. To his relief, it had been some weeks since she had tried to show how much she disliked him, and said nothing when she dragged down his clothes off the hangers, or recently, when some sketches he had done of her had been torn up and littered the floor of the studio. Losing his temper that first time had been a mistake.

His phone rang. It was Vincent again, and Jack could visualise him as he wandered around the gallery, dressed in a style reminiscent of the eighteenth century. Bright-coloured frock coat, silk cravat and perhaps a cloak as well, waving his cigarillo in its gold holder. He had phoned at three o'clock, four-fifteen and now at four-fifty-three, with queries which had to be answered, and always that add-on at the end of their conversation. 'What time can I expect you? I need you here, like yesterday.' He made Jack nervous. Like an actor, he was always uncertain as to how well his work would be received, and this year it seemed to be even more important. He had a daughter now, and must make sure that there would be enough money to give her the best of everything. His relaxed nomadic existence of the last few years was no more.

He caught sight of himself in the long wall mirror. The sudden thought that his tall dark figure might still remind Marie Elaine of the man who lived with Mia made him decide to buy some brighter clothes as soon as he could. He wondered what Kate would think of this and smiled to himself. She had thought his dark taste far too sombre at times. Suddenly, his heart thumped with anticipation. Although she hadn't replied to his letter, perhaps she might have waited until this evening to meet him face to face before - before what? He asked himself. Don't get carried away. Don't be a fool. You've no right to expect anything. 'Marie Elaine, we must go, the taxi is outside,' he called.

The door opened slowly. She stood there dressed in her blue denim skirt and fur-trimmed pink jacket. But one matching boot was held up, and it was obvious that she couldn't manage to pull it on herself. Lately there had been little triumphs here and there which gave him hope that they would eventually grow closer. While she still declined to talk, preferring to chat with the dog, he had almost got used to that. Now she sat on the end of the bed and he helped her on with the boots.

'They look really pretty on you, stand up and I'll zip your jacket,' he smiled, another first.

'Right, let's go.' He hurried out on to the landing, but then doubled back when there was no sound behind him, to see her in the doorway unrolling a sheet of white paper. He waited until she held it up, astonished to see a drawing of Chancer, sitting on the grass with his ball between his paws and tongue hanging out. 'Marie Elaine, that's wonderful, and such a good likeness of him!'

The sheet of paper was lowered slowly. Her dark eyes appeared, then her nose, and smile, wide and joyful.

The exhibition was a great success. A number of paintings had already been sold before it even opened. The rest were picked up very quickly, much to Jack's relief. As the gallery became more crowded, he found his eyes straying constantly beyond people in search of Kate, but he didn't see her and was disappointed. The display of Mia's work drew a lot of comment, and many substantial offers, but it wasn't up to him to accept, they belonged to Marie Elaine.

For the first time his mother was there with Gay, Rose, Kathleen, Chris, and Gerry. Kathleen's eldest daughter stayed with his father, who couldn't be left alone. Over the past few weeks he had physically improved, but he was still depressed and increasingly forgetful. Jack called to Inchicore almost every day now, and although his Dad still didn't know him, he always seemed delighted to see Marie Elaine. This eased Jack's pain somewhat, and he knew that probably for the foreseeable future there would be no improvement, if ever.

'Thanks so much for coming, I really appreciate it.' He hugged his mother. 'Would you like something to drink, Mam?'

'Nothing for me, thanks, I'm just after my tea.' Mrs. Linley looked well this evening in her beige camel coat and blue silk scarf tied at the neck. But she had lost weight, and Jack was concerned. 'Where's my Marie Elaine?' She immediately reached for her granddaughter.

'Hey, no hugs for us?' his sisters laughed and he obliged. When everyone had a glass of wine, they moved to stand in front of the various paintings hung around the walls. The series of family groupings painted in dark tones were very different to his previous vibrant works.

'They're a bit gloomy for me,' Kathleen remarked.

'Thanks!' he laughed.

'I love them,' Chris said.

'Culture vulture,' Rose grinned.

'At least one of us appreciates his talent.'

'What other people think doesn't matter a damn, once they sell!' Gerry guffawed.

Jack didn't respond to his remark and brought them over to where Mia's bronze pieces were displayed.

'They look lovely,' his mother said, 'did you do them?'

'No, they were done by Marie Elaine's mother Mia; she was a sculptor.'

'I'm not sure what they're supposed to be.' There was no pretence on his mother's part.

'You can decide yourself.'

'They're my Mummy's,' Marie Elaine said, 'that's the sunshine!'

She pointed to a beautiful composition which even Jack hadn't quite understood. And then ran to another. 'And the sea; a horse; and I think that's a cat!' she giggled.

Yes, he could see it now.

'They're very nice.' Mrs. Linley nodded.

'And they're all mine.'

'I think Marie Elaine might be an artist too, she drew a lovely picture of Chancer,' he smiled at her, but she was whispering something to his mother and didn't hear.

'There is a stillness, or something about them which I really like,' Chris murmured.

'Mia had a very special talent,' he said, suddenly excited when he spotted Carol among the crowd. 'Excuse me for a second, there's someone I must see. Mam, would you look after Marie Elaine for me please?' He pushed through the people. 'Thanks for coming, Carol.' He kissed her lightly on the cheek. 'Is Kate here?'

'No, I'm sorry Jack, she couldn't make it.'

'How is she?'

'Good. These are wonderful, I love them.' She nodded towards the paintings.

'Thanks,' he smiled, longing to talk.

'Jack, there are some people I want you to meet,' Vincent interrupted.

'Go and talk to those prospective buyers, I'm no use to you,' Carol grinned.

'I'm sorry. Tell Kate that I ... I ... '

'I know, I know.'

Vincent drew him across the room and introduced him to an elderly couple. He was forced to chat with them for a while, and then one person led to another, until finally he had to excuse himself and see if the family was still there.

'Mam wants to go, I think she's a bit worried about Dad,' Chris said.

'You don't mind, Jack?'

'Not at all, Mam, I'm delighted you came. We won't be staying much longer, anyway.'

'I think I'll take Marie Elaine home with me,' His mother smiled down at the little girl who held her hand tightly.

He waved them all off in a taxi, but as he turned to go back inside, Marie Elaine pulled at his jacket.

'What is it?' He bent down closer.

'Can we see the lights again, please?' she whispered. It was one of the few full sentences she had ever spoken to him without anger and simply couldn't be refused. He had asked the taxi-driver to take them to the top of Grafton Street on the way in, and obviously the glittering display had made an impression on her.

He made his excuses to Vincent, who really didn't mind since by that time most of the work had already sold. Still reluctant to hold Marie Elaine's hand, he kept a tight grip on the hood of the jacket as they walked along, watching her stare up at the bright lights above. The street was packed with people, musicians, and carol singers, an air of anticipation on their faces. He was enjoying her excitement, until she brushed against someone walking towards them, and he apologised automatically, still keeping his eyes on her. But there was a sudden scream of surprise. The hood was jerked out of his hand, and he looked up to see Kate standing there, Marie Elaine's arms wrapped tightly around her.

'How's my little princess?' Kate smiled, bent down and hugged her.

'Look at the fairy lights, look!' She pointed upwards.

'They're beautiful. That's Rudolf and the reindeer over there, and Santa Claus.'

'Kate ... I was thinking of you. I was wondering if ... ' he stuttered, longing to reach out and touch her face, press his lips against hers, like he used to do.

'We went to see the pictures. There was a lady with no clothes on. And a man with a big hat. And you get a red star for a prize. I made a picture of Chancer!' Marie Elaine chattered.

'Would you come over at Christmas?' he asked.

But Kate didn't look at him, all her attention concentrated on the animated child.

'And I saw you in the paper,' Marie Elaine smiled.

'Did you?'

'You looked beautiful,' he added.

'But Chancer tore it up. Are you coming home to see my picture of him?' She swung out of her.

'Not tonight, pet. What's Santa bringing you for Christmas?'

She reached up and whispered in her ear and Kate smiled.

'Now I must go, I have to meet my friends.' She kissed her and the little arms were thrown tightly around her neck.

'Will you bring me with you?'

'I'm sorry, it's only big people tonight.'

'We have to let Kate go now,' Jack said gently. Although he would have given anything to throw his arms around her, and beg her to let him come too.

'Happy Christmas, and I hope Santa brings you everything you want,' Kate said and, with obvious difficulty, extricated herself from Marie Elaine's grip, pushed through the crowd and disappeared.

'Happy Christmas,' Jack said, staring after her. Loneliness swept through him and he felt quite bereft, reproaching himself for not using this one opportunity better. Then he looked down at Marie Elaine, but couldn't see her. He called out her name. Turning in a circle, his arms banging against people, suddenly worried that she had fallen on the ground and would be trampled. But she wasn't there. Panic spiralled through him.

'Marie Elaine? Marie Elaine?'

Chapter sixty-eight

Kate hurried towards George's Wine Bar in South Frederick Street, barely able to see where she was going through the tears. It only took a few minutes at the half-walk half-run, difficult enough in high heels, heart racing at twice its normal pace. Her response when she met Jack and Marie Elaine again had shocked her. Except for those occasional treacherous breakdowns, she had managed to keep herself together since discovering he was her father. But tonight, in a matter of seconds, she had been reduced to an emotional rag. Suddenly aware that she really wasn't in a fit state to join the girls, she dabbed her eyes with a tissue and wandered past the entrance and around by the Setanta car park. But it was rather dark and isolated, so she turned back again, and slowly went down the steps into the bar.

Pushing open the door she spotted the girls immediately in an alcove near the piano. 'Pour me a drink quick!' She flopped into a comfy bucket chair. Carol handed her a glass of red wine. 'God, I need this.'

'What's wrong?' May asked anxiously.

'I just bumped into Jack on Grafton Street.'

They glanced at one another. No-one said anything.

'Have you ordered?' She took off her brown suede jacket.

'Yes, there are a couple of platters of tapas on the way, tortilla, olives, bread and those gorgeous peppers stuffed with mozzarella.' Olga waved her glass in the air.

'Sounds delicious.'

'Cheers, Happy Christmas!' The others raised theirs in a toast.

Kate gave her jacket to the waitress who was standing by. 'Excuse me girls, I'm just going to the Ladies.' She picked up her velvet purse and went through the restaurant to the back. In the mirror she could see that her make-up was streaky and shakily repaired it. Praying that she could last the night before breaking down again. A woman joined her. Their eyes met and she smiled.

'Are you?'

Kate looked quizzically at her.

'The person on that television programme?'

'Oh yes!' Kate laughed, taken aback.

'We really enjoy the show. Would you come over and give us a few ideas? My house is in an eighties time warp and badly needs to be updated.' She sprayed perfume.

'Certainly I could.' Kate opened her bag and gave the woman a business card. 'Just give me a call.'

'That's great, I'm thrilled. What a surprise to meet you here!'

On her way out she stood back to allow someone else pass, and she gave Kate a familiar glance also. 'Sorry, I can't remember the name. I've met you somewhere recently, I'm sure of it.'

'We've all got a double.'

'I remember now!' she grinned, 'you're on TV!'

'Yes,' Kate felt embarrassed and wondered would she ever get out of the Ladies tonight.

'Are you one of the newsreaders, or the weather?'

'Eh no.'

'Give me your autograph, anyway, will you? I collect them.' She rooted in her purse and pulled out a piece of paper. 'This is so exciting.'

Kate scribbled a note.

'Kate Crawford!' The girl read the few words she had written. 'Now I know! You're the designer?'

Kate nodded.

'Thanks so much. When I tell the girls, they'll be green with envy.'

'I'm not exactly a celebrity,' she smiled shyly.

'We all love the show, and have applied for tickets.'

'Good, hope you enjoy it. I'd better get back.'

330

'I've been keeping you, sorry!' she gushed.

'Where were you? We were going to send out a search party!' Carol laughed.

'Met a couple of people, got chatting.' Kate sipped her wine.

'Who?'

'I didn't know them.'

'But they knew you, is that it? One of the joys of being famous. Girls, we're only in the halfpenny place. No-one knows us.'

'It's one of the disadvantages.' Kate glanced around, hoping that none of the other patrons would recognise her. It was the negative side of appearing on television. She didn't like it and had begun to feel very self-conscious.

'Who are you fooling! You know, girls, we might become notorious ourselves from rubbing off her nibs here!'

They all laughed.

'And because we don't want to be interrupted by the outside world, are all our phones turned off?'

'I left mine at home,' Debbie said.

'Yes, I did that when I was on the Luas,' Kate confirmed.

'Check, check.'

This evening, the wine bar was packed with Christmas revellers, the atmosphere electric. A young guy played jazz on the piano. People sang, and in the space between the tables couples danced. It was a great night, although Kate found it extremely difficult to join in the hilarity, her mind still back on Grafton Street with Jack and Marie Elaine.

Chapter Sixty-nine

'Have you seen a small girl wearing a pink jacket? She's got dark curly hair, and she's only five ... it was just a few minutes ago ... ' Jack was gripped by an intense fear for the safety of Marie Elaine.

The man shook his head. As did the young couple. The crowd of youths. The two skinny girls with short skirts. The burly Santa Claus. And any others he approached. All the time he kept calling her name. Marie Elaine! Marie Elaine! But there was such noise in the street with the voices of people, the sound of a choir singing *Adeste Fideles,* a couple of guys on saxophone, a classical quartet, he had to believe she would hear his voice. 'Marie Elaine!' He pressed the key on his phone for Kate. There was nothing. The line dead. And then rang the Gardai.

'She's not in here, I'd have noticed her straight away, a kid on her own. Don't worry, we'll ring around, the security men will all keep a look out. Why don't we announce her name from the Information Desk?' The Brown Thomas concierge, Ciaran, dressed in top hat and tails, was very helpful. The staff quickly relayed a message which echoed throughout the shop, but there was no sign of Marie Elaine. He waited there for a short while, watching the crowds of people surge past, laden down with bags of Christmas shopping. He thought of the presents he had bought for her. Baby Born. A Barbie Horse. A set of make-up. And numerous other small things which he had hidden away in the studio. Eventually, he had to leave his phone number with them, impatient to get out into the streets again. He went into the other shops and did the same thing, and then, suddenly, through a gap in the crowd he saw a pink jacket. A huge wave of joy swept through him. 'Marie Elaine?' he yelled and ran. But his happiness was short-lived. This little girl had fair hair, blue eyes and stood behind her mother, afraid of him. He was devastated.

'What are you doing?' The woman held tight on to her little girl. 'Get away from us.'

'I don't know where my daughter has gone.' He stared back in the direction from which he had come. 'I can't believe I've lost her,' he whispered, ashen-faced.

'What was she wearing?' The woman's attitude changed slightly.

'The same. Pink jacket.'

'I'm sorry, we haven't seen her.' She moved away.

He stared after them. But in a matter of seconds they had disappeared. He didn't know what to do. Which way to turn. He wandered back down the street, tears clouding his vision.

Suddenly a Garda walked past and he rushed towards him. 'Have you seen a little girl?' He was out of breath.

'Who?'

'One minute she was there and the next - I'm terrified somebody might have taken her. Maybe some...oh God!'

'Who are you talking about?' The young man was immediately concerned.

'My daughter.'

'How old is she?'

'Five, just five.' He indicated a height with his hand.

'When did this happen?'

'A few minutes ago, maybe ten, fifteen, I'm not sure,' Jack said, still frantically scanning the people passing, searching for a small child either held by the hand or carried in arms.

'What was she wearing?'

'A pink jacket, with white fur. I think. Yes. Definitely. And blue jeans. No. A skirt. With diamonds on it. Blue leggings, boots, she couldn't put them on, I had to do it, and ... ' He almost choked.

'Can you give me a description?'

'She's dark, quite tall for her age, with curly hair. I'll give you a sketch.' He pulled a pen from his inside pocket and quickly drew a

333

fair likeness of Marie Elaine on the back of a business card.

The Garda looked at it and spoke to someone on the radio.

Then he heard the siren and a sigh of relief swept through him. They would be able to find her. Surely.

The two officers asked him to sit into the car and went over every detail. What had happened from the time they had left the house this evening, to the time Marie Elaine had disappeared.

Another car swept past and stopped. The officers discussed the matter with them and they disappeared.

'We'll find her, don't worry,' one of them said.

'Where is this woman, Kate? Can you make contact with her?'

'I've already tried, the phone is off.'

'How well do you know her?'

'She's my ex-girlfriend.'

'Is she the mother of the child?'

He shook his head.

'Where is her mother.'

'She died.'

'Is there a possibility that your ex-girlfriend took the child?'

'No!'

'Perhaps she might have some ulterior motive?' A pen was poised over a notebook.

'What are you suggesting?' he burst out angrily.

The pen was lowered.

'People do strange things. Perhaps it may be for financial reasons, or revenge, or…'

'Kate isn't that sort of person. How long more is this going to take? I must look for my daughter!'

'We'll need this woman's address.'

'You think she's kidnapped her?'

'We have to eliminate every possibility.'

'Ridiculous. You have to concentrate on strangers. Men. Paedophiles. The sort of people who have an unhealthy interest in small girls!'

'Mr. Linley, this woman was the last person to see your child.'

'She's not involved.'
'Did she ask to take her?'
'No!'
'The address, please.'

Chapter Seventy

The girls climbed up the stairs from George's, a laughing group, all planning to head over to El Noches.

'It's the newest club in town, the place to be seen!' Carol quipped.

'I'd like to be seen there with you, let's go.' The tall Scottish guy ushered her into the waiting taxi.

'Kate, are you coming?' His friend asked.

She hesitated. Really not in the mood for extending the night any longer. It was after three now.

'Come on!' May pushed her into the second taxi. 'It's Christmas!' She laughed.

The club was thronged with people. The noise level shattering. They couldn't even hear each other above the noise of the crowd and the booming music. The two Scots, Bob and Ian – were in Dublin for a business meeting. They had had a lot of fun during the evening and now they made their way into the back of the club, found a corner and ordered drinks. Kate watched the others. They were all in fantastic form. Sinead, Debbie and Olga were already on the dance floor. Even quiet May seemed to be having a ball; Carol was particularly animated as she chatted to Bob.

'Let's dance.' Ian took her hand and they pushed through and joined the others on the floor. Twisting and gyrating to some modern rock tune Kate was almost having a good time. A few glasses of wine had blanked out her earlier upset somewhat and she didn't want to spoil the party by leaving early.

'I'll be in Dublin again in the New Year, would you meet me for dinner?' Ian asked when the music quietened to a romantic ballad, and they danced slowly.

Kate was taken aback.

'I'd like to see you again. Just the two of us.'

'I'm very busy, I don't have much free time at all.'

'No-one's that busy,' he smiled.

'You look at my diary!'

He was quite attractive, sandy-haired, a rugby player, and the first man she had met since Jack who had shown any interest in her. She quite liked him.

'I'll give you a call when I'm over,' he grinned.

'Yea,' she had to laugh.

Chapter Seventy-one

A Garda car took Jack home to pick up a photograph. A quick race through the streets. The siren noisy. The blue light flashing. He stared out through the window, praying he would spot Marie Elaine. But the darkness and speed at which they travelled made it impossible to see anything more than shadows. They reached the house and going in, he had a crazy hope that through some miracle she might be there, and that the events of the last hour were simply a nightmare. But the house was as he had left it. Dark. Empty. Although the dog whined as soon as the door was opened. He found some photographs of Marie Elaine taken at her birthday party, wincing when he saw them. His darling child was out there in the darkness of a December night. What had he brought her to? If he hadn't come into her life? If ... if? The thoughts of what could have happened to her filled his mind with grotesque images. He pushed them away and hurried into the kitchen. The bundle of black fur jumped up and down, but he ignored him, quickly filled the water bowl, threw half the packet of dog biscuits on the floor, and rushed out again.

Back in Grafton Street, he gave the photograph to a Detective Inspector Traynor who was in charge now.

'I'll see this is put on to the computer.'

'I'll kill the bastard who puts a finger on her,' Jack muttered.

'It may be a kidnap attempt. Successful well-known people are targeted because they're the ones that can pay the ransom. Plenty of petty criminals are only interested in making a fast buck and they

338

think this sort of thing is easy.'

'Or it could be one of those … ' His dark eyes grieved. He wasn't able to verbalise what was going on in his head.

'The street was very crowded. She may have wandered off.'

'Or just ran away. She doesn't like me very much. It's taking some time to get used to one another,' he was embarrassed.

'We're covering all eventualities.'

He followed the Inspector into Brown Thomas and joined in the search. Frantically looking for his little girl. In every nook and cranny. Under counters. Behind displays. Racks of clothes. Fitting-rooms. Store-rooms. But she wasn't there. He tried Kate's mobile again. And then the house. But couldn't make contact. Frustrated, he decided to retrace his steps back to the Nestor Gallery, relieved to find that Vincent was still there with a small group of people.

Rushing in, he was unaware that he presented a rather wild figure. In the high-ceilinged room, his words echoed loud as he asked if anyone had seen Marie Elaine. Heads turned slowly. Eyes fastened on him. Puzzled. The rumble of voices died. The only sound in the ensuing silence was the tap of Vincent's footsteps as he detached himself from the group. A glass of champagne in his hand; a cigarillo in its gold holder gripped between his lips. 'What did you say?'

'Marie Elaine is gone.'

'The little one?' Vincent asked.

A young woman raised her eyebrows in shock. Red lips open. Hands raised.

'How old is she?' another asked, and the black feathers quivered on the small hat she wore.

'Five. Did she come back here?'

All the heads were shaken as they looked at each other, perplexed. He ran into the adjoining rooms. Into the hall again, taking the stairs two at a time up to the next floor. He tried all the doors but they were locked.

'Can we do anything to help,' Vincent asked from below.

'If you see her, keep her here and phone me immediately please?'

'Certainly, dear boy.'

Outside on the street again, he searched behind refuse skips. Piles of black bags. Cardboard boxes. Praying that Marie Elaine might suddenly appear. Although praying was something he hadn't done in a long time. A very long time. He circled Grafton Street. Trying to cover all the streets which ran in a radius. Now the shops were closed. Shutters had come down. But bars and restaurants were packed, and as the weather was reasonably mild, crowds sat outside and created a festive atmosphere. He talked to stern-faced security men. Drinkers. Smokers. The ones probably on drugs. But many of them couldn't even understand what he was saying.

At one point he stood on a corner, frenzied with worry. The Gardai were searching the shops and he had seen how they had combed through every inch and was satisfied that if she was there, they would find her. He tried to get himself together, and behave in a more logical fashion and continued on towards Trinity College. There he asked the porter about Marie Elaine, and showed him a photograph. The man was sympathetic and Jack began an extensive search around the various buildings, across the green areas, the courtyards, but it yielded nothing. After that he crossed the street, passing the Bank of Ireland, continuing on to Westmoreland Street, O'Connell Bridge and the quays. He looked over the wall at the swiftly-flowing River Liffey. Lights reflected in the dark swirls of water. He stared down. His mind playing tricks. Was that a pink jacket floating? A small hand stretched up. Dark curls plastered wet on a porcelain face. Eyes closed. He went over the bridge and it was only then that he realised how far he had come from the point where she had disappeared.

He turned back. There was a sudden gust of wind. A spattering of raindrops. And a distinct chill in the air. He shivered and wondered was Marie Elaine cold too. Had she fallen somewhere? Was she hurt? A group of young men and girls slouched across the street, barely avoiding a fast-moving car with screams of laughter, high on alcohol and whatever else. He went over.

'Have any of you noticed a little girl wandering alone? She's wearing a pink jacket.'

They stared at him. A girl screeched with laughter, and a couple of the others joined in.

'Lost your bird? Has she ditched you?' one of the men leered, his voice thick.

'Run off with some other fella?'

'You mustn't have treated her right.'

'Wouldn't put up with that if I was her.'

'Good enough for you,' they laughed again and pushed past him.

He glared after them furiously. Wanted to shout. Idiots. Pissed out of your brains. Useless shits. But curbed his wrath. It would be a waste of valuable time. He pressed Kate's number again, but still the phone was powered off. Rain fell heavily now. The shower of sparkling drops was caught in the streetlights. Visibility reduced. But it didn't seem to affect the young people spilling in and out of clubs and bars. He pushed through them. On a corner, a young girl retched. Another was dragged along by her friends. A boy lay comatose up against the door of a shop. A group of girls dressed in skimpy fancy dress shouted and laughed as they stumbled along. Gangs of men wearing football shirts punched the sky and chanted. Remembering his previous encounter, he decided there was probably no point in approaching any of them.

But a noisy group had gathered a short distance away. Curious, he pushed through to see a man being badly beaten up by a few others. There had been a young man killed recently in this way and Jack wondered what to do. If he intervened, he'd probably be attacked himself, so he put his head down and got out of there. A moment later he spotted two uniformed Gardai and rushed over to them, asking first about Marie Elaine, relieved to find that they knew about her, and then directing them to the fracas across the street.

The phone rang. It was the Inspector. His heart thumped with sudden anticipation. 'Have you found her?'

'No, I'm sorry, we're still searching.'

'Are you checking the CCTV cameras on the street?'

'We're in the process of picking up the tapes.'

Jack sighed. 'I'm going to get the jeep and drive out to where she

341

used to live.'

'Where is that?'

'Kimmage.'

'Could she have made it that far?'

'I'll go along the route.'

Slowly he drove towards Margaret's flat. Turning down deserted side streets. Stopping. Peering between parked cars. Into gardens. The night had turned stormy. The wind had picked up and trees swayed, casting dark shadows. He heard dogs bark. Cats mewl. And other weird shufflings and noises in the shadows which startled him, never mind a small girl. God, she must be so scared. Approaching the flat, he phoned. But it went through to the answering machine. He drove up and jumped out of the jeep; pressed the doorbell hard. Once. Twice. He pounded on the knocker. Pushed open the letter-box and shouted. 'Karen? It's Jack Linley. I'm looking for Marie Elaine, have you seen her?' His voice sounded very loud in the stillness. 'Karen?'

He straightened up. A noise drew his attention, and he was aware of a neighbouring window opening.

'What's going on there?' A man's voice shouted.

Jack ignored him. He wondered how long he should wait here. Perhaps the girls were away too. Was he wasting his time?

Suddenly, a light was switched on inside. He could see it gleam through the stained glass window, a pink rose in the centre. Pink. Pink. Pink jacket! His heart thumped. The door was opened a few inches, held by a chain.

'Karen?'

'Yes?'

'Jack Linley here. I'm sorry for disturbing you so late, but Marie Elaine's missing, and I wondered if she had managed to make her way here?'

'No I haven't seen her; Mum's away.'

'I know that, but I just thought ... '

'If I see her, I'll let you know.'

'You have my number?'

342

'Yes.'

'I'd appreciate that, thanks.' Disappointed, he watched the door close. Another dead end.

'Will you shut up or I'll call the Gardai!' the voice from the window echoed again.

Chapter Seventy-two

'Bye! Thanks for a great night,' the girls called as Kate climbed out of the taxi.

'Why don't we go in now and start work, it's not worth trying to get a couple of hour's sleep,' Carol suggested with a laugh, 'or we could kip down on the board.'

'No way, Jose!' May showed a new side to herself. The shy serious person had completely disappeared under the influence of a few jars. 'I need to shower, and have a decent bit of breakfast – then I'll be able to face the day.'

'There's no hurry this morning. You'll have to wake me up probably.' Kate waved goodbye. It was just after six o'clock. They had lost all track of time in El Noches, and had to wait almost an hour before they managed to get a taxi. But it had been very enjoyable, and strangely now she didn't feel tired. Walking up the driveway, her mind still whirled with thoughts of Jack. In the dark she fumbled for the house keys, when a sudden sound caused her to twist around nervously to see two Gardai standing behind on the step.

'Kate Crawford?' The tall one asked.

She nodded nervously, suddenly expecting them to tell her some awful news. Had someone been involved in an accident? A vision of Shane or Conor lying in a crushed car flashed across her mind. Or Jack. Marie Elaine. Baby Abigail? She felt sick.

'We'd like to have a word with you.'

'About what?'

'Could we come inside?' He stepped closer and she had no option but to agree, although she wasn't too sure whether they were genuine Gardai or not.

'Is something wrong?'

'We're searching for a young child who has gone missing.'

'Which child?'

'Marie Elaine Ekman Linley.'

She stared at him, shocked. 'But I saw her only a few hours ago. What happened?'

'Where have you been since that time?'

'I've been out with friends.'

'Would you mind if we take a look around the house?'

'Why do you want to do that?'

'We're checking all possibilities.'

'You think she's here?' she asked angrily.

'As I said, we have to clear everyone who had any contact. It won't take long.'

'Did Jack say that I took her?'

'We're from the local station.' They looked at one another.

'I'm going to ring him straight away.' Kate turned on her phone. Keyed in the pin-number and dialled Jack. But the line was busy.

'May I?' The tall Garda indicated the sitting-room.

For a moment she hesitated, hating the thought of giving them the run of the house. Why did they need to search? Why would she bring Marie Elaine here? It was ridiculous. Fury, anxiety and terror all boiled inside her, a crazy mix of emotions.

The other man produced a notebook. 'Where were you this evening between eight and nine?'

'Shopping.'

'Where exactly?'

'Grafton Street.'

'Did anything happen?'

'No.' She was puzzled.

'Did you meet anyone?'

'Marie Elaine and her father.'

'Could you tell me what occurred?' He stared at her with his rather small dark eyes, whose colour she couldn't ascertain.

345

'I talked to the child mostly. He and I ... ' She was aware that there was a slight tremor in her voice and hoped that it wouldn't give the impression that she was particularly anxious or had something to hide.

'For how long?'

'Two or three minutes.'

'And then what did you do?'

'I met some friends at George's wine bar.'

'Where is that?'

'South Frederick Street.'

'Who did you meet there?'

'The girls who work with me, it was a night out for Christmas.'

'Could you give me their names?'

'Why do you want to know?' Her voice rose anxiously.

'And I'll need phone numbers and addresses.'

In the office, Kate checked the address book. Fuming when she heard footsteps upstairs. Hating the thought of the man rooting among her clothes and personal possessions. Feeling really under threat she hurried back up, and gave him the details. He left her alone then. She was anxious to phone the girls to explain what was happening, but was afraid to interfere now. Carol, May, Sinead and Debbie would get the fright of their lives. And, because she was a foreign national, Kate couldn't imagine how Olga would react.

'We need to have access to the building at the back and also the attics.'

She handed over the keys and with a tissue dried the moisture which had built up along her hairline and temples. One of them went up the stairs, and she could hear his footsteps echoing as she stared out through the kitchen window into the dark back garden, her heart pumping very fast. Eerily, the light from a torch flashed in the shadows as the Garda searched among the trees, but it disappeared as soon as he entered the mews and turned on the main light. He spent a short time there and then returned. The other had already come back downstairs.

'Thank you, Miss Crawford.'

She stood silently watching as they walked down the steps and disappeared. They must have had their car parked up the road, she thought angrily. Probably just in case I might have noticed it. She closed the door and tried Jack's phone again. This time, he answered immediately.

'Did you tell the Gardai that I might have taken Marie Elaine?'

'No, of course not. I told them it had nothing to do with you.'

'But they were here waiting when I got back and they've searched the house from top to bottom. You must have said something!'

'Of course I didn't. They thought because you were the last person to see her that maybe you might ... '

'Might?'

'It could be a kidnap attempt.'

'Why on earth would I kidnap her? It's crazy!'

'It's just the way they work, evidence, witnesses, all that sort of thing. For God's sake, Kate ... ' his voice petered out.

'Bloody hell, a kidnapper!' She cut off the phone.

Chapter Seventy-three

Kate's anger only added to Jack's distress over Marie Elaine. How could she think for one minute that he would suggest such a thing to the Gardai. He rang back immediately. But the voicemail bade him leave a message and that was all he could do. Stumbling up George's Street, the futility began to get to him. The rain pelted down now. Earlier he had tried to be positive. But now his worst imaginings came back with a vengeance; worse than any horror movie.

Every shout or scream from a drunken teenager was Marie Elaine. Crying out for help as she was grabbed and bundled into someone's car. Dragged by the hand into a grimy flat. Held in a dark room. Without food or drink. He passed a doorway. A homeless person huddled there in a sleeping bag, a sheet of cardboard the only protection from the elements. He stopped and moved closer. Imagining how cold it must be to lie there on a night like this. He didn't notice how wet his own clothes were at this stage.

A man stood on a corner watching him. He pulled on a cigarette and the red tip glowed in the shadows. Jack asked him if he had noticed a child walking alone.

'Have you got a fag?' He cut across him as he attempted to describe her.

'Sorry, no.'

'A euro for a coffee?'

Jack put his hand in his pocket.

'Someone stole my wallet.'

He pulled out some notes. 'If you see a little girl, would you tell the Gardai?'

'Yea.'

He gave him the money.

'Thanks.'

Was he the type that might take a five-year-old and demand a ransom? One of those people who sell children abroad for large sums of money? Or, God forbid, one of those others who ... ?

Two women grinned at him from a doorway.

'Hi there!' They beckoned him to come closer. Dressed in bright-coloured mini-skirts and glittery low-cut tops with lots of jewellery. 'Doing business?'

'No thanks.' He went on to explain about Marie Elaine.

'How awful, poor little thing.' They were both very concerned. 'We haven't seen any children around.'

'If you do, report it immediately, will you? And don't let her go.'

'To the fuzz?' They laughed.

'Here's my number.' He scribbled it on a piece of paper. Gave them some money also, and trudged on. Suspicious of everyone he saw.

Chapter Seventy-four

'Are you all right?' Carol asked, hugging tight when she arrived at Berwick Road.

'I have a hell of a headache. But I don't care about myself,   it's … Marie Elaine.' Kate sniffled into a tissue. 'And Jack thought I had kidnapped her. Can you imagine? Me!'

'Surely not?'

'He must have given the Gardai my address. I'm furious with him.'

'But what reason would you have for taking her?'

'Exactly!' she snapped, and then dissolved into tears. 'I love the little scrap.'

'I keep thinking of what might have happened,' Carol whispered.

'Don't go there, Carol, please, I couldn't bear it.'

'Have you had something to eat, or even a cup of coffee?'

'No. I just want to get into town.'

'Did Jack give you any idea of where they had already searched?'

'No. I think we should take it from where I last saw her.' Kate pulled on her jacket.

'How about we make a plan?'

'I can't think straight. I just want to get back to Grafton Street!'

'Bring a photo – we'll need it to show people.'

It was a miserable morning with a steady downpour of rain. They went back to the spot where Kate thought she had met Jack and Marie Elaine the night before. 'Let's retrace my steps on the way over to George's, check out the shops.'

'We'll have to wait a bit longer, it's not eight yet. There's a cafe over there, come on, we'll have something to warm us up.' She took Kate's arm, and guided her across the street. Inside they sat at a table in the window. There was an aroma of freshly-baked bread in the place, and Carol ordered two coffees, warm rolls, butter, and marmalade.

'Have something to eat.'

'I couldn't. The poor pet might be hungry. Thirsty too. I pray she's not out in the open.'

'Come on, just a little.'

Kate shook her head and stared out through the window. The street surface was shiny with puddles. People hurried past on their way to work, heads down, sheltering under a multi-coloured sea of umbrellas battered by a gusty wind. 'I should ring the girls. Explain what's happened. It must have been terrible for them. And you too. The Gardai calling at all hours. They can be so aggressive.'

'No worries, we're all made of staunch stuff, didn't take a feather out of any of us!' Carol grinned, 'anyway, I've spoken to them already and they said not to worry, they'll handle everything and work on if necessary.'

'Don't know what I'd do without you.' Kate could feel her emotions coming to the surface again. 'It's the strangest thing, but suddenly I don't give a damn about work. All that excitement about Rome, and Paris, and being on television - I couldn't care less if I never went anywhere again. If we never got an order again. I thought that was all I wanted. All that mattered in my life - God, I've been so vacuous.'

'Enough of that! Let's go, the shops will be opening up soon.' They walked out into the street. 'We have a few minutes yet and I think a prayer wouldn't go amiss,' Carol suggested.

Kate stared up at the altar in Clarendon Street church. But she was unable to pray, suddenly brought back in time to her own childhood. Trying to imagine how a little girl might feel to be lost at night. To see things through her eyes. Buildings stretching high above. People rushing past. Big feet thumping. Heels clicking.

Strident voices. Music. Strange noises. Pushed. Shoved. Panic. Screams. Crying for a Mum who will never be there for her again. She talked to her own mother then. A whispered prayer. Please find Marie Elaine, please?

'Thanks for bringing me in here,' Kate murmured, as they lit candles.

'If I'm in town, I often pop in for a few minutes.' Carol pushed up the umbrella as they walked down the steps of the church.

'I wondered if she might have been attracted into a shop that sells Christmas toys and decorations, she was all exited about the lights.'

'And why don't we get some extra copies of this photo and put a message on it?' Carol said.

'We could offer a reward for information! I should have thought of it before now, I don't know where my brain is.'

'You've been up all night.'

'So have you.'

'Let's do that before we search the shops.'

They handed out copies of Marie Elaine's photograph with the message offering a reward of ten thousand euro, and Kate's telephone number printed underneath. But no-one they talked to had seen a little dark-haired girl dressed in a pink jacket wandering alone. More than one person recognised Kate, and for the first time she saw that as an advantage. Although she also received irate looks and muttered curses as she hurried ahead of Carol, twisting in and out between pedestrians. 'I'm sure I saw a Christmas shop around here, I'm positive.' They came to the end of the street which led into the Grafton Arcade, but decided that she mightn't have gone that far, and turned back, disappointed. They went into Hibernian Way then, but it proved equally fruitless.

'Try the other direction, up towards South Anne Street.' Carol was out of breath now.

'I didn't go that way.'

'No, but how long do you think she could have kept you in sight among the crowds in town last night?'

'Not very long.' Kate slowed down a little.

'Following other people she thought looked like you?'

'I wish to hell I had something on me other than these stupid heels,' Kate groaned and almost fell stepping down from the path on to the street, trying to avoid a large puddle.

'Buy a pair of trainers somewhere?'

'No time! Danker Silver, cheese shop, Nijou.'

'Boutique,' Carol added, 'maternity wear.'

'Jewellers.'

And then they stopped suddenly, both staring like children into a wonderland.

'I knew it was here, I just knew it.' Kate leaned against the glass door and peered into the shop. It was a bright Aladdin's cave of colour. Glittering silver and gold. Exactly the sort of place a child would love. 'She told me Santa was going to bring her a panda.'

'There's one.' Carol pointed to the large black and white bear in the window.

Kate tried the door, but it was locked.

'Is there anybody inside?'

'I can see a girl at the back.'

They both knocked loudly on the door.

The shop assistant waved them away, pointing to her watch.

'Doesn't she realise that there are sales to be made?' They pounded this time, but received no response and stared at each other, frustrated.

'We'll have to get her attention.' Carol took one of the last photocopies out of the envelope and held it close to the glass pane in the door, while Kate used her key to knock sharply. But they received a very angry look from the girl, who then disappeared.

'Bitch!'

They kept knocking until finally, to their relief, a man came out. He unlocked the door and peered at them through the narrow gap. His expression was unsympathetic. There was a scowl on his long pale face.

'We're looking for a child, and we think she might be in your shop.'

'She was wearing a pink jacket.'

'There's no child in here,' he muttered.

'Please let us in to look, please?' Kate begged.

'We're not open yet.'

'We'll ring the Gardaí if you don't.'

At that, he became more amenable. 'I suppose so.'

Inside at last, they searched quickly along the narrow aisles which had been created between the displays. Traditional teddy bears in every colour and size, dogs, cats, rabbits and any other strange animal you could think of. A huge range of toys for both boys and girls, and an amazing collection of other gifts and Christmas decorations. But there was no sign of Marie Elaine, and after all the initial excitement they were both desperately disappointed.

Kate's phone rang. She fumbled to find the right key. 'Hello?' She could hear the clink of a coin.

'Are you the mother?' A hoarse male voice enquired.

'No - I mean - yes, I am.'

'You giving the money?'

'Yes, where is she?' She pulled Carol towards her and they both listened.

'That would be telling, wouldn't it?'

'Is she all right?'

'Yea, she's fine. Now, are you going to give me the ten grand?'

'Yes, sure, if you take me to her.'

'No, you'll have to give me the money first, and then I'll tell you where she is.'

'Hold on.' Kate put her hand over the phone. 'We can't get hold of that amount now,' she whispered to Carol, who grabbed the phone from her.

'We'll give you a thousand when you tell us and the rest when we find her.'

'Put it in the skip on South William Street in ten minutes.'

'Where exactly?'

'There's one about half-way down. But I'm warning you, don't ring the bloody cops, or you'll never see her again.'

Chapter Seventy-five

Jack stared at a computer screen. A fuzzy greyish image of Grafton Street appeared but it was crowded and hard to differentiate one person from another. Suddenly, his phone rang and he was ecstatic when he heard the news from Carol. But he was concerned about the girls dealing with this man, whoever he was, and immediately told the Garda even though she had warned him not to. This was the first breakthrough, and they reacted immediately, rushing out to the cars, and heading to South William Street.

'The girls shouldn't have done this. God knows who is claiming to know where your child is. It's our job to deal with it.' The Inspector was tight-lipped.

'I hope they'll be all right.'

'Phone and tell them to back off.'

Jack tried Kate's number, but she didn't answer. 'It's probably too late,' he said.

'Taking the law into their own hands. Crazy!'

They walked up Wicklow Street, the Inspector talking on the radio to the Gardai in the area.

'We'll wait until he appears.'

'But you don't know what he looks like.'

'He won't show himself until Kate puts the money in the skip, then he'll pounce.'

Chapter Seventy-six

After they had been to a couple of cash machines to get the money, they rushed into a shop and asked the assistant for a bag and pushed the money inside.

'That's it, there, has to be. It's the only one around.' Kate pointed to the yellow skip, filled to overflowing with rubble from a building which was being renovated.

'There's no sign of the Gardai.'

'Thank God.

'How do we do this?'

'We'll just walk up and throw the bag in.'

'What if it goes right down into the rubbish?'

'We'll try and place it at the top. Then we have to wait for your man, he's supposed to tell us where Marie Elaine is.'

'I'm terrified. What if he's some sort of weirdo?' Carol slowed her pace.

'Have to take a chance on that.'

'I'd never be any good as a spy.' She shivered.

'Don't run out on me,' Kate warned.

'What do you think I am?' Carol looked around nervously. 'Hope no-one else grabs the money.'

'Who else knows about it?'

'How can you be so calm?'

'Slow down, act casual.'

They approached the skip, and just as Kate was about to put in the bag, someone pushed from behind and it was grabbed out of her hand.

'Hey, you, hey!' She ran after the figure in black jacket, jeans and a baseball cap, who sprinted quickly ahead. 'Stop that man!' Kate yelled, but no-one took the slightest notice.

'Bastard!' Carol shouted, showing no fear now as they hurtled down the street, but they came to an abrupt halt when two Gardai appeared and cut off his escape. Then with unexpected speed he wheeled around and ran back towards Kate and Carol. They immediately tried to block him, Kate managing to grab the back of the jacket as he pushed through. In the struggle the cap fell off to reveal a shock of red hair.

'You're a woman!' Kate was astonished. 'How could you, how could you!'

'Bitch!' Carol leapt on her, grasping hold of the hair and hanging out of it, until the woman was overpowered by the Gardai, pushed up against a wall and handcuffed.

'Kate! Carol!' Jack suddenly appeared around the corner, followed by more uniformed Gardai, and a man in plain clothes. 'Are you hurt, my love?'

She leaned up against the wall, out of breath. 'I'm all right.'

'You shouldn't have done this. It was dangerous,' he said anxiously.

'We had to take a chance on it. You have her now and she'll tell you where Marie Elaine is!' Carol smiled broadly.

'That's probably highly unlikely,' the Inspector said.

Kate covered her face with her hands.

'Thanks so much for helping to look for Marie Elaine, Kate - Carol. And I'm so sorry about the Gardai searching your house, Kate - I didn't suggest that you had anything to do with it - believe me.' His eyes burned out of his pale drawn face.

'I would suggest you go home now and leave this to us. Never take the law into your own hands. If there are any further calls let us know immediately,' the Inspector was curt.

'I'd better get back. I've been looking at security tapes,' Jack explained.

'We'll keep searching, you go on,' Carol said.

'Thanks again.' He moved towards Kate, but she had turned

away, and for a few seconds he stood looking after her, his expression forlorn.

'I hated the way that plain-clothes bod spoke to us. Like we were kids!' Kate was angry.

'Well, I'm certainly not going home. Are you?'

'No way! And there's still a chance that the woman may know something.'

'Bitch!'

They walked along Wicklow Street.

'Jack looks rough. Worn out,' Carol said.

Kate didn't reply.

'Let's go in here for a few minutes, take the weight off our feet and regroup.' Carol led the way into a small coffee shop, and Kate followed meekly.

'Right!' Carol finished her latte. 'Let's make a note of the streets we've covered.' She scribbled a map on a serviette.

'I don't know where we've been, I'm all confused now,' Kate sighed deeply, and pushed her damp hair back from her face.

'You're too tired for this.'

Kate's phone rang, and immediately a sparkle of hope brightened her eyes.

'They were just after the reward,' Jack sounded very dejected.

Tears filled Kate's eyes. She couldn't say anything. Carol took the phone.

'The Gardai knew that woman, and the man too apparently. They're just petty thieves, and not up to much more than shoplifting. I really appreciate your help.'

'Not at all, Jack, it's nothing. Do you want to talk to Kate?'

'Yes.'

But she had already stood up and left.

'Have you called on anyone else to help?' Carol asked.

'Yes, some of the family are coming in.'

'Kate?' A familiar voice said from somewhere to their right.

358

She turned, surprised to see Grace walking towards them.

'I'm trying to do some shopping before it gets too busy, I'm so looking forward to spending Christmas with you.' She kissed them both.

They told her what had happened.

'That's terrible. The poor wee thing,' she was shocked.

'We're continuing to search, you never know.' Carol stared along the busy street.

'I'll come with you,' Grace offered.

Their initial impulse and certainty that they would find Marie Elaine had vanished now. The frantic rush was replaced by a steady walk, probably in deference to Grace. They went from shop to shop, showing the photograph to the staff, who were always very helpful. But as time passed, they became more and more dejected.

Grace stopped at Anne's Lane. 'Have you looked up there?'

'Yea, earlier on. But we'll have another look, no harm,' Kate called out the names of the various establishments as they passed. 'Venu. Chilli Club. A dental clinic. and up there is The Sporting Emporium.'

'It winds a bit, until it comes to a dead end.' They followed the street again turning left and right. The area was deserted. The lock-up garages closed, cars parked, rubbish left out for collection.

'There are coloured lights outside a building, look, down at the end.' Grace pointed.

'We didn't notice any lights the last time.' Kate walked unsteadily on her spiky heels.

'It's a shop!' Grace exclaimed.

'Never even knew there were any down here,' Carol said.

All three stared into the window. On display was a large wooden doll's house, in that fairytale Disney-style with turrets, tiny mullioned windows and balconies. It was a most colourful and fantastic piece of work. Silently they pushed open the door and a bell dinged. There was no-one there and they stood looking at an amazing collection of houses. Reproductions of every possible type, all jammed together on the floor area and on shelves around the walls.

'This is unbelievable,' Kate whispered slowly, 'it's just the sort of place.' A surge of anticipation burst through her.

'Can I help you, ladies?' A middle-aged man appeared, brushing sawdust from his hands.

'We're searching for a little girl.' Kate handed him the photograph.

'Do the houses open? Would it be possible for a child to climb inside?' Carol asked, excited.

'Oh yes, they are empty now. I make the furniture to suit customers' requirements.' His chubby face was very concerned. 'They can be used for storage space also.'

'I never knew you were here.'

'This is my workshop, and we only opened for the Christmas trade a few weeks ago.'

'Some are too small, it's really only the bigger ones. Can we look?' Kate asked.

'Certainly.'

'I'll check the back.' Grace hurried away.

Carol opened and closed doors at speed.

'What about the one in the window?' Kate asked.

'Let me help you.' The man reached forward.

'It's very close to the front door, and she could easily ... ' Kate held her breath as he grasped the little brass knob.

Chapter Seventy-seven

'There she is!' Jack shouted, and leapt up out of his chair, pointing to the image on the screen. Grafton Street was a mass of movement at 20.23 on the evening before. People gathered together so tightly it was very difficult to see an individual. The rather fuzzy pictures were partially obscured by the Christmas lights which glimmered brightly.

'Maximise that,' the Inspector instructed the operator.

It was enlarged, but on closer inspection was obviously not his daughter. Another disappointment. He had been staring at the screen for hours. More than once thinking that this person or that was either himself, Kate, or Marie Elaine. He rubbed his eyes, exhausted, frustrated and losing hope now. 'It's hard to recognise anyone,' he said wearily.

'We'll go back to where you were standing. Examine each frame again.'

The image filled the screen, suddenly much clearer.

'Stop! I think that's Kate.' Jack jerked forward. 'I'm sure of it. Look ... there!'

A person who looked very like her moved through the swaying crowd. Then she turned into a shop. They waited until she reappeared and began to push her way through the crowd again. With breath held Jack watched, praying it was her, finally rewarded when she stopped.

'That's when she met us,' he whispered.

'There you are.' The Inspector pointed to the screen with a pen.

'I can't see Marie Elaine.' He peered closer.

361

'You're blocking our view of the child. But we have you now. The images can be enlarged.'

Jack watched Kate move away. Immediately, she was swallowed up by the mass of people as if in a swamp. 'We'll never be able to see where Marie Elaine went in that crowd.'

'Give it time, Jack, give it time.'

Chapter Seventy-eight

Kate sank down on her knees and leaned into the doll's house. 'Marie Elaine!' she whispered, 'Marie Elaine!' A huge euphoria swept through her.

She lay there, curled up, but at the sound of Kate's voice, raised her head, dark eyes large and scared, face grimy. Immediately, she burst into tears and reached out her arms.

'Marie Elaine, my love, are you all right?' She held her close.

'I was afraid to come out.' Her sobs grew louder. 'And I'm wet ... and it was all dark!' She clung to Kate. 'And I couldn't find you.'

'Ssshhh, you're all right now pet, I have you.' Kate rocked her soothingly.

The others rushed up and hugged them both. 'I can't believe she's safe!'

'It's wonderful!' Grace kissed her.

'I'll get a rug.' The man ran into the back. 'Thanks be to God I left the heating on all night.'

'This is fantastic, we've found her, oh my God, we'd better phone Jack. What's his number?' Carol asked excitedly.

Kate called out the digits and she dialled quickly.

'Come into the back, it's warmer there.' The man tucked a red tartan rug around Marie Elaine, and helped Kate to stand up. He hurried ahead of them, and pulled a chair out. 'I'm sorry it's not very comfortable, but customers don't come in here normally.'

Carol held the phone to Kate's ear. 'We've found her, Jack, we've found her!' she gabbled, 'in a doll's house!'

The man handed her a cup of milk and she held it to Marie

363

Elaine's lips as she drank thirstily.

'My God, I can't believe this, Grace, you brought us luck,' Kate smiled at the child cuddled in her arms.

'It's fantastic!' Carol hugged them again.

'I am so happy we have found her, so happy!' Grace dabbed her eyes with her handkerchief.

'Should we call an ambulance, have her checked out?' Carol asked anxiously.

'I don't think so. Are you feeling better now, pet?' Kate stroked her hair.

Marie Elaine nodded, and clung even closer.

The sound of sirens from the Garda cars drew their attention then, and Jack was the first person to appear, hurtling into the shop. He wrapped his arms around them both, his face buried in the tangle of soft dark and fair hair. All of them were in tears now. After a moment, he stood back a little, a smile of wonder on his face. Still holding tight to Kate, Marie Elaine immediately reached out to him, 'Daddy?'

'Let's go home ... ' Kate said softly and kissed Jack.

The End

364

CYCLONE COURIERS

Cyclone Couriers – who proudly support the LauraLynn Children's Hospice Foundation – are the leading supplier of local, national and international courier services in Dublin. Cyclone also supply confidential mobile on-site document shredding & recycling services and secure document storage & records management services through their Cyclone Shredding and Cyclone Archive divisions.

Cyclone Couriers
With a fleet of 35 pushbikes, 120 motorbikes and 45 vans, they can cater for all your urgent local & national courier requirements.

Cyclone International
Overnight, next day, timed and weekend door-to-door deliveries to destinations within the 32 counties of Ireland.

Delivery options to the U.K., mainland Europe, U.S.A., and the rest of the world.
A variety of services to all destinations across the globe.

Cyclone Shredding
On-site confidential document and product shredding & recycling service.
Destruction and recycling of computers, hard drives, monitors and office electronic equipment.

Cyclone Archive
Secure document & data storage and records management.
Hard copy document storage and tracking - data storage - fireproof media safe - document scanning and upload of document images.

Cyclone Couriers operate from 8, Upper Stephen Street, Dublin 8.

Cyclone Archive, International and Shredding operate from 19/20 North Park, Finglas, Dublin 11.

www.cyclone.ie   email: sales@cyclone.ie   Tel: 01-4757246

THE PASSIONATE WOMAN

By

FRAN O'BRIEN

Bel has an intense passion for life and her husband Tom. They are the perfect couple, with successful careers, a beautiful home, and all the trappings. But underneath the façade, cracks appear and damage the basis of their marriage and the deep love they have shared since that first night they met.

Her longing for a baby creates problems for Tom, who can't deal with the possibility that it might be his fault. His masculinity is questioned, and he is swept up into something far more insidious and dangerous than he ever could have imagined.

Finally he arrives at a point of no return and Bel has to contend with the consequences.

*